BEAUMONT

The Second Book of The Architects' Club Series

Sam Earner

Copyright © Sam Earner 2024

Sam Earner has asserted his right under the Copyright, Designs and Patents Act 1988 to be identified as the author of this work.

All rights reserved. No part of this book may be reproduced or modified in any form.

This novel is a work of fiction. Names and characters are the product of the author's imagination and any resemblance to real persons, living or dead, is purely coincidental.

For my parents, who showed me the meaning of happiness

Acknowledgements

Once again, it has been a pleasure to work with Helen Fazal, copy editor for this book and *Rothwell*. I have a deep appreciation for her keen eye and creative perception in crafting a worthy finished product. My thanks go to Fleur Currie, for reviews of draft manuscripts and field notes from travels in Mongolia. Finally, my gratitude to Michael James for providing guidance on rotary wing aviation.

1

Bruce Noble sat at his desk on the tenth floor of Eaton House, Kowloon, Hong Kong, contemplating the memories of eight years earlier. Now a captain in British Army Intelligence, he shared an open-plan office with the United Nations Military Observers' team. He looked past his drab surroundings and out across the manicured lawns and exotic vegetation of Kings Park, through the gap between the staggered high rises stretching away along Nathan Road, to the forbidding skyline of Lion's Rock. He pondered how the events at Rothwell in 1988 could have slipped so quietly into history, how the anticipation of an exciting career in military intelligence had been met with dull routine.

Dull, except that his thoughts had been stirring of late. His mother, Jenny, still missing, never confirmed dead; Lady Margaret Cadogan-Brandt, last seen about to drown under Serpentine Lake; his best friend Rory McIntyre, tragically killed in a mountaineering accident; his brutal fight with Jez Picher. And then there was Mr James Tavener, whose proximity to Rory at the time of his death and sudden disappearance after Jenny had vanished had sealed the suspicions growing in Bruce's mind.

He let out a breath, returning to the present to find himself staring at the large regional map on the wall, peppered with blue map pins showing the UNMO stations across Asia. His eyes were drawn to a pin set high above the others: Poklonny Krest in the northeastern corner of Mongolia, the UN's remotest observer station. Lying on the border with China and Russia, the siting of the station might be seen as largely symbolic, a view over a junction of vast countries. But, as part of the intelligence community, Bruce knew the real reason for it: it was only a hundred kilometres from Hulunbuir, home to China's secret biological weapons facility. The Chinese did not object to an UNMO station so far from Hulunbuir. What could anyone see? But British and US intelligence fancied the choice of a forgotten site as a point from which future capabilities might be used, or future operations mounted.

Beside the map was a wall calendar. Chinese New Year was a week away: 19 February 1996 would herald the Year of the Rat. Tavener. Rat.

'You volunteering, Bruce? We could use someone at PK over New Year.'

The words broke into his introspection. From behind a mahogany desk, its green leather top adorned with a turned brass paperweight, fly-fishing trophy and framed photo of his Sandhurst platoon, pointless clichés of a thoroughly institutionalised existence, Bruce's officer commanding had caught him eyeing the map.

'Perhaps, Alastair. Is a volunteer required?' he replied.

BEAUMONT

'Over Chinese New Year? You bet, stupid. Who'd want to be on duty when we're in Hong Kong? Battalion has been bleating that we don't visit the outstations enough. Covering the north over that period would earn big brownie points for the unit – and the volunteer. You up for it?'

Bruce capitulated, but to instinct, not authority. 'Okay, if it's so important to placate the bosses at home, I'll go.'

*   *   *

It was late evening on Sunday 18 February. What should have been a day's journey from Hong Kong's Kai Tak airport to Poklonny Krest via Ulaanbaatar had taken three, thanks to long waits for connecting flights. The final two-hundred kilometre leg from Choibalsan airfield was courtesy of a UN Gazelle helicopter flown by a blue-eyed Army Air Corps captain called Skip, who was keen to show off his flying skills over the expanse of flat land.

When they landed, he shut the aircraft down and pointed towards the block where Bruce should report.

'Book in there. Oh, and welcome to Corimec Castle.'

Bruce thanked Skip, grabbed his kitbag from the back and closed the aircraft door. As he tramped across the helicopter landing site he looked around him. Corimec Castle was set on a foothill of a seven-hundred metre peak, with panoramic views over miles of open steppe. The accommodation comprised rows of white containerised units – Corimec units – like posh shipping containers.

These were set among a handful of converted farm buildings on the eastern side, the side that bordered China, the side that mattered. A tall perimeter fence topped with barbed wire enclosed the compound, which was about the size of a football pitch. In the fence were two breaks: a simple pole barrier to the road from Choibalsan and a pair of wire gates facing the Chinese side.

Next morning, Bruce entered the mess room and joined the queue at the servery for breakfast. A tang of body odour and dirty clothing emanated from the young soldier ahead of him. He noted the man's dust-covered boots, so early in the day; his rifle slung over a shoulder like a handbag. A wide stretch of the arms and gaping yawn didn't offer a clue as to whether he was just off night shift or trying to wake up.

Bruce looked across the room with a ready smile but was met with suspicious glances from the three or four tables where the soldiers were tucking into their food, the hubbub becoming a hush. He figured that word had got round about his usual beret being that of the 'Green Slime' – the Intelligence Corps. In such a remote place his hosts would think the only thing he could spy on was them.

'Did you get some sleep?' asked Captain Jansen, the station OC, who appeared beside Bruce at a side table beyond the servery. 'Not as comfortable as Hong Kong.'

BEAUMONT

Bruce set his tray down and poured a mug of tea from the urn, unsure whether Jansen was being objective or oblique. 'It was fine. Thanks for having me.'

Over the next couple of hours he went through the formalities of liaison, scratching around for any intel that a crew experiencing Groundhog Days might have missed. Nothing.

He decided to take the only motorcycle for an excursion around the locale. In an hour's riding he reached only one tiny settlement of three *gers*. To Bruce's Western eyes, the scene was a curiosity, the circular, white canvas-covered structures with their wooden frames resembling great truckles of camembert, speared by drinking straws and set upon a vast dirt platter.

He stopped the bike, kicked the side-stand down, lifted his goggles, spat and patted dust from his clothes. A man emerged from the middle hut. For a moment he just stood and stared, but then he waved, bidding Bruce to come inside.

Bruce's brief encounter with the locals seemed to be mutually intriguing, as the family observed the man on the motorcycle, in his green uniform and white helmet, trying to swallow the smell inside their humble tented home. Yak products make for potent food smells and the *gers* were rank with an odour like stale cream. Bruce nodded, bowed and smiled frequently, realising he hadn't done his cultural homework, as the leather-faced elder showed him around. The man was proud of the crafty beer store hidden under the felt floor. He pointed to the dozen bottles lying in the dirt and roared with laughter. Bruce laughed with him, while inwardly praying they weren't supposed to share them before his ride back.

On his return journey he took in the consuming expanse that stretched to an unreachable horizon. The sun slipped away and chill gripped the air. He crossed chalk-white rivers that ran with suspended particles of glacial melt from distant mountains as the bitter cold cut around his goggles and the last light faded into night.

Corimec Castle was still when he got back. Banter had struck up in the crew room, with a handful of off-duty soldiers crammed around an Uckers board sinking Fosters under a haze of cigarette smoke, while those on duty looked on. Bruce headed to the ops room to view an empty shift log, then out across the few metres to the east observation platform, from where he peered through a pair of binos into the night towards China.

'Hoping to see much?' came the voice of the corporal on sentry duty beside him, as the pair faced the blackness.

Bruce put down the binos and ignored the jibe. 'Just curious ... Maybe bored, I guess.'

Instead of pretending a fake interest, pointlessly staring through the binoculars, he decided to indulge his real curiosity. He closed his eyes and allowed the heat picture of the scene to register in his mind's eye. The corporal glanced at him and turned away with a dismissive sniff, wondering who this weird intelligence officer was, with his apparent ability to invoke psychic powers. He raised his own image intensifier to scan the area.

Suddenly a pinprick glow of radiated heat broke through Bruce's inner quiet. He focused as the image began to swell, revealing a human torso some two hundred metres away, emerging over a gentle rise.

'What the hell?' said the corporal, as he tweaked the controls on the nightscope before pressing his radio's transmit switch. 'Control, this is East Tower. We have someone approaching on foot. No. Two people. Over.'

The first two people ever to approach the station from China started a panic of activity. In the crew room, chairs scraped and toppled to the floor as duty staff rushed to their posts. Bruce kept watching the action across the plain. The corporal on the tower switched on a powerful searchlight, flooding the area with white light.

As the figures came closer, Bruce could see both were men. They were running up an old dirt track that led past a disused barn towards the station's eastern gate. One was lagging behind, struggling to keep up. Bruce silently urged them on. *Come on! You're running for a reason. Keep going!*

Suddenly the horizon came alive, lit up by white headlights and red and blue flashing emergency lights. The chorus of engines built as the pursuers closed in, maybe five or six vehicles in all.

Bruce leapt down from the observation tower.

'Get the gates open!' he called to two soldiers stood-to on the fence line.

'No, leave them,' shouted Captain Jansen, who had run over from his accommodation block. 'We're not authorised to access Chinese territory.'

The first shots thudded near the escaping men, who were now close to the barn. More shots rang out, a couple striking a Corimec hut.

'*Verdomde idioten!*' Fucking idiots, spat Jansen as everyone ducked for cover.

'Get these gates open!' Bruce repeated.

Jansen hesitated.

'It's why I'm here, I have authorisation to extract them,' Bruce lied.

Jansen nodded, then signalled to the waiting soldiers to open the gate. They ripped the binding from the latch and kicked the gates free from a tangle of weeds. Now Bruce had a clear view of the fracas.

Rounds continued to search for their targets, thumping into the ground ahead, accompanied by sparkles of muzzle flash and deafening cracks in the air as stray bullets streaked overhead. The slower man went down, silhouetted by the headlight beams. Bruce sprinted through the gate towards the fugitives, right into the teeth of the fire, and into Chinese territory.

'Captain Noble! What the hell? Are you crazy!' Jansen shouted.

Bruce glanced back over his shoulder.

BEAUMONT

'Get that bloody light off!'

'But you don't have a gun!'

As the area returned to pitch black, save for the haphazard sweep of lights from the closing vehicles, Bruce summoned his heat vision again and dashed for the barn.

Inside he found the first Chinese man, panting furiously and cowering behind a stack of wooden crates. Bent over with hand to chest, he was clearly exhausted. As Bruce approached, he flinched. Bruce dragged him into cover at the rear of the barn, away from the glare of a Chinese police four-by-four searchlight flooding the entrance. Out on the track his companion lay motionless. He hadn't moved since being hit.

Bruce held the man firmly by the shoulders.

'Stay calm. Quiet!'

Over a loud hailer a voice called in Mandarin. No doubt an invitation to give themselves up.

Three Chinese crept through the entrance, their long shadows stretching inside. Bruce spotted a possible way out through a gap in a corrugated metal panel a few feet away, but they couldn't move. The men were armed and their willing trigger fingers had convinced Bruce that taking prisoners was not their priority. He watched as the policemen swept their rifles around.

Another shot burst through the night air. A high-powered rifle from the UNMO station shattered the Chinese searchlight, sparking a mini firefight. Shots were exchanged before the vehicles pulled back, leaving the three police in the barn without support.

Bruce placed a steadying hand on the shaking runaway, indicating he should stay put, then slipped behind a dilapidated tractor. Panicked exchanges broke out between the officers. One yelled an order and fired two rounds into the darkness.

Bruce felt for the knife on his web belt. With a clear heat image he detected that the shooter was the closest to him. He stepped out behind the man and cupped a hand over his mouth, pulling him back and off balance, then thrust the blade down through his carotid artery and into his windpipe. The muted squeal, gargle of foaming blood, and thrashing of feet on the straw floor broke the silence, sending the other two policemen into retreat. He let the body thud to earth.

He returned to the terrified fugitive, grabbing his arm.

'Move!' he commanded, before smashing the metal panel aside and leading the man away in the lee of the barn, out of sight of the vehicles.

Seconds later the police opened fire on the barn. Machine-gun rounds punctured the corrugated sides and stray bullets cracked above their heads. But they made it, crossing the unmarked border into Mongolia, round to the far side of the station perimeter and safety.

2

Captain Jansen was waiting at the front gate when Bruce arrived with his new guest. He had watched the action unfold in horror.

'You can't bring him in here. It could be a trick,' he said.

'A trick? The other guy was hit, you moron! He's my client now. Search him if you're concerned about security. He's unarmed, for God's sake.'

Two soldiers swept the exhausted and dishevelled man for whatever he might be hiding. When they went for his trouser pockets the man refused and a scuffle broke out.

'Stop!' shouted Jensen. 'Show me.'

Reluctantly he pulled a 3.5 inch floppy disk from his pocket and handed it to Bruce. Jensen reached for it.

'My client,' Bruce said again, as he stowed the disk inside his combat jacket. 'Happy now?'

Without waiting for an answer, he started to guide the man away towards an empty dormitory, keen to discover what this was all about before anybody else got to him. As they went, another call crackled over Jensen's radio. Bruce could hear the panic in the voice as it shouted that a cluster of military vehicles was approaching, spreading out around the compound. The army must be taking over from the police.

Once in the dormitory, Bruce began a hurried debriefing.

'Can you speak English? What is your name?'

'I am Ying.' The Chinese man took a deep breath to steady himself. 'You must keep the disk. They will come here, but they will not search you.'

'They can't enter this site. It's UN.'

'They will break all rules to get me!'

'Okay, I'll get it to my people. But first—'

'No! It must not go to the authorities. We tried years ago to warn you.'

'What do you mean? So, who should I give it to? What's on it, anyway?'

'You must tell no-one. *No-one!* Years ago I, and my friend who they just shot ...' He paused to swallow his emotions, still trembling. 'We went to Hong Kong and met MI6. Only one man, the head of MI6 station. Nobody else. He tried to make us work as his agents. But that was too dangerous. We refused, but we gave him the information. Now you have the latest information. Much has changed. This is to stop a great war.'

Bruce's eyes widened. He blanked, his mind spiralling at the magnitude of what he had uncovered. What should he do?

'You must take it to England,' Ying continued. 'To the Lady of Rothwell. Nobody else.'

BEAUMONT

Bruce felt paralysed by the impossibility of the words: *Lady, Rothwell ...* Lady Margaret. He stayed his impulse to ask the obvious – *Who else should I give it to, if she is dead?* His intuition told him to do as requested, or at least try. He shook his head in an attempt to clear it.

Outside, the noise of armoured vehicles had drawn close. A loudspeaker was shouting demands in Mandarin.

'We need to get you away to safety, otherwise your information might not be worth much for very long. Wait here and stay down.'

He strode out into the yard. 'Someone get Skip!'

*   *   *

Bruce hustled Ying across the landing site to the helicopter, arriving to find Skip strapping himself into his seat. He opened the rear door, pushed Ying inside then clambered in after him. He slammed the door shut as the drone of vehicle engines grew around them.

'Skip, you need to get this thing airborne pronto. Can't say what will happen if they reach us.'

'What the hell is going on? This place never has incidents, let alone a shoot-out.'

'Move it!'

Skip didn't even bother to fasten his chin strap as he started the single engine. In the back Bruce worked on securing Ying before donning his own headset.

The aircraft's instrument console lit up as Skip flicked switches and yanked levers. The engine turned, ignited, then accelerated to operating speed.

'Hold on!' yelled Skip.

Scanning all around, he pulled the collective lever firmly upwards. Bruce felt the thrust as they began a rapid ascent.

The downwash from the Gazelle was all that kept the advancing Chinese soldiers from rushing in to grab their man. Bruce and Ying peered down at the shrinking figures below as Skip pulled max torque, stuffed in some rudder and span the aircraft into a rapid ascent. The few tufts of grass visible in the HLS lights spread flat and a dust bowl spat outwards at the hapless troops as the aircraft lifted and turned for Choibalsan.

Once they were straight and level, Skip interrupted the brief calm that had settled in the cabin.

'So Bruce, you gonna let me in on what this is all about?'

Bruce flicked his headset mic down in front of his mouth. 'Negative. Most secret, old boy. Sorry. Not much reward for your sterling efforts, I know.'

Bruce's words prevented Skip from asking more questions as he pressed on at full throttle, with one eye on the fuel gauge and the other on the nav computer.

Bruce reached into his combat jacket to retrieve a copy of the theatre resupply flights schedule. He studied the dates and times for the weekly Pacific Ghost Shuttle, a USAF C-17 Globemaster III from 17 Airlift Squadron, which flew from Guam to Ramstein Air Base in Germany via Kathmandu. The shuttle was due to arrive at Choibalsan midday tomorrow. Would that be soon enough to escape any crazy attempts by the Chinese to intercept them? Would they get away to Europe before the diplomatic storm erupted in Asia? Bruce prayed so.

The Gazelle landed in the dead of night. Nobody came to ask questions, which suited them just fine. Choibalsan was just a stop for refuelling and basic engineering services; there were no administrative facilities for checking passports. Skip helped himself to a refuel, took a comfort break, then headed back to the action at PK, while Bruce and Ying bunked down on the floor of the maintenance hangar, sandwiched between a perished rubber gym mat and a fusty blanket.

Sore and cold from a short night they awoke early. The remaining hours waiting for the flight gave Bruce time to form a plan. Soon the knot in his stomach abated, both because no enemy had appeared on the skyline, and also because he had conceived a cover story to get Ying onboard.

At midday the roar of the C-17 grew in the eastern sky. It kicked up a mass of dust in its wake as it landed, before turning off the runway and rolling to a rest outside the hangar. The rear ramp was lowered and logistics troops began ferrying supplies off using forklift trucks. They were joined by a local crew of four, who appeared around the hangar doors as if by clockwork. They had wasted no time waiting for the flight to arrive.

Bruce ushered Ying towards the plane. He knew he had to look confident as he escorted his 'associate' onboard. A goliath of an airman standing halfway up the ramp was already examining Bruce and Ying as they approached.

'Good day, sirs. And who do we have today?' he asked. A hand was extended, inviting identification documents to be presented. Neither was on the manifest.

'Captain Noble, British Army Intelligence Corps attached to UN Military Observers' Asia headquarters, Hong Kong. I am escorting Mr Ying.' Bruce felt a pulse of tension in his stomach as he heard his words aloud. *A Chinese name. That will raise suspicions.*

Bruce studied the man's rank insignia: he was a USAF master sergeant. He took Bruce's identity card then looked back sternly.

'Where is Mr Ying's ID?'

Ying said nothing and stared at the ground, his hands clasped in front of him.

'Mr Ying had rather an accident and nearly drowned after being swept away in a flash flood on the steppe. We were lucky to save him. Regrettably we could not do the same for his papers.' Bruce waited for a reaction, feeling the coil in his stomach tighten.

'Hmm, so why are you not booked on the flight? Can't let you on if you don't have paperwork.'

BEAUMONT

Having opened his dialogue with the master sergeant, Bruce was surprised how well the story then flowed. But thank God for thinking it through, he thought.

He presented Ying as an attached soldier from UNMO's Cambodian group, en route to the UK on leave. It was agreed that he would access suitable UN administrative services to obtain temporary ID at the first opportunity after landing in Germany. To further placate the master sergeant, Bruce agreed to complete a NATO travel order so there was some paperwork to back up his story. Further fabrication.

The three men moved aside as a pair of forklifts crossed with cargo, one struggling up, the other speeding down the broad metal gangway. The master sergeant returned Bruce's ID card in exchange for the signed travel order. He looked them both up and down again, not really buying it, Bruce guessed, but knowing not to ask too much when the 'intelligence' word was involved.

He raised an arm, inviting them aboard. 'That's good enough for me, gentlemen. Have a good flight.'

As the colossal jet got airborne, a huge weight left Bruce. He attempted to make conversation with Ying amid the din of engine noise, trying to gather any information that he was willing to share.

'So, what will you do when you get to Germany? Do you have somewhere to go?' he asked.

'I have a place in mind, but not in Germany. Somewhere with a loyal Chinese community.' Bruce took this to mean somewhere he would blend in without being dobbed in to the Chinese state. 'Somewhere with good ice cream too,' Ying added with a smile.

Six hours later, the aircraft reached Kathmandu, easing down into the wide bowl within the Nepalese mountains. The stop allowed for an hour's leg stretch during refuelling and cargo exchange. Ying headed off to the washrooms to get cleaned up and Bruce went in search of coffee, hot food and a telephone, unsure how to sell the last twenty-four hours to Alastair in Hong Kong.

An hour and a terse phone call later, he was waiting at the foot of the aircraft ramp for Ying to return. He was nowhere to be seen. Alastair had given strict instructions for Bruce to hand him over to the British authorities in Nepal and return as soon as possible, but Bruce knew he had crossed a red line when he had allowed Ying to tell him his cryptic plans to get away. When he let him head off alone, he had passed the point of no return. Now he had disobeyed a direct order. This would deepen the crisis and constitute the second charge on a court martial sheet – after the unauthorised facilitation of defection from a communist country.

Yet, amid his turmoil and panic, Bruce connected with a quiet resolve to maintain course. His thoughts ran to Lady Margaret and Rothwell. Was it all too much to believe? Too much to hope for? The only certainty seemed to be that there was too much at stake not to try and reach her, to reach *someone*.

He entered the C-17, waved to the air loadmaster that all was well, and sat back as the ramp was raised and the plane lurched onto the taxiway bound for Germany. Now the clock was ticking. Now *he* was a fugitive.

3

Trying to do the right thing would be worse than constant deception, Bruce considered. He had given the British authorities a lead when he and Ying had embarked on the C-17 in Choibalsan: they were on the flight manifest and therefore on the authorities' radar. That meant he would be pursued when his ETA in Hong Kong passed. His stomach churned. He would face disciplinary proceedings and likely lose the disk to faceless men in overcoats when intercepted at a UK port of entry. The thoughts spun in his mind while he tried to rest.

At Ramstein Air Base he slipped through arrivals without challenge and again phoned Alastair. He swallowed hard before his performance, feigning a bad line, inadequate local currency for the payphone necessitating a brief one-way conversation, and something about being delayed … *Did you say you are still in Kathmandu?* asked Alastair.

He bought himself at least twenty-four hours, but only if Alastair didn't contact the embassy in Nepal and discover that Ying had not been delivered to them.

After switching to civilian clothes, courtesy of Ramstein's PX, Bruce got himself to Frankfurt, then

BEAUMONT

Heathrow on a red-eye service with Lufthansa, arriving at 03:30 the next day. The terminal was almost deserted, which Bruce thought could work for or against him. His trepidation at passport control was short-lived, however, as a jaded official slid his passport back through the window without as much as a glance. Onward. He withdrew the daily maximum allowance of cash, took a Europcar hire and set off for Rothwell, all the while resisting instincts to smash the speed limit.

As dawn broke and Bruce drove along the main road beside his hallowed sixth form college estate, he was met with an incongruous scene that contrasted with his lasting memories of Rothwell's expanse and beauty. Through sections of overgrown foliage stood a tall fence with *Danger* and *Keep Out* signs dotted along it. The main entrance was closed by equally tall, ugly green metal gates and more warning signs. Bruce's belief that Lady Margaret had died eight years prior returned. He was furious with himself for not insisting Ying suggest an alternative contact.

In front of the wide entrance was a workmen's shelter – set over exposed pipework or cables, Bruce presumed. Parked beside the shelter was a works van, unmarked save for amber roof lights. Bruce didn't stop. Something was wrong.

As he drove past, in his side mirror he caught sight of two men sitting in the van. At ten past seven in the morning. Two hundred metres further on he swung into a narrow lane on the right. A gap between bramble bushes on the side made for a good spot to conceal the car. He got out and surveyed the area to orientate himself. The high security fence covered this, the northern side of the estate, too. He presumed it must run for miles.

Bruce was pleased that the fence was cheap, put up by someone on a budget. That meant it could be climbed. He removed his bomber jacket, clambered up to within reach of the barbed wire at the top, and flung it over as protection. He wasn't surprised when it tore as he tried to retrieve it from the other side, but he muttered a curse when he saw fibres of grey shell and white filling stuck to a barb and wafting in the air.

The sun was rising into a clear sky, revealing a carpet of dew and a layer of mist that covered the meadow up to the estate buildings. It was unnaturally still. Bruce recalled stories that birdsong was never heard at former Nazi concentration camps. He pressed on, trying to ignore the surge of emotions he felt as the semi-circular corrugated roof of the Elephant Hut came into view.

He crossed the main drive, threaded past the workshops and old college hospital, and went down the hospital road towards the house, before stopping in cover of undergrowth to observe the Oxford wing. Nearly every window was boarded, the once pristine sandstone walls weathered to a dirty teal green. Evidence of the firefight of 1988 remained in pockmarks on the walls. The ornate gardens were a mess, overgrown, gone to seed and suffocated.

As he approached the windows of the former Wessex common room, he saw a figure ahead, reclining in a deck chair beside a table, wearing a Panama hat and reading a broadsheet. Out of options, he gave up sneaking, straightened up and walked over. The man did not look up from his paper. Bruce scuffed the grit under his feet and cleared his throat.

'Please don't patronise me. Especially when you look so cold and lost,' began the stranger. He put down the paper and turned to Bruce.

'Oh ...' Bruce was lost for words. The man's face was leathery and lined. Long pointy features were framed by gleaming blue eyes that sparkled and stared hypnotically. A beauty and danger like Odysseus's sirens. 'Er, good morning ... um ... apologies for disturbing you.'

He continued to watch Bruce, as if contemplating what he had just heard. 'Well! I don't usually allow visitors, but I think I must make an exception for you. Why don't you sit and allow me to pour you a cup of tea.'

'Thank you,' Bruce replied, pulling up a rusty metal patio chair and taking a sip of cold, black tea.

'I knew something was coming. Could feel it. But what chance to meet you again!' the man continued. 'Do you remember ... this?' Pulling his tweed waistcoat aside, he yanked his shirt up to reveal a single scar between the ribs on his left side.

Bruce took a moment to connect. He turned white.

'Oh, please. Relax. I mean you no harm. I ate yesterday, anyway. I was most impressed, you understand? Do you know how dull it can be, never meeting a worthy opponent? The delight – and surprise, I might add – to realise you could see as I could in the pitch black of down there.'

Bruce felt light-headed. He was straining to comprehend their encounter.

'Well? Speak! How may Quentin Saxelby be of service?' the man asked in well-modulated tones that contrasted with the blood-curdling shrills of all those years ago in the deep of a tunnel.

'I came here to see her ladyship. However, the place seems rather deserted. Apart from yourself, of course.'

'And has been since perhaps a year after the curious episodes of, now … let me see … yes, it must be eight years ago. What a summer! It was not so very long after I ran out of American SEAL meat that the fireworks came – all the shooting above ground. You'll recall, I'm sure.' Bruce listened intently, reliving the whole thing. 'Then, not one week later and more hijinks, with new intruders creeping around my domain. And they must have really spooked her. First time ever, as I understand it, that anyone hit the panic button. Flooded the place! And that forced poor sickly QS to the surface like a scuttled sub. But I never saw *her* again since.'

BEAUMONT

Bruce hoped against hope. 'If Lady Margaret did somehow survive, where might she have gone?'

'Ah, naughty boy. Smitten, eh? She's much older than you, you know. But she must have been fond of you. Saved you from me. Both barrels of the Purdey! No love lost there. Yet we were so close once. Did so much for … Well, there it is. Another time, perhaps.'

The image of Quentin standing in the underground hall after being shot twice without apparent injury was branded in Bruce's memory, like so many things from that time. It seemed his host did not wish to speak further, though, at least not about trade secrets.

'Do you have any idea where she might have gone, sir?'

'Sir? … Don't. I am no sir,' He paused for a moment before continuing: 'Her *real* affections have always been with an associate whom we all knew, her fencing coach, a Monsieur Lucien Martell.' Bruce sat up. 'But only after dear old hubby Edward passed, I'll give her that. Monsieur Martell was a wealthy but private man – getting the pattern? His wealth has no connection with the cognac, by the way. He had a chateau in France, eastern border with Switzerland. Small place called Beaumont. That was years ago, but then I rather lost touch with life, so he might still live there, for all I know. Anyway, try it, if you really must.'

'And if not there?'

'If he is there and she is not, then she is probably dead.'

4

Five hours after leaving Rothwell, Bruce reached Dover, abandoned the hire car in a back street and headed to the ferry terminal. As the Tuesday afternoon sailing eased out of port, anxiety became relief. He was about to escape the UK undetected, the disk still in his possession, and now with a prospect of reaching Lady Margaret or Lucien Martell. Checking around him on the sunlit outer deck he didn't sense anyone among the day-trippers and business people paying attention to him. But he knew time was running out.

He devoured a pile of fish and chips, made sporadic attempts at rest, changed his remaining sterling, and looked through a cheap fold-out road map of France before Calais drew into view. As the vessel approached to dock, everyone had taken their places for a swift exit, with queues down to the car decks and along the passageways.

Then it came, the message over the tannoy: 'Would Mr Bruce Noble please report to the ship's information desk. Mr Noble, to the information desk, please.'

His heart nearly stopped. An image of Colchester military prison flashed through his mind and his stomach turned to water. He involuntarily moved a step in the opposite direction but checked himself. A woman with two children next to him picked up on his disquiet.

'Alright, love? Lookin' a bit peaky … Nearly there.'

He had to conjure a way out. He left the queue and started walking around the inner deck, past the toilets and lines of empty faces watching him.

Ahead he spotted a member of the crew in a hi-vis waistcoat carrying a walkie-talkie. A glance outside confirmed they had docked. He could hear the scraping and clanging of metal as the bow ramp was lowered. The engines fell quiet and the crowd stirred to push forward and disembark. Now was his moment.

'Excuse me!' he called. The crew member turned. 'I'm Mr Noble. Could you tell me which way to the information point please?'

'The information desk is deck above, forward of the galley,' she replied.

'Thanks.'

As Bruce headed past, he heard what he had hoped for: '*Control, Sally. Mr Noble is on his way.*'

That seemed to do the trick. The vehicles began to roll off and the foot passengers were shuffling out. Having ascended to the next deck, he promptly descended another staircase, then another, in a desperate attempt to reach a lorry at the back of the queue.

The vehicle deck was emptying fast. At the back, in the far corner, was an unmarked eighteen-wheeler with a curtain-sided trailer, on French number plates. Bruce trotted behind the lines of other vehicles and saw the driver in his cab watching for when to go. He cut around to the rear of the truck and hoped to God the driver wouldn't check his mirrors while he peeked under the curtain for a gap, unclipped the straps and clambered up. In the moments before moving off, he did his best to secure the lower edge of the side sheet and pin the straps so it wasn't flapping loose.

The truck was waved through customs. French bonhomie for one of their own.

It was two hours later, around 5 p.m. and getting dark, before they stopped. Bruce waited for the driver to head away, then jumped out. They had stopped at a roadside services. Making his way into a back street of the village, he read a sign above a filling station: *Hettencourt*. He checked the map. It was just off the A1 to Paris.

He had been scouting around for ten minutes when he came upon a tired old Triumph 650cc Bonneville, complete with kick-start. It was in a cluttered alleyway, a few metres along from the back door of a shop – a bakery, judging by the aromas emanating from within. The deserted setting explained why the owner had left his crash helmet stowed on a mirror. Alas, no keys.

Bruce did a double-take, realising that the ignition was not near the 'bars between the clocks but below the seat. An old bike. He checked around, took out his Leatherman utility tool and tried the thinner screwdriver in the ignition.

BEAUMONT

The lock was as worn as the rest of the bike, loose enough for the screwdriver to find its way in. After some waggling, it turned, bringing on the ignition light. Bruce opened the fuel tap and slipped the helmet on. He quietly turned the bike around, jumped a couple of times on the kick-start and sped away. Just before he rounded a corner towards the A1, he checked his mirrors to see the bakery's back door fly open.

Seven hours and three fuel stops later, a freezing Bruce Noble thrummed into Beaumont, breaking the midnight silence like an uninvited Spitfire. Another vehicle hidden, abandoned, he started a hopeless search for the chateau in the dark. At the centre of the village a woman was wiping down tables in a bistro. He tapped on the window.

'*Bonjour, Madame!*'

She threw down her cloth and came to the door. '*Bonsoir, Monsieur.*'

'*Je cherche le château de Monsieur Martell.*'

He was met with a frown, then she pointed up and along the road to the east. '*Un kilomètre.*'

'*Tres bien. Merci.*'

She forced a cough, and held out a hand for Bruce to make payment. He produced his wallet and fumbled a ten franc note into her palm.

'*Merci, monsieur. Bonne nuit.*'

Château Beaumont rose against a cavernous indigo sky, its single conical spire piercing the stars, the ink-black slate roof bathed in moonlight. The few dim lights showing behind the windows gave Bruce hope that someone was home. Being so close to delivering the disk was torture. Images of being sent away – *No Monsieur Martell here* – started to gnaw at him. He tramped up to the enormous front door and yanked the bell mechanism.

Eventually, it opened.

'*Oui?*'

The man was still up, dressed in black trousers and black roll-neck sweater. Bruce's fatigue was draining him, his brain clouded. He began in English.

'Sorry for disturbing you, sir. Are you Monsieur Martell?' The man said nothing. 'I am here to see Monsieur Martell. It's very important.'

'Your name, *s'il vous plaît.*'

'Noble. It's Bruce Noble. From Rothwell.'

'One moment, please.'

The door closed. Bruce tugged his tattered jacket tightly about him to stave off the shivering that was taking hold. It intrigued him that the man showed no surprise at his late arrival, nor his tone.

A few minutes later the door reopened and Bruce was invited inside to wait in a capacious living room. He suddenly felt exhausted, slumping into the plush grey fabric cushions of the Lawson-style sofa and staring up at the dark wooden beams crossing the white ceiling. Across from him was a matching sofa, both set beside an imposing limestone fireplace with broad mantel and tapering chimney breast that reached to the top of the room. The embers lay dying in the grate. Much like the way he was feeling, Bruce decided.

Ten minutes later the door opened and a man in a burgundy towelling dressing gown and Barbour check slippers came into the room. Bruce guessed this must be Lucien Martell, a tall, brawny, well-groomed man of around fifty with black, wavy hair, whose slight excesses were neatly brushed back around a tough face of strong bones and weathered skin.

He stood up and extended a hand, which was received, then the man gestured for Bruce to sit.

'Thank you for seeing me, Monsieur, at this very late hour.'

'What can I do for you, young man? And please, call me Lucien.'

'I have very important, very urgent, news for Lady Cadogan-Brandt.'

Lucien immediately sat back and let out a long breath. He looked away towards the fire, pursing his lips, breaking eye contact. Bruce's gut tightened. *She's dead.*

'That could be difficult, *mon ami*. I presume you didn't hear what happened to her? How do you know her?'

Bruce outlined their history, but held back from speaking about the last few days as best he could.

'It would help us both if you could share something of what has brought you here now, otherwise I cannot help you,' said Lucien.

'I was told in the strongest terms that it was only to her that I should speak,' Bruce replied.

'Then speak to her, you shall,' came a voice behind him, as Lady Margaret rounded the sofa and sat down.

5

Bruce stared at the woman sitting before him. It was some moments before he willed himself to react. With reserves near empty, he was running on adrenaline. Seeing her brought a torrent of conflicting emotions and memories. The years since their last encounter had established the grey in her hair, which now dominated the blonde, although it still ran long and luxuriant. Her physique remained trim and athletic. The radiant blue eyes continued to cast a spell upon her subjects.

'You're alive!' he said, finally.

'Very much so, thanks to you, I believe? I always thought it was you who sent the arrow. Impressive shot, by the way. I was somewhat stuck until you intervened. Thank you for saving my life.'

'I saw the door closing and you hadn't got out of the tunnel. I thought you wouldn't make it.'

They paused, just taking in for a moment that it was a happy ending.

Then Bruce couldn't hold back from asking the burning question of the last eight years. 'I don't suppose you have heard anything more about my mother – what happened to her?'

Lady Margaret waited. Bruce continued, 'I know you had nothing to do with her disappearance, but your words stayed with me – about letting go and moving on. It's counterintuitive, though. To tell me I should put it behind me suggests you *might* know something. I always wondered.'

'Very well, I will do my best to go back over that conversation with you. Tomorrow, may I suggest? After you have rested. For now, should we talk about the "very important" matter at hand?' she said, raising an eyebrow.

Bruce reached inside his jacket to retrieve the disk. He set it on the table.

Nobody spoke for a while. They eyed the small square of black plastic that beckoned to be viewed.

At last Lady Margaret said, 'It needs to be checked before we do anything. Please follow me, Bruce.' She led the way from the living room, with Lucien following behind.

During the short walk to the basement, Bruce outlined the essentials of how the disk came into his possession. They passed through a wooden door under the main staircase, then descended a set of smooth stone steps which led to an open area under a low arched ceiling.

The space was quiet, private, as if even echoes knew not to enter. Under the soft yellow glow of a central bulb set in a conical metal shade, a line of desks and a couple of chairs ran along the wall opposite, plus computers, a bank of monitors of various sizes, a pair of telephones and a VTC system, filing cabinets and other office equipment. To Bruce this had the hallmarks of a mini operations centre.

There they were joined by the man who had answered the front door. He was introduced as Marc Arnaud, Monsieur Martell's personal assistant. Marc sat at the computer on the far right with the three watching over his shoulder. A stocky, muscular man with thick chestnut brown hair and equally dark eyes, he gave Bruce flashbacks of Rory. The resemblance was sufficient for Bruce to feel a wave of sadness wash over him, something he hadn't felt so much of late, but which touched him whenever he recalled his best friend at Rothwell.

The computer was stand-alone, not connected to the internet. Marc inserted the disk into a separate drive to check for viruses and trojans. He looked over his shoulder to Lucien and Lady Margaret in turn. '*D'accord?*' With their nods of approval he opened the only file. The document was entirely in Chinese characters.

'Ah,' Lady Margaret remarked, 'no surprise, I suppose. However, we have no Chinese linguists present, unless by chance ... Bruce?'

He shook his head.

'We will have to find a fluent Mandarin speaker we can trust to decipher the document,' she said thoughtfully. 'It will have to be an insider.'

They returned to the living room, where Bruce ran through the whole chain of events, this time with every detail he could recall, from his impulse to visit the UNMO station at Poklonny Krest to ditching the Triumph in the woods outside Beaumont. At this, Marc was duly despatched to get rid of the evidence.

'At least with the motorbike disposed of the police should not come here, unless they plan on conducting door-to-door enquiries across all of France. It was fortuitous that you rode by night, Bruce,' said Lucien. 'And you used cash after Heathrow. Smart.'

'My lady, am I allowed to ask why Ying specified you and no-one else?' Bruce asked, unable to contain his curiosity any longer. 'I mean, setting aside the previous encounter with MI6, what is it that you can do that they cannot, or would not?'

Lady Margaret and Lucien exchanged anxious looks. She circled the room, lost in contemplation, before replying, 'Ying isn't his proper name, Bruce. It's a pseudonym, it means Hawk.' Bruce's expression set with bewilderment. 'He is allied to us, and we are a group of people spread around the world with a common interest for mankind's peaceful evolution. Can I start with that, without sounding radical or alarmist?'

Bruce puffed his cheeks as he blew out a breath. 'Wow. That's a start alright.' His mouth opened to form his next words, but didn't quite know what they should be.

'So Quentin Saxelby, your resident caretaker at Rothwell, is he a member of this group?' he asked at last.

'He is ... or was. I am not quite sure now. Tell me more. You said you just sat and spoke. In the open air?'

'Yes, the man who once stabbed me was most ... convivial. Even buoyant. Curious chap, too. Very unusual voice, not weird, almost enticing. Which *is* weird, I guess. And how did he survive you shooting him that night?'

The questions were mushrooming.

'I think we should retire to bed. There is much to cover and tomorrow could be a long day. Do we agree?'

The next morning, with Bruce sporting fresh but rather oversized clothes, courtesy of Lucien Martell, they gathered for breakfast in the kitchen. Everyone was sat around an antique French oak table, their small talk interspersed with sounds of croissants being munched and cutlery scraping plates. As they finished eating, Marc, who apparently doubled as the cook, untied his apron and threw it onto a black granite worktop. He picked up a wad of paperwork from the dresser. Now it was his turn to lead events.

'Madame, Messieurs, I have used a prototype translation programme recently sent by our associate in Seoul to view the file. Here is a printout.'

Marc presented two copies of the thirty-three page report. It helped, partly.

The chatter and eating stopped. Lady Margaret's brow furrowed as she scythed into the pages. Bruce peered over her shoulder and she tilted the document towards him. The more brains the better. Lucien was likewise engrossed in his copy.

The minutes ticked by. Her ladyship flicked through the final pages, almost without looking at them, before returning to the front page. She frowned as she reread the title, slowly vocalising the key word.

'What's a *Fùjiàn*?' she asked.

'In this context, I think appendix or similar,' said Marc, referring to a Mandarin dictionary. 'The software isn't perfect. Sometimes it only translates proper nouns to Pinyin, not English. It says Appendix D: *The People's Medicine.*'

'So this document is just a part of something much bigger,' said Lucien.

Silence resumed as they read on. Bruce remembered Ying's words on the plane, that the disk was the means to stop a great war. He looked on anxiously as sheets were turned back and forth.

'*Mon Dieu!*' Lucien exclaimed at last. 'On page four ...'

Lady Margaret turned to the page and read. She raised her head to engage with each in turn. 'Can this be right? A plan for the economic subjugation of the West? Using a genetically engineered virus? That's biological warfare!'

'Soft power,' Lucien mused. 'Winning without fighting. Without your enemy even realising there *is* a war. Very clever.'

'Smacks of Sun Tzu,' Bruce put in.

Lady Margaret shook her head quizzically then looked up. 'Bruce, tell me again what Ying said about trying to inform MI6 in Hong Kong years ago.'

'He said they spoke to only one man, the head of the Hong Kong station, who tried to recruit them to work as agents. They declined, but handed over the information anyway.'

'I see. Please wait while I fetch something from the study.'

Lady Margaret headed off and returned minutes later, thumbing through a dossier in a burgundy cover.

'I didn't think I liked the sound of that,' she said. 'Guess who was head of MI6 in Kowloon between 1980 and 1984? James Tavener. It's right here, in his resumé.'

'*Non!*' said Lucien.

Bruce felt himself reddening. 'Just a moment. Are we talking about the James Tavener I knew – Jim Tavener, so-called lab technician, TA lieutenant, arsehole of Rothwell College, so up himself but failed to save Rory on Crib Goch? The Jim Tavener who disappeared at the same time my mother vanished ... left the college and nobody said a word. Tavener is ex-MI6?' He thudded a fist on the table. 'So this is all connected!'

'Please, Bruce,' said Lady Margaret. 'I know it's big shock for you and a lot to take in. Just bear with us for a moment. This is serious.'

'What do you mean, my lady?' asked Marc.

She took a deep breath and began to recount what happened in the days after the dramatic events of eight years before.

'Soon after Tavener left Rothwell, a Roger Gleeson of the Security Service appeared at my door, asking about Mr Tavener. On a number of levels that was understandable. It was possible that Tavener was an actual missing person then. But Gleeson was MI5, not the police. I suspected that Jenny Noble-Franks' disappearance and her connection to Rothwell as mother of one of the students, plus Tavener's employment there and his history in the intelligence services, were dots that Gleeson had joined. But it was a small slip in his questioning that caught my attention. He asked whether Tavener ever discussed his former career. Then, becoming more specific, whether he had ever mentioned times or places of which he was fond. *Fond.* "What about the Middle East or South America? Or Hong Kong?" asked the good Mr Gleeson. *Hong Kong!*'

Lucien snorted.

'Can you see the glitch there, Bruce?' she asked.

'What? that he would never discuss his career in intelligence?'

'Not really. It's the last part. The Middle East and South America are regions. Hong Kong is not. He didn't say Asia or the Far East. He was leading the witness. He knew what he was doing and it felt desperate.' She thought for a moment before continuing: 'One is led to infer that Tavener possessed information of similar magnitude to this document all those years ago in Hong Kong, thanks to Ying. And coming from the same source makes me suspect that the plans were of a similar nature. His interest wasn't to save the world from catastrophe, however. I expect his actions were only motivated by self-interest – how he could trade the information for his own financial gain.'

'Ha! Retirement planning,' said Lucien.

Bruce stood up and paced to the back door, deep in thought, then spun on his heel.

'My lady, I don't doubt Tavener's deceitful character – certainly not any more – yet I must play devil's advocate for a moment. How do we know that his attempt to recruit Ying wasn't normal practice? That he didn't act honourably? After all, there has been no biological attack or outbreak of any significance to threaten the West. On the other hand, if he did act as you suggest, what if he has already sold the intel? He would have to do it sometime, before it became outdated.'

Lady Margaret got up from the breakfast table.

'All valid points, Bruce. And the essence of it is that we don't know, and therefore we must find out. You see, Ying was adamant that the disk did not go to the intelligence services. He must have had suspicions about Tavener's motives, a reason to distrust him, which leads me to believe Tavener did not act honourably. He may have sold already, but sometimes the most valuable intelligence can be just knowing intent. Details inevitably evolve, so knowing intent becomes king. It appears that has not changed, which means Tavener's retirement plan would endure till conditions provided either opportunity or imperative to sell. The events in Mongolia could certainly fit the bill.'

'So this is double bad. Not only do you – your group or whoever – have to save the world from economic meltdown and global conflict, it has to happen before Tavener cashes in on his intelligence. He will sell to the Chinese, presumably, as the most interested party and therefore the highest bidder. Otherwise he will threaten to sell to the West. Once the Chinese discover that their secret is out they will double down on security leaks – big purge of personnel and a foreign face not getting within five hundred miles of Beijing. They will change their execution plans, Enigma-style, so our intelligence becomes useless. After that it would be almost impossible to infiltrate Chinese sites to find a way to combat the threat.'

Lady Margaret smiled at Bruce's analysis. 'Therefore?' she said, encouraging the last step.

'Therefore, a great war will likely follow, just later. And for what? Tavener will be sat with a pile of cash on Anthrax Island.'

'That's why it's called blind ambition, Bruce.'

6

They took a break to allow the bad news to register. Lucien and Marc went to the study in search of contacts to advise on biological warfare, virology and other expertise that would be required for a forthcoming operation. Lady Margaret led Bruce outside to walk the grounds and get some air.

'We were to speak about your mother, Bruce.'

'Yes. Thank you. Well, as I said last night, at Rothwell I failed to grasp the logic behind your advice to look forward and get on with my life. I always wondered whether there was more to it, whether you knew something but couldn't tell me.' He stopped short of saying *wouldn't tell me*.

'I see. I think you may have read too much into my words. I was offering advice so that in the worst case you didn't suffer further loss – loss of your life's opportunity – and compound what was already happening.'

'Oh, so that's it?' said Bruce with a sigh.

'Our paths crossed, Bruce, and we have helped each other – saved each other's lives, no less. That bonds us, even though you haven't seen me in years and we did not relate as friends. But what matters to you, Bruce, matters to me, which means I would always treat your mother's well-being as top priority in any way I could. I hope you will understand and accept that. It's as much as I can offer.'

Bruce welled up. The slimmest prospect of hope had again evaporated. The most he could manage was to bow his head in acknowledgement, unable to get any words out.

They crunched along a gravel path beside a broad scruffy lawn that had not been tended through the long, cold winter. Ahead of them the peak of the Salève, crested with fresh snow, rose above a screen of mixed conifers and birch trees.

'Do you plan to stop Jim Tavener? How will you locate him after all this time?' he asked.

'With great difficulty. He could use anyone as a proxy. And he could choose any time and place to sell his information – assuming he knows what happened in Mongolia.'

'He *will* know, if his plan requires specific conditions to trigger it. The absolute decider for him will be whether he learns it was Ying who escaped – if his name gets out. There's a diplomatic shitstorm in full swing waiting for my return. I broke quite a few international rules, thanks to going with my gut. I'll be thrown in Colchester, no shadow of a doubt, so I hope it's been worth it, as I officially have no future now.'

Bruce looked to the ground and shook his head, shocked by his own words and what they meant.

Lady Margaret turned to him, her eyes full of compassion. Then Bruce looked past her, up to the Salève.

'What is it?' she asked.

Bruce pondered. 'Ridiculous really, and wishful thinking, given my situation, but …'

'But what?'

'You say Tavener would use a third party to conduct a sale.'

'It would be standard practice, and for someone with his morals, a given. He would control proceedings remotely and the proxy would be little more than a courier and a mouthpiece. But if things went wrong, they would take the fall, not Tavener. I doubt whether they would ever meet him in person.'

'If he has a history in intelligence, then using unsavoury characters from his past runs the risk of being traced. It's still long odds, but his service file would give the likes of MI5 somewhere to begin. To my mind, what he wants is someone who could carry out his instructions, someone he could control, but with no obvious link to him.'

'Sensible enough, I suppose. And ...?' she said, watching Bruce closely, sensing a nascent psychic intuition at work.

'Jez Picher. Would Jez Picher fit the bill?'

'The boy who threw you over the balcony?'

'And the reason we all ended up in the Principal's office, where you wiped everyone's memories clean with your chemical smoke bombs. Yes, him,' Bruce replied. 'That's it! That's what all the angst was about back then. Why I felt a compulsion to let it go. And you backed me, remember? It fits, doesn't it? Against all odds, he could be the only chance of getting to Tavener.'

She grinned at Bruce wrestling impossibility and actuality. 'Providence ...'

'My gut says that's why. I don't feel any other possibility. Let's face it, your world seems to operate on an entirely different plane, doesn't it? I mean ... here I am, again!'

Bruce developed his hypothesis. 'Picher got commissioned, but he didn't last long, so I heard. He was thrown out of the army after a string of misdemeanours finally caught up with him. A friend saw him at a careers fair in Tidworth, said he made contact with a US private defence outfit called Terrain Ops Corp. There are many such players in the defence market. They do some legitimate work, like providing support services in conflict zones, as a cover for the grubby, off-the-books stuff that pays the big bucks. Apparently he's muling dodgy cash around the globe for this so-called military logistics company.'

'That *would* fit the profile, but only if Tavener took note of him at Rothwell, which I believe he might have done. He would have been planning it all along and Picher's character made him an obvious candidate.'

'Naturally I would be only too pleased to assist in checking up on Jez, and well placed to do so, as an old ... um ... associate. But it does look like I will be locked up and therefore incommunicado for a few years.'

BEAUMONT

'You would be perfect for such a task. He wouldn't suspect you. Might hate you, but not suspect you. And perhaps you *could* be available, if we swung circumstances in your favour.'

Bruce puzzled over what she meant but said nothing as they returned inside.

*   *   *

Forty-eight hours later, a suitably rumpled Captain Noble walked through the gates of police headquarters Kathmandu to report being mugged. His invisible return had been orchestrated by Marc Arnaud, and included a first-rate false passport, since discarded, in the name of Christopher Brown.

By the time Bruce reached Eaton House five days later, the initial diplomatic ructions had subsided. Without any papers or passport, the delays with police interviews and time taken to recover him to Hong Kong meant that the fuss had died down.

As the lift doors opened onto the tenth floor he swallowed hard and braced himself. He would do his utmost to keep a low profile, but he knew that wouldn't allow him to escape being the centre of attention in the office.

He was immediately grounded, pending ongoing enquires ahead of an expected court martial for trashing international protocols, including the alleged murder of a

Chinese police officer and aiding the defection of a Chinese official. Bruce guessed that Alastair had already convicted him in his own mind. He gave him all possible demeaning, non-sensitive duties to conduct from his new abode away from confidential material: the storeroom. Bruce had expected things to be serious but he was not prepared for this passive bullying, this form of humiliation *ante*. It was moronic and sealed in Bruce's mind his conviction that he had to tackle the much bigger crisis that lay beyond the goldfish bowl of the Hong Kong office.

Days of torrid legal wrangling dragged on. An Army Legal Services solicitor, who evidently had failed to secure a career in civvy street, was appointed to represent him. The brief did get the decisive outcome Bruce was hoping for, however. He was given the opportunity to resign, rather than stand trial by court martial. Extenuating circumstances were cited: Bruce had acted to preserve life where a clear threat had been identified, for which there were many witnesses. Beijing didn't pursue the killing of a Chinese police officer. Although furious, they were also embarrassed by the whole affair. No murder weapon was found and nobody had witnessed the alleged killing, so there was no concrete evidence to bring charges.

Bruce kept his head down and his mouth shut. He satisfied his chain of command by forgoing all entitlements to resettlement services and remaining leave. In a month he was gone from Hong Kong, out of the British Army and heading to northern Cyprus.

7

The Chinese new year had started well for President Tao Wei. The towering hulk, who always wore a fixed smile, no longer merely overshadowed, but had finally eclipsed all his former peers in the National People's Congress and the Chinese Communist Party. He was satisfied with the fruits of his labours, the reward for his courage, acting for the good of the Party and all Chinese people. They had left him no choice but to coax and bully his way through lesser men who could not see the way.

He allowed himself a moment of proud reflection, taking in a lungful of fresh morning air. His masterstroke had been to achieve the constitutional amendment which allowed his unlimited term as President. But his good humour was soon marred when his thoughts returned to the news that two officials at the Hulunbuir bioweapons facility had sought to defect, and caused a large fire at a sensitive phase of his programme.

As he soaked up the early morning sun on the terrace of Changchungong, the Palace of Eternal Spring, Tao attempted to settle his frustration by watching his two children play around the trunk of a pagoda tree. Since

1980, government policy was a maximum of one child per family, for most people. But Tao was not most people.

The sprawling site of Beijing's Forbidden City, in which Tao had established his private residence, was about half a mile wide by one mile long. The basic layout dated back to the early fifteenth century, under Emperor Yong Le. The imperial hierarchy of the time applied to geography too, and the City was the centre of a system of concentric proximity, where the highest ranking in society lived closest to its walls. But Tao had no time for such nonsense. Opened to the public in 1949, Tao closed it after coming to power in 1993 to repurpose it for the domestic needs of China's ruling communist party officials. The shift was driven by a need for unity, identity and security, Tao had asserted. But his peers suspected that such notions ran in many directions.

He left his children under the care of their *bǎomǔ* and returned inside to his presidential suite. This setting, away from the distractions of the main parliament in the National Assembly and Great Hall of the People, was his preference when contemplating matters close to his heart.

He looked to the head of his palace guard, who snapped to attention as the President entered.

'No disturbances.'

The man bowed and swept out of the room, closing the doors behind him.

Tao went to the safe behind his desk, dialled the six-digit code into the rotating lock, and removed a file bound in a cover of the distinctive scarlet of the CCP. In some matters, he preferred the old ways, like his dated safe. Its system of mechanical wheels, pins and slots made for a type of safe that most could not open first time, even when they knew the combination. It meant no instant defeat by electronic hacking. He unfolded the A3 plan on his desk and cast his eye over the strategic map of *Fènghuáng* – the Phoenix Programme.

Tao smiled to himself as he surveyed the array of red triangles spread across the map of China, marking one hundred underground sites now in top-secret development. Each was a nuclear protective facility, capable of sustaining ten thousand people for two years. He swelled with pride at his grand scheme, which was moving ever closer to fruition. This would be the greatest achievement of his life. In fact, it would be the greatest achievement in the life of any Chinese ruler throughout history.

So secret was the programme that Tao dealt directly and separately with his hand-picked team of scientists and engineers. All were sworn to allegiance by the honour of personal direction from the President. Such secrecy, however, meant that his military leadership, and especially Marshal Lin Xiangquin, the chief of the People's Liberation Army, were only familiar with parts of Phoenix.

The rivalry that had grown between Tao and Lin had begun as a healthy competitiveness and mutual recognition during their university days in Beijing. They unwittingly promoted each other's careers by levelling criticisms that marked them out as larger-than-life characters who got results by bending the rules, bold splashes of colour in a sea of grey men. The effect was complementary because they moved along different paths – the soldier and the party official. Early differences faded from sight in their mid-careers: Tao, having been raised in privilege as the son of a senior communist party official, was accustomed to life within sight of the Forbidden City; Lin had risen from the poverty of Lanzhou amid brutal industrialisation that displaced families and flattened homes. It was ideological differences that caused tensions between them. When both reached senior positions by their late forties it was ironic that the soldier was a man of reason and the party official was a fanatic.

In 1979 Lin was a thirty-five year old infantry major in the Battle of Cao Bằng in Vietnam. There he learned hard lessons about war: its unpredictability, the political perversions that can cause and undermine it, and the acceptance of compromise. The Chinese were victorious but suffered heavy losses at the hands of local militia, while largely failing to locate and engage Vietnamese regular units. After only seventeen days they declared that they had achieved their war aims and withdrew. The scorched earth tactics of their exit left Lin with a lasting sense of shame.

Tao, by contrast, had never felt the collision of ideology and reality. He had an unshakeable conviction that Chinese communist doctrine was founded on principles that were intrinsically superior to those of a liberal, decadent West. The relative inferiority of China's standing in the world, its struggles with poverty and the failure to mobilise a huge population to be the leading industrial power in history all gnawed at his very being. It was an enduring humiliation that he was bent on overturning.

Tao's first term as president had brought modest territorial gains through military muscle-flexing. Disputed areas met with renewed Chinese sovereign interest: unpopulated reefs, shoals and atolls in the South China Sea underwent development to enable military power projection; there was manoeuvring to install Chinese political leadership in Tibet; skirmishes ensued in border areas with northeast India, and intimidation of Taiwan with fighter incursions in its airspace became a regular occurrence. But these were ultimately little more than distractions and exercises for the development of his geopolitical strategy based upon campaigns conducted at sub-critical intensity. Tao fine-tuned his successes by using limited means that achieved results without generating tangible resistance. And that gave him his big idea.

He returned to the safe and withdrew another file: Appendix D: *The People's Medicine*.

Its thirty pages felt heavier than they should. Compared with a map of protective bunkers on home ground, Appendix D brought home the prospect of rolling the die. It did not elicit the warm glow of pride. President Tao placed the file on his desk and stood upright for a moment, his hands at his sides, to compose himself, to remember his destiny.

The People's Medicine had begun as an initiative conducted at his behest within China's three bioweapons research facilities. They had prototyped the mutation of a respiratory virus that was relatively harmless to ethnic Chinese, having no more effect than the common cold. Other races were likely to experience more severe symptoms.

Tao's masterstroke was that such a virus could be cultivated with limited lethality and then be surreptitiously released. Too severe a pathogen would kill so many that investigations would be pursued to confirm an act of war. The optimal lethality would more likely be accepted as another natural mutation within the animal kingdom and freak transfer to humans – a zoonosis. Better still, when many became ill globally, and some died, it would be treated with heightened caution. That would bring normal life and productive output in the West to a standstill. It would cause economic turmoil and, ideally, economic collapse, as government debt became unmanageable, supply chains stalled, and the social order imploded. The West would suffer total systemic failure. It would literally eat itself alive. Its ideology would be dead.

However, the programme was not complete, and the laboratory fire at Hulunbuir was a substantial setback. With the lead virologist killed trying to escape and the project leader now a defector, their deputies would try to recover the work and get back on schedule. Tao was frustrated and uneasy, knowing that a miscalculation could cost him his leadership and set China back decades.

He would not have the opportunity again that he had been creating over the past three years – the opportunity to engage the US and its allies strategically in the South China Sea and the Western world over trade. The US and international carrier group exercises to be held in 1997, in what Tao held as Chinese waters but which the West declared as international waters, would provide the perfect conditions for the next part of his military campaign. And when Appendix D became effective, years of Western companies enjoying profits from cheap Chinese labour would be undone. The skills, know-how and technology learned by that cheap labour would be the dominant force in global economics. Hard power and soft power would be brought to bear.

The teams at Hulunbuir would have two months before President Tao ordered *The People's Medicine* to be released.

8

James Tavener was lucky. A year later, after the reunification of Hong Kong in July 1997, he might not have heard the news about Hulunbuir so easily. Soaking up the mid-morning Sardinian sun with a cappuccino in hand, he read and reread the sensational coverage of the incident at the UNMO station in Mongolia and the fire at the bioweapons lab. The new Hong Kong paper *Apple Daily*, set up by Jimmy Lai in 1995, was controversial, but it had reach. That meant it was available on the island, in an outlet near the San Benedetto market in Cagliari. With its extensive use of paparazzi, *Apple Daily* had become one of Tavener's most reliable intel tripwires, even with a day's shipping delay.

He looked up from the page and across the broad terrace that once belonged to Signore, reflecting on his double masterstroke in 1988: cracking the Rothwell vault and turning disaster into victory here in Sardinia. But it was the latter – his second and final visit to Signore to hand over the product and collect his bounty – that came back to him so vividly.

He had arrived at Cagliari airport on a sticky July morning, an envelope of photos safely tucked inside the money pouch he wore round his waist, hidden under his linen jacket. He made his way to the familiar pickup point, round the corner from the Caffè Antico, and was once more ushered into a waiting Mercedes. As before, he was blindfolded and squashed between two men for the drive to the crime boss's remote villa in the mountains.

This time the reception was cooler, even brusque.

'This way, James,' Signore said, leading him to the familiar side room with the Hockney original, *A Bigger Splash, 1967*, hanging opposite the windows overlooking the pool. The two heavies followed. 'So James, you have it?'

Tavener took out the photos and handed them over. Signore studied them, a few seconds on each of fifteen prints.

'So, what do we have here exactly? Explain it to me.'

Tavener glanced back at Signore's men, both powerfully built, wearing dark suits and ties, stood one behind each shoulder.

'What you have here, Signore, is the most up-to-date portion of an extensive but otherwise outdated index of everyone involved in Lady Margaret's organisation. As you know, the organisation has variously interfered in your world and those of your business associates, including collaboration with state security services.' He reached into a pocket to retrieve a breath freshener and some mints. 'Do you mind?' he continued, raising the mints in request. 'I love garlic, but it doesn't love me.' He forced a chuckle which was not reciprocated.

Signore waved a hand to do as he pleased, then continued with his questions. 'So we have codenames, tied to family names, locations, current employment and ... what's this?' He squinted at a photo, trying to make out the tiny words. 'Contact protocol?'

'It's just an indicator of the preferred way of covertly making contact. To meet or exchange information. That sort of thing.'

'*That sort of thing*,' pondered Signore, as he looked past Tavener into space. 'My concern is whether all of this is "that sort of thing", James.' Tavener blinked in surprise. 'Yes, James. How can I trust this information? How can I trust *you*?'

Tavener glanced again at the guards who stirred behind him. He chewed another mint and twisted the nozzle on the breath freshener nervously, while contemplating a response.

'Well? answer me!' Signore snapped.

'I don't understand. What do you not trust?'

'You! I don't trust you because you lied to me, James. During your previous visit you said you shot the man and the woman in the multi-storey and left them for my men to remove.'

'I did. That's what happened. The police found no bodies.'

'That's right, James. They didn't. But my men did not take them. I had no men watching you. Someone was on to you, James. But who? Was it *her*. Did she outsmart you?'

Tavener felt the adrenaline flood into his arteries; his pulse started to race. He heard the smooth brush of metal on leather after the pop of a catch as a guard readied his pistol.

With the mints in one hand and breath freshener in the other he raised his hands in submission. 'I don't know what to say, Signore …'

'Of course you don't.'

'Apart from ... Goodbye!'

Tavener sprayed over his shoulder, casting the VX nerve agent towards Signore's men. They choked and fell almost instantly, clutching at their throats as faces flushed and eyes watered and bulged in paralysis. Holding his breath, he turned the spray on Signore, then ran for the door, slamming it as he went out into the clean air of the corridor.

The antidote in the mints would buy him time, but Tavener knew he would need to shower and change his clothes as soon as possible to avoid the persistent threat from the VX.

He slipped into the next room, grabbed a cast-iron bookend from a nearby shelf and listened for the first passing guard. The man entered the corridor and wandered through. Tavener emerged behind him and struck the back of his head with the bookend, killing him instantly. He searched the body, taking a gun and silencer and a short-wave radio. He fitted the silencer, dragged the body out of view and crept upstairs.

Moving from room to room along the pool side of the villa, Tavener spotted the remaining five goons. He estimated a further six people to be on site in addition to the guards, including a gardener, cleaning staff and cooks. From an end window he had a clear line to fire on the two guards at the main gate some thirty metres away. There was nowhere for them to take cover if he missed with his first shots, but it would probably consume half of his ammo to take them both. He slid the magazine from inside the pistol grip to check the contents. It felt full, thirteen rounds.

He opened fire. Two double taps took down the man on the right. Only one pair of shots was needed for the guy on the left, who was slow to realise what was happening, thanks to the reduced noise of the shots. As he hoped, someone inside the house saw the guards go down. The screaming started. Another pair of hoods rushed out to the aid of their comrades, thinking the danger was outside the gates. This time Tavener waited till the newcomers stopped moving: one crouched over a downed man, the other tentatively peering over the wall from a wooden platform. Tavener took his time, lined up each shot and dropped them both. Five rounds left.

The screaming from domestic staff was halted by the remaining guard shouting at them to shut up and stay inside.

BEAUMONT

Tavener headed out of the bedroom and squatted behind an armchair at the end of the landing with a view of the top of the staircase. He extended his aim over the chair and waited. The minutes ticked by and he felt the first signs of nausea. Would the last guard sweep the house alone? He would have to find out what had happened to Signore.

Tavener crunched another mint as he moved along the landing and inched his way down the stairs. His nausea was worsening. When he arrived at the side room, the door was open and the final guard was breathing his last next to Signore. He had become contaminated after touching the body.

Tavener ran to the kitchen and in broken Italian shouted for the staff to leave. They were under attack from another boss's crew. They were never to return, nor speak of this to anyone, or they would all die, their families too.

Now, eight years later, Tavener was satisfied, but perplexed. He was satisfied because he had kept a steady hand after killing Signore and his men, cleaning down and clearing up. After disposing of the bodies and decontaminating to remove all trace of VX, he had raided the computer files and safe. He soon realised that the constant threat from other crime syndicates had meant his late host had valued privacy so highly that nobody outside the criminal world would miss him, know his men or lay claim to the villa. The deeds of ownership were in a false name, which Tavener was content to perpetuate.

As for his bounty, the acquisition of a luxury villa, an eclectic collection of original art and all of Signore's financial assets, plus sensitive information on criminal operations were orders of magnitude greater than his agreed half-million dollar final payment. On top of that, he still had financial reserves aplenty from selling the Rothwell lists on the black market.

Tavener had settled in, making the villa self-supporting for energy and food as far as possible. He exercised contact with the outside world via occasional trips to Cagliari and the use of a postal box at the Poste Italiane, Via Giuseppe Biasi.

Now he was in a dilemma. The news from Hulunbuir brought opportunity for more gain. The intel he had kept safe since the early eighties now needed to be sold if he was to capitalise on it, but the window was closing. It was the Chinese government's protests about the UN aiding their official's escape that had completed the puzzle for him. He sensed that the lab fire was sabotage. The escaped official was a risk to his long-term plan to sell to the Chinese what others knew about them, and James Tavener was not given to wasting years of careful preparation. As he contemplated his position, he felt a brooding frustration, a determination deep inside to bring this one home too. He wasn't done yet. But he needed to make the sale soon, which, aside from a multitude of logistical and tradecraft preparations, meant recruiting a proxy.

9

Bruce was intrigued but not surprised that the summons to his first meeting with her ladyship's organisation came not by post or email but in a dream. In fact, in a repeated dream, with precisely the same form and message over three consecutive nights. He did as requested, yet in the back of his mind he prepared himself for being the biggest fool on the planet when it turned out to be a figment of his imagination.

Having arrived at Larnaca airport, he hired a car and headed for Turkish-occupied northern Cyprus. The car rental company's rules forbade taking the car into the north, but Bruce paid the ten Cyprus pounds for a worthless, but mandatory, insurance at the Black Knight crossing. Ninety minutes later he crunched down the stony track to the coastal outcrop at Ayfilon on the north shore of the pan handle.

Ayfilon was remote, desolate, beautiful, and sun drenched, even in March. Bruce pulled up in front of a group of ramshackle modern buildings comprising six small chalet rooms, shower block, restaurant, and outside dining area which overlooked a white sandy cove. Nearby were the ruins of an ancient chapel set under tall palm trees that rustled hypnotically in the warm Mediterranean breeze.

Bruce wandered over to the only people around, all sat at a lunch table under the dappled shade of vines growing across an open-framed roof. He was relieved and excited when Lady Margaret turned to face him. The other three looked up and smiled as he reached the table.

'Welcome, Bruce. You got my invitation. That's good. Important, too,' said Lady Margaret. 'Refreshments?' She indicated the cold drinks and meze snacks neatly set upon the table.

'Hello everyone. Yes, my lady, the most intriguing message I have ever received.' The others chuckled. Bruce helped himself to the dolmades. 'So, the chef is actually Greek?' he said, raising the stuffed vine leaf.

'Our chef is a Greek Cypriot. We have this place to ourselves for a few days. Self-contained, as you might have expected.'

Her ladyship introduced Bruce to the team and, as his senses settled from the journey and the reality of how he came to be there, he realised he had met all of them before, bar one.

'Bruce, you know Lucien Martell from Beaumont, and Quentin Saxelby, my unexpected guardian of Rothwell.' Each nodded politely.

'And this is Martine Kruger, one of our team from Germany.'

BEAUMONT

Bruce strained to maintain a professional demeanour, while underneath feeling his emotions starting to swim with stimulation overload. Under a clinging fine white woollen roll-neck sweater, the thirty-something's sculpted physique was unmistakeable. She sported cropped and styled blonde hair, ice blue eyes and a withering smile. Her eye contact was so direct it was almost unnerving, even odd. She seemed to look at Bruce but then defocus and look through him. She suppressed a grin and reciprocated Bruce's bow of the head.

'Before we launch into the task at hand, you will need a period of induction, Bruce. I suggest a mix of one-to-one and group sessions, so you learn something about working with us and what it means in practical terms for your personal life – getting paid, and so forth,' Lady Margaret continued.

And so it began. Bruce spent the next two days strolling along the beach or engaged in practical exercises with one or more of the team, to hear the essentials of how they operated and plug any gaps in his otherwise ideal background in military intelligence.

At the end of the first day, Lady Margaret caught up with Bruce as he walked with Martine from the beach. Martine waved to her ladyship and headed off towards the showers. He was covered in sand, dripping with sweat and sporting scratches and bruises from an unarmed combat refresher session.

'Looks like you're making good use of the time,' Lady Margaret said, watching him dab a streak of blood from his knee.

'Thank God the sand is soft, because she is not.'

'Quite, but I'm sure she has your best interests at heart.' Bruce raised an eyebrow but said nothing. 'Well, it's my turn now, if you can bear a few minutes more. I know you must be tired. I want to share some background about our organisation, for you to sleep on.'

'Actually, it's what I most want to hear. The drip feed of knowledge has been eating me,' said Bruce.

Lady Margaret led him away from the buildings, and as they ambled back along the beach, side by side, she started to talk.

'Since the dawn of civilisation, humankind has navigated all manner of external and self-made trials, tribulations and existential threats as it struggled to evolve. As far back as Jesus Christ, advanced thinkers and practitioners, who saw the dangers at hand, faced their own dangers by being too far ahead of the crowd and advocating ideas that others couldn't accept. Too far ahead, or too far behind, and you could end up crucified.'

She turned and saw that Bruce was listening intently, his head down, gazing into the sand.

'As the centuries rolled by, and the world shrank through technological and cultural advances, like-minded movers and shakers began to connect and form groups to share their emerging ideas. By the turn of the twentieth century, when the first global body was established, some of the members were descendants of generations of covert actors. More recently, the collection of ideas that described our philosophy was brought together most effectively, as far as I for one can tell, by the American thinker Ken Wilber and his writings on Integral Theory. What this boiled down to became the organisation's core mission: a version of something called the Prime Directive – which is about enabling humanity's harmonious navigation of the evolutionary process by tackling existential threats.'

'Saving mankind from itself,' Bruce interjected.

'Mainly, which is why I was careful to say a *version* of the Prime Directive. We are firefighters rather than midwives, although we seek opportunities to act as both. Where democracies and their instruments of state are constrained by bureaucracy, hamstrung by politics, or thwarted by time and capability, our global network of assumed good souls seeks to act decisively, covertly, and most of all, in time.' She paused, allowing Bruce to comment.

He lifted a bottle of mineral water to his lips and pondered her description, then gulped some water down and asked, 'What about the part with folks' special abilities – me and heat, you and psychic communication, and so on?'

'Well, those who understand and subscribe to such a philosophy tend to be advanced thinkers themselves. And their highly developed cognition – which resides in the realms of transpersonal consciousness – is the kernel of abilities that made many such people suprahuman.'

Bruce's exhaustion finally caught up with him. He screwed his face in bewilderment.

'Hang on. Suprahuman? You mean, essentially, that these people – meaning us? including me, presumably – have some form of higher consciousness going on which can manifest in a variety of ways? Ways that make us different.'

'Very different, Bruce.'

After dinner, Martine sidled up to Bruce. 'I hope you are not in too much pain from our sparring earlier. How about a quiet walk along the shore, so we can chat properly this time?'

They roamed past remnants of turtle nests. Both were careful as they stepped over the ghosts of excavated sand from where tiny flippers would have struggled towards the water. The evening was calm, the white sand lying in luminescent crests under a rising moon and clear sky.

'So what's your thing, Bruce?' she asked.

'What do you mean? Like hobbies?'

Martine shrieked with laughter. 'No, not *hobbies*. Your special abilities – to be on the team. Like, mine is that I can sort of read people's minds. Well, more detect their true emotions.'

Bruce felt himself blush, not knowing where to look. 'How on earth can you do that?'

'I can sense the electromagnetic fields around people's heads. Not see them with my eyes – wrong part of the EM spectrum – but sense them, as tiny as they are, like microvolts or something. I realised it when I was a teenager. It was like I could close my eyes and see halos around everyone's heads. Then, as I grew older, I learned that these were matched to their emotions. So, when people try to hide their emotions they can keep a straight face, but no way can they keep a straight *head*. But I can't read actual thoughts. Really annoying.'

'So there's some hope then,' Bruce muttered, as Martine grinned back.

'Well?'

'Ah, yeah. My skill is seeing in the dark using heat pictures. Started when I was at sixth form. Like you, I don't see with my eyes, I feel with my skin and that forms mental images – like an inner vision. It fascinated me and I suppose practice has improved it. I can now almost see through the insides of buildings, like a layered 3-D model. As long as it's not a cold store or ice hotel.'

'That's so cool! Or is it hot? You need both, presumably!' They laughed. 'And your physical skill? What are you good at?'

'You mean relevant to this type of work? Not really considered it. I guess it would have to be something I'm not proud of, which is combining seeing in the dark with, er, stabbing the unsuspecting.'

'Well, you're in good company there. Sounds like Herr Saxelby could offer some advice,' said Martine.

'Yeah, we traded techniques some years ago, you might say. But I don't know anything about his background. Only met him twice. What's his story?'

'Well, we were first introduced yesterday. The rest of us arrived a day ahead of you. He goes by the code name Rostam, you know, after the hero in Persian mythology.' Bruce didn't know but nodded his agreement anyway. 'He was quite the surprise, but very open. I think he was pleased to be back and wanted to tell everyone his story. Apparently, he's one of the longest serving and most dedicated of the Club. He sees in the dark, too, but I'm not sure how. Haven't got to that yet. Years ago he volunteered in a bioengineering experiment, which was both a success and a failure. Whatever happened, his dermis somehow absorbs and dissipates energy from blunt trauma, including bullets. It uses the energy to instantaneously solidify, and as soon as the energy is dissipated it returns to normal just as quickly.'

Bruce raised his eyebrows but could not deny what he had witnessed when Lady Margaret fired two shotgun cartridges into Quentin at Rothwell.

Martine continued, 'The trouble was, the drugs messed him up psychologically and physically. He became paranoid and blamed the closest authority figure for his suffering.'

'Lady Margaret.'

'Correct. Also, he could not withstand sunlight, he told us. It gave him terrible skin irritation, so he goes underground. And it all happened at Rothwell, where there's plenty of underground. He was down there for five years, living off venison which he hunted at night with his famous dagger. You know, just like the real Rostam's dagger.'

'So, what changed? He's okay now, isn't he?'

'He was forced out of the tunnels. They flooded, or collapsed or something. He went outside and realised he no longer had problems with daylight. And he wasn't crazy any more. The drugs must have finally worn off.'

'Yes, I knew about the last part,' Bruce mused. 'Eccentric but not crazy. So is he still ... well ... bulletproof? I mean, for the mission. We've got a rather skewed set of skills, with two people who can see in the dark and one whose trick is being bulletproof but might not be.'

'That he doesn't know. He hasn't been shot in a while and probably isn't keen to find out. And you need to understand that with team composition we don't have access to any skill we want, it's who is the best fit overall and who is available and willing. Rostam's real trick is that he speaks Mandarin fluently, plus more than a dozen other languages too.'

'That would be vital on this operation.'

They circled away from the beach and started along the track back towards the buildings. With every passing minute more gaps were being filled in for Bruce. As in any insecure communication environment, the organisation used codenames to protect identities and as a crude confirmation of identity when meeting others. Such concepts weren't alien to him from his time in military intelligence; the difference was they were theory then and a reality now.

He pondered another reality – the tension over how much information could be shared, even within a tight-knit team. Ideally, folk would know as little as possible about what everyone else was doing and could do. However, according to Martine, the organisation was so small and fragmented by the mid-eighties that need-to-know became virtually pointless. When a mission team was formed everyone's skills had to be declared anyway.

As they walked a gust of wind sent palm leaves tumbling and rustling across the stony track, grains of sand chasing and dancing upon their dry skin. The hairs on Bruce's forearms stood up, whether from the excitement of his induction into this special order, or Martine's electric presence, or perhaps just the cooling night air, he couldn't quite tell. Probably all three.

But then it came to learning what was the biggest secret of all to him, the actual name of this thing they called 'the organisation' or 'the Club', something her ladyship had curiously omitted to mention. But, like meeting your heroes, this so-called secret proved to be a salutary anti-climax. He asked Martine why a group who could psychically communicate with each other would even bother to state a name for itself that would only help others to identify and pursue them.

'Exactly,' she said. 'For many years there was no proper name. What happened was our pursuers gave us a name anyway– many names, in fact – the favourite in recent years being The Architects' Club. Rumour was the CIA called us that as an insult, because apparently we think that we are the architects of mankind's destiny. It seems to have stuck. What the CIA didn't know was that the Czech contingent found this hilarious, because they used to meet in a secluded basement bar, Klub Architektů, in central Prague.'

10

The next morning, Friday, 29 March 1996, Lady Margaret led the group away from breakfast to the outside seating area to brief on the operation.

'As I see it, we have four initial objectives comprising phase one,' she commenced. 'Firstly, Quentin and Lucien will deploy to Beijing to set up an operating base and conduct reconnaissance of relevant government and residential sites.'

Spread over the table was a map of central Beijing. Everyone shuffled their chairs closer and leaned in as her ladyship highlighted key areas with a laser pointer. Bruce could see the Forbidden City, Tiananmen, the Great Hall of the People, and to the east the Jianguomenwai Embassy Compound where a number of western embassies were located.

'Quentin and Lucien, or rather Rostam and Peridot, will rent a low-grade apartment a few miles from the centre befitting a travelling language lecturer and mature postgrad student of international culture,' she continued. 'Secondly, Martine will lead Bruce in a speculative line of enquiry to locate James Tavener. This will give Bruce some real experience in our kind of tradecraft. I will visit

BEAUMONT

London to approach a dormant contact to see if she can help me find out what Roger Gleeson may have on Tavener. It could inform whether he is a risk and therefore needs to be managed. And, finally, Marc, at Beaumont, will set about locating our Chinese official, Ying. He will be key to this whole thing. Any questions?'

Bruce held back for a moment to allow others to speak first, but none was forthcoming.

'My lady, a couple of points, if I may? What do you mean by "managed", regarding Tavener?'

Across the table, Quentin Saxelby's expression set with a moue.

'That entirely depends on what we discover. It might mean nothing – he is no threat. Or, the other extreme, he must be forcibly stopped from jeopardising the operation,' she replied.

'We'll put him on the lunch menu,' said Quentin, before roaring with laughter. 'In which case, best to avoid mid-week. I've never much of an appetite mid-week.'

Bruce checked his previous conviction about where on the crazy–eccentric spectrum Quentin was right now. Images of flashing daggers and spurting blood flitted through his mind. The orange blur when Quentin speared his shoulder years before brought a pang of phantom pain. At least the scent of rotting flesh had left his breath.

'Quentin. Thank you. That's quite enough.'

Bruce attempted to move on. 'What do you expect to happen after the first phase in Beijing, my lady?'

'We will need to infiltrate and access further information about the biological threat so we can develop means to counter it. That might involve passing key information to governments so they can enact containment measures, initiate testing regimes, or develop a vaccine if we cannot disrupt or eliminate the virus at source.'

Bruce's face washed with shock. 'You're going to enter Chinese government sites? In the heart of Beijing?'

'That's what we do, Bruce. And what's more, depending on how your task with Tavener goes, you might well be joining us.'

*   *   *

Jez Picher was far from James Tavener's preferred choice of proxy. But time had taken its toll on the limited list of candidates he might lean on, come the day. Sat in the office at his Sardinian villa, he stroked the padded leather desktop while taking stock. Long-term maintenance of potential proxies was a chore and a liability. Each periodic check of candidates' locations and status risked alerting them or others to his interest.

Suitable individuals usually had criminal backgrounds or dubious morals, which meant leverage could be used. Information on them was not publicly available: no listing in a company annual report, for instance, although the internet was starting to spawn social communications for the masses.

BEAUMONT

Tavener had conceded defeat with his top three hopefuls, all off limits. Dominique Sanchez languished in a Spanish prison on terrorist charges. Chao Shanyuan had somehow got himself under investigation for money laundering in Hong Kong. And Chad Branson had six months left with terminal cancer. So, to Plan B.

Only a few factors had to align to narrow a field of potentials from hundreds to a handful. Tavener needed someone open to off-the-books dealings, whose character he knew, whom he could control, who would be available, and who would never guess they had once met the ghost that was directing them. And someone he could burn if the deal went sour.

Rothwell College was fertile ground for finding someone whose character he was familiar with, but all bar a few of the students from his time there were now serving officers in the British Army. Of the few who were not, all but one had failed to complete their commissioning course at the Royal Military Academy, Sandhurst. Which left only Jez Picher.

Picher must have had the grit and intelligence to get through Sandhurst training, so he was robust. Tavener imagined it was his inherent flaws as a young officer during his first two postings with the Royal Engineers that undid him. Likely career breakers for army officers could be failures involving any of alcohol, money, ammunition, personal relationships, and confidential information. Jez had probably strayed with some or all of them, making for a string of disciplinary dealings by commanding officers that forced his decision to take premature voluntary release. It was all conjecture on Tavener's part, but the fact remained: Picher had left the army very early in his career.

Tavener kept in touch with significant developments of Rothwell students through the *London Gazette*, which listed commissions and retirements, and copies of *The Officers' List for the British Army*. That was how he knew when Jez would do the obvious and head to the Tidworth careers fair in search of his next employment. And a CV as short and ugly as his meant only one company would likely entertain him: Terrain Ops Corp, a US-based private military company specialising in logistics support to military contractors, and a regular at Tidworth's careers events.

Once Tavener found Jez on the Terrain Ops Corp online staff list, he pondered whether a 'global facilities manager' meant flying around the world with suitcases of money, depositing and receiving under-the-radar tax-illegal sums that far exceeded cross-border limits. It didn't matter. With his work email tapped and a watch list of twenty-plus Hotmail addresses running permutations starting 'Jez' and 'Jezza', Tavener set about profiling Picher's working and personal lives.

* * *

BEAUMONT

Bruce Noble was surprised to find himself sat at a computer, not heading for a succession of airports, as Martine Kruger's mentoring began.

'Homework first, Bruce. Otherwise we are just running about like idiots,' she asserted. 'And this internet is going to be a gift, but maybe not so much yet.'

They had returned to Beaumont. With ample accommodation, it made sense to do the homework at the temporary hub of the Club's global operations. Bruce did as instructed, working to develop an intelligence picture of a target, something that fitted naturally with his former employment. Terrain Ops Corp's online presence made a good start point, but determining specifics about Jez's tasking and locations was another matter. And so the long hours began.

Lady Margaret, meanwhile, reflected upon the cycles of life which now found her once more underground, once more searching the Rothwell archives for a name. Secreted away behind Beaumont's generous wine cellar was a vault that served as a makeshift replacement for Rothwell's wrecked strong room under Serpentine Lake.

She rifled through the neatly ordered files, so expertly organised by Roberts, her faithful aide. Quickly finding what she was looking for, she stopped for a moment and a shadow fell over her face. Dear Philip, how she missed him, his life so cruelly cut short at Tavener's treacherous hands. She closed her eyes to clear the spark of rage that had ignited in her thoughts, then opened them to read the vital information.

> *Entry: 1 Jul 90. Shepperton, Dawn (F); Code: Jade; Orgs: British Army (WRAC) (75-81); UK Security Service (MI5) (82-); Thames House, Millbank, London SE1; Contact: Protocol FOXTROT.*

She let out a deep sigh. Protocol Foxtrot was a pain, and risky. Because MI5 might have operated internal security measures, such as random or periodic tapping of home phones, or trailing individuals to see who they met, convoluted measures were required to make contact.

The next morning she left Beaumont and its considerable comforts to return to England, where the task of confronting one of the greatest perils the world had ever faced rested heavily on her shoulders. She prayed that things would work out, from travelling on a false passport to reaching her asset undetected.

It was late afternoon when, wearing a plain grey raincoat, her platinum-blonde hair covered with a navy blue scarf, she inserted the key into the door of the Club safe house in an unremarkable street in Ware, Hertfordshire. The house, which she owned through a cover company, had a working, but ex-directory, phone number. It was well located, outside London but close enough for ready access, and near to Luton airport.

BEAUMONT

*   *   *

Tuesday, 2 April 1996 started overcast and damp. Dawn Shepperton tugged her cashmere scarf higher around her neck and pushed along the pavement, away from Victoria station.

She went through the motions of varying her route to work, which felt pointless after going to the same building for fourteen years. Her role in the Security Service archives did not afford opportunities for exciting assignments or travel to exotic places. Nonetheless, at least twice a week she would pass by the Regency café, glancing in the window for a four-by-six-inch notice asking anyone to report if they had spotted a missing dog. Not any dog, but a dog guaranteed not to be confused with another – an Australian Silky Terrier called Tiny. Small, rare, nickable. That meant the only call to be made to the number on the notice would be by Dawn herself, which she would do for the first time from a public telephone on her way home that evening.

'Hello, I'm calling about a missing dog, the one in the notice in the café window,' she said from a stinking call box near the Grosvenor Arms in Stockwell.

'Well, that's wonderful news! May I check that we are talking about the same dog, though? What did the notice give as its name, if I may ask?' said Lady Margaret.

'Jade.'

'That's it! And her sister is so missing her! She's called Amulet, you know.'

'I think I might have seen her. How can I help?'

The explanation of help curiously ran off-course and into an analogous conversation about the paperwork that might be required to report the sighting of the dog to the police. Because even a public phone could have been tapped, however remote the possibility, the obscure discussion was necessary to hide what Lady Margaret required: a search of evidence holdings between November 1987 and February 1988 submitted by Roger Gleeson. The message was coded via specific locations, the only locations, in fact, where the dog owner had ever seen another Australian Silky Terrier. The latitudes and longitudes in degrees, minutes and seconds would identify a pre-determined book, plus page, lines and letters therein that spelled the brief message.

Less than twenty-four hours later, Dawn posted her reply to a London PO Box.

*   *   *

At the safe house, Lady Margaret set her cup onto the coffee table and opened the envelope. The contents were from a teenage hopeful, giving the answers to the quiz in the unnamed maths enthusiasts' newsletter. Ergo, a coded reply, which her ladyship hastily decrypted.

BEAUMONT

MSG START. ONE ITEM FOUND. 16 FEB 88. PHOTOCOPY FROM MICRODOTS. SIS FILE HONG KONG STA JUL 83. ORIGINAL MISSING. TITLE QUOTE PLA VIROLOGICAL THREAT ENDQUOTE. CONTENTS ACCESS RESTRICTED. LAST ACCESS R GLEESON 28 FEB 96. END.

She set the letter upon the table and released a breath, glad that Martine and Bruce were already working flat out to find Tavener. So it's true, she thought. You really are a threat.

11

Bruce was quietly relieved when the time came to actually do something. For all its promise, the internet soon dried up with leads for Jez Picher, so he and Martine headed to Geneva airport, bound for Blighty.

He thought it quaint and inevitable that in his new exotic world of suprahuman saviours the path of progress was consistently prosaic. The only solid plan they could devise for locating Jez started with getting his registered address, or at least the one he left with the careers transition staff at Tidworth over a year earlier.

The pair arrived at Heathrow, then hired a car and drove to Andover, Hampshire, where they were soon settling into a small B&B on the western edge of town. Under their cover story as conservationists from Manchester University, they explained that they might arrive back late some nights after a spot of wildlife watching on Salisbury Plain, which was no trouble for Mrs Grant when the balance was paid upfront in cash.

Tucked in the tiny room allocated to Martine, they began detailed planning for the task.

'I will register *post hoc* for resettlement services,' Bruce said. 'It's plausible and shouldn't cause a stir, seeing that

I'm long gone, as far as the Intelligence Corps is concerned. My trick will be to claim that I actually registered before but didn't complete the process, so they should have my details, including address.' Martine nodded, while removing a tea bag from a cup as she made them a drink. 'Then, I hope, the person on the desk might go to check their records and thus give me a clue whether they're kept in a filing cabinet or on a computer. The former, please God.'

'Okay, I like it. Then I guess you will go back later to search for information on Jez?' said Martine.

'Correct, although we haven't covered how to get in when the place is closed, or what happens if the information is held on a computer. Live records for serving soldiers are all on UNICOM.'

'That depends on your reconnaissance. I assume the Intelligence Corps didn't train you to case a joint, *nein*?' Bruce shook his head. 'From the moment you enter Tidworth you are watching *who* and *what* is *where*. Who might be sent out to arrest us if we fuck up, for example. At the building, take in all details, like layout: which rooms connect to which? Door locks, which way doors open and which side are the hinges? Windows. What type? Double glazed? Fireproof? You can't break those. How are they locking? Which windows are out of the way and people might forget to lock? And cameras. And patrols. Then there's potential entry and egress points and routes. Got it?'

'Wow, I'll try my best. What will you be doing when I'm registering?'

'We'll go together, but I'll drop you first so we are not seen together by gate guards or MOD police. I'll go for a walk around the area and do my own recce.'

'Sorry to ask this, but are you gonna tone down your look a bit, so you're less, well ... less eye-catching?'

Martine gave Bruce a sideways look. 'I will wear a headscarf. That should add about forty years.'

They began the next day, Thursday 4 April. Bruce was intrigued by the culture shock of his first arrival at a military garrison as a faceless civilian. No salute. No more yes, sir, no, sir. But being ignored was one step away from being forgotten, which suited him fine. The gate guard mumbled an instruction to join the visitors' queue and book in. Bruce thanked the soldier and stepped over to the line that spilled out of the security hut, tradesmen in high-vis jackets and retired officers in pinstripe waiting in turn alike.

The resettlement offices were in a low security area, away from the resident military units. That allowed Bruce to walk there unescorted, so he was free to make mental notes without the distraction of small talk. He entered the building and presented himself at the sliding window in the reception, ready with his story.

The woman through the glass rose to her full, skinny height and looked down at Bruce. She pulled the glass aside and studied him for a second with accusing eyes alight behind school teacher's spectacles.

'Yes?'

'Good morning. My name is Bruce ... Bruce Noble. I tried to register for resettlement services last year—'

'Tried?'

'I did so via your online portal, but I don't think it worked. You see, I have an interview—'

'Noble, you say?' Before waiting for confirmation, she had spun on her heel and was halfway down the office to a filing cabinet, an ubiquitous grey four-drawer cabinet, the second in the row.

Jackpot! That would be where Jez's records were also held, Bruce hoped. While the woman flicked through the dividers inside, searching for his file, he observed everything possible to inform an overnight break-in.

She returned, her demeanour as charming as before, clutching the file. It had only one sheet of paper within. 'You appear not to have been granted access to our services.'

'Oh ...'

'Need to take it up with your commanding officer.'

'Right, well—'

The window slid shut and the woman withdrew to her cup of coffee.

I hope it's gone cold. Bruce left the reception area and stepped out into the sunshine.

They waited till the Saturday night to enter. Martine had spotted posters at the NAAFI about a live music night and figured that a raucous knees-up would help draw the guards' attention away from the deserted offices on the opposite side of the site. Their concern would be that things stayed good-natured. They didn't want high spirits to boil over into a pitched battle between the resident infantry and cavalry units. Such developments would draw duty staff onto site, cause a full security sweep and greatly increase the chances of being detected.

At Shipton Bellinger, one mile south of Tidworth, they hid the car in a quiet lane and headed across country to the woods on the western fence line. Ninety minutes was enough observation time to confirm that the patrols, each consisting of two armed guards in combat uniform, didn't vary their route, checking along the fence and then the buildings in a similar pattern every hour.

Martine stood on Bruce's shoulders, spread the razor wire on the top of the fence apart and laid a piece of doubled tarpaulin sheet over it to clear the way. They scaled the fence then sped across the open ground to the building which housed the resettlement office. Twenty yards to the left of its main entrance were the toilets, Bruce's Plan A for an entry point. Martine moved to a secluded spot under some conifers that offered a wide view of the area, from where she could keep watch.

Bruce kept to the shadows, hugging the walls, and shuffled along to the target window. The ancient metal frame was thick with layers of white gloss paint. He slipped off a small rucksack and took out a jemmy, which he used to prize window and frame apart, then opened the latch with a hook. He went in head-first, clambering down on his hands and knees onto the toilet lid and floor. Exotic.

He entered the reception office and tried the cabinet. Locked. He took a moment and let his mind's heat picture come to full intensity. Soon the small silver key appeared as a cold spot, tucked in a shorter section of a pen-holder on Mrs Charming's desk. Once inside the cabinet, the paperwork was all at the same temperature, so Bruce lit and held in his mouth a thin Maglite torch fitted with a red filter to subdue the beam and preserve his normal night vision. He worked hurriedly, fathoming the filing system to move through year and alphabet and get to Jez Picher's record.

Third drawer down, bingo!

> *Picher, Jeremy Steven.*
> *DOB 4/7/69.*
> *322 Cranford Drive, Hayes, Middlesex.*
> *UB3 7HJ. 0181 756 4972.*
> *Unit: 28 Engineer Regiment, Royal Engineers.*
> *Shortlist: Terrain Ops Corp; Combat Systems Ltd.*

Against protocol, Bruce reached out a gloved hand, snatched a Post-It and pen from the desk, placed the Post-It sheet upon the hard plastic surface and scribbled the details down. He stowed the paper in his jacket pocket. Everything was returned to its proper place, closed and locked. Five minutes after crawling through the toilet window he let himself out of the front door, the Yale mechanism locking after him with a clunk that echoed around the concrete walls outside. He froze and listened. In the distance he could hear the muffled bass of drums and peaks of guitar from the NAAFI concert. Otherwise all was still.

Martine appeared beside him. 'We need to move, before they get to the fence again.'

Half an hour later, safely back at the B&B, Bruce felt for the first time the effects of adrenaline working over an extended period. He was drained.

He laid back in a bath of bubbles, peering across to a shelf with a spare toilet roll under a crocheted white wool cover that was crested with a ballerina figure. *Why?*

Next door, Martine was already fast asleep, recharging before tomorrow's sprint to discover whether the Hayes address was current or a dead end.

*   *   *

Cranford Drive, Hayes, Middlesex was so close to Heathrow that Bruce felt certain it would be Jez's current address, but he gambled that Jez would be away. The area was a low-rise sprawl of 1970s builds, with cars covering every pavement and green verge. Number 322 was near to the end of the road and presented both opportunity and challenge for observation and entry to the narrow mid-terrace house.

Martine reversed into a parking space about a hundred metres from the front door, where they could keep eyes on, but were obscured from view. The curtains in the house were half-drawn. Bruce had to go further into an attempted disguise, adding to his unshaven look by pulling up his sweatshirt hood in case the unthinkable happened and Jez appeared at his window to ask him how come he was here.

They waited for an hour until it was a quarter past two. Martine reached into her bag for the mock ID card of a Christian fellowship group member to ward off any questions from neighbours. But this didn't feel like a neighbourly area.

'I'm going to take a look round the back first, to see if there is access from Wilkins Close,' she said. 'Then I'll see what mail is lying on the mat. I reckon he's overseas.'

'I'll radio if I suspect a problem,' Bruce replied, the short-wave unit in his lap.

Martine popped her earpiece in and set off.

The back of the property yielded nothing of interest, apart from further confirmation that no-one was home. The curtains were semi-drawn there as well. There was no building opposite the front of number 322, only the red-brick back garden wall of a property around the corner. Martine checked for an external alarm unit – there was none – then knocked at the door and waited. No reply.

She checked around, then peeked through the letterbox. The hall was dark, with the kitchen door closed ahead. She produced a small mirror on a telescopic handle and fed it through the opening to view the doormat area. A pile of mail lay inside.

She checked about her again, confirming no movement in the street, then switched to a set of skeleton keys to gain access. Once inside she donned latex gloves and checked for surveillance measures, such as motion sensors or tell tales on doors. Nothing obvious at first sight.

She thumbed through the mail, which was all addressed to Mr J. Picher. *Target confirmed.* One item caught her attention – a patchy foreign postmark. Did it say *Sardegna*? She went to the kitchen and put the kettle on, then went back into the hall. She started to walk up the stairs. *Which steps creak, Martine?* The first, audibly, the second, slightly. In the bedroom was a computer terminal and modem.

Martine went back downstairs to the kitchen and steamed the envelope open.

> *Dear Mr Picher,*
> *Please be advised that your travel on 12 April is authorised. Upon arrival further guidance will be left for you in Deposit Box 1172.*
> *Regards*
> *[Unsigned]*

BEAUMONT

She photographed the single sheet of paper, wiped the glue back and resealed the envelope with a neat application of Pritt Stick.

Bruce's voice crackled in her ear: 'We might have company. A car just went into Wilkins Close. What's round there?'

'Garages for the houses. They can come in through the back entrance.'

'Then you'd better leave, in case it's Jez.'

'I need to place the devices first. Out.'

Out. Which really meant: *Stop distracting me*. Bruce slid across into the driver's seat and started the engine.

Martine crouched as the garden gate squeaked open, then noticed the kettle. Hot kettle. *Scheisse*.

Mind in overdrive, she scanned the kitchen window, spied a spare key in the tray under a cactus plant, shoved it into the lock and turned it partly to secure it. Just in time. As the fiddling and tutting began on the other side of the door, she kept low and slowly added cold water to the kettle, hoping it would cool before he got to it. Then she moved back upstairs.

Behind her she heard the back door handle being twisted back and forth and a shoulder being thumped against the troublesome door. She grabbed the computer base unit, a vertical stack style by Time Computers, and threaded the microdata transmitter through a cooling vent close to the modem port till its tiny magnet fixed it in place. She looked at the landline on the desk but had no time to fit a bug. The front door suddenly slammed open.

She listened from the top of the stairs, praying that he, whoever *he* actually was, would do the logical thing and go check the back door. Wrong. A loud creak signalled an abrupt ascension of the stairs, footsteps stomping up two at a time. Martine drew back behind the bedroom door and held her breath, ready to fight.

The sound of relief came from the bathroom as urine plunged into water, accompanied by a loud sigh. Martine ducked past the bathroom and down the stairs, missing the last two steps, then let herself out.

12

Ying had provided a generous clue about his intended destination during the flight from Mongolia when he told Bruce he wanted to go somewhere there was good ice cream. Marc quickly took the obvious reference to Italy. If Ying sought refuge in a Club safe house, the relevant one would be in Milan's Chinatown, and this was where Marc was now heading to locate him.

The safe house was a two-bedroom apartment above a Chinese reflexology clinic on Via Luca Signorelli, a back street in the centre of Milan, one kilometre north of Castello Sforzesco. A near continual flow of scooters, cars and vans scuttled along the one-way street, kicking up dust and rattling shuttered windows. Echoes of doors slamming, televisions playing too loudly, cats yowling and folk shouting to each other bubbled away in the background as Marc and Ying made themselves comfortable around an old wooden table in the small kitchen.

Marc took a sip of coffee, pursing his lips in approval.

'How are things working out here? Are you happy?' he asked.

Ying was a small man with a cheerful face but whose natural expression had been overcome by exhaustion.

'You mean, have I been followed? No. But happy? I have no family here, or friends.'

'You didn't have family in China,' said Marc, realising his insensitivity too late. 'But we appreciate your selfless contribution,' he added. 'The world will have you to thank, God willing.'

'And let's remember Qiang. He paid the greatest price for this.'

'Of course. Who can forget his courage. Maybe he will be honoured in a future China, if we succeed.'

Marc paused in a moment of reflection, acknowledging the human cost of their endeavour. Then he returned to the mission. He needed to collate information for Quentin and Lucien in Beijing.

'For now, my concern is that you can sustain your life here. Live, be content, or as content as you can be. Stay low, stay safe. Until this is over. Can you do that?'

'What else can I do? I'm a dead man if I am caught. We must succeed, for everyone's sake. I will tell you everything I know.'

They ran through a wealth of detail, sketched out plans, listed routines and discussed key players: anything that might aid Quentin and Lucien in their endeavour to identify vital information from within a highly secure and hostile environment. Ying's access to the computer system would have been removed, but his knowledge of his former colleagues' habits for storing passwords, the standard location of keys to cabinets and rooms, the way to access data and other inside information, gave crucial clues to infiltration methods.

But Ying was sceptical. 'The problem is their faces will not fit. No matter whether they are posing as tourists or academics, if they stay in the city for more than a few days the authorities will notice them. The new leader has conjured an atmosphere of intimidation and fear. Everyone reports on everyone. Nobody dares to break ranks.'

'Apart from you. The brave few. And if Mr Tao has got things wound so tight, he will get a tidal wave of false alarms. Nothing more than hearsay. Let's hope that obscures things and buys time for our team.'

Ying shook his head, unconvinced. Marc suggested they eat before he headed back to Beaumont to write a brief for the men in Beijing.

*   *   *

Martine and Bruce had arrived in Sardinia a day ahead of Jez. The stakes were increasing for Bruce, who had continued to grow his beard to reduce the risk of being identified. He had gone from designer stubble, through 'rugged', and now verged on 'vagrant'.

Jez's Alitalia flight touched down in Cagliari just after 11a.m. In the arrivals hall, Martine hung back along a wall of car rental desks, absorbed in a copy of *L'Unione Sarda*, while outside, Bruce sat in the short-stay zone behind the wheel of an Alfa 156 GTA.

As the passengers began to emerge from the flight, Martine peeked over the newspaper, trying to spot Jez through the crowd, while recalling Bruce's description. She knew she would have to allow for the passage of time and deliberate alterations to his image in trying to identify him. At last he came into the hall. The yellow Titleist golf cap, a rash of blonde hair breaking out underneath, was an attempt to cover up, but only served to amuse Martine. Jez's inane grin confirmed him as the target.

'We're on,' she said into the mic beneath her blouse collar.

'Ready,' Bruce replied.

A few minutes later, Martine rounded the exit doors and watched as Jez joined the tail of a queue boarding a bus to the city centre.

'Fuck!'

'What's up?' asked Bruce. 'Pick up now?'

'*Ja*, but take your time. He's getting on a bus into town.'

'Roger.'

Tailing the bus was like a reverse game of cat and mouse. Bruce adopted a driving strategy that attracted more than one frustrated blast from a local's car horn when he appeared to be on a go-slow. They had hardly gone a couple of miles when thickening traffic and a bus-only filter lane forced them to watch as the bus disappeared around a bend and into the central bus station.

Martine sighed in frustration. 'Stop for a moment. I'm going to have to go on foot. Stay on comms.'

'I'll try and pull in somewhere.'

She lost sight of Jez's bus for about a minute while she jogged along the pavement and into the station. There were seven buses in bays, with swarms of people coming and going. By the time she recognised the number of the service he had taken, the last two passengers were struggling their cases out of the doors. She continued through the station, checking exits, and then waited by the washrooms in case he showed. But Jez had vanished.

Ten minutes later, she called Bruce to pick her up by the piazza opposite the station.

'He's gone. He must know his way around, because he isn't wasting time with directions,' she said, pulling the car door shut.

'Plan B then. Over to Giuseppe Biasi and stake out the postal boxes,' said Bruce.

'Yes, they're the only ones I could turn up in my research. But they definitely don't go up to 1172.'

'Probably the right ones then. And I'm guessing that he isn't going straight there. Long walk, unless he takes a taxi.'

Bruce spun the Alfa around and onto Via Roma.

A twenty-minute crawl later, they pulled up short of the roadway entrance to the complex containing the Poste Italiane facility. It was under an apartment block in which they had rented a studio holiday let.

Bruce took a small backpack from the boot.

'Back in five,' he said.

Martine sipped from a Perrier bottle and watched the area while she waited. When he reappeared in the side mirror she got out and unloaded their bags. They headed inside together, she to the bathroom and Bruce to the dining table where he opened a laptop, connected the transceiver and activated the video camera that he had positioned on the roof of the block opposite the entrance. Then it was a matter of watching, waiting and replacing camera batteries at four-hourly intervals – the acknowledged weak part of the plan in the event of Tavener running counter-surveillance.

Martine returned from the bathroom. 'Is it working?'

'Appears to be.'

'I hope this shit holds up. Talisman is always getting some new tech from his nerds.'

Talisman. Marc Arnaud's code name. As operations coordinator and Club tech expert, his role was much more than Lucien Martell's PA and cook, Bruce had come to realise.

'Looks like pretty good kit,' he said. 'Resolution and zoom are better than anything I've used.'

'Wait till it falls over. *Kaput*. Then it's back to basics and we are running the risks again.'

The evening rolled on. The Poste Italiane was due to close at ten. Bruce checked the time in the bottom corner of the screen: 21:48. They huddled in front of the laptop, expecting Jez to turn up at any minute. But 10 p.m. came and went.

BEAUMONT

Bruce slumped back in the sofa and drained his cup of tea. Martine put the TV on.

With one eye on the video feed and one on the telly, at first Bruce didn't take much notice of the little white van trundling up to the front of the Poste Italiane complex. He glanced round to see what was happening. A tall male in faded blue overalls and white cap got out of the van, took out a bucket and mop and thumbed through a bunch of keys on a chain. They could only see his back view.

'Cleaner's arrived for his night shift then,' Bruce mumbled.

'What's that?'

'Cleaner.'

Martine laughed.

'What's so funny?'

'Italians! They won't pay more for cleaning out of hours. No way. They clean around you in work time.'

'Well, not this one apparently.'

Martine turned to examine the picture. As she watched, the man entered the building and closed the door behind him. The camera angle and zoom allowed a view of the first few postal boxes but was too elevated to see more than three metres inside at floor level. She could just see the man's legs as he stood in front of the boxes.

'What's he doing?' Bruce asked.

'Stopwatch! Are you recording?' said Martine.

'Yes.'

Bruce hit the start button on his Seiko and watched as the legs drew back a step, then turned away and out of sight. Moments later the figure reappeared. Bruce stopped the timer.

'How long?' she asked.

'Eight seconds.'

'What could he do in that time?'

'Deposit instructions? Return a key? I'm not sure.'

The figure reappeared, walked out and locked the door, then put his equipment in the van and departed.

'We need to open that box,' said Bruce, his tone emphatic.

'But we don't know exactly which box, Bruce. No, we stay back and wait for Jez.'

'Then what? We could lose him again, without a clue where he's heading.'

'Then we don't lose him. Simple.'

They took turns monitoring the video all night, popping out at changeovers to replace camera batteries. At 8.45 next morning, Bruce was staring into the small laptop screen, rueing that they could not just raid the postal boxes when Jez entered the picture.

'Martine, he's here!'

She rushed across the room to glimpse Jez's back as he strolled into the Poste Italiane facility.

'Let's go!'

They burst into action, grabbing their kit and sprinting downstairs to the car parked on the street outside.

'Get the engine running. And keep your head down,' she instructed Bruce. 'I'll get the camera.'

Every second felt like a year to Bruce. At any moment Jez could reappear, hop into one of the many cars and vans strewn around the locale and drive off. At last Martine appeared from a side door of the building opposite, a duffle bag under her left arm. Bruce sighed as she reached the car and got in.

'Where are you, Jez?' he said under his breath.

'Maybe he has to show proof of identity and then collect a key to the box,' Martine pondered.

Suddenly Jez stepped into view, carrying a large envelope and reading something as he went. He crossed the street and got into a white Fiat Cinquecento, where he continued to study the sheet of paper.

Bruce turned to Martine. 'I'm still hazy about the part where we tail him – eventually to the airport, I guess? Then he disappears through a departure gate and we lose him. How does that work?'

'If his next move is to leave the island by plane, then he must book a flight first, which means going to an agent. Then we get Talisman to hack the manifests for tomorrow's flights out of Cagliari. And we go wherever he is going.'

'Which works as long as he travels under his own name. And it's tomorrow.'

'The note at his house used his real name.'

'If Tavener gets slippery, gives him false travel documents, then we're stuffed.'

'The fallback is we just tail him, see which flight he checks in for and request an asset to track him at the destination airport.'

'Still not great. What if there's nobody available? One missed step and he's gone. We need to get ahead of this, Martine.'

'And how are we going do that?' she asked, looking Bruce in the eye.

For a moment they were quiet, watching Jez as he sat in the car, flicking between the piece of paper, his phone, his watch and a map.

'Do you think he could be under observation now?' Bruce asked.

'It's possible. But I would expect that Tavener needs to be ahead of him, so he's probably on his way to wherever is next. They're not going to try anything in this town, that's for sure.'

'I have an idea.'

They had to act before Jez set off. Martine moved just in time and appeared at Jez's car window.

'*Ciao. Lei parla inglese?*'

Jez snapped the sheet of paper face down and looked round in surprise. The large envelope was on the passenger seat.

'Er, yeah, I'm English. What do you want? I'm kinda busy, actually.'

She leaned forward and met him with a long gaze. 'My car, over there … Can't get it to start. It was fine earlier. Do you think you can take a look for me? I thought you might be the sort of guy who could help a girl out. I would be so grateful, just to have a look …'

She sensed the field around Jez's head light up. He was torn. He flicked his watch over to check the time. Again.

'Two minutes. That's all I've got,' he said, stuffing the paper under the seat and stepping out of the Fiat. 'If I can't see anything obvious you'll have to call someone. Okay?'

As Jez and Martine crossed back to the Alfa Romeo, Bruce emerged by the Fiat and reached through the open window, all the while checking in case Jez looked back. His mouth ran dry.

He grabbed the envelope from the passenger seat and peeked inside, trying to steady his shaking hands. *Breathe, Bruce.* It contained a wad of fifty-dollar bills and a couple of typewritten A4 sheets. He looked around for the sheet of paper, which he found under the driver's seat. A quick scan suggested it was the key. He returned the envelope and took the piece of paper, pinned a corner under his toe, and snapped four quick shots with a Ricoh digital camera, before slipping it back and disappearing behind a row of vans. Beads of sweat on his forehead broke into streaks that ran into his eyes. He wiped them clear while crouching out of sight.

A minute later he heard the Alfa break into life and an overjoyed Martine pouring praise upon Jez.

As the Fiat sped off in a cloud of dust, Bruce and Martine examined the camera images.

> *Dear Mr Picher,*
> *You have been booked into the Hotel Alt, Düsseldorf, for two nights commencing 14 April. Please confirm room number by usual means after check-in, so that conference materials can be sent to you.*
> *Pre-conference reading and expenses for services to date are enclosed.*
> *Regards*
> *[Unsigned]*

'*Nein!*' cried Martine. 'Düsseldorf! My backyard, pretty much. *Dummkopf.*'

Bruce ignored Martine's excitement. 'He's come all this way for money – and something else, but not the file that Tavener wants to sell.'

'It could be a situation brief, cover story, things like that. Stuff you wouldn't send by mail. Tavener isn't gonna let the file out of his control until as late as possible, when everyone is in place for the sale. Looks like it will happen in Düsseldorf.'

Bruce looked out of the car window, deep in thought. 'Makes sense, though. Tavener and Jez are white Europeans: they will blend in there, Chinese faces less so if the agents are ethnic Chinese. And the escape routes from Düsseldorf are myriad, in all directions. And conference materials? I agree, he's gonna try to sell.'

'Düsseldorf!'

13

In Beijing, Quentin Saxelby and Lucien Martell, aka Rostam and Peridot, had set up shop in a single first floor room with flimsy plasterboard walls, which verged on being an infested squat. Buried within a migrant worker enclave in the Fengtai district of western Beijing, they had accepted the risk of a random state crackdown on ethnic villages for the gain of obscurity among a population not loyal to the authorities.

Fengtai was eight miles from the centre. Quentin had almost forgotten the joys of travel in Chinese cities since his early days sourcing textiles for a Savile Row gentlemen's tailor, and after a few appalling bus journeys he had quickly refined their arrangements. Even in April the overcrowded buses reeked with perspiring passengers, and navigation between stops that were far apart was made near impossible when they couldn't see out of the filthy windows. A combination of cycling over the dead flat terrain and the subway proved better ways to get around.

Quentin's mastery of languages and Lucien's photographic memory combined to produce a rich intelligence picture from only a few excursions. The only snag was the President's decision to return the Forbidden

City to sole use – and access – by senior Party officials. The men didn't flinch from the notion of infiltrating the compound in search of secrets, but its sheer scale meant they could spend a month looking for where information might be secured, even if they were given free rein.

The briefing that had arrived by post into the safekeeping of an associate at the Jianguo hotel was, therefore, a godsend. In their apartment, Lucien opened the padded envelope containing a copy of the Lonely Planet guide to China. The code giving the start of the page range with hidden content had been sent via secure text, another of Marc's technical coups. Lucien turned to page 714 and began the process of scanning pages into the laptop with a hand-held device. After a few minutes the software reconstituted what was invisible to the human eye, and out popped Marc's brief from Ying.

'Has it worked?' Quentin asked, lowering his newspaper with a snap. 'What does the mystical doctor have to say?'

Lucien said nothing and continued his intense reading of the text. Quentin tossed the paper onto the floor and moved to look over his shoulder.

Lucien paused. 'It's not good. Ying has never seen the main document of which the appendices are parts, and he doesn't know where it's kept. He says he had access only to previous versions of Appendix D: *The People's Medicine*. The President would frequently amend the master copy with handwritten notes, which were fed back to Ying as part of regular updates.'

'Ying was working on it with his team, with the President sticking his oar in, presumably. So it's President Tao's brainchild really. No doubt there. Where was Ying's appendix kept?' replied Quentin.

'Um …' Lucien flicked to a map of the Forbidden City. '*Jio-tai-dian* … the Hall of Union. Here.' He indicated the building, which lay near the heart of the vast site.

Quentin broke away, slowly pacing the threadbare remnants of carpet that didn't even fit the room.

'That's got to be it,' he mused. 'This is the President's baby. Where is *his* residence?'

'*Un moment* … Ah, here. The Palace of Eternal Spring. Wow, these names are going to make communication interesting if things get wild. Here, look.' Lucien indicated the building, two rows west of the Hall of Union.

'Short commute to work then,' said Quentin. 'That's where the main directive document will be – in the President's home. I'd bet anything.'

'I agree. And if a bioweapons operation is only an appendix, then what on earth else is there? I bet Tao wants to keep this close to his chest. He is probably the only one who has the whole picture.'

Quentin looked back at Lucien, for a rare moment lost for words.

The pair returned to the laptop screen and reread the brief. The silver lining for infiltration of the City was that the price of reclaiming palatial accommodation was its antiquity. Once past the palace moat and the outer wall, inside the compound the buildings had only rudimentary security measures: guards on some doors, locks but no guards on others. Some without either. And no CCTV or passive infrared motion detection. Who would dare to enter the Forbidden City uninvited? There were few details about the President's quarters. Ying had only been inside once.

'What bothers me most is what's happening on the other side of the world,' said Lucien. 'What's going on in Düsseldorf? Is Tavener about to sell his intel? If he makes contact with Chinese intelligence, it could precipitate a lockdown here.'

They agreed there was no time for a final recce of the site – exfiltration routes to escape and dead drops to stash product would have to stand as previously identified. The aim was always to extract information without trace, which was laudable but dangerous. Copying took longer than stealing.

* * *

It was Saturday evening, 13 April 1996. The piece of information from Ying upon which the mission hung was a contradiction between the President's avowed devotion to all things traditional Chinese and a penchant for the culture of the romantic West. Mr Tao occasionally ordered European foods for his Saturday evening, often on the moment, something to which his staff had become accustomed.

Quentin and Lucien thus planned to enter the Forbidden City as delivery chefs from Maxim's. They would run the risk of conflicting with a real food order which might come from one of the few fine restaurants able to supply such cuisine, but that, as Quentin's logic had it, would only assist the mission: the haphazardness of *more* French food turning up at the gate, or French food in addition to Italian, would be consistent with previous presidential demands. Combined with a narrative of eloquent, high-handed Mandarin from Quentin, plus a diatribe from a very busy and important French chef by Lucien, the pair hoped to be through the gate without the guards bothering to call the restaurant, nor highlight to the President that *they* were the reason for his food going cold.

So, to meet a dinner schedule alien to Westerners, their plan began at 4.30 p.m. with a special collection from Maxim's.

Motor vehicles were kept well back from the Meridian Gate, the entrance to the Forbidden City, but a pair of Chinese tricycles could roll right up to the checkpoint.

The exchange with the guards went largely as expected, with just one surprise.

'Which is for sampling?' asked a rotund officer, adjusting his cap and signalling for the lids to be opened on the food.

Quentin was taken aback. Was this humour or serious? He looked quizzically at the guard.

'For security. We need to check it's safe! Which one?'

BEAUMONT

Quentin thought he must have overlooked something obvious. How could *he* decide which to check? He selected an entrée of chicken liver pâté and lifted the small cloche. The guard grabbed a piece of toasted crusty bread and dug in. Lucien gave a small nod, realising what was going on. The seconds crept by to the sound of munching.

The guard licked his fingers and gestured for their papers, which his colleague checked.

'This way,' he said. 'The officer will escort you.' Quentin paused, waiting for their papers to be returned. 'These when you leave,' the guard ordered.

The three started into the complex, Quentin and Lucien on their tricycles and the escorting officer walking in front. They tried to note every building, square, passage and doorway, but were overwhelmed by the continual twists and turns through the labyrinthine sprawl. Where the major buildings barged their way to dominate open spaces, the result was cavernous and deserted. Staggering feats of construction and ornate red-washed precision rang as empty vessels that reflected nothing bar the dull thud of the guard's clumpy rubber boots.

Lucien looked over to Quentin. 'The food will get cold at this speed. Can't we ride ahead?'

The guard spun round and spat an instant rebuke. 'Inside the City you do not speak unless you are spoken to.'

Ten minutes later the trio emerged from the alley between the President's residence and the Western Palaces into the wide courtyard of the Palace of Eternal Spring. The men's minds went into overdrive as they scanned the building's elevation for clues to its layout, to enhance the fragments that Ying had described.

'Wait here,' said their escort.

They watched as he approached two sentries stood atop the broad stone steps to the entrance. They hardly dared to breathe, the possibility of being exposed and arrested suddenly very real. The sentries' faces signalled the inevitable surprise that no such food had been ordered. The escort thudded back to Quentin and Lucien, fury building in his face at the humiliation they had created.

'Who did you speak with in His Excellency's staff?' he said.

'We did not make the arrangements,' Quentin replied. 'I believe they are a special gesture, a surprise, extended personally to the President by Monsieur Cardin.'

The escort's expression twisted in conflict. He stared at the floor, a finger set across his lips in deliberation, before returning to the sentries. After conferring, one of the sentries went inside. Moments later he reappeared, waving for them to bring the food.

Baskets in hand, they entered the hallowed halls, taking in the polished dark stone floors and intricately carved blackwood arches, side tables and fine antique vases. The sentry led them to the kitchen where the cooks were preparing dinner, heads turning to see the reason for the interruption and insult to their efforts. They donned latex gloves and unpacked the dishes in silence. The sentry gave

Quentin a long look then turned away, leaving him to speak with the chef.

'I will need to warm some of these for His Excellency,' Quentin said. 'Your exquisite cuisine will not be wasted. This is more of a sampling menu.' The chef huffed and walked away.

Everything appeared to be going to plan.

Quentin asked Lucien, 'Would you fetch the finishing ingredients from the tricycles while I warm the sauce?' He took his time decanting the glossy brown fluid into a pan.

Lucien slipped out of the kitchen into a dark corridor, checked about him and headed for the President's study. The halls and rooms away from the dining suite and living area were cloaked in a deathly silence and Lucien's heart quickened as he spied places to conceal himself. He readied his excuse for the bathroom for when a guard appeared ahead or behind him. But there was nothing. Nobody. He intuited the culture at work here. The enterprise focused on the man, protected the man, honoured the man, not the territory. Spirit mattered, not objects.

He found the study from Ying's account of a curious perspective painting of a corridor, which hung near the door. It was like the optical effect created by standing between a pair of tall mirrors that faced each other – a corridor stretching into infinity. He listened for anyone inside the study, then entered.

Once within he glanced around the generous space. Beyond a conference table was a smaller painting hung behind a broad desk. Lucien headed straight for it and removed the picture to reveal the safe. He let out a breath – that was precious time saved. The safe was small, although large enough to hold D4-sized papers. It was opened by a purely mechanical action via a single rotating numerical dial.

Lucien tried to ignore his peril. Thoughts of Club operating procedures to circumvent interrogation and torture by precipitating one's own demise – because everybody broke in the end – flitted at the back of his mind. Cyanide was not a pleasant way to go. He felt his whole body getting hot with the pressure.

He retrieved the thin electrical cable secreted within his belt and connected the probe and earpieces – disguised as parts of an ornate beaded wrist-band – to construct an electronic stethoscope. He noted the dial's current setting, plugged in, and began to unlock it using the faint tell-tale sounds from backlash and geometry in the mechanism. On the eighth rotation he conquered the code and was in.

Quentin was making haste slowly. He felt the eyes of the cooks upon him as he moved through the menu items, simmering here, keeping warm there, heating bowls and tasting flavours. He was buying every second possible but he felt the initiative slipping from them as the chef stepped over to ask exactly when he planned to serve His Excellency.

'The President, of all people, knows that good things sometimes require patience,' said Quentin.

'Well, you should know that he has little of that, for anyone or anything.' Quentin looked up and gave a curt nod. This was no time to overplay it. 'And where is your colleague?'

'I sent him outside to fetch some items.'

The chef looked about him but would not lower himself to go and check on Lucien.

Quentin sensed time was up and he could perhaps create more room for Lucien by drawing attention to the act of serving the President.

'I am ready. Would someone assist me, please?' he said to the chef.

But that was not how it was done. Waiters were called and Quentin stood back as they carried the items that he indicated.

Then a new voice sounded at his back.

'Your friend. Where is he?'

Ah, so now I am being graced with the attention of a presidential close protection officer, Quentin thought.

'*Ici, Monsieur. J'ai les articles,*' came Lucien, carrying salt and pepper mills, truffle oil and a garlic crusher. '*Ah, trop tard.*'

They waited under the gaze of the protection officer as the waiters took away the last dishes of coq au vin.

Quentin noticed spots of blood on Lucien's left hand. He picked up a napkin, absentmindedly swirling it around as if just passing the time before giving it to him with a furtive glance towards the problem. Lucien took it and covered the bleeding.

Twenty minutes later an official entered the kitchen.

'His Excellency sends his gratitude and congratulations to Monsieur Cardin for a most enjoyable experience. You may leave now. Take all your items with you.'

14

The only way Bruce and Martine could get ahead of Jez in the race to Düsseldorf was by private charter. A check of available flights indicated that he would probably be booked on the only connecting flight for the next 24 hours. There were no direct flights from Cagliari.

Bruce settled back into the leather of the Gulfstream business jet, bemused by Martine flashing the cash, courtesy of a Club credit card registered to a cover company. They touched down around midday local into a drizzly North Rhine-Westphalia, running six hours behind Beijing time. The plane taxied into a private hangar where they sped through a dedicated customs check before grabbing a hire car. A fast one.

They were using the Steigenberger hotel as a base for operations. It was comfortable and only half a kilometre away from the Alt hotel, where Jez would be staying.

An hour after they arrived, they were joined in Bruce's room by Marc Arnaud, who would provide technical support to the op, as well as being another experienced Club player. With tea and coffee cups steaming in the background, Marc unboxed four different styles of briefcase.

'Interesting. I won't even try to guess at the play for this one,' Bruce said with a frown.

Marc threw the cardboard packaging aside and set the cases in a neat line.

'We need to find a way of replacing the information Jez will be handing the Chinese. They need to think Tavener's intel is shit. This also means he will be taken out of the picture for a while with the MSS pursuing him. The plan is to swap his case with an identical one containing our disinformation – concocted courtesy of Amulet and me back at the office. I got these two from local outlets.' He pointed to a black Samsonite and a brown leather Antler case. 'The others I brought with me. Now, I might be wrong, but I'm guessing a classic trade scenario: "You transfer the money and my guy opens the case" sort of thing.'

Bruce's puzzled look returned. 'That's all good, but what if he carries the paperwork in some other way? Like, no briefcase.'

'We watch Jez's hotel and try to confirm such details. But, think about it, Tavener will not want Jez walking the streets with his prized file unprotected.'

Martine smiled. 'Nice work. It'll save time if things turn out that way. And we'll soon know, depending on exactly what "conference materials" are delivered to the Alt hotel.'

'It figures,' Bruce said. 'With Jez as his proxy, Tavener will want to be close by. But he isn't going to travel far with extra bulk like a briefcase when he can pick one up locally, and that limits his choices.'

'Okay, you both happy with that?' asked Marc. They nodded. 'Then I better head over to the Alt hotel ready for Jez's arrival, while you work through the options for how to track and intercept him en route to the sell. We will only get one chance.'

*   *   *

The Alt was a traditional hotel, its quaintness marred by the large plastic board running across its frontage displaying its name. The hotel entrance was situated on Hunsrückenstraße, a pedestrianised alley containing various boutiques and eateries, with a handful of tables outside that belonged to its café.

Marc considered it likely that Tavener would be observing the scene, so he made an effort to disguise his appearance in case he was needed for another live role later. With jacket collar up, baseball cap and a pair of aviator sunglasses, he took a seat at the café to wait for Jez to arrive.

He looked at his watch. The flight had landed half an hour ago, and Jez should appear in twenty minutes, traffic allowing. He had bagged a position near to the entrance, from which he could both see the pigeon holes for room keys and catch snippets of conversation between reception staff and guests. Perfect. He sat back, reading a copy of

Bild and dragging out his first coffee. Passers-by came and went as if he was invisible.

At just before 4 p.m. Jez panted his way into the alley, past Marc and into the lobby. He looked stressed and tired. Marc focused on the discussion with the receptionist less than five metres away. 'Room 114.' That was all he needed to hear. First floor, room 14. Standard dumb key, no electronics.

To avoid making a temporal connection between Jez's check-in and his departure, Marc ordered another coffee. Tavener would spot a coincidence like that a mile off. The delay was fortuitous. Ten minutes later a man in a shapeless brown jacket and tie approached, casually swinging a metal-clad briefcase in his right hand. He swept past the café tables and into the Alt. The crown jewels. Marc stifled a sigh of relief as he saw that the case matched one of his.

To extend the charade and buy more time, he produced a biro and began scribbling on a page in the newspaper that was advertising a competition. He observed the delivery of the case, the call to Jez's room and his subsequent prompt collection. Jez was already on a mobile as he tramped out of reception with the case under his arm. *Formidable!*

When the waitress asked Marc if he would like another coffee, he politely declined, picked up his belongings and handed her the cash. She bade him farewell and began clearing the table.

BEAUMONT

A diversion though the Galeria Kaufhof allowed Marc to shed his disguise before returning to the Steigenberger. In the hotel room he was jubilant.

'We have the case. This one,' he said, raising the hardened briefcase, a type often used for carrying camera equipment. 'But one detail, *cependant* ...'

'What?' asked Martine.

'I saw a barcode label on the underside. The courier was trying to look casual and went too far, swinging it everywhere. I took some photos.'

Marc extracted the button lens and recording unit from his jacket and connected it to a laptop. Bruce picked up the briefcase and turned it over.

'You mean this?' He pointed to the sticky label. 'Why is this important? It's a new case. The guy didn't bother to remove it.'

'*Non*. Look closely. Two numbers there. A product code and a serial number,' Marc replied.

'Who puts serial numbers on briefcases?'

'The Germans,' said Marc, looking to Martine. 'No offence.' She grinned back at him and waved away his apology.

'So, maybe it was left there so Jez could check it to make sure the case wasn't switched,' said Bruce.

'It's precisely for that reason,' Martine interjected.

Marc brought up the first, blurry image from his button camera, then ran through a series of photos, back and forth. 'Here, this one is clearest.' He zoomed in and adjusted contrast to sharpen the image. '*Merde*, I can only see some of the numbers.'

'That's a ten-digit number,' said Bruce. 'Jez won't remember all that. And I doubt he will be allowed to write anything down. He'll just go for the last three digits is my guess.'

'True.' Marc zoomed in closer. '387.'

'Then let's craft another sticker ending 387,' said Martine. 'Okay, Bruce, we need to go.'

Bruce and Martine headed out to monitor Jez's movements, leaving Marc to prepare the briefcase.

He worked meticulously, running through a range of fonts till he had the best possible match with the barcode sticker on the case. He placed a sheet of gloss paper in a portable printer and out popped the new label. Next, he put on a set of magnifying glasses and brought to hand his instrument tool set, with which he modified the locks so that any combination would open them. A false panel was inserted inside the case, behind which was placed an electrochemical weight-adjusting device. A miniature microphone, GPS unit and short-range transmitter were hidden behind the weight mechanism. Finally, he put in the file of disinformation for the Chinese. This should appear sufficiently credible at face value to satisfy exchange and payment, but when subjected to proper scrutiny the contents would be discredited.

BEAUMONT

If the plan worked, Tavener would be hunted by Chinese intelligence and any potential security clampdown in Beijing would be stalled or avoided.

*   *   *

Bruce blew out a lungful of tension. While the Club had extraordinary people, wealth and next-generation technology, it also felt small, thin, lacking. Extraordinary people were rare. It made for scarce resources, its Achilles' heel. If he messed up there was no cavalry to rescue the situation.

With Martine at the south end of Hunsrückenstraße and Bruce at the north, they watched the hotel entrance, communicating through their earpieces and hidden microphones.

A light rain began to fall and the sky between the city-centre buildings darkened into evening. Bruce pulled his cap down against the wet and pressed himself into a doorway. He was in uncharted territory. He had never been properly trained in live surveillance of human targets. On foot. And worse still, Jez would surely recognise him up close, never mind the attempted disguise. But they needed at least two for the job and Marc had a host of other tasks to cover. Bruce had to be a ghost.

At 6.50 p.m. Martine saw Jez emerge from the hotel into the alley, briefcase in hand. Game on. He was striding in her direction, head down. She opened proceedings in Bruce's ear.

'Contact.'

'Roger.'

Bruce felt his stomach lurch as he spotted Jez heading away in front of him.

Jez reached where Martine was standing. She let him pass while she pondered the window display of a boutique, her reflection confirming that her flowing chestnut hairpiece, scarf and voluminous tote bag were in order.

Jez hung a left, then a right onto the broad tree-lined Heinrich-Heine avenue.

'Heading east, towards hotels,' Martine announced.

Bruce trailed some fifty metres behind. Jez darted across the lanes of crawling traffic, with a couple of horn blasts sounding at him as he went. Nerves and naivety were showing. This was a fine way to attract police attention.

'He's turned into Theodore-Körner Straße. I reckon it's the Breidenbacher hotel.'

'Copied,' replied Bruce.

'He's looking up ahead. I'm sure that's the venue. Need to move now.'

'Moving!'

Bruce grappled with the scenario they had rehearsed. The Breidenbacher Hof was one of Düsseldorf's finest, and largest, hotels. It was also just one block from the Steigenberger, where they were based. Lady Margaret had concurred with the team's guess that it would be a likely location for the exchange.

He could see extensive roadworks and a contraflow traffic system outside the Breidenbacher. This caused a bottleneck on the pavement, which held Jez up while Bruce slipped around him on the opposite side of the street. He crossed over, rounded the boarding erected to enclose the works, and joined a throng of people heading towards Jez, squeezing past the hotel on the narrowed pavement. The rain was now falling heavily and darkness was near total. He had rarely been so grateful for poor weather.

'Ready?' he said into his collar mic.

'Ready.'

Bruce peered around the line of bodies ahead of him, spotting that Martine was a few paces behind Jez. Both were now fast approaching, head on. Seconds later, they crossed. As Jez tried to push past in the column of oncoming pedestrians, Bruce feigned avoiding something on the ground, swerved and shoulder barged him. But he overdid it, sending Jez into the construction boarding, which gave way with a resounding snap of tearing chipboard before clattering to earth. Jez careered into a pile of stone chippings inside the enclosure and ended up flat on his back, as the briefcase caught the exposed end of the next board and skidded to the pavement a few feet from him and out of his sight.

The crowd concertinaed to a halt, and those nearest clutched each other to prevent themselves from falling.

Martine leaned over the case, let her trench coat hang open to cover it from view, and quickly exchanged it for Marc's case, which she had stashed in her tote bag. Bruce said nothing, but pressed on through the crowd and away. A bulky passer-by, eager to reach in and lend Jez a hand, pushed Martine aside. She moved behind the Good Samaritan and watched to check that Jez picked up the case.

'*Danke! Danke!*' Jez exhausted his German vocabulary. 'Fucking arsehole! Who the fuck ..? What was that about? Blind or something?' he spat as he grabbed the case and tried to dust himself down, his hair dripping wet and rain soaking into his jacket.

'*Kein problem,*' said the helper, patting him on the back.

Jez shoved his way out of the crowd and ascended the steps into the hotel, flipping the case over briefly to check the barcode.

Martine continued past the hotel entrance, then turned into a side alley and out of view. With her back to the street she took out Jez's case and hung it on a set of hand-held digital scales.

'Team Zero, this is Team One. I have the package. It's 2.92,' she said.

'Copy. It's in range. Adjusting now,' Marc replied, signalling that he would remotely activate the electrochemical device in Jez's new case so the weight matched the original. 'That's net 158 grams. Maybe twenty-five to thirty sheets, plus a cover. Not a bad guess.'

'Great work. Let's pray they buy the contents,' she said. 'Team Zero going mobile.'

15

Marc entered the Breidenbacher. He checked his watch. Six minutes had elapsed since Martine radioed with the weight measurement for the briefcase. He had to estimate how long to wait until Jez had met with the Chinese intelligence officers. It wasn't certain they would sweep the briefcase for electronic emissions – it wasn't their briefcase, nor their show. But Marc had to assume they would. He couldn't activate the GPS or microphone until after such a check. When was a total guess. The rub was that these hidden devices had only small batteries and therefore very limited range. They might not connect with his receiver if they were too far away, even in the same building. He steeled himself to let sufficient time pass before switching on.

He walked through the lobby and took the stairs to the third floor in an attempt to place himself centrally within the hotel. He found an alcove with a view of the street, plugged in a second earpiece for the briefcase's microphone, and when ten minutes had elapsed he activated the electronics.

The GPS suggested they were on the top floor, which was little surprise. Harder for the buyer to escape with the goods if the deal went sideways. Marc increased the earpiece volume and listened.

The first voice he heard was a man, clearly Chinese, speaking in a business-like tone. He caught the tail end of what he was saying. In reply, Jez sounded nervous.

Chinese voice: ... *authorised to represent your associate?*
Jez's voice: *I am, although I will be following his strict instructions.*
By telephone?
Yes, this phone.
How can we verify the product?
My associate will answer all your questions though me.
[Pause]
Then let us begin.

Martine's voice crackled into Marc's ear. 'Team One and Two are back.'

'Okay, I'm tuned into the game now. Get tidied up there. Speak later.'

Jez: *Hello? We're ready.* [Pause] *My associate requests fifty percent payment prior to presenting the product.*
[Muffled voices]
Very well.
These are the account details for wire transfer. [Sound of writing on hard surface.]

One moment.
[Mandarin being spoken in background]
The funds are being transferred.
My associate is checking now ...
[Long pause]

Marc looked up. Damn, a maid was approaching, pulling a housekeeping trolly. She stopped. Was everything okay? Yes, he was speaking on his mobile. Apologies, she didn't realise. Sorry to disturb.

He returned his focus to the room two floors above.

... appears to have been received. Thank you. [Briefcase being clicked open] *Here is the file.*
[Paper being handled. Long silence.]
[Speaking in Mandarin.]
This suspect is dead ... We knew about him. Wanted ... Ah, okay. There is more ...
Yes, still here... [Pause] *My associate asks if you are satisfied that this meets with your expectations.*
We know some of this already and some parts are quite out of date, but there is new material for us to investigate.
[More Mandarin exchanged.]
We accept.
Great.
We will transfer the balance now. Yes?
Yes, please.

BEAUMONT

Is this the only copy?
[Pause]
No. My associate has one more copy. As insurance.
Of course he does. At least he does not try to lie.
So, is our business complete?
Almost. May we see the case please?

Merde! Marc killed the electronics and ran for the stairs. He hurtled down, bounding four steps at a time as he spoke into his mic.

'Team One. Zero. Package is about to be opened. Prepare to move.'

'Team Zero, you leaving the show?'

'Affirmative. Using VIP access,' he said, referring to an exit route through a service entrance at the back.

Ten minutes later Marc swung into the room at the Steigenberger to find Bruce and Martine standing over their kit bags and rucksacks, all packed and ready to go.

'What happened?' Martine asked.

'They were about to inspect the case, with Jez still there.'

'*Scheisse*. Tavener will know he's been rumbled.'

'Hmm, but maybe good too. Nothing will happen in Beijing now. And Tavener will go into hiding.'

'The other crumb of good news is that I can get rid of this beard,' said Bruce, dragging his fingers through the tangle of hair, scratching feverishly along his jaw. 'No more Grizzly Adams. Bloody itches too.'

'*Maintenant allons-y,*' said Marc, waving his arms towards the door.

The trio hauled their equipment downstairs and headed out without another word. They would travel separately back to Beaumont.

Marc pushed along the street, then rounded a corner, leaving Bruce and Martine behind him. He went down into an underground car park, set his heavy bag down and sighed as he opened the van. The operation had gone well enough, rather than well. The bonus of having the Chinese chasing Tavener without his knowledge would have been the icing on the cake. But life wasn't like that.

* * *

In Beijing, Quentin and Lucien arrived back at their apartment, unable to shrug off their suspicions over how easy it had been to access the presidential palace.

'We could have just poisoned him,' Lucien said.

'I doubt it,' Quentin replied. 'We didn't see what happened in the dining suite. It wouldn't surprise me if someone tasted every dish prior to him eating it – for every meal from the outside, that is. To suspect the food cooked by his own chefs would look ridiculous for someone who wants to present a strongman image to the world.'

'I can imagine that he likes to think of himself as the embodiment of some Sinitic spirit.' Lucien mused. 'He probably considers himself to be special, precious. But having someone taste your food, wherever it comes from, diminishes the demi-god image.'

'Quite,' said Quentin.

Lucien unwrapped the napkin from around his hand, the white cotton soaked with red. 'Better clean this up.'

'You did that while recording the information? How?' asked Quentin.

'When we get back home, I'll show you.'

Lucien's mobile pinged. A secure text had arrived.

'Oh.' He held the phone up for Quentin to read: *ABORT Z.*

Z was code for *Zhōngguó* – China. Leave the country. Not the target, not Beijing. China.

'Ah,' said Quentin, reading the message. He frowned. 'Perhaps our worst fears are about to come true. They could be on to us. Departing after this mission was the plan anyway. But we'd better make it snappy.'

'Snappy? It's seven hundred kilometres to the Mongolian border.'

'But only two hundred to Bohai Bay.'

'I still don't like that option,' said Lucien, shaking his head. 'We'll never get out. The navy would intercept us.'

'It beats a long walk in Mongolia. There are no pickup points or airfields for half a continent. In Bohai we can strike a deal with smugglers. The Tianjin gateway, remember? The authorities don't pick up the guys who bring in their contraband goodies.'

Lucien looked away, still shaking his head.

'Trust me,' Quentin said.

'We travel together?'

'I suggest so, at least till we're clear of China. Riskier but also safer, if that even makes sense. And with what's in your head you're too valuable now.'

'Better switch to these,' said Lucien, placing new passports on the table.

*   *   *

It was Thursday 18 April before Quentin arrived at Beaumont, nearly a week after Lucien received the text telling them to leave China. After completing the sea journey from Tianjin they had separated. Quentin amused the others as he recounted the tale of their escape on a slow boat from China. They had followed an old smugglers' route that originated in the silk trading days and ran across the Yellow Sea to Incheon, South Korea.

By mid-afternoon, Lady Margaret, Martine, Bruce, Marc and Quentin were gathered in the living room for afternoon tea, complete with silver trays, ornate cake stands and fine bone-china cups. They were waiting for Lucien, who was due at any moment. Bruce eyed the macaroons but held back from taking one.

BEAUMONT

The thump of a car door heralded Lucien's return. Bruce wandered to the window, curious about who had driven him the final leg of his journey. Probably a local taxi. Monsieur Martell and his chateau could not be a secret here after so many years, generations indeed. Bruce contemplated the outline of long dark hair, obscured by reflections upon the driver's window, as the Citroën turned and drove away. No taxi markings though.

Lucien entered the room looking jaded and a little ruffled. He set his bags down. *'Bonjour mes amis!'* He received a chorus of welcomes before everyone helped themselves to the spread.

'Now we are assembled, I would like to say a sincere thank you and job well done to both teams. Missions accomplished, as far as things go,' Lady Margaret opened. 'And congratulations to Bruce for a good performance on his first task.' A ripple of applause went around the others.

'Just did what I was told,' said Bruce. 'Thanks to Martine for excellent mentoring.'

Her ladyship then summarised the outcome of the Düsseldorf operation, for the benefit of Quentin and Lucien. They learned that the text message telling them to vacate Beijing was indeed a precaution, taken when the briefcase was compromised by the Chinese intelligence operatives.

'Now to Beijing,' she continued. 'Lucien and Quentin were also successful in their task. After reconnoitring the government buildings and residential area of the Forbidden

City, they pulled off a rather audacious infiltration of the presidential palace. Lucien ...?'

'*Ah, non. Continuez, s'il vous plaît,*' he said, dropping his head, exhausted.

'*Bien sûr.* Well, they cooked up a plan – sorry – to deliver a take-out meal, unannounced, pretending to be from Pierre Cardin's Maxim's restaurant. And somehow they ... well, they blagged it. Lucien cracked the President's safe and located what we think is the main planning document, of which the appendix is a part.'

Bruce raised a hand. 'May I? That's incredible, of course. Do you mind me asking, what do you mean by "think"? Can't we tell if it's the main document?'

'*Non*, I cannot read Mandarin,' said Lucien.

'But Quentin is fluent—'

'We don't have a copy, old boy,' Quentin interjected. 'Haven't seen it. Yet.'

Bruce looked around at the others, confused.

'Bruce, allow me to continue and perhaps your questions will be answered,' said her ladyship. 'The copy is in Lucien's head. He has a photographic memory.'

'Oh. Right. Apologies. I'll shut up and listen.'

'No, it's fine. He can't *tell* us anything. We have to extract his images and read the Mandarin.'

'Christ! What does that entail?'

Nobody replied. Evidently, this was something Bruce did not need to know.

BEAUMONT

* * *

Thirty minutes later, accompanied by Marc and Quentin, Lady Margaret led Lucien to the basement, to a room that resembled an operating theatre. An array of ceiling lights beamed uniform bright light into the space, and a cluster of LEDs on an adjustable arm hung above a padded table long enough for a tall adult to lie upon.

Lady Margaret stood aside while Lucien reclined on the table. Next to it was a video camera on a tripod, a computer terminal and two monitors. Marc attached a web of electrodes to Lucien's scalp, with a paste to improve electrical contact across his forehead, then sat at the computer.

He looked over to her from his desk.

'Please, proceed,' she said. He nodded then turned to Lucien.

'*D'accord. Prêt?*'

'*Oui.*'

Lucien closed his eyes and let out a long, steady breath. He clenched his left hand, with the nail of the index finger in contact with the side of his thumb. A minute passed, then, as the left monitor registered the range of alpha, beta, delta and theta patterns, images began to flicker on the monitor to the right.

'*Enregistrer* ...' Marc confirmed that the images were being captured.

'*Bien?*'

'*Ah, non …*'

She watched as Lucien tightened his fist. Blood began seeping from around the nail. 'Easy does it, Lucien.'

Marc looked around the monitors at Lucien's side and saw what was happening. 'It's to help him recall.'

'*Et maintenant?*' asked Lucien.

'*Mieux qu'avant. Assez bien.*' The images were clear now.

The process lasted for five minutes. Lady Margaret stepped in with a bandage and dabbed away the drips of blood that ran from Lucien's hand. She looked to Marc, raising her eyebrows.

'*Terminé!*' cried Marc. He stood and looked at Lucien, whose jaw muscles were writhing in his face, beads of sweat across his forehead mingling with the paste.

Lucien gasped and opened his eyes.

16

Marc's reverse EEG machine had been purloined from an advanced research programme in the UK private sector. It had been adapted and developed as a working prototype by a small core of engineers and a medical physicist on Lady Margaret's payroll. Bottom line was it worked.

Lucien had recalled the images using a physical stimulus to which a cognitive association had been made – an anchor in the jargon. That enabled what he could easily access, but not understand, to be output for others to see. Outputting this way had its trauma but was less error prone than attempting to write or draw what he pictured.

Marc had printed eleven sheets containing the main body of a presidential directive. Skewed in some places, blurred in others, there was sufficient material for Quentin to give an initial reading. Later he would prepare a full transcript.

It was just before 7 p.m. Lucien had recovered from his EEG session and was sitting beside the fireplace with a glass of cognac in his right hand. The left had been re-bandaged. One by one they filtered back to the airy high-vaulted space of the living room, which by normal standards would be considered a hall. Bruce sat on an end of a sofa beside Martine and opposite Lucien, Quentin and Marc, with the fireplace to his right. Her ladyship stood to Bruce's left, facing the fireplace. She invited Quentin to present his initial findings.

'Thank you, my lady. It's bad news, and worse than we could have contemplated. We really wanted two things – call it cake and eat it. Not that I'm much for cake,' he added with a chuckle. 'We wanted details on the suspected virus programme *and* to identify what it's a part of. The virus plan was an appendix, remember. So, an appendix to what?'

The room was silent, save for Lucien tipping back his glass of cognac with an audible gulp. Bruce felt intrigue wane and trepidation begin to coil inside him. This was real, and real sounded bad.

'Lucien found nothing more in His Excellency's safe about the biological details we require to identify the virus,' Quentin continued. 'They're probably in the lab up in Hulunbuir, or maybe another research facility. We don't know, but at least Ying's copy of Appendix D provides the essentials for Western virologists. The main document is called *Fènghuáng* – the Phoenix Programme. The appendices are a series of measures that, from my reading, are intended to make China *the* global superpower.'

Groans sounded around the group. Bruce was at sea again, dislocated and a step behind them. The others reacted as though they had already figured it out. What the hell was it the Chinese were intending to do?

'The sub-plans in the appendices seem to constitute a strategy of escalating measures, moving from what the wonks would call soft power or passive measures to, well, the very opposite.' Quentin paused to see how his words were being received.

'My God, what does that mean?' Martine broke in.

'It means a progression of growing regional influence and expanding economic influence, meaning ownership, meaning control. That evolves to military hegemony, like building more bases across the South China Sea, dominating shipping routes, and challenging disputed territories, such as the borders with India, Tibet and Taiwan.'

'Christ, he's going to invade Taiwan?' The penny had dropped and now Bruce couldn't hold back.

'It runs further and deeper, in all directions really. A prime goal is transformation of organic Chinese tech capability – silicon-chip production, mobile communications and data networks, AI, and so on. Own, develop, control. You can see the attraction of Taiwan, with its semiconductor production. But I must hand it to the President, he saves the best till last.'

'What! upsetting the international order by every and all means isn't enough?' said Martine. 'His ideology is economically unviable, so infect the West to destroy production and escalate state debt so we are dominated by

Chinese sovereign wealth. Build tech production from stolen corporate secrets!'

Her face flushed, she was almost shouting. Bruce went to place a calming hand on hers but withdrew when she glowered at him.

'Then brace yourself, Martine,' Quentin continued. 'Tao's calculation is that the West is impotent and divided. It will not have the backbone to oppose China. And Russia ... Russia is still grappling with an aspiration for democracy and free market economics. But will it break free from its cultural and ideological past, from the gravitational pull of the KGB?'

'And if he's wrong? What if America and its allies, such as Japan and Europe, what if they move against, say, a Chinese invasion of Taiwan?'

'Then we end up at Appendix H.'

Bruce's eyes widened. He had never seen Quentin check himself. Never a flicker of doubt would ever cross the man's face.

'Well? What the hell is Appendix H?'

'Nuclear conflict.'

The atmosphere felt like a nuclear detonation had sucked the air from the room.

'Madness!'

Martine stood up and went to the sideboard. She turned her face from them, and Bruce thought he spotted her wiping away a tear as she poured cognac from the decanter. She glanced round at Lucien. 'Another?' He raised an empty glass and sighed heavily. She served them both a full measure and returned to the sofa.

Quentin cleared his throat. 'The nuclear strategy is not what it seems either. It's not a simple last resort if conventional conflict escalates and the Chinese are losing. I mean, can you imagine the scale of it by that stage? No, it's to spark a first strike by the US. Tao has ordered the construction of a hundred nuclear protective facilities across China. But these are a kind of Noah's Ark. If my interpretation is right, they are to preserve a selected one million Chinese to survive and inherit the world after total nuclear annihilation.'

Nobody said a word. The only sound in the room was the fire crackling in the grate. Bruce's long stare of disbelief at what he had just heard shifted to check the others' faces. Her ladyship had locked eyes with Lucien, as if he might make it all go away. Martine appeared to have aged in minutes, the intensity of her gaze deepened by the reflections of the flames. And Quentin? His silence said everything. It was Bruce who spoke first. As in times past, his turmoil had reached its limit and instinct took over.

'I get the idea. Fucking nuts, but I get it. Almost. I don't get the ending. One million people in the ark? That's ... that's nought point one percent of the population. Why cause the deaths of nearly all your people by provoking the US to go first?' He took a breath. 'And inherit *what*? The world will be in nuclear winter and radioactive for how long? ... decades ... centuries?'

'Ah yes,' replied Quentin. 'They're expanding ground-launched nuclear silos across the country and developing a new warhead that carries short half-life fissile material. The land will be inhabitable ...' He flicked to the printout and ran a finger down the sheet. '... inhabitable in around two years.'

'Two years? In bunkers with ten thousand people? They'll have eaten each other alive by then. No offence, Quentin,' Bruce replied.

'None taken. And what about the Americans, you may ask. They don't use short half-life warheads, do they? I think that is an example of strain in Tao's thinking. He believes the US will respond proportionately, that their first salvo will be a limited strike, and therefore the consequences will also be limited. Crucially, they will go down in history as the aggressor. The Chinese counterstrike will be total and annihilate the US, the entire population, before further exchanges occur.'

'Fucking nuts. How can so many people allow one man's madness to even see the light of day?' said Bruce.

'Simple. They don't know the whole picture. He controls the narrative and plays them all like puppets in a regime of fear and paranoia.'

Martine's exasperation caved in to hopelessness as she looked to heaven. 'But *why*?'

This time she reached out and took hold of Bruce's hand.

'It's his Atman Project,' said Bruce. Everyone turned to him. 'That guy you were telling me about, my lady, when you were explaining the philosophy behind the Club – Wilber? – the one whose concepts seems to make sense to you all. A friend at Rothwell used to read his stuff. One of the things he told me was about people's Atman projects.' He waited, unsure if he sounded ridiculous or if they were even interested. But surely it fitted, he thought. After all, they all knew about Wilber too.

Lady Margaret circled a hand, inviting Bruce to continue.

'Well, how did Shaun used to put it? It's like we're all part of an evolutionary process. What we seek, as the Buddhists might have it, boils down to the avoidance of suffering and the pursuit of happiness. And that's the word: *pursuit*. What we need is to evolve our consciousness to *realise* or connect with that sense of knowing, wisdom, feeling complete. I don't quite know how to put it. Shaun referred to Atman as a label for this idea. Am I right?'

'I believe you are along the right lines, Bruce.'

'The point is, if we don't seek to evolve our consciousness, we inadvertently pursue happiness through substitute experiences: a bigger house, a better car, a new lover, a promotion. Whatever. The substitute activity is what Wilber calls Atman projects: false substitutes for what we intuitively seek.' Bruce paused, watching their faces.

Quentin started clapping slowly. 'The boy's got it. And I agree. History is full of men – usually men – seizing power in the pursuit of glory and legacy. That's the stock Atman project for the megalomaniac. With all the usual clichés applying: power corrupts, idle hands make the devil's work.'

'So what are we going to do about it?' asked Martine. Her eyes were still red and watery but her tone had found its fight again. Bruce squeezed her hand.

Lady Margaret was staring at the floor, her brow furrowed. Bruce guessed that she was wondering where next. 'Let's stay with the good Mr Wilber and his Integral Philosophy for a moment,' she said, 'because, for me, it's the starting point to knowing we *can* do something. And, just like gravity, there are rules at work.

'When he was debriefed by Marc, Ying painted a rich picture of President Tao. Tao's reign is all about the virtue and pride of the Chinese people, the superiority of his ideology and political system. But his true intentions are not virtuous. In fact, they are the polar opposite of the ideology, so there exists the potential for his removal. Were his plans to be exposed, it would be impossible for the Chinese Communist Party to look the other way. Add to that whichever eager presidential successors wait in the wings, and there is a route to derailing this so-called Phoenix Programme.'

The others listened, relishing a glimmer of hope in the face of doom.

Lucien stood up. 'I like that. It's why we acknowledge Integral and use it as our compass. Works with the universal design, with evolutionary flows. Any hard response would just energise and escalate the problem. But this concept, it's a soft approach, works from within, uses the situation's *dynamique* to resolve it. Smart.'

'If we are contemplating exposing the President, then would it be an idea to bring Ying in, to have his expert advice at hand? If that's safe to do?' said Bruce.

'Yes, Bruce, that would indeed be the intention.' Lady Margaret scanned the faces of her team. 'Now we have the unenviable task of devising a solid plan from an ethereal concept.'

17

James Tavener ended the call with Jez and hurled the cut crystal brandy glass at the wall. Achieving his aim to sell intel for a negotiated two million dollars was little solace to being upstaged and taken out of play by an unknown party. If it *was* unknown.

He sat in his room in the princely setting of the Gut Dyckhof country house hotel, five miles west of Düsseldorf. He had been enjoying his time savouring fine dining in the barn restaurant set beneath an imposing black tower and taking in the majesty of the gardens' famed topiary. The exercise in cashing in his chips from a long-planned intelligence scam was a retirement fund boost. No need for unnecessary risks, no need to be too close. Things had been going so well.

He had conducted a clinically clean operation through Jez, who had never met with him, did not know his name, and had only heard his voice once – during the sell. Even then it was disguised through an audio module. But Tavener seethed over how easily it had unravelled at the end. The Chinese foreign intelligence officers had worked quickly, stripping the briefcase to identify the electronic tricks. They had even attempted to sweat Jez, but that was short-lived. He imagined their dilemma. They were not on home turf and if they stopped to interrogate Jez they could be hit once they started. No surprise they got out fast, abandoning both briefcase and man to lessen any incentive to intercept them.

If Tavener wanted revenge, his only leads would be Jez and the substituted briefcase. In the moments after the Chinese left the Breidenbacher, Jez had followed protocol and texted RED. Tavener called him, heard the news and instructed him to return to the Alt hotel with the case for a phone debrief.

It wasn't long before Tavener had uncovered Jez's previous inattentive reports confirming all being well. On recollection, he *did* come into contact with a lady in Cagliari who wanted him to look at her car. But that was nothing. It took seconds, so didn't cross Jez's mind as a risk. There *were* people at the café outside the Alt hotel when he arrived. What was unusual about that? But he couldn't be sure if the same people were there when the briefcase arrived. Then there was the incident outside the Breidenbacher, which shouldn't have mattered because he didn't lose the case, and the barcode was right. Wasn't it?

He had attempted a description of Martine in Sardinia, which didn't need to be much. Beautiful woman with short blonde hair would be sufficient to mark her out in any future contact. And the guy who barged him through the boarding? He didn't see his face, but not a big guy. He didn't speak, either.

As for the case, Tavener had wanted to see it for himself, but that was impossible. Jez was hot. He couldn't leave it anywhere for fear of surveillance. Instead, Tavener did his best to build a picture of the tech from Jez's description. The electrochemical weight adjuster was contained in a sealed unit, however, and he directed Jez not to break it open because it could contain explosives, much to Jez's delight. The microphone, GPS and transceiver were easier to identify. These seemed to be modern but not revolutionary. Perhaps CIA, maybe MI5, or 6. Had he fallen out of favour with his old employer at last? Or was Roger Gleeson back on the case after the events in China reached the papers? Possibly.

But at the back of his mind, Tavener felt a lingering doubt about selecting Jez, about Rothwell, Lady Margaret and the Architects' Club. After all, it was a curious outcome. Jez had not been intercepted, nor detained. Tavener had got his money, and one set of lies was doubtless substituted with another. But now he was a wanted man.

He gave Jez one final instruction: dispose of the case. Not leaving to chance how he might do this, he specified the means of weighing it down, and from which bridge and when he would drop it into the Rhine.

James Tavener kicked back in his armchair and looked out across the rolling Lower Rhine countryside. A grin flickered across his face, whether in acknowledgement of a worthy adversary or at the prospect of murdering that person with his own hands, even he could not tell. He had no choice but to embrace his fury and follow any potential lead.

*   *   *

Marshal Lin Xiangquin, chief of the People's Liberation Army, had been summoned. Of medium height and slim build, his face was drawn and lined, with bags under his eyes that bore witness to years of internal, as much as external, conflict. President Tao Wei stood behind his broad blackwood desk in his office within the Great Hall of the People and invited his head of armed forces to sit.

'I wish to hear how our activities in the Strategic Development Initiative are progressing from a defence perspective. I know I get regular reports from Congress, but I want to hear it from you, man to man.'

Marshal Lin felt a familiar sense of unease about the President's motives – the man was unpredictable and scheming.

'Could you be more specific, Your Excellency? I mean, everything is going broadly to plan, and I believe we will achieve our goals.'

Lin did not even say 'the Phoenix Programme' out loud, which is what he meant, so wary was he of his superior's sensitivity over the subject.

Tao looked down at Lin, his expression flat for a moment. Then he stepped from behind the desk and began to slowly pace the room.

'Very well. How is the expansion of our land-based nuclear deterrent going? Site development, the short half-life warheads, test launches?'

'We have completed sixty-two launch silos, with the remaining fifty-eight all under construction. I expect them to meet the revised—'

'Barely over halfway. You should be at seventy-five percent by now,' Tao cut in.

'Remember, we revised the schedule, Your Excellency, to accommodate the redirection of expertise to the Phoenix facilities.' Lin paused, watching the President's reaction. 'We have very limited expertise in the construction of nuclear protective sites like these, which are at the cutting edge of such enterprise.'

'Continue.'

'The warhead programme has challenges but is moving in the right direction. The shorter half-life material needs to be compensated with greater yield, otherwise we would require many more warheads to defeat an aggressor.' Another check for reaction was met with a wave to continue. 'The next test launch is scheduled for one week from today.'

Tao turned to face him. 'The test. Where?'

'Firing from Yichang, northwest into the deserts of Qinghai, Your Excellency.'

'Distance?'

'Two thousand kilometres.'

'Just the delivery system?'

'Yes, Your Excellency. They will use a dummy warhead for representative weight and aerodynamics.'

Tao said nothing, circling slowly about his desk and staring around the walls, deep in thought.

'I want you to fire into the Philippine Sea.'

Marshal Lin's face widened in shock. 'Your Excellency ... over Taiwan? But that would be highly provocative. It could hit shipping. And we would have incomplete test data.'

'You will have all the data you need if it reaches the sea. I leave collateral deconfliction to you, Marshal. The world must know we have arrived. I will not wait for China to be afforded the respect it deserves, when the evidence is plain to see, right now!'

'Your Excellency, surely under your leadership China's rise is evident and continues to become more so with every passing day. But I must counsel caution. Firing over Taiwan will attract an ... unhelpful reaction in the West. Their fear will drive them to act against us, to shun us even. Your wisdom is in the quiet economic and technological advances that you have set in motion. We should trust in those. Give them time to evolve.'

'I have no time for evolution. You speak from your heart, Xiangquin, I have no doubt. But this is about timing. The West is in decline, in turmoil. Russia is a source of hope and fear for the US and her allies. A distraction too. We do not have the luxury of waiting to *evolve*. We must take our place while fortune extends itself to us.' Tao paused. 'You will do my bidding, Xiangquin.'

'As Your Excellency commands.'

An hour later Marshal Lin returned to his headquarters in the Central Military Commission, a few kilometres west of Tiananmen. His growing unease at the President's appetite for global recognition and power had become a malignancy that grew in the pit of his stomach. Was Tao bold or mad? He walked through his outer office and waved away the staff assistant, who stood offering a clutch of papers for signature. 'Just bring me tea, and Phoenix Appendix H,' he said. 'And no calls for one hour.' That would get him to lunch.

Lin skimmed through the pages, trying to reconcile the conflict between his gut and his logic. Appendix H: *The Nuclear Strategy* was large and comprised two parts: offensive, so-called retaliatory measures, and defensive, survival measures. Both were under rapid development. The logic ran that as a rising nuclear power you simultaneously became a potential threat and therefore a target. So your attack capability should be matched by a survival capability, which in the precept of the Cold War's Mutual Assured Destruction – commonly shortened to MAD – increased the deterrent effect. If you got hit, you could still emerge as the victor. So best not to attack.

BEAUMONT

What gnawed at Lin was the scale of the defensive measures. A first one hundred sites were under development, top-secret facilities that could each support ten thousand people for up to two years. But that was a fraction of the population of over one billion people. Information was scant about a second phase to increase the number of facilities.

Lin ruminated. How would the people be chosen for the Phoenix facilities? Many more would be needed to protect the population. Other nuclear powers had facilities only for government and military purposes, there was no protection for the general population. Perhaps his one-time friend, now his superior, had honourable intentions and grand ideas, but he was, after all, human. He too would struggle with earthly matters, like the realities of time and cost to make China the world's most nuclear-protected state.

The aroma of steaming tea brought Lin from his trance. He took a sip and looked out to the Fuxing road, watching the traffic scuttle along the dusty highway under a permanent haze of pollution.

The other thing that intrigued the marshal was the President's enthusiasm for short half-life fissile material. As if in the event of a nuclear exchange China would benefit from access to inhabitable land. But that would be in the West. How would that work? Move the populace from a radiated Asia and live in America amid the ashes?

The big issue was that Lin's old friend did not see fit to include him, the head of the armed forces, in the central plan. That remained the sole preserve of His Excellency. Tao's vision was unfathomable and bizarre. With the elaborations stripped away, it smacked of being borderline insane. Lin accepted the value of good security, but this was nihilism. Tao's ambition was clear to see. A fanatical assertion of Chinese superiority that was founded on undermining the West and its systems. A dirty tricks campaign. But without sight of the main document, Lin was left to imagine all the ways the appendices could come together. When, where, against whom, in what order and to what extent? It was all a mystery, but the consequences of miscalculation for the Chinese people for centuries to come were becoming terrifyingly plain.

He tipped down the last drops of tea and tried to clear his mind. Now he had to focus on the matter at hand: how to fire a nuclear missile into international shipping waters without proper consultations, warnings or fatalities.

18

Having possession of the MI6 file Tavener had intended for sale to the Chinese was simultaneously a gift and a torment for Lady Margaret. Sat at the desk in Beaumont's study, she worked through the pages with deliberation, anxious over what she might find. A gust of wind shook the tall sash windows, making her flinch. She resumed, doing her best to stay her trembling hands.

Tavener's foresight and cunning had to be appreciated. The kernel of his ruse was, in fact, truth. Ying and his dearly departed associate, Wu Qiang, had indeed secretly approached MI6 in Hong Kong in 1983 to alert the West to research into engineered viruses that could be used as vectored bioagents. The file gave no names of MI6 operatives, of course, but the phraseology implied a single point of contact and no input by analysts or other persons. Tavener had kept the matter under wraps. So, had this been a one-off endeavour for retirement planning? or had he been a bad apple for years prior? She couldn't tell, but suspected the latter.

When she reached the end of the file she exhaled in relief. Her worst fear was allayed. Probably due to the passage of time and the diminished condition of the

Architects' Club in the 1980s, none of its operatives or associates had been identified as such in the file. What Tavener had done was to use the reliable identification of the Chinese officials as the centre of a fabrication set in a narrative that had genuine hallmarks of time and source. Conjecture, complemented with informed guesses based on recent events, supplemented the original material. It was supposed to amount to something that appeared real. The grey areas might disappoint the Chinese after proper investigation, but they passed muster in the time-limited setting of a black market sale. Clever Jim. Rotten scoundrel.

Lady Margaret closed the document, locked it in a desk drawer, then stepped out of the study to see how her team was getting on. In the living room Quentin and Lucien were sitting with Ying, who had just joined them from Milan. The three stopped conversing and looked up when she entered.

'I don't mean to interrupt,' she said. Then she addressed Ying. 'Are you settling in?'

'Thank you. Yes. Everything is most excellent,' he replied. A concerned expression flickered in his face. 'My lady.'

'Ying has just pointed out a potential gift! Absolute gem,' Quentin said, his voice raised in excitement. 'He was involved with the development of a Valkyrie-style decree – the CCP's emergency powers provision for the military to take control in the event of a critical breakdown of governance. It's a great opportunity!'

'So, under the right circumstances, power could be wrested from President Tao?'

'Yes, my lady. I will work with Lucien to manipulate the operation order. Thus we should achieve our key mission objective: to expose and incarcerate the President in a single, very public, action.'

Quentin looked at her and beamed a wide grin.

'It sounds very promising. Let me know when you have got further and have confidence that it will offer a concrete option for the operation.'

Lady Margaret smiled warmly, bowed her head in acknowledgement of their progress and withdrew into the corridor, making for the basement.

As she descended the steps, a wall of monitors came into view in the operations area. The larger three were switched off. To their right two smaller screens cycled with CCTV images of Beaumont's grounds and key approaches. She heard muffled voices coming from behind, so she turned left and headed back on herself. After the operating theatre on her right, she came to the equipment store, where Bruce, Martine and Marc were engrossed in conversation. Theirs was the responsibility for logistical and tactical preparations, covering everything from surveillance to transport to combat muscle. They had a lot to talk about. The conversation trailed off when they saw her ladyship.

'How are the preparations going?' she asked.

Marc wiped the back of a sleeve over his damp brow.

'Okay, but we will struggle for space, and if our shipment is compromised, getting replacements will not be quick.'

'This is some of the most sophisticated kit I have seen,' Bruce interrupted. 'Like this …' He held up what resembled a lightweight motorcycle crash helmet. 'Head-up display, integral night vision, radio comms, video feed, auditory enhancement … I mean, wow!'

Marc gave her ladyship a furtive grin and raised his eyebrows.

'I'm pleased you approve, Bruce.' She looked to Marc and Martine in turn. 'Is there anything you need me to do?'

'*Non merci*,' Marc said, looking at Martine who shook her head.

'Very well, I will leave you to your preparations and I shall continue with mine.'

As she climbed the stairs out of the basement, Lady Margaret let out a long sigh. Hers was a weighty responsibility: to direct – and have final call on – strategic decisions from the operations room at Beaumont. But first, she needed to alert the relevant authorities about the impending viral threat, which meant another contact with Ms Shepperton in London.

* * *

BEAUMONT

Roger Gleeson was as pleased with his career as he could reasonably expect to be. From head of a programme in the late 1980s he had advanced to what he considered would be his career ceiling in the Security Service: Deputy Director, F Branch (International Affairs). As the registry trolley squeaked its way down the corridor and into his office on the fourth floor, Gleeson hadn't a clue that this was going to be no ordinary Monday. It was 29 April 1996.

Marcia placed files and envelopes into his in-tray, but for some reason chose to afford a brown paper package special treatment, setting it down directly in front of him. She seemed not to comprehend her instinct to do so, and Gleeson looked up at her, wondering why she had placed it on top of a memo he was reading.

'Um, okay. Thank you, Marcia,' he said quizzically.

She left without replying, without even making eye contact, which was out of character and added to the surreal mood. Gleeson shook his head and gave in to his curiosity. The package was addressed to the Head of International Affairs. He went to pull the string ties aside and rip through the paper, but hesitated, as if it might be a bomb, or infected. But it would have been scanned. What was he thinking? So in he went.

The cover was possibly the blandest, most widely available document binder it was possible to purchase in Britain, which piqued his interest. He opened it and began to read. The contents comprised five typed pages in the form of a summary report. It contained no details about sender or author, no date, no signature or any means of attribution or verification. Doubtless the paper and ink were equally ubiquitous, as would be the printer from which they came. He flicked back to the torn packaging, which showed a London postmark. Not helpful. The document was credible – absent of any translation gaffes by foreign intelligence services – and it was compelling.

The report read that sources had informed of an expected outbreak of a new viral respiratory disease in southeast Asia. What made this important was the unknown pathogen, whose lethality and transmissibility meant it could spread rapidly and disrupt normal life on a global scale. In other words, become a pandemic. Some loss of life was anticipated, such that the social and economic consequences would be enduring and severe. In the worst case it could lead to such interruption to production and macroeconomic function that markets would collapse and democratic order would be critically undermined.

Gleeson paused reading. His head was spinning. Experience told him to stay cool and take his time. This would turn out to be a prank, albeit a well-written one. He turned the page. A series of figures and tables followed that were replete with chemical symbols and formulae. The narrative continued into an outline of intervention measures: testing, isolation and containment, sampling and genetic sequencing, vaccine development.

If experience told him this was probably a prank, his instincts ran strongly in the opposite direction. He felt nauseous. Thoughts of where to go next rampaged through his head: UK healthcare authorities ... researchers ... the World Health Organisation ... governments around the world, starting in Asia. But how to convince others about what could not be corroborated until it might be too late? And why had it reached him under these circumstances? It suggested foul play. But by whom? The sender was withholding information. Why?

Gleeson put the report down and noticed his sweaty palms. He loosened his tie and shrugged off his jacket. He could be sitting on the intelligence coup of the decade. Get it right and maybe he might make Director. Wrong, and he would collect his pension early, or worse.

He stood and moved to the window, taking a moment as he looked out over the Thames. As his mind calmed, he recalled a recent visit to the archives. The Tavener microdots. Those tiny grains set upon a square of soluble acetate film had been hidden by cunning Jim in a bath tap in his flat at Rothwell. Gleeson had always wondered whether the enigmatic golden boy of Vauxhall Cross was not just shrewd and ruthless but also ambitious to the point of narcissism, only ever out for himself. Now he knew. When the miniaturised photographs were reproduced into a readable paper format they contained images of a Hong Kong station file reporting a programme to develop a targeted virological capability by the Chinese.

The file hadn't come to light when it was created in the early 1980s. Now the hullabaloo at the Chinese bioweapons facility and the defections of the two officials had prompted Gleeson to dust it off. It was all circumstantial, but the file and the events at Hulunbuir would strengthen his hand in getting the warning to be taken seriously.

*   *   *

James Tavener had returned to Sardinia to lick his wounds and plot revenge. In the absence of any other substantial leads, he decided to go with his gut and follow the Rothwell legacy. His initial trawl of information started with Bruce Noble. Bruce was Jez's sworn enemy, taken to hospital by her ladyship, attended at the Principal's enquiry by her ladyship, best buddy of Rory McIntyre, and doubtless the other party to shenanigans in the tunnels. Most of all, he was Jenny Noble-Franks' son. There were too many coincidences to ignore around Mr Noble, and James Tavener was not a believer in coincidence.

It turned out that Bruce had recently left the Intelligence Corps, which, like Jez, was a very short career for a Rothwellian. But where he worked now was a mystery. However, as the internet continued to develop, things were becoming more connected, which was milk and honey to Tavener. The resettlement services office at Tidworth had recently set up a public email address, because service leavers had no digital means to contact it using internal MOD systems. When Tavener hacked the machine used to access the internet, he found that it hosted details on ex-army folk, since it was not considered to be confidential military information. He discovered that Bruce Noble had tried to register for resettlement services weeks *after* leaving, when that would normally happen months prior. No home address was listed, nor any company names of prospective employers. Why?

He was starting to suspect, starting to imagine.

Tavener wandered through the vast, empty villa. It was showing signs of neglect. Rooms that he didn't use were abandoned under a growing layer of dust, cobwebs had appeared on ceiling pendants, and a stale odour lingered in the absence of regular cleaning. He made a cappuccino and went out onto the terrace. Outside showed similar neglect. A once perfectly tended Mediterranean garden was becoming overgrown. Weeds had broken through at the edges of the terrace. Evergreen shrubs were losing their ornate shapes. The grass was nearly a metre high, but the summer would return that to dust. Under the warm Mediterranean sun, the cypress trees rustling in the breeze, Tavener contemplated how to track down the suspects.

The first significant point to consider was his presumption that Lady Margaret was dead. He had witnessed how slowly the vault door opened and closed when she had acquiesced to his request to see inside. He knew that its keypad was also the means of activating the tunnel flood system, a destruct button for her and a failsafe against code breakers. To activate it was surely to die.

Without either of the assassins coming out alive he could not be sure whether he had overlooked something, another setting or mode maybe, that enabled the door to open more quickly. His working hypothesis had to be that she was alive.

He sat back in a creaky garden chair and mulled over the possibilities. Say she exited through the vault and the auxiliary tunnel, which could have served both as a means to drain the place after flooding it and as an escape route. She would immediately have gone into hiding, so the world would *think* she was dead. Now she was a ghost, which meant she could pursue him, stop him from selling the lists he stole from the archive seconds before it was destroyed by the booby-trap explosion. But that hadn't happened. The lists were sold for a tidy sum within six months. Maybe she wanted to get clear of organised crime – there would be any number of syndicates, cartels and gangs after the bitch who had screwed them all those years. It made sense.

So where did she go? Brazil, to dearest Giles and Henrietta, waster socialites whose privileged status would stand out anywhere? No. That really only left Monsieur Lucien Martell, fencing coach, confidante, lover.

He's the only option to pursue, Tavener decided. How many Lucien Martells in France ...?

19

The international reaction to the missile test firing over Taiwan was not the shitstorm that Marshal Lin had expected, even if it did lead the evening news on most Western channels. The test proved the deployment vehicle modified to carry the new warhead was reliable and accurate: it fell without incident some three hundred kilometres southeast of Taiwan into the Philippine Sea. Now work could continue to upgrade the Dongfeng missile, whose intended range of twelve to fifteen thousand kilometres would be capable of reaching far into mainland United States.

But Marshal Lin was not celebrating. As his driver returned him to his residence in one of the Western palaces within the Forbidden City, a spectre was growing in his mind. He knew how these things worked. Japan had woken a sleeping giant at Pearl Harbour and the world had learned to spot tyrants that were existential threats to the global order. As President Tao's longing for dominance became a reality, so the West would be moved to oppose him. America would redeploy some of its Pacific fleet to the South China Sea to provide a regional presence, assert international waters, and seek to reassure and gather allies to its cause. It would press matters of nuclear non-proliferation at the UN. It would threaten sanctions and withhold access to key technologies to curb advancement in Chinese military applications. It would likely defend Taiwan, for reasons of principle and practicality: the Taiwan Semiconductor Manufacturing Company was key in global semiconductor development and production. The West would want to deny China's ownership of it as much as Tao dreamed to control it. Was he ready for all that?

Tao would argue that the developments were to bring a balance of power, to level the field, to create an equilibrium that was currently absent. Lin didn't buy it. He was beginning to feel that his old classmate was close to running away with things. It was an itch he could not ignore. He knew that if he ever wanted to know another proper night's sleep then he would have to get ahead of whatever the President really had in mind.

Lin made a decision. He would tour the country on the premise of ensuring that everything was running to schedule. He would talk to the leads for the workstreams that comprised the appendices of the Phoenix Programme. He would talk to their subordinates too, and get behind the facade that Tao had conjured. It was time to investigate.

*   *   *

BEAUMONT

Ying found relief at Beaumont. His familiarity with Beijing's suffocating environment – its hordes of people, the acrid air – had not translated into making Milan with its elegant streets and pleasant climate any more tolerable. He was a country boy who enjoyed the outdoors. It was the pretext of a fishing trip with his close friend Qiang at Hulun Lake, their humble way of celebrating Chinese New Year, that put them over halfway to the Mongolian border from Hulunbuir that night. When the lab went up in a fireball, they had a head start on their pursuers.

Most of all, Ying loved to walk around Beaumont's extensive grounds. But he could not explore further. He would be noticed and tongues would wag.

It was eleven o'clock in the morning on Friday, 3 May 1996, and Ying returned indoors to resume his work with Quentin and Lucien. Quentin was studying the notes they had made on the CCP's emergency powers provision.

'Are we getting this right? I'm sensitive to a misunderstanding of culture becoming a misstep in execution,' he said, frowning. 'Ying, would you mind talking us through the ways that this order is intended to be used?'

'The Party has named this order *Dēnglóng*,' Ying explained. 'I am familiar with *Dēnglóng* from when I served as a member of staff in the National People's Congress during its five-yearly review. Either the President, the leader of the Standing Committee of the CCP, or the head of the PLA can order it. The effect is a militarisation of essential government functions and control of critical national infrastructure, like power and telecoms. It would lock the country down and keep the lights on, while removing the threat and maintaining stability as normal governance was restored. That is the theory.'

Quentin pondered Ying's explanation. 'How did they choose the name?'

'In China *Dēnglóng* is very important mythical creature. It drives away evil, protects people and master, and can tell truth from lies. But there are many ways to interpret who it serves.'

The confusion was understandable to Quentin. The very events that enabled revolutions to succeed in China were to be prevented from recurring by enshrining in law provisions to protect the constitution in times of crisis. But Ying's description made it sound like the order could work in several ways: it could be invoked by the Party acting in the interests of the constitution, but also by the President to protect the government. The ambiguity had never been an issue, probably because both entities saw it as serving them, and to the people, the Party and the government were one and the same. Moreover, in the event of a revolution it became academic, because opponents would fight the military if they thought it was defending a corrupt regime. That is, if the military were not leading the revolution themselves. After all, what defines revolution?

Bottom line: it had never been tested.

The game now was to go as far as possible preparing sections of the order that would create the desired result: to allow a showdown exposure of the President to succeed. They had to ensure he could not order arrests before his true plans were revealed in all their grotesque and undeniable glory. The problem was that Ying could not remember the detailed structure sufficiently well to fabricate an entire substitute order. Nor did he have the secret knowledge of codewords and verification serials to prove the identity of the person giving the order. That would all have to be resolved in China.

The test firing over Taiwan, and Tavener's attempted sale of intel, had raised the stakes for the Club's return to the theatre of operations. Never mind that by now Maxim's had probably denied sending a dinner to the presidential palace that Saturday evening. But then again, possibly not.

20

Before dinner that evening, Lady Margaret called a meeting. Everyone gathered in the living room, making themselves comfortable while she and Ying took their places in front of the fireplace. Bruce sat beside Marc and studied the serious expression upon her ladyship's face. In the room was a sense of anticipation, the usual chatter replaced by silence.

'This afternoon's work has been intense and productive, as you may have noticed. It has thrown up an unexpected opportunity that will form the basis of our plan for deployment to Beijing,' she began. 'I will now invite Ying to explain.'

She smiled to her guest and motioned for him to speak. Ying took a step forward, hands relaxed by his sides, posture upright, as if he had found an equilibrium. He was among friends now.

'The Jianguomenwai Embassy Compound is three kilometres east of Beijing centre. It is home to many Western embassies. I have visited some of these embassies and what is basic knowledge for me could be valuable to you.'

Bruce leaned forward in his seat and made brief eye contact with Marc before they both looked back to Ying, intrigued about what was coming.

'The more secure embassies, like the US Embassy, use their own people, rather than local Chinese, for facilities management work, like catering, cleaning, minor maintenance, and sometimes more technical work. Many others contract out such services. The only good thing about that type of work for contract staff seems to be the money. It is well paid, much better than their home countries, but not, how you say... life-changing, and separation from home, and the regime in Beijing, mean that the money soon does not look so good, and the drawbacks are felt.'

It was a familiar theme: staff retention a problem and turnover high. That presented an opportunity for the Club to enter and remain in Beijing as a group, taking obvious precautions about where and when individuals would work.

'Well, it fits the circumstances,' said Quentin. 'I mean, good tradecraft prevents anyone returning to where Lucien and I were based in the Fengtai district. And if the game is up with the President's dinner, courtesy of Maxim's, then the authorities will be checking out any suspicions about longer-term visitors wherever they might be, whether in migrant ghettos or hanging around fancy restaurants. So we have to look elsewhere.'

'Correct, that is exactly what is likely to be happening,' Ying resumed. 'But the good news is that some embassies have become more flexible in their hiring regimes, fast-tracking security checks or allowing people to join on an escorted basis, where they have to work under supervision while waiting for full clearance. But this is not strictly enforced. During my visits to embassies, I often saw contractors going about their business on white passes without anyone watching them.' He paused and made eye contact with each person, inviting questions.

Bruce raised a hand. 'What about logistics? Like, where do contract staff live?'

'The support workers are accommodated in the residential districts neighbouring the embassy compounds, with all expenses paid. There are normally many roles and shifts to choose from.'

'But wouldn't the MSS suspect everyone in a foreign embassy of being a spy, regardless of the legitimacy of their entry to China?' Bruce asked.

'A good question,' said Ying. 'This is why it should work so well for you. Yes, you will be watched, but as part of a very large group. It is true that embassies are the obvious places for intelligence operatives to work, but real spies need roles that give them reason to move around outside the embassy on business. Contracted support roles do not allow this. And in any case, private intelligence organisations like the Club are extremely rare in China. You would not be on the MSS radar.'

Ying then ran through what was required for a work visa in China. When he finished, Lady Margaret confirmed the next steps in their preparations.

'Bruce will assist Quentin with arranging the various false proofs of identity needed to apply for roles and obtain clearances, from passports to bank details and utility bills.'

This was a stock in trade for the Club and valuable experience for Bruce. Then she looked at Martine and Marc in turn.

'Equipment preparation?' asked Martine.

'Quite. Sensitive equipment that cannot be substantiated as personal belongings will be smuggled into Beijing via commercial freight to our associate at the Jianguo hotel. Marc will lead on this task. Meanwhile, Lucien and I will make the operational plans.'

* * *

After a week of relentless activity, both teams had done as much preparatory work as possible. Technical kit was packed and shipped, identity documents had been created, references fabricated and job applications submitted. Now it was a matter of waiting.

As if Lady Margaret needed reminding, on Tuesday 14 May the BBC World Service reported the outbreak of an unidentified respiratory virus in Foshan, a city of around three million people, lying a hundred kilometres northwest of Hong Kong.

Once more gathered with the others, she watched the news channel in the living room, propped on the arm of a sofa and clutching a cup of Earl Grey tea. She was full of trepidation. It was no surprise, but it was still a terrifying prospect. The newsreader's tone reflected the mood among those who did not know the truth: this was small beer, a few cases, nothing more than a curiosity.

'So it begins,' she lamented.

'When did the file go to MI5?' asked Lucien.

'They've had barely two weeks. I doubt that anyone of adequate seniority has even made space in their diary for a briefing.'

For a moment she deliberated on her choice of Roger Gleeson as the MI5 figure to deal with this. He was a deputy director, a man of considerable experience and uniquely placed to join the dots, she reassured herself. That was her assessment. She hoped it would not turn out to be a bad bet.

'They'll probably only react when they see something happening on the ground,' said Bruce. 'This should spark some action.'

The news pictures showed medical staff wearing only the most basic protective equipment.

'Why on earth would they risk infecting their own people?' said Martine, shaking her head.

'Don't you think it's deliberate?' asked Lucien.

BEAUMONT

'I agree,' said Quentin. 'The Chinese are playing a finely calculated game. Initiating the outbreak on home territory would complicate accusations of deliberate intent.'

Lady Margaret surveyed her companions' reactions over the rim of her raised cup, which she held in front of her mouth absentmindedly, like some barrier against the unfolding reality.

The newsreader gave more information. 'The location of the outbreak has led some experts to suspect transmission or mutation from animals to humans. About forty percent of cases have been associated with people involved in physical contact with animals, from trading livestock to slaughter and preparation for wholesale.'

Marc's laptop pinged.

'Martine, it's an email from the German Embassy. Your application for the position of IT store assistant had been accepted. Looks like you could fly out on 20 May for an immediate start, subject to final administration. They ask *Do you accept?*'

'Yes, she does!' Martine exclaimed.

It took another two weeks, until Thursday 30 May, for the entire team to join their new employers in various embassies in Beijing. Each had menial roles on variable shifts, which gave the flexibility required to operate covertly and also take some rest.

Bruce arrived last and started work as an assistant office manager in the Australian Embassy. A fancy description for the guy charged with replacing chairs, setting up workstations and ordering printer paper. On his first morning he walked into the compound and was checked off a list by gate security.

'Thank you,' said Bruce as his passport and papers were returned to him.

'You want the large door in the middle, top of the steps,' said the man in uniform, pointing towards the embassy. 'The reception staff will guide you to registration.'

As he crossed the car park he gawped at the embassy building, a hulk of grey concrete with vertical strips of windows that would likely steal more daylight than they gave. His senses tingled with the flood of new information and experiences coming to him. He felt isolated and vulnerable. What if a mistake in the team's planning led to him being exposed? He could find himself facing questions, even end up in custody. He hated how quickly his mind ran to the worst-case scenario: the brutish faces of two Chinese prison guards glaring back before throwing him into a stinking cell and slamming the door with a resounding boom.

He had almost forgotten where he was when the embassy front door pierced his nightmare, thudding closed ahead of him as people entered and exited the building. He tried to swallow, but his mouth was dry. His mind turned to the others. Quentin would have the challenge of pretending to be engaged by his role as a cleaner at the New Zealand Embassy. Bruce imagined him behaving differently on an operation, a serious player who would give an Oscar-winning performance as the old guy nobody paid any attention to. Marc's technical expertise meant his job with facilities management, fixing electrical and building-related faults, should be a doddle at the Belgian Embassy. Lucien had joined the Canadian Embassy's catering staff, where peeling vegetables and dishwashing would replace crafting Maxim's gourmet cuisine. Then there was Martine. She would take her store assistant duties at the German Embassy in her stride. They all had the burden of maintaining cover while doing what they came here for.

Ying remained with her ladyship at Beaumont. As a wanted man, setting foot on Chinese territory would be suicide, but his continuing expertise and insider knowledge was gold dust for the operation.

By time they were all in country, the virus outbreak had been registered more widely: in nearby Hong Kong, then Taiwan and Vietnam, and as far away as Alaska. The World Health Organisation was heading the response to the new disease, which, as predicted, was making some people severely ill, while others showed few symptoms. As expected by the Club, few critical cases had been registered among the ethnic Chinese population. It had now been given a title: Polymorphic Respiratory Disorder or PRD.

The Club members took a hit via salary deductions to upgrade from shared accommodation to private rooms or studios. All had bagged places within a square kilometre east of the compound. After completing Phase One of the plan: to establish themselves in their work roles, they were ready to embark on Phase Two: linking up to co-ordinate reconnaissance and develop the intelligence picture.

21

Despite Ying's encouraging words, the fact remained that even as support workers Lady Margaret's people were in the spotlight. Their coming together had to be through a natural flow of events. It was the coincidence of being new to Beijing and common personal interests that provided plausible opportunity for paths to cross and friendships to form.

Bruce, Martine and Marc apparently loved tennis, for which facilities existed on the residential complex: four hard-surface courts surrounded by a high chain-link fence. On the third day after Bruce arrived they met there at a prearranged time. Bruce headed to one end of a court and Martine the other, with Marc starting as umpire.

'Ready?' asked Martine.

She threw the ball high and fired a serve that skidded past Bruce before he had raised his racquet. Fortunately, it was out.

'Maybe a little slower next time, or I'm not going to give you much of a game,' he said.

Bruce cut the image of the beginner, with two left feet on court, suggesting he just wanted to try anything to pass the time. At least seeing that the fence was there to catch his stray shots rather than imprison him provided some comfort.

Quentin and Lucien were wilier, opting for a mutual appreciation of beer. Quentin had advised against wine, which both would have preferred, because of its generally poor quality. The Chinese predilection for excess yields meant that peanuts were often planted between vines as a cover crop out of season. The result was nutrient-depleted soils, made worse by unripened grapes in cooler years. The beer, however, was acceptable. Tsingtao, the most popular beer, was once a German concession that had been taken over by Chinese brewers. Besides, blue collar workers drank beer, not wine.

They met in a corner of a bistro-cum-bar called Little Venice, situated on site within the embassies' residential quarter.

'I hope you can suffer this,' said Quentin, as he returned to their table with a pair of tulip-shaped glasses overflowing with frothy beer.

Lucien drank a mouthful and wiped the foam from his upper lip. '*Bien.*'

Quentin surveyed the bar to check for anyone taking an interest in them and that no-one was within earshot.

'Where do we begin? The mission, I mean. Not the beer menu.' He winked at Lucien.

'First, the Headquarters of National Defence. No surprise there.'

BEAUMONT

They had gathered information about the headquarters during their previous operation, with a focus on personnel and vehicles that could be used as a quick reaction force to bolster government facilities and residences in an emergency.

'We need to break in to locate the *Dēnglóng* order and its verification codes,' said Lucien. 'Only then can we complete a revised version of the order and execute it.'

'Well, the clock is ticking and we have no Plan B as I see it. Failure is not an option.' Quentin turned his attention across the room again.

Behind the bar a television was showing reports of the spread of PRD into other countries, with maps indicating outbreaks in India, Turkey and Italy. Numbers ran along the bottom of the screen: estimated global deaths had reached ten thousand.

'Goodness! This thing is really taking hold now,' said Quentin.

'It's as we suspected – exponential.'

Over the course of two days Marc swept his team's accommodation for eavesdropping devices. Quentin did the same for him and Lucien. None were found.

The benefit of working some night shifts was that they were often free during daylight hours to tour the city. After a week, Lucien judged there would be a diminishing MSS interest in them as new staff. He felt comfortable that they could become more active in their preparations, so he suggested they go sightseeing in their sub-teams, a next new step for Bruce.

'Photographing government sites is strictly forbidden and a guaranteed shortcut to prison,' he said, 'but judicious swapping to telephoto lenses where the target is at a distance should allow us to capture elements of buildings' structures, security measures and layout. The trick is not to be caught with such images.'

Bruce couldn't shake his apprehension over doing more things in their sub-teams in public. After all, until a week ago they were supposed to have been strangers. The cover stories for how they came together, and how that might extend to more than tennis, seemed tenuous, risky. *That is how it works, Bruce*, Martine had explained to him, in her usual empathetic way.

During the first excursions Bruce got the hang of how he, Martine and Marc could look innocent, milling around in various spots and taking plenty of snaps on each other's cameras, with the required backdrops including a target building, first and foremost being the Headquarters of National Defence.

'No, to the left a bit. I want to get the cute dog in too!' Martine said, acting the excitable tourist as a scruffy *tugou* cocked its leg in the background. Bruce and Marc duly shuffled across, always aware that they were never out of sight of someone in uniform. This time, about a hundred metres to their right, a lone municipal policewoman strutted up and down a section of perimeter road bordering Yuyuantan Park.

To throw off any authorities who took an interest in them, they embellished their cover with a vignette of two single males subtly vying for the female's favour. Bruce found this a struggle. It wasn't easy to be frivolous under the pressure of acting out a cover upon a cover.

By the third week of June, enough data had been gathered about the HQ to marry with Ying's clues as to the precise location of the secure files containing the master copy of *Dēnglóng*.

The teams established meeting places away from their residences. They would arrive as separate groups of friends at one of three bar restaurants, to a varied pattern. As usually happened in Beijing, waiters would intercept foreigners and usher them past the hubbub of the open restaurant to plusher booths in the back. The price for this experience ballooned, but the quality of the food did not. They weren't concerned about budget, though, and the further cover of being ripped off like any other gullible foreigner, while having greater privacy, suited their needs.

It was just after 6 p.m. on Wednesday 19 June, three weeks after their arrival in Beijing, when they gathered at the Small Duck restaurant on one of the two nights a week when they were all free. Quentin and Lucien were joined by Martine, Marc and Bruce at a secluded table in a booth on the first floor, set back from the windows on

Chongwenmenwai Street. The restaurant was Quentin's idea: an acceptable spot as far as tradecraft was concerned, but also acceptable cuisine that was cooked in a closed oven, a relative novelty in Beijing.

Marc completed his sweep around the table and booth, slid the RF detection device into his pocket and gave a nod to Lucien. *All clear*.

Lucien, as in-theatre lead, opened proceedings. 'We have narrowed down the target area to the third and fourth floors of Building C, near the centre of the headquarters. The files should be in a secure room near a service cupboard containing a hub for the air-conditioning system. Access to site is by identity pass at manned entry points, whether on foot or in authorised vehicles. Prior authorisation is required for visitors. That's during normal working hours. After 6 p.m., electronic card passes can open pedestrian access gates, one at the main entrance on the south side, one on the north. Guards still cover vehicle access and have visual on the pedestrian gates. Entry to buildings is same – swipe a pass. And Ying thinks some internal doors are covered by Simplex-type number locks. Perimeter is a four-metre-high security fence, topped with wire. CCTV covers two metres inside the fence along the whole perimeter. Night patrols of four pairs of guards circuit every thirty minutes.' He paused to allow for questions.

'What's the regime regards out of hours working?' Bruce asked. 'Do many people do it? Can folk work alone in offices?'

Quentin looked up. 'If I may?' Lucien gestured a hand for him to continue. 'I had that conversation with Ying. Like many a headquarters, one would imagine, you'll get your minority of staff who either must work late or stay on for an attendance promotion. It depends on whether there's a need. The site is home to around two thousand people. We estimate ten percent will work through to, say, 10 p.m. and then maybe one percent till gone midnight. There's duty staff on all night, but Ying thinks not too many, maybe a dozen.'

'Well, that's going to be challenging. Between two and three hundred on site till 10 p.m.?' Bruce said.

'But we would go in much later, maybe at 3 a.m., when whoever is left is feeling it,' said Martine.

'So that leaves us with two real choices,' Lucien resumed. 'An overt entry, using cloned passes. That will ping on someone's screen, so it's still a risk, setting aside the obvious issues of disguises and that only Quentin speaks Mandarin. Or we go for covert entry. An even bigger risk.'

For a moment nobody responded.

'Surely option one is a non-starter? I know that's effectively what you did at the presidential palace, but we won't be masquerading as cooks this time,' said Bruce.

'Well, either way we need to get a plan together. We go in this weekend,' said Lucien.

22

Back at Martine's apartment, Bruce puzzled over Lucien's autocratic tone. Going into the Headquarters of National Defence on Saturday night was not up for debate, that was a done deal. The imperative to achieve the mission before things escalated with the West was not in question. But Bruce was concerned about rushing a one-time opportunity. Mistakes multiplied when people rushed.

Martine popped the caps on three bottles of Tsingtao. Bruce eyed the cold bottles, condensation already forming and running down the sides. Beer always made ideas flow, but not necessarily good ones. He gulped a quick mouthful of the fizzy lager.

'Do we really have just the two options for going in?' he said. 'Neither sounds solid to me. Firstly, overt entry. We walk into the site using passes and wearing uniform. I suppose passes would be cloned by temporary theft from an off-duty member of staff, using Marc's whizzy electronic device to read the embedded data on the magnetic strip?'

He looked to Marc for confirmation but was met with a shrug of the shoulders. *Who knows. Continue.* Bruce carried on talking, thinking aloud.

'Hmm, the uniforms would need to be those of the CCP internal affairs inspectorate, who are not based at the defence HQ and who are feared by other departments. Fewer questions asked.'

Marc and Martine kept straight faces and sipped their beer occasionally but said nothing. Bruce had now got into his stride.

'The problems might come with time of entry and not having full knowledge of the internal layout,' he said. 'For instance, if we encounter a door with a manual combination lock, we could be in trouble trying to defeat it if anyone else was nearby. In my experience, inspectors would be escorted, anyway. Alternatively, we could go in late, like 3 a.m., on the premise of a snap secret inspection of some kind. But that would still register identities on the security system and could raise alarm bells if inspections never happened like that. Oh, and who exactly would go in? We would need a heavy disguise and good Mandarin skills.'

Bruce chewed his lip, annoyed with himself for brainstorming and critiquing simultaneously. Option one was not looking good.

Marc grinned, took another swig of beer and smacked his lips in satisfaction.

'Okay, what else?' said Martine.

Bruce took a breath. 'Second, covert entry. A basic approach, obvious if you will, would be to scale the fence, having disrupted the CCTV and perimeter lights on opposite sides of the compound. In the control room it would look like it's all gone dark, but outside eyes will be drawn to where the lights have gone out. We scale the side with lights but no cameras. That's *if* you can exercise such control.'

Marc raised an eyebrow but did not answer.

As a final effort to produce more than two options, Bruce scrabbled to generate ideas off the top of his head. 'Then there is a range of more quixotic means of entry,' he said, his tone edging towards imploring. 'Perhaps if we can get the kit we could access the roof using hang-gliders from a nearby tall building. There is an adequate landing area on the roof, and Beijing has some very tall buildings, although I don't know whether any are close enough to make the flight, even on a twenty-to-one glide slope.'

Martine suppressed a giggle. 'And don't forget you've got to get the glider to the top of whichever building you're going to jump from,' she said. 'That would look good when you walked through the front door of the Jing Guang Centre. Did you bring hang-gliders, Marc?'

'*Non.*'

This time she couldn't hold back the laughter.

Bruce shook his head and gave a wry smile. 'I'm glad to be of service,' he said, unabashed. 'Last wildcard idea, then. I saw an advert at the entrance to the Small Duck restaurant for *Beijing by Night*, an experience comprising dinner followed by a balloon flight over the city. Did you see it? Apparently it's an exotic way to marvel at Beijing's skyline. Let's assume that maybe two or three such trips go on a Saturday night. It's a regular thing. We can hire our own private ride but the flight plan is to our requirements. It would launch from a suitable place for the prevailing wind to carry us over the target area, close enough to drop onto the target using highly manoeuvrable sports chutes. We need conditions to be right. Must stay clear of controlled airspace, mainly into the capital airport to the northeast. Then again, we could just charter a plane and parachute from out of area using HALO. What do you think?'

Martine pursed her lips. 'You're getting more adventurous, so that's something. Balloons can't be controlled for direction much if the wind changes and I doubt whether the authorities like them going over military sites. And any parachute entry has the problem of transitioning and landing without being seen or heard, like when the canopy washes over the side of the building, for example. It's bound to happen. And what are you going to do with it? Stash it and leave it? We can't leave any trace. And then you've got to get out.'

'Well, it seems that none of my ideas will work. How else can we do it? I'm not firing myself out of a cannon.'

Everyone erupted into laughter. When it had died down, he said, 'Okay, then what? Your turn.'

Martine looked at Marc. 'I'll let you explain.'

'Tomorrow, Bruce. We'll go the shed and I'll show you tomorrow.'

BEAUMONT

The next morning Marc sneaked Bruce in through the back of the Jianguo hotel. It was quiet. The breakfast service had finished and guests had gone out for the day, whether sightseeing or on business. At the back of the basement, past a sprawling parking lot and a wide ragtag area containing spare conference chairs and tables, bellhop trolleys and broken wardrobes, was a pair of dull metal doors. Marc opened one and ushered Bruce inside.

'*Un moment.*'

The fluorescent lights buzzed into life, illuminating a dusty corridor. They headed to the far end, to another door which was secured by a hefty padlock. Marc undid it, reached inside and switched on more lights, and in they went.

Bruce couldn't believe his eyes. The room was about the size of two ISO shipping containers set side by side, and it was chocked up with equipment.

'Whoa! How did you—'

Marc raised a hand for him to be quiet, checked back down the corridor and closed the door.

'How did you get this lot here?' Bruce continued in a whisper.

'It's one of the most important things to our organisation. It takes a long time to make friends who don't ask too many questions, friends who can be trusted.'

Bruce almost had to pinch himself. He had a flashback to Rothwell and its tunnels, its secret spaces and places that would surprise. He scanned around, spotting everything from sleeping bags to GPS handsets, thermal imagers, clothes for disguises ... and guns. Lots of guns, whether 9mm Glocks, Heckler and Kock MP5s, or Franchi Special Purpose Automatic Shotguns.

'I officially admit to being impressed,' he said. 'What's this? A Glock 17C? I didn't think they were out yet.'

'Coming out now, sort of,' Marc said with a wink.

'First dibs to the Club, eh? Hang on ... parachutes? You two were enjoying taking the piss last night, but you brought some anyway.'

Marc sniggered. 'Right, let me show you what we have come here for. All this stuff you like so much – it's ancient tech. Why would nobody try to break into Chinese Defence Headquarters? Because they would get caught. Probably get killed. *Not us.*'

Bruce shuddered to hear Marc hand fate a VIP invitation to the mission.

Marc went to a large storage box at the far end of a rack and took out a suit. He held it up for Bruce to see. It was an all-in-one full body suit, in a tough but flexible black material. There were sections that appeared to be armoured, and various networks of cables or tubes integrated into the skin.

'Er, okay. Motorcycle leathers?'

'*Non.* Anti-gravity suit.'

Bruce looked at Marc briefly, but before he could respond, he broke into fits of laughter. He was convulsing with the effort of suppressing his amusement, eventually squatting down then rolling onto his side on the floor as the emotion consumed him. He couldn't help himself. *Was this for real?*

'Would it help if I called it something else and we skipped the technical explanation?' said Marc.

Finally, Bruce stopped laughing, drew in a great lungful of air to try to regain his composure and got up. Marc had been patient. He had indulged Bruce's reaction and now met him with a stone-cold stare.

'You need to listen because we haven't got all day for you to get your head around this. *D'accord*? I'll try to explain. Are you good at physics?'

'Got an A at A Level, if that helps.'

'Okay. This is very advanced shit. It could really help the world, as you can imagine, except if technological secrets like this get out, some serious people will guess where we got the materials for it. Besides, the mad men of this planet would start wars over this type of thing. The world's just not ready for it.'

Bruce felt like he was entering a parallel universe. *This can't be real.*

'I can't tell you what this is made of, where we got it, how we developed it,' Marc continued. 'Nothing like that. We're open about many things but not stuff like this. Get caught with this and they're going to get it out of you.' Bruce stared back, his face set with astonishment. 'So, you know the Earth has a magnetic field which you can detect with a compass needle. It aligns with the field. And ferromagnetism is a physical property of elements like iron, cobalt and nickel.'

'Yeah, good so far.'

'Compare that with gravity. Earth, everything, has a gravitational field. This suit uses a material that behaves with gravity in the way iron behaves with magnetism. It responds to the Earth's gravitational field to produce a reactive force, and that force that can provide lift. The other components in the suit allow for control of the lift force in the vertical plane. Compressed air is used for lateral motion.'

Bruce looked more closely. The suit was an all-in-one set of motorcycle race leathers with collar, cuffs, shoulder, elbow and knee pads. Under the leather was a body harness incorporating the special material. On the back was a slim profile backpack unit with neatly routed electrics and metal braided cables that he presumed would carry fluids.

'So, the force makes you weightless, hence the anti-gravity label,' Bruce said. 'Increase that force and you move upwards in the Earth's field. But then you need a paddle to move where you want to go, so the air acts like thrusters on a satellite?'

'Exactly. The electrics activate the material. Turn it on and off and set how much lift.'

'How much thrust does the compressed air generate? I mean, how fast can you go?'

'Well, you're not going to shoot about like Iron Man in the comics. Maximum forward speed is about twenty kilometres per hour. But remember, ascent and descent can be a lot quicker, which is why, yes, these are motorcycle leathers, for when you fuck up. You get a helmet too, but not so bulky as a motorcycle helmet. It's to protect, but also give you comms, amplified hearing, head-up display and image intensification.' He paused and grinned at Bruce. 'You might not need that, of course.'

'Image intensifiers can't see through walls, so I think I'll stick to my thermal vision, thanks,' Bruce replied. 'Although, that said, it depends on how the suit affects my skin's ability to sense the environment around me.'

He wandered over to a chair and sat, eyeing the suit, taking a moment for it all to sink in. He pondered the limits of his imagination. The Earth was once believed to be flat. Man wanted to fly like the birds. He stared at the moon in wonder. There was a time when nuclear energy was unheard of. Unimagined. All that changed. So why was it so hard to accept another physical discovery?

'What about size? Who is the suit for?' he asked.

'I picked the sizes to fit the team: two medium and two large, for you, Martine, Lucien and Quentin. They have stretch panels and can also be adjusted,' said Marc, indicating the cuffs and ankle closures. 'They've got impact protection under the shoulders, elbows, knees and hips. That's smart, too. Non-Newtonian materials, really tough. Finally, Kevlar plates for the chest and back, but they are not very big, just for vital organs.'

'Wow, more surprises!' Bruce stood up and meandered around the space, grappling with his curiosity. 'This really works? So, why can't I just stuff a load of iron into a suit and use the Earth's magnetic field?'

Marc tilted his head. 'I thought you were good at physics. The Earth's magnetic field is much weaker than gravity. A lot weaker.'

'But I never heard of any element in the periodic table that has gravitational properties like this. Did it come from a meteorite?'

'I never said it was an element. Anyway, who knows?'

'You do, but I get it. Right, assuming I am on the team to go in, I'd better practice with this thing. Where do we do that?'

'Right here. Now. That's all we can do. You're going in two days' time, remember.'

'You're joking. I'm only going to get six inches off the floor here before going five storeys up in the pitch black, into the most heavily guarded building this side of the Pentagon?'

'*Précisément.*'

23

In China's northeast, seven hundred kilometres from Beijing and just over a hundred kilometres from the North Korean border, is the city of Shenyang and the nearby Beishan Mountain. Marshal Lin would usually fly such distances, but that would mean filing a flight plan. He suspected that President Tao had tabs on him, which is why he put up with the eight-hour road journey. His diary, and all staff except his travel party, were told that he was visiting military garrisons, not one of the Phoenix nuclear shelters.

The marshal's BJ80 SUV was a rip-off version of the Mercedes G-Class. It was good off-road, but more importantly, better on-road. Fast, quiet and comfortable, by Chinese standards. His support team, including close protection, rattled along behind in less plush vehicles.

At 6 p.m. on Thursday 20 June, his convoy swung off the main road from Shenyang and headed along the fresh tarmac to the entrance gate of the secret facility. Three checkpoints existed to make the transition from a straightforward restricted military site to a top-secret one under construction. Covered by forest on either side, they drew up to the first barrier. Lin's staff assistant, Master

Sergeant Bao, rolled down the window and presented passes for the four in his vehicle. The guard peered into the back and glanced at the passes before handing them back and snapping to attention. A crisp salute followed as the barrier was raised.

Lin had calculated his arrival time to coincide with the end of the day shift and handover to a smaller night shift contingent. The vehicles rolled up to the parking area in front of the edifice of reinforced concrete set into the mountainside. The flurry of panic was evident even before he got out. Phone calls from the gates had everyone scrambling like termites. *To do what?* he wondered.

The site director appeared through the huge blast doors, wearing a high visibility jacket and hard hat. Lin recognised him from a photo on his file. The man pushed through the workers to meet Marshal Lin halfway across the parking lot.

'Sir, good evening. Welcome. We were not expecting you. We are honoured,' he began.

'Thank you, Comrade Cheng. I am here on a purely informal basis, to keep in touch with my portfolio of responsibilities, not to conduct any inspection. Please tell your people to go about their normal business.'

'Very good, sir.' Cheng motioned a hand back and forth, signalling to a colleague who was waiting at the entrance for everyone to carry on. 'May I offer you refreshments? Something to eat, perhaps? Have you come from Beijing? Such a long journey.'

'That is most hospitable of you, comrade. However, we stopped about an hour ago, so I would like to proceed with a tour inside, if I may?'

Cheng bowed briefly, stood aside and swept his arm ahead, inviting Marshal Lin to lead.

The two men walked inside and climbed onto the first of a line of golf buggies that had been modified for use in the facility. Lin's staff and one of Cheng's assistants followed. They sped off along the broad internal highway that led into the mountain.

'Is there anything particular you wish to see, sir?' asked Cheng.

'Just enough to have an idea of the contents and layout of such a site. I believe the functions and facilities are similar across all the Phoenix sites. Correct?'

'I believe so, although I have not visited any others. Consistency is maintained by the President's hand-picked team of architects, engineers and inspectors.'

Lin nodded. *Consistency.* Is that what His Excellency called it?

'Of course, individual site layout will be influenced by local topography,' Cheng added.

After passing a series of internal blast doors and various service hubs with offices, refreshment points and vehicle stations, they reached the start of the residential facilities. The scene was extraordinary in its scale. Lin had never seen anything like it. It was vast. Brightly lit by arrays of tube lights within translucent white encasements, the arched concrete walls reached away from either side to high above them. The chasm would swallow a five-storey building. The highway itself was three motorway lanes wide. Along the ceiling ran all manner of pipes and ducts, presumably for electricity, water and air conditioning. People scuttled back and forth on foot and in buggies, the majority heading out, off shift.

'Perhaps we should stop here, sir,' Cheng said. 'From here on, in that direction is the first residential neighbourhood. In the office is a map of the facility for your convenience. Shall I wait for you here, sir?'

'Very good, Mr Director. Yes, please allow me to look for myself. Thank you.'

Lin stepped off the buggy and his staff assistant, Bao, automatically followed him. The marshal raised a hand. 'Wait here. I will explore alone.'

He strode away to the office, knowing his men's eyes were on him for his protection. And Cheng's eyes would be on him for reporting to the President, no doubt. He spotted a water point in the office and poured himself a beakerful from the tap. On the wall opposite the water point was a large map, about two metres wide by one metre high. Lin lifted the paper cup to his lips, slowly taking a drink while he studied it. His eyes narrowed as he followed the multitude of coloured lines, the matrix of rooms and spaces. There was a wealth of services, some of which would be alien to whoever got to shelter here: fire-fighting stations, decontamination areas, medical centres with operating theatres, a radiological lab.

He took a step forward, reached out and ran his fingers over the map, as if to check it was real. There were five neighbourhoods, each housing a fifth of the nominal ten thousand population. He turned to a map hanging further along the wall, which showed the area in which he stood in more detail. A warren of living quarters stretched for a kilometre, running on both sides of the central highway and stacked two-high. Then his eye was drawn to four huge supplies stores. Was this food and equipment? What about cold stores? He set off to view the closest.

Marshal Lin startled the young soldier inside the vast warehouse. Wearing a white coat, with clipboard in hand, the junior sergeant jumped to attention and they exchanged salutes as Lin walked by.

He stopped in quiet awe. The space was vast, even bigger than the central highway, being of similar height but wider, and darker too. It contained countless shelves. Each structure must have been fifteen metres high, ten shelves to a stack. He stopped counting after getting to seven pairs of stacks that were each at least a hundred metres long. They disappeared into the distance.

Then it hit him. Never mind the scale of the operation. The shelves were already full. His stomach turned. Was this right? So much stock already in place? He walked a few paces back to the soldier by the entrance, motioning a hand downwards. *Relax.*

'What sort of material is in here?'

'Sir, all is non-perishable food. Tins, dried packets, bottled drinking water. Also, household consumable items, like cleaning materials. Sir!'

The marshal let out a breath. Perhaps that was understandable.

'I assume there will be no fresh produce?'

'Correct, sir. Only non-perishable and frozen. There is an area for growing some essential foods under artificial conditions. That is in Neighbourhood 3, sir.'

'Where is the cold store? Does that have any stock yet?'

'Cold store is next hall along on opposite side, sir.'

'Very good, Sergeant.'

'Also fully stocked, sir.'

To settle his nerves, Marshal Lin wandered out of the warehouse and into one of the habitation suites. It was about five metres square, with sleeping and living areas and bathrooms. No kitchen. Food would be provided at central canteens. On the back of the door he saw a map of the neighbourhood showing fire escape routes and emergency assembly points. He noticed that the habitation suites shown on the map were not all the same size, some were much larger.

He headed back out to the central highway. Five doors further on, he came to one of the larger suites. He stepped inside and noticed that it had beds for up to six people, a larger bathroom, larger living area and a kitchen. He tried to figure out the architect's logic. Perhaps this would house individuals who had no family in the facility, or maybe a team of staff who needed to live together, emergency respondents or members of a quick reaction force? Having more people in one larger suite kept the area per person similar to the smaller suites, which he believed would be for two adults and one child. He puzzled the permutations and returned outside again.

Another soldier was passing in a buggy. Lin put out his hand and ordered a gruff-looking old captain to stop.

'Sir! How can I assist you?'

'Can you tell me why there are two sizes of accommodation suite? Who will live in them?'

Confusion crossed the captain's face. 'Er, I do not know, sir.'

'What do you mean, you do not know? Some are small, some are larger. I ask, why is that?'

'I understand, sir. All habitations are allocated according to the list. I am not authorised to access the list, sir.'

'What ..?' Lin checked himself. 'What is the logic for the larger ones? The small ones sleep a family of three, presumably.'

The captain's expression darkened. 'The large ones are for officials and their families, sir ... with more than one child.'

Lin returned the salute drearily and started back to the waiting buggies. The picture crystallised in his mind. There was already a list of families selected for the shelter. Food stocks were in place, here at least. They would never build further facilities to protect any more than point one percent of the population. The elite and their families would survive. The rest would perish. So much for communist ideals.

24

The team selected to infiltrate China's Headquarters of National Defence was Lucien, Martine and Bruce. They needed a means of recording information quickly, as a fallback if the tech malfunctioned, which meant Lucien with his photographic memory. They also required combat skills – that would be led by Martine and backed up by Bruce.

All three had a night-vision system, whether provided by their equipment or, in Bruce's case, naturally. Because his organic night vision was thermal it could also see through walls to detect heat sources with sufficient temperature contrast. Lucien had considered using Quentin as back up. He was a formidable combatant who also had a natural night-vision and perhaps might still have been able to shield the others in a gunfight, but the preference was to leave no trace, and Quentin delighted in executing undesirables, whether it was avoidable or not.

It was Saturday evening, the twenty-second of June, and back in the bowels of the Jianguo hotel they were making their final preparations. Marc had constructed a crude model of the target from cardboard boxes set at one end of a trestle table. Beside the boxes were displayed photos and floor plans. Radios, firearms and pyrotechnics were laid out on the floor alongside three anti-gravity suits.

As they assembled round the table, Marc checked one of his laptop screens, which gave camera views of the corridor and basement outside. All was quiet.

Lucien kicked off. 'This is to confirm tonight's mission. The target is the *Dēnglóng* order file, thought to reside in Building C, fourth floor, west side offices, along here.' He indicated areas on the model with a laser pointer, then flicked to the corresponding stills and floor plan. 'I will lead, with Martine and Bruce in support. Marc will run mission control and tech support from a mobile station on Luilinguan Road, with Quentin assisting and ready as tactical reserve. Okay so far?'

There were no questions as Lucien ran through what they had collectively planned. Entry would be aerial. From leaving Marc's van, they would fly up to one hundred and fifty feet and over to the headquarters' roof in close formation. Flying higher risked appearing on radar; lower, and somebody might spot them from the ground. The met conditions were perfect. There would be no moon, and no cloud cover meant no light pollution from the ground being reflected to cause silhouettes. The sky would be pitch black. Light winds would not hamper progress.

'How will we avoid being seen from the windows once we get onto the building?' asked Bruce.

'Good question,' said Lucien. 'There are external fire escape stairs providing access to all floors. We can fly down beside them so we are shielded from view. Best of all, no-one should hear us coming. The AG suits enable quiet movement, with short bursts of compressed air coming through nozzles tuned to minimise noise.'

'The trickiest part will probably be getting into the building from the fire escape,' Quentin added. 'The emergency doors won't have any external handles, locks or hinges. And they will be alarmed. So we attempt window entry first.'

Bruce looked up. 'That's gonna be tricky to pull off without damaging the frame or glass.'

'Then look at these shots, and these ... Windows left open, would you believe it? But whether and which is a lottery,' said Quentin, pointing to the still photos on the table in front of him. 'If that doesn't work out, be aware of two service hatches on the roof. Western buildings often have these accessed by an internal vertical ladder set within a utilities room. That might provide a covert way in.'

'That's a no-brainer, surely?'

'No, Bruce, it's not,' said Martine. 'We would probably have to bust in through the hatch. You leave any trace and they'll know about it. Then they'll check everything to see what's been taken. They would tighten security, making later infiltration more difficult. They might even conduct a search to account for all the embassy staff, and we could be absent.'

With the briefing and questions done, everyone switched to admin routine, eating, sleeping and conducting final kit checks.

Quentin was not much for rest. He woke the team at 01:30, a full hour before the start so circadian rhythms could adjust. No place for sleepy heads tonight.

They kitted up, climbed into Marc's Great Wall Motor van and slipped out of the hotel basement.

'Still can't fathom this stuff,' said Bruce, squeezing a section of the material sewn into his leather suit. 'Is it liquid?'

'Marc would know. I think he calls it an electromorphic alloy,' Martine replied.

'Still no wiser. But thanks,' said Bruce, before continuing in a low voice, 'When I asked him he wouldn't even say if it was some mystical element from another world, it's so light.'

'*He* didn't want you knowing too much, for your own good,' said Marc, peering at Bruce in the rear-view mirror.

After a ten-minute drive along a circuitous route to check for tails, they pulled up by a derelict warehouse.

Marc turned to the infil team. 'Head through the fence and around the side. You should be unobserved. Launch from there. I will be in position in five minutes. Remember, we will have eyes on the roof and top floor only. Wait for radio check on Channel 1 secure.'

BEAUMONT

In the dark of an old grain store Bruce checked his suit, ensuring the harness was tight so his sensitive parts didn't suffer when he lifted off. He donned his helmet and flicked the radio and external microphones on, then grasped the suit controls that protruded on short stalks from under his wrists.

A flash of trepidation came over him, like being in a dream where you're about to fall. Would this really work? Would he be able to cope, to control it and stick with the team? Too late now. He took a long breath and invited his heat picture to develop. Within seconds his surroundings morphed to shades of orange. He was ready.

'Team One, this is Zero. Radio check, over.' Marc was in position.

'Team One. Received and ready,' replied Lucien.

'Zero. Launch in five, four, three, two, one ... Go!'

Lucien's helmet tilted and his voice sparked in their ears. 'With me!'

Bruce closed the middle three fingers of his left hand around the lift control and eased into the night sky. They were ranged in a flat line a few metres apart, with Bruce in the middle because he was the novice. He used his right hand to direct a small lever that controlled direction. A soft hush of air expelled from behind his shoulders, sending him forwards.

The suit worked brilliantly, giving comfortable, balanced support. He felt like a string puppet. Light lift was effected at his forearms, so he would not tire holding them horizontally. That allowed the controls to be operated in a natural orientation to the direction of flight. He relaxed his thermal vision briefly to obscure the view below when height exposure brought a moment of panic. It was unnatural. Sailing along engulfed in darkness offered a strange solace.

'Team Three, all okay?' asked Martine.

'Affirmative, thanks,' Bruce responded.

They had transited for barely three minutes before the massive bulk of the headquarters rose into view, outlined by a twinkle of security lights along its fences.

'Increase altitude to one hundred and fifty feet,' Lucien ordered.

Bruce's head-up display showed they were at ninety-five feet. He eased the lever and climbed effortlessly, wondering what would happen if he pulled it violently upwards.

'I see nobody on the roof, although the fence lights are dazzling the night vision picture a bit,' said Lucien. 'Team Three, what's your view?'

'Same. Roof looks clear of human heat sources. No movement.'

'Phase two begin.'

They descended swiftly to within two or three metres of the metal roof for a controlled landing. Bruce almost got left behind, then overshot and impacted with a thud a short distance away from a satellite dish and a cluster of antennas. He looked up to see the others anxiously scanning around for anyone who might have heard it.

'You okay?' Lucien asked.

'Yeah, sorry.'

Out of sight, far below, they heard guards shouting to each other. Each froze, listening for whether it was coincidence or a reaction to Bruce's landing.

Martine whispered into her mic: 'Zero, are you picking up the shouting?'

'It's echoey, but I think they're talking about shifts,' came Quentin's voice. 'Doesn't sound like they're bothered by anything else.'

'*Bien. Merci*,' said Lucien. He signalled to Bruce. 'Check out the hatch. Is it secured?'

Martine checked again for observers, near and far. They kept low, and Bruce crept over to inspect the cover.

'It's accessible both ways. There's a handle.' He slowly applied pressure and it moved with a screech. 'Bollocks! It opens, but probably hasn't been used in ages.'

'Go in and check if it's connected to corridor 5B.'

Bruce lifted the cover carefully, checked inside, then stepped onto the vertical ladder and clambered down, with Martine following. His vision showed exactly what they had expected to find: an enclosed space containing utilities pipework and controls. At the bottom he eyed the door and its lock. He tapped a menu select button on the side of his helmet to show his position superimposed on a plan of the top floor in the head-up display.

'Think this is viable,' he whispered on the radio. 'It's off 5B.'

Lucien descended inside, closed the roof hatch behind him, then floated down past the ladder and landed next to Bruce. He examined the door fastening. 'Crap security measures. This is set up with safety in mind, so you can't get locked in. I'm surprised. I would have bet my life it would have been the other way round.'

'Let me scan outside,' said Bruce.

He closed his eyes and concentrated his internal picture to form a 3D view of the building's interiors, within a radius of about twenty metres. A succession of transparent cuboids edged with hues of orange described the corridor and adjoining rooms. Bright spots pricked where electrical or air-conditioning services had concentrations of heat. But the picture waxed and waned, which was unusual.

'I think it's clear,' he said.

'You think? Not sure?' Lucien replied.

'The suit and helmet are blocking my skin's ability to sense the temperature differences. I get images, but it's in and out. There's no movement in the corridor or nearby, though.'

The trio crept out of the utilities room and made for a set of stairs to the floor below, which had a similar layout. Bruce removed his helmet to aid his thermal vision. He soon gave a thumbs up to signal that the stairway was clear. They scurried down to the door on the fourth floor, with

Bruce leading. Another thumbs up, this time for the next corridor.

Lucien signalled to proceed. The corridor was in darkness. A few metres to their left on the other side was the entrance to the offices that should contain the secret files. Bruce and Martine covered Lucien as he went to the door.

'Room clear,' Bruce whispered.

The door was access-protected by a mechanical keypad combination lock. Lucien took out a couple of slender crooked metal implements, inserted them into the latch bolt housing, prized the bolt back and opened the door.

A large office with a jumble of desks and computer terminals lay inside. Tall windows ran down the opposite side, some covered with venetian blinds, a couple with broken blinds hanging in tatters. Broad fans hung from the high ceiling, and some at the far end still creaked slowly round. Stale body odour lingered and so much dust hung in the atmosphere Bruce could almost taste it.

To the left, set in the centre of a dividing wall, was another secure door. Lucien soon defeated its Simplex-type lock to reveal what looked like a registry containing shelves of classified files.

Bruce watched the corridor from the first door and Martine took post by the registry entrance while Lucien headed in.

'Zero, Team One. We are in target location. I need Rostam to guide now. Switching video feed on.'

'Zero. Roger.'

Lucien activated his headset camera and began a systematic sweep along the shelves for Marc and Quentin to see on their monitor.

Quentin spoke. 'Back out a little and focus on the labels above the shelves.' Lucien complied. After a minute, Quentin spoke again. 'There. Second shelf. Go right.'

Martine came on the radio. 'This is Team Two. We got company. Artemis is signalling movement, people ascending the stairs.'

'*Merde*. Any idea why that might be, Zero?' Lucien asked Marc.

'Not sure. Perhaps your comms interfered with the antennas on the roof.'

'Okay. Let's keep going. Rostam?'

Quentin guided Lucien to a box file under a shelf heading that translated as *Contingency Orders*. It contained two paper files. Lucien held each in front of the camera.

'One on the left, old boy. That's it! *Dēnglóng.* Bingo!'

'*Fantastique!*' exclaimed Lucien.

'We got about twenty seconds at most,' Martine interrupted.

Lucien set the file down on a nearby table, produced a compact digital camera and snapped as fast as he could, turning through the pages. His video feed was also being recorded.

'Hide!' said Martine.

BEAUMONT

Numbers were being punched into the keypad on the outer door.

Lucien clicked the last three images and returned the file into the box and onto the shelf. He pressed back behind another row of shelving and into the darkest corner he could find.

Bruce had concealed himself behind a desk at the far end of the outer office. As the door from the corridor opened, its outline contrasted by a bright torch beam, he withdrew slightly to get a view from under the desks. He watched the light and a pair of feet move into the office. The visitor went straight for the registry.

Martine held her breath as the door swung back. She was floating, horizontal above the door, thankful that the guard's peaked cap restricted the view above his head. The torch beam pierced the gloom, revealing racks of files, stationery and a cutting table with guillotine. She reached a hand down, held it close behind the man's head and closed her eyes to concentrate.

There is no-one here. All is well. I should leave now and continue my checks. There is no-one here. All is well. I should leave now and continue my checks.

She repeated the mantra, intuiting that what mattered was the sentiment, not the language. The man stayed still, not going further to look behind the shelves. He let out a sigh, then backed out and closed the door behind him. They heard the outer door clatter shut.

Bruce brought his helmet to his mouth and breathed into the radio mic: 'Room clear.'

Lucien and Martine reappeared from the registry. 'Zero, what's going on outside?' asked Lucien.

Marc crackled into life. 'Men are vacating the roof.'

'Bruce?'

'Yep, five guys heading down. Looks like they've checked all the floors. Upstairs is clear now.'

'Okay. Let me finish photographing the file, then we leave,' said Lucien.

Three minutes later the team retraced its steps back to the roof, keeping radio silence. Once outside they rose together as shadows into the welcoming night sky.

25

The instant his convoy swept into Defence Headquarters, Marshal Lin knew something was up. Even a humble gate guard can salute in a manner that presages trouble. Most perplexing was that Lin did not know what the trouble was. His staff would normally give good warning of such things.

All became clear as he passed through a silent outer office and into his own to find the President waiting. Sprawled in one of the two leather armchairs, President Tao had helped himself to a tot of twelve-year-old McCallan. Lin knew this was a bad sign. Tao wasn't normally given to drinking alcohol.

'The phoenix returns to its nest,' he said.

'Your Excellency, this is an unexpected honour. How may I—'

'Oh, cease the platitudes, Xiangquin. And spare me any sycophantic excuses when I ask you why you disobeyed my orders. Why you had your staff lie for you.'

Marshal Lin had the presence of mind to try to keep calm, to control the pace of their engagement. He removed his cap and jacket, poured himself a glass of water and sat in the armchair opposite his superior.

'Very well. Then you know where I have been, which was not my original plan. Why would I suffer such a long road journey, after all?'

Tao appeared unmoved and made no reply. He was probably enjoying the torment.

Lin looked about him, his eyes darting here and there, searching for a response that would be believed. He allowed his air of frustration, even pressure, to show, and he let out a deep sigh. 'Your Excellency, the events which I counselled you against seem to be moving very quickly. I feel unprepared. You have entrusted the Phoenix facilities to your construction and nuclear directors, I understand, yet I am still charged with the military effectiveness of the overall campaign. I need to be informed about what is happening, the status of the programme elements, otherwise how do I assess strategic pace?'

Tao grinned to himself and tilted his head from side to side as if weighing up a roulette placement.

'So, what did you learn, Marshal?'

'That, in the one facility I visited, preparations are advanced. The design is good, well concealed, well protected. And very well stocked. Of course, only you can say whether the other sites are similar.'

'And that is my point, Xiangquin. I will tell you precisely what you need to know and when you need to know it for our great emergence to succeed. I do not require you to do so for yourself.'

Lin maintained eye contact. 'Yes, Your Excellency.'

'On which note, you should be aware that our biological initiative is not going to plan.' Lin raised an eyebrow. 'The rumours of PRD outbreaks spreading rapidly across southeast Asia have been confirmed, with cases now being exported worldwide. But the situation already has the attention of the World Health Organisation. Cases appear to be getting managed more effectively than we had anticipated. Testing and sampling is underway in a number of countries and many cases require little more than paracetamol to ease the symptoms.'

'But we made great efforts in the bio vectoring programme. Was there a miscalculation?'

'After the traitors attempted to destroy our work at Hulunbuir, our new lead virologist reconstituted the virus from the records, but we suspect these had been falsified. As you know, there had to be a balance between severity and transmissibility, but the substitute virus appears to be too weak and too easily contained,' said Tao, slapping the arm of his chair in frustration.

'And there will be enquiries. The WHO will want to know how it happened, the source, the reasons.'

Tao shook his head, dismissing the comment. 'We will open our arms, then stonewall them. Peasants. Who do they think there are? The world's policemen?' He took another sip of whisky. He was looking flushed. 'No, this is a blessing. Providence is telling me to press on, not to wait. The time for being patient and subservient has passed.' Marshal Lin swallowed. *What was coming now?* 'We move to the next phase,' said the President. 'Take control of the Taiwan Strait.' Lin didn't speak. This time he knew to say nothing. 'They are Chinese waters. Taiwan is part of China, anyway,' Tao continued. 'We will control all international shipping passing through, initially on the premise that it is for safety reasons because we are carrying out a series of naval exercises in the region.'

'May I ask your direction regarding the inevitable challenges that will arise in respect of the UN Convention on the Law of the Sea?' Lin asked.

'Simple. What is it they say in the West about possession and the law? We declare that UNCLOS stands. We are not in violation of its terms. We are acting responsibly towards the international community while exercising our sovereign right to maintain defence forces. With time, that will become the new way and they will lose interest. They will accept the status quo or find alternative routes.'

'I assume that the controls will make passage all but impossible? The consequence being sole occupancy of the Strait?'

'Correct, Marshal Lin. Then we will have set the conditions for unchallenged access to Taiwan itself.'

'For an invasion?'

'Repatriation, Marshal Lin. Repatriation.'

*   *   *

BEAUMONT

Beaumont's halls had a melancholy about them, lessened by the addition of another companion her ladyship had invited to join her at this critical time. It would have been unwise and against protocol to be without support at the Club's headquarters during a major operation. Were enemies to appear, all could be lost, and Lady Margaret had tasted nearly losing all once too often for a lifetime.

Moonstone's willingness to drop everything and head to eastern France bore testament to the Club's renewed health. Around the globe old acquaintances had been rekindled. People recognised that each new chapter in world affairs brought some form of peril. There was more than an acceptance that the Club should lead the way to tackle global threats, there was a hunger for it.

This contrasted with the depressing days after Moonstone had watched over Jenny Noble-Franks for nearly a year, finally withdrawing when the situation looked safe. The tragic timing of her shooting was an open wound for him. What if he had hung on a little longer? His departure was followed by the test of motive and loyalty that her ladyship had conceived for James Tavener in Bristol. The test had worked, all too well. Tavener's true colours were as vivid as the blood that ran from Jenny and dear Philip Roberts.

His name was Gregory Pitman. He was a former Royal Marine, who had taken roles in various defence companies dotted around Bristol and the southwest of England. Another of the Club who was in his fifties, he followed the marines' way, staying fit, alert and sharp in his skills. No middle-aged spread for Greg. He was tall and wiry, with angular features and piercing blue eyes.

In the operations room in Beaumont's basement he sat alongside Lady Margaret for the VTC debriefing with Lucien and Quentin. The relative comfort of the cool, quiet basement contrasted with the view of the men in Beijing. They were in Lucien's studio apartment, huddled in front of their laptop, with streaks of sunlight breaching the window blinds behind them. Reflections of the weak electric light in the ceiling fan pulsed as it turned, moving just enough air to cool the sweat around their shirt collars.

Lucien was outlining the daring operation at the Headquarters of National Defence. When he concluded, Lady Margaret sat for a moment processing what she had heard.

She looked up, her eyes wide with amazement at their achievement. 'It was a great effort indeed, and saved by Martine's quick thinking. So, we now have the *Dēnglóng* order and what we think are the verification codes required to activate it. My main interest is whether we can validate the codes. What if they are now hosted on a computer and we have accessed a defunct file?'

'My guess would be that something of this importance wouldn't be left to fester,' said Quentin. 'If it went digital, the file would be archived, and it would have markings to make that clear. I reckon that since they never expect to enact such an order the codes wouldn't be changed, or at least not frequently.'

'Well, I appreciate your estimation. Nonetheless, we will need a strong Plan B if it goes wrong when we pull the trigger on this. Do you have everything required to initiate it when you have written the revised order?'

'We can forge Lin's signature from other documents,' said Lucien. 'Clearly it would be unwise to make an exact copy. That might be detected. We must also create a voice file: a model of his speech, built from sampling his voice, which I can operate through processing software – with Talisman's technical support, of course.'

'You mean to speak as if you are Lin to initiate the order?' said Lady Margaret, momentarily puzzled.

'Correct. And to deal with any questions that might come back,' said Quentin. 'Whoever receives the message will be under extraordinary pressure. I need to be able to respond to that, or pray the protocols save me from too much chit chat. It should be cut and dried. An order, a verification of identity using a code. Done.'

'Greg, what do you think?' she asked.

'We can never be sure – about any of it. The logic holds, as far as it goes. I didn't hear of any such order when I was in the MOD. In the UK the army would only ever be on the streets to protect the public, never to keep a government in power. As you say, we need a good backup plan, because the tide will turn against us in a heartbeat if we get this wrong.'

'We also have wider conditions to address,' said Lady Margaret. 'My instinct says that *Dēnglóng* is doubled-edged. Use it too soon and Marshal Lin will be taken down for treason, never mind his denials about not ordering it. He will be accused of bringing slanderous accusations against the President that he will be unable to prove, even if he wanted to. The only evidence would be a copy of Phoenix itself, which Tao would deny as a subversive fabrication, and after that nobody else would dare to stand against him. Use it too late, and the game will be over. So that means other conditions need to be met for it to work.' She took a sip of tea. 'Ideally, we need overwhelming evidence of Tao's plans to destroy the world, evidence that could be exposed at the right moment to outmanoeuvre any of his contingencies.'

Lucien and Quentin exchanged looks.

'Dare I ask what overwhelming evidence you have in mind?' Quentin asked.

Lady Margaret coughed, more in apprehension than need.

'Gentlemen, I am deeply grateful for the two sterling successes you have managed thus far, both in the President's personal residence and at the Defence Headquarters. And I shudder to send you in for more. But I fear what we need in our possession is a verifiable copy of the list of people selected for a place at the Phoenix nuclear shelters. That will mean that Tao will have no escape come the moment.'

Greg turned to her. 'Do we even know if there is such a list?'

'By my reckoning, provision for only a tiny proportion of the population means there must be a list. This could be exposed in session at the People's Congress if we trigger *Dēnglóng* at the same time. Ying reports that the conference hall has been refurbished – at the President's direction, no less – with new desks and monitors, which would facilitate displaying the list to senior officials. When the party members saw who was and was not on it, Tao would be finished.'

She hoped.

They agreed.

26

In Beijing, the team gathered once more at a safe watering hole to discuss the next operations. It was a muggy Wednesday evening in the last week of June. A round of cold beers sat in the centre of the table while they waited for their food. From the kitchen wafted the aroma of spices and hot oil, the clang of a wok, the sizzle and eruption of flames from a pan, whenever the saloon doors squeaked open and the waiters hurried through.

All five were present: Quentin sitting with hands clasped upon the straw trilby he had set upon the table; Bruce reclined, arms folded, looking jaded around the eyes; Marc, ever alert, was scanning around them for anywhere that surveillance devices might be lurking; Martine, aglow in the sultry atmosphere, her elbows propped on the wooden surface, hands joined under her chin, set with anticipation. Their attention was on Lucien who was debriefing on the VTC with Lady Margaret. After five minutes covering the essentials, he paused for questions and handed out the beers.

Martine ran a finger in circles in the pool of water at the base of her Tsingtao. 'I shouldn't say the obvious, but for the first time I am seriously contemplating that we will probably give our lives to this one. We've got to go back into Defence HQ and plant our version of *Dēnglóng*, get a copy of the Phoenix list, then pull off what will effectively be a military coup against the President. How do we expect to get through all that and stay alive and free?'

'Don't worry, my girl. Where's the Martine fire gone, eh? Not growing a sense of vulnerability, are we? Look at it this way, if you're caught we will find you and bust you out. If you're killed, well, you won't care.' That was Quentin's take on paternal wisdom.

'If she's killed, I'd care,' said Bruce. He blushed. Why did he say that? It came out before he could stop it.

Martine didn't react. The others said nothing, but Lucien and Marc looked at each other and raised their eyebrows.

'If any of us comes to harm or gets caught, the whole thing could fail anyway,' Bruce continued. 'We have to accept the stakes. Our safest approach is probably to be bold. Hold no fear.'

'Sounds like you just invented our motto, old boy,' Quentin said, with a pat on Bruce's shoulder. 'Better in Latin, though.' He closed his eyes for a second, his lips silently forming the words. '*Nolite timere* ... That would be close enough.'

'I'll drink to that,' said Lucien, lifting his bottle for the rest to clink. '*Santé!*'

The following evening, Lucien came to Quentin's apartment to assess the findings of their trawl through the available information. They sat across the Formica table under the familiar pitiful light and creaking fan. A mosquito buzzed overhead.

'Where to begin?' said Lucien.

'We've got to think like the man. This is intended to play out exactly as Tao wants. He must delegate, but he also wants to maintain a high degree of control.' Quentin rubbed his chin, pondering. 'Who is in charge of the construction? Top level, I mean.'

Lucien turned the pages of their copy of the Phoenix directive to find the senior appointments list. It indicated that the Director of Works was responsible for the allocation of protective space.

'As the *de facto* chief construction engineer, he is like Noah, deciding which animals get to go into the ark,' Quentin said. 'But he has to act in accordance with God's wishes on which types of animal are chosen. Few will be.'

'Let's check him out.'

An hour passed, with secure messaging exchanged between the Beijing team members and between Lucien and Beaumont. Research by Marc, corroborated by Lady Margaret and Greg Pitman, indicated that the Director lived in Shanghai. And he lived well, in the penthouse of a swanky new development on the east bank of the Huangpu river. His main office was in the People's Urban Planning Directorate next to the Shanghai People's Government building on Renmin Avenue.

'That's got to be it. Probably the location of the master copy,' said Quentin.

Lucien sucked his teeth. 'Better prepare for a trip to Shanghai.'

Shanghai presented a problem. It was twelve hundred kilometres from Beijing, a distance that meant whoever undertook the mission would have to eat into their holiday time. It was common practice in most Western embassies to limit holiday bookings in the first few months of the financial year to prevent excessive early consumption. And holiday allowance wasn't generous anyway.

They posited the options. A million names on a list suggested electronic format only, so the target would be a computer system. Sure, Mr Director would probably have an office in the People's Congress, which would obviate the need to make the long journey south. But would the computer there be synchronised with that in his main office? If not, it would mean taking risks for no gain, and worse, wasting time. The silver lining of an infil mission on the People's Urban Planning Directorate was that security might be lighter.

'My proposal is for Bruce and Martine to head south, with me directing the op from the basement of the Jianguo hotel,' Lucien said. 'Marc will also go to Shanghai, to give technical and tactical support, and that will be critical. After Bruce and Martine have conducted a recce of security measures, Marc will have to figure out how to get around them.'

'Well, you can offer expert guidance on that front, Lucien,' said Quentin. 'Or should I call you Raffles, after you managed to crack the President's safe.'

Lucien met this with a self-deprecating smile. 'Then there is the small matter of accessing what must be the most highly classified computer server in China,' he said.

*   *   *

Martine, Marc and Bruce took the van for the overnight trip to Shanghai. They planned to use the cover of sightseeing to make their cheap backpacker accommodation and presence around the city centre plausible. They checked into the Pujiang hotel, but had no intention of using its flea-bitten dormitories. Bruce eyed the stained carpets and tatty drapes and suppressed a groan. What could you expect for seventeen yuan a night? Martine looked at him and smiled. 'Have faith,' she whispered.

After dropping some dummy luggage upstairs the team returned outside.

'The good news is that the Shanghai Museum puts us within a couple of hundred metres of the Urban Planning building,' said Marc. 'Plan is to park nearby, go inside to stare at a few bronzes, Ming vases and terracotta figures from Xian. Then we have reason to be in the area to conduct our recce.'

Once again, the doldrums of a Saturday night into Sunday morning would be the mission period, once they had completed their target reconnaissance. Bruce thought back to three months ago when he and Martine stayed up all night watching the post office in Cagliari, waiting for Jez to turn up.

He listened without comment as Marc explained that the aim of the recce phase was to identify the security measures protecting the target. They would have to locate a specific computer network entry point, ergo a computer terminal. But how would they check out all the security measures without actually getting past the first one ... without going inside the building? Bruce wondered.

Next morning, Friday, 28 June, he woke after an uncomfortable night spent in the back of the van. Throwing back his light blanket, he sat up next to Marc and reached for the winder to let in more air through the side window. Martine was awake, binos in hand, sat in the passenger seat under the minimal cover from the lowered windscreen visor.

'Is that it?' he asked, pointing through the windscreen.

They were parked beside Huangpu Park, across the bridge from their hotel with a view of the Urban Planning building through a narrow gap between trees. The building was an unremarkable concrete and glass construction, about fifty metres high.

'That's it,' said Martine.

Marc sat up, ran a disposable wipe over his face and started to explain the day's agenda.

'It's a bit too cosy in here, I know, but at least the operation should be a short one,' he said.

'And smelly,' said Bruce. 'This city's a bakehouse. Must be high thirties already.'

'We can use the showers at the Pujiang, communal or not,' Martine put in.

'If we can proceed now?' Marc resumed with a tut. 'We've got a big chance. The Director is in his office today, but I'm guessing he's going to stop work mid-afternoon at the latest. If we can do the security recce *and* get his computer access today, then we're on for tomorrow night, which would be a result. We could get back to Beijing sooner, too.'

He reached behind his seat to produce an aluminium camera case, then opened it to reveal his next curiosity.

'This is it, how we will do the first phase.'

Bruce stared into the foam-lined case. 'Er, mate, I see some wires and a hand controller. Suggest you remove that hornet, though. Presume it's dead.'

Martine laughed.

'*Zut alors!* I will assume that you really know nothing from now on, okay?' Marc exclaimed. 'You're correct. That *is* a type of wasp. But not a wasp as in insect, it's a W-A-S-P – a Wide Area Surveillance Parasite, a flying robot that will do your job for you.'

Bruce had that sinking feeling of being the class dummy. Again. Would he ever catch up with this bunch who operated ten years ahead of the best government technology he had ever seen?

Marc explained that the WASP was another serious prototype device. This time the focus was not on big and powerful, but small and stealthy. And small meant tiny. The artificial insect was roughly twice the size of a thumbnail and could fly for up to five hundred metres carrying a micro camera and transceiver. He would pilot it into the Director's office where it would literally be a fly on the wall. He would use it to record the Director's password key strokes and observe any other means used to access his computer – biometrics, for example. 'It's amazing,' he proclaimed. 'Not just the aeronautical aspects, but the range and capacity to transmit video in real time. The key is the lithium ion battery.'

'Let's hope we don't need fingerprints or retinal scans. But if it's just passwords, then whoopee, we're in!' said Bruce. 'Although, how will we navigate the folder structure? It will be in Chinese characters.'

'We will be live-linked to the guys up north. Quentin will read from your headset feeds, like before.'

'So we're using the AG suits?' Bruce asked.

'*Non*. We use only when necessary. This target is easier than Defence Headquarters. Get caught wearing one of those and … well, you know what happens.'

Bruce listened as Marc confirmed the rest of the plan.

'So, now you are aware of another of our capabilities, Bruce. We will use the WASP to visit potential access points, like doors, windows, the roof and the basement. It should send live images to record and analyse. That will determine the route in and out, plus alternatives.

'You and Martine will wear subdued colours. If you are challenged near the target building you must look like normal civilians, not Power Rangers. You will carry casual backpacks with some tourist paraphernalia, like city guides, sandwiches, and the inevitable one size fits all cagoule masking the emergency escape item.'

Bruce screwed his face in confusion. 'Cagoules in summer?'

'Dumb tourists always carry them. It's de rigueur. Like Wellington boots at Glastonbury.' He reached down and took two packs from a side compartment. He held one up. 'In here is another piece of advanced tech. Okay Bruce? Your tourist stuff goes at the top. Make sure if you are going to deploy this thing you clip into the chest harness and leg straps or you'll fall out.'

'Go on.'

'If you are pursued you get to the roof. It's fifteen storeys high. This is like a parachute, but not. Fifteen storeys is not high enough for a normal chute, but this is a wing – for what we call LALO, low altitude low opening.'

Bruce sat back. 'Somebody pinch me. So the SAS does HALO, but we do LALO. And this thing really works? Cos I'm gonna admit that I'll be shitting myself if the first time I give it a try is off a fifteen-storey building.'

BEAUMONT

'You clip in, find a clear space with no other buildings nearby – and there are none around this one – and jump. It has an accelerometer with altimeter back up. When it detects you falling it will open in one second. I estimate that you will be at around a hundred and thirty feet up when it opens, which means you can fly the wing maybe a hundred metres away. It's to get you clear and leave the goons on the rooftop. I will be nearby in this van, remember.'

Bruce's mind ran the inevitable disaster video. Accelerometer: fail. Altimeter: fail. No reserve chute: too low anyway. How fast would he be travelling when he hit the concrete?

'I'm not convinced.'

27

They pulled up under cover of Shanghai's exotic plane trees, immediately north of the Directorate of Urban Planning building, on one of the many tracks crossing the People's Park. Marc had chosen well. They blended into the fluid, bustling scene of small cars, vans, bicycles and people moving and mingling in the area.

'I'll go mobile,' Martine said, as she inserted an earpiece and stepped outside.

She had covered up with a headscarf and ugly sunglasses to hide her blue eyes and blonde hair. Staring squads were less of a problem in cities where folk were used to seeing foreigners, but her image was so striking that crowds would be drawn regardless.

While Martine made like a tourist and scanned for hostiles, Marc set up the WASP. He lifted it with a father's tenderness from its resting place, teased the rotors apart to deploy them and set the machine upright upon the lid. With the laptop and device synced, he asked Bruce to lower the passenger window then activated the handset. The tiny mechanical insect lifted off, drifted through to the front of the van with a subtle hum, then darted out through the window.

'That really *is* something,' said Bruce. 'How fast can it fly?'

Marc was concentrating on the video feed and telemetry on the laptop. He managed a distracted reply to Bruce.

'Oh, maybe ten metres per second, which is good because that's about what a real wasp can do.'

'Let's hope nobody swats it.'

Marc broke from his screen to look at Bruce with disdain. 'It's the only one we've got.'

Less than a minute later the WASP was on station.

'Come, see,' said Marc.

'Where is it?'

'Sat on a street light outside the front entrance.'

'That's incredible! What camera has that thing got?'

'The best in the world at this scale – an acquaintance works in Carl Zeiss labs. Watch this …'

Marc zoomed in and peered down inside the high glass frontage into the reception area to see how people entered.

'Perfect. They just check passes and go in. Old tech. That's good.'

Marc flew the WASP up the side of the building, keeping it at a distance so it wouldn't be noticed. 'I'm going to start at the top. I figure the boss will have his posh office there. No ground floor rubbish in this hierarchical state.'

'So much for communism, eh?' said Bruce.

'Complete bullshit. The people are expendable. Fodder for the ruling classes. Anyway, here, what's this? Is he our guy?'

The WASP had a view through the window of a top-floor office where a lone individual sat hunched behind a desk with a computer monitor, keyboard, two phones and a photograph. It wasn't any standard office desk, but a large mahogany affair with inset leather top, where the overweight figure toiled away reading something, alternating his attention between document and screen, seemingly distracted, somehow anxious.

The room was more than twice the size of the next office, which Bruce guessed was for the Director's outer office staff. It included a polished mahogany conference table around which were ten chairs. Beside that was a trio of brown sofas and coffee table. Behind the Director, facing into the corner, was a computer workstation. Bruce felt like a real spy, a tradecraft voyeur. He watched a staff member enter, set a file upon his master's desk, bow his head and withdraw.

'Bruce?' Marc jolted him from his absorption.

Bruce pulled a photo from a folder and held it for Marc to compare with the video images. 'The hair. Same side parting? And the pudgy, scowly face. I reckon it's the Director.'

'Well, it is the boss's office and he seems to own it. Now the difficult part. I need him to go over to the terminal in the corner and use it. The secure comms will probably be on a different system and that could be it. But it's no good if he doesn't use it.'

They had to wait. To conserve power Marc landed the WASP on a ledge, concealing it beside a window frame. He would have to bring it back for a recharge at some point, which would risk missing what they needed to see.

'He must have to check stuff all the time, with all that's happening. Christ, they fired a dummy nuke over Taiwan recently,' said Bruce.

They kept watch. The Director looked busy, stressed, now moving about between desk and filing cabinet and phone with quick, impatient motions. A darkening sweat patch was growing around his shirt collar. He wore a fixed grimace with mouth downturned, lips refusing to open to let in more air, which he evidently needed to do, judging by the pulsating expansion and contraction of his nostrils.

A female assistant entered the office with a cup and saucer, steam just visible rising from it, then left, closing the door behind her.

Marc perked up. 'Here we go.'

The Director settled himself in front of the computer terminal in the corner. Marc moved the WASP in through the open window and parked it on the frame of a picture of President Tao, which gave a clear view of the keyboard. They held their breath.

'Come on,' Bruce muttered. The notion that every step in their plan had to work loomed in his mind. He focused on the man's chubby fingers, his heart thumping as the Director began prodding the keys.

'Got it!' said Marc. 'Two passwords. I guess a mix of characters and symbols, but that's for Quentin to work out. At least eight digits each'.

He brought the spy insect back to the van, eyes fixed on its video feed as he thumbed the two small joysticks of the hand controller to fly it home.

'Ready?' he asked Bruce as the faint buzz became audible at the van window.

Bruce opened his hands for it to land, then offered it to Marc. He took it and gave it a little kiss before setting it into its box and plugging in a fine recharging wire. 'Beautiful creation!'

Moments later Martine reappeared at the open van window. She stuck her head partly inside and looked at the pair in the back. 'Get anything?'

'You bet,' said Bruce. 'You?'

'Other than hot, you mean? There's not much to report. Looks like a soft target compared to Beijing.'

In the afternoon Bruce found a secluded spot in the park away from the van and played the part of a Westerner snoozing on the grass in dappled shade with a copy of a tourist map of Shanghai draped over his face. Meanwhile, Marc ran another WASP recce, this time checking all entry points and getting a good look at the roof. When he had finished, Martine rejoined them and they gathered in the van to chat through the options while slurping and munching their way through chicken noodle soup and *popiah* rolls.

'I suggest going in here, on the ground floor, then taking the emergency stairs all the way to the top. There's no CCTV covering those stairs,' Marc said, moving a pencil over a sketch he'd made of the floor plan.

'That's an emergency exit, right?' Martine said. 'How will we get in? It opens one way, surely – and it'll be alarmed.'

'True, and true.'

Bruce raised his eyebrows, but he was learning to wait till he had heard more before speaking. Marc talked them through making an electrical bypass for the alarm circuit contacts in the doorframe and forcing the securing bolts. 'Can't have it both ways. The door opens outwards, and the construction means we can attack the bolts.'

'Better work out a Plan B as well,' Martine suggested.

By the early hours of Sunday morning, 30 June, the team was set to go. They had talked their plan to death over dinner in Shanghai's glittering centre. The exciting concept had become a terrifying reality for Bruce. It brought a sense of foreboding which curbed his appetite. Having a good meal spoilt was a cardinal sin for him in itself, but knowing it was also mission critical to have sufficient energy on board had made forcing himself to eat doubly unpleasant.

'The disadvantage of doing this in the middle of the night is that people will notice this van much more easily, so after you depart I will head out of the centre and return via a different route to my covert position. You'll be on your own for about ten minutes till I get parked again,' Marc said.

'That's fine. We'll still be on comms so you'll know if there's a problem,' replied Martine.

Bruce and Martine checked that their earpieces were securely inserted, donned their backpacks and eased their way from the van in the shadows of the People's Park. They kept a low profile, walking steadily with hoods up and heads down, saying nothing, ready with their cover story of tourists returning from a late Saturday night on the town. Even at 2 a.m. there were still people wandering around. Bruce was grateful that some were well-oiled and not making any effort to keep their laughter at bay. A welcome diversion.

As they approached the emergency exit door on the north side of the building, Martine whispered, 'This is bloody dark. We need to see what we're doing. Talisman said there are street lights here, but they haven't lit.'

'Stay close,' said Bruce. 'Conditions are good for me tonight.'

They watched to check no-one was observing them as they paced the final yards to the doorway, which was set into a recess. Bruce brought his thermal vision to life, then slipped his pack off and took out the metal bridging strips to bypass the alarm circuit. He felt along the top edge of the frame with a small current-detector probe and located where the circuit ran to the door. After some pushing and pulling, he overcame the layer of grime and the strips went into place.

'Still clear,' whispered Martine.

Bruce used Marc's specially crafted tools to engage and shimmy the internal lock bolts, finally standing and hanging on a pair of short crowbars to overcome the mechanism's resistance until the bolts were clear of the door, both at the top and the bottom. Glancing behind them they quickly entered and closed the door.

Martine placed a hand on Bruce's shoulder to stop for a moment. Marc's voice came over the radio.

'Team One and Two. Zero. Radio check, over.'

Martine clicked twice on the transmit switch in her jacket cuff. *OKAY*. They were in business.

Bruce gazed around his deep orange hologram view of the interior, checking nearby on the ground floor and ahead up the stairwell. They began climbing the fourteen levels above.

There were no internal locks on doors, not even on the top floor, evidence that the Directorate was primarily an institution that dealt with civil matters and thus had less security.

When they reached the door to the Director's office Bruce was breathing heavily, trying to control his intake of air so he remained calm and quiet. Martine appeared to have no such concerns.

They entered the office, Bruce feeling modest relief on seeing the familiar objects that he'd watched on the WASP's video feed: the shiny conference table, the sofas, the tidy desk and the computer workstation. They checked about them, then made for the workstation. Martine got out a 3.5 inch floppy disk.

'Zero. Team One. We're at the target,' she whispered into the mic.

'Roger. Remember, we assume the account is monitored. I will deploy our friend to watch the night shift. Two minutes to leave once you log in,' Marc replied.

The WASP would be positioned at the entrance to the building to observe the security guards in reception. Bruce knew they would come. It was just a matter of how soon. He and Martine slipped on headsets with side-mounted mini cameras.

Marc confirmed that comms were working. 'Patching in Rostam now.' Quentin and Lucien were receiving the radio and video feeds.

'Here we go,' said Martine. She turned the computer on and they watched as the hard drive spun up.

First screen: a solitary cursor blinked at the left of ten underlined spaces. Green on black. Martine typed in the key strokes, which she had memorised. She hit enter. The computer came to life, then the modem automatically began dialling. That wasn't meant to happen. Bruce could hear his pulse thudding in his ears.

'I didn't start that,' she said.

'Got no choice. Just continue,' said Marc.

Second screen: a Microsoft window opened, requesting user ID and password.

Microsoft? So much for home grown, thought Bruce.

Martine entered the details. They were in.

'Two minutes,' she said to Bruce. 'Go!'

A standard File Explorer view opened. She waited, keeping her camera trained on the screen for Quentin to examine.

'Ninety seconds,' Bruce whispered.

Quentin's voice cut in. 'Scroll down ... Stop ... Second row from bottom of screen. First folder, left-hand side.'

Martine double clicked and the folder opened. It contained about twenty sub-folders and hundreds of files. '*Scheisse*. This is a mess.'

'Stay there. I'm checking the folder titles,' said Quentin. 'Try second one down.' She opened it. 'Sort by date modified ... There! Top file. Open it.' She double clicked as instructed. '*Fènghuáng. Xiàngmù míngchēng lièbiǎo* ... That must be it – the Phoenix Programme list of names. Ding dong! And it's got a red hot classification marking. How many pages?'

'Sixty seconds ...' interrupted Bruce. A bead of sweat had reached its critical size, rolling down his back before being absorbed into his shirt under the backpack. Beside him Martine's crystal blue eyes were strained, alight in the reflected glow from the computer screen, tension in every facial muscle.

'There are 2,164 pages,' Martine said.

'Copy it. Then go up a level and take as much as will fit on the disk.'

'On it!' She dragged and dropped the file to the floppy drive. The progress bar began creeping along.

A phone started ringing behind them on the Director's desk.

'Leave it,' Martine said, before Bruce had even turned to look at it.

The seconds ticked by. The phone kept ringing. Suddenly Marc's voice cut in over their headphones.

'Team One, Zero. I got movement in the lobby. Folk are on phones and double checking their monitors. They're grabbing radios and flashlights ... and guns.'

'This is so fucking slow. It's not that big a file. Just text, I think,' said Martine.

'But what processor is it running? Maybe *that's* home grown,' Bruce said. He watched the progress bar. It had reached fifty percent.

'They're heading for the lifts,' came Marc's voice in their ears. 'And no, I can't stop the lifts.'

'Ten seconds ...' said Bruce, counting the clock down as per protocol. But it was academic now. It evidently took less than two minutes for out of hours system access to attract attention. He looked to Martine for a reaction but she was fixated on the progress bar. Seventy percent.

'Shall I stall them? Buy you some time?' he asked.

'How? Remember – no trace. That's what we do. I must get this. Think we're screwed, though.'

'*No trace* went out the window the moment you logged on. We'll have to settle for *not identified*.'

28

Eighty-five percent. Bruce felt the savage reality begin to tear at him that one hundred percent was no good if you were wearing handcuffs. He forced a deep, steadying breath, and pushed aside the rising doubt about Martine's judgement – was she now lost in the moment, fixated? He had an idea.

'When you get the files, go to the roof and get away. I'll stall them. You *must* get away, Martine.'

'I know. But you're gonna get caught if you're not slick about it.'

Bruce sprinted out of the office and turned right along the corridor. He passed the main staircase on his left to reach the lifts, same side and a few metres further on. Mercifully one of them was only three floors below. He pressed the call button and watched as the numbers above the doors lit in sequence. A second lift had started to ascend from the lobby.

11, 12, 13 ... at last his lift reached the fourteenth floor. As he waited for the doors to open, Bruce's mind was working at lightning speed. Which floor to choose? The doors slid apart with a loud ping. He reached inside and pressed 10, jumped back into the corridor and waited for the doors to close. The lift started its descent. Bruce stood motionless, watching the progress of the lifts on the digital display above the doors, waiting for the movement to be registered by the crew in reception.

The lifts crossed just before his reached the tenth floor. As he hoped, the ascending lift stopped soon after, at Floor 12. He guessed some of the guards inside had jumped out and would run down to check Floor 10. When their lift didn't continue from the twelfth floor, he figured that the rest of the guards were on their way up the stairs. They would race the last two levels in no time. But which route would they take? the fire escape or the main staircase?

He looked along the corridor to the exit from the main staircase. The doors had a pair of D-shaped vertical handles. He grabbed a fire axe from a cabinet next to a large mains-fed hose reel and pushed it through the handles. It was a loose fit but it would buy time.

He could hear the rumble of boots on the main staircase. He ran back to the office to check on Martine.

'You done?'

'Just getting some other files, too.'

'You gotta go. They're here. We'll be blown!'

'*Schtimmt.*'

She ejected the floppy drive, closed File Explorer and did a hard shut down. She dashed past Bruce and turned left along the corridor to the fire escape stairs, just as the guards began rattling and pounding at the doors. The fire axe shook and slid out within seconds, clanging to the floor as Bruce disappeared into the stairway after her.

The escape stairs swept down to the left. Ahead rose a vertical steel ladder to a trapdoor in the roof. Martine had nearly reached the final couple of rungs, her steps resonating upon the metal. She disappeared from view. The trapdoor banged shut, its thunderous impact ringing around the walls.

Could he follow her? Bruce started towards the ladder, but the thud of boots closing on him drove his instincts to head down, to stay out of reach. Out of sight.

Their blood was up. Shouts and radio chatter echoed at his back as he descended, sliding along the handrails and leaping entire sets of steps. On the tenth floor he changed the pattern, exiting the fire escape route and moving inside to the main stairway. His mind was electric, streaking between thought and emotion. He pictured Martine making her leap into the night. Above him echoed the noise of radios as the guards called to each other to trap him. He winced at what it would mean if he was caught. They would skin him alive for the truth.

Two floors lower and he switched back to the fire escape stairs. He stopped to listen. Above him all was quiet. From the heart of the building came the faintest base tones of boots thudding in chaotic pursuit. The drumming of the pulse in his ears had liquified to a raging hiss. Adrenaline and sweat overwhelmed his body. He felt weightless, charged with power.

He pressed on, light of foot, quickly descending the next seven floors. Each time he passed a floor it was like roulette. Would the door fly open? Would he run into the muzzle of a captor's gun?

He reached the bottom, the door by which they had entered the building. Again, he stopped and listened. Nothing. He eased his weight against the push bar and the door gave way with a creak. Once outside, Bruce closed it as best he could and ran into the park. He removed his headset and threw it deep into the bushes. The break-in tools followed.

Moments passed. Up ahead a couple were chatting and walking towards him, not a care in the world. Then a voice in his ear shook him from his trance.

'Team Two, Zero. Situation? Over.'

Bruce wasn't clear yet. He clicked twice on the transmit switch. *OKAY.* He needed to be further away before he dared to speak.

At the end of the broad path beside the park he turned the corner, heading for the road so that Marc could pick him up. Two guards appeared.

'*Tíngzhǐ!*' Stop!

Bruce curled his left hand to hold down the transmit switch. He hoped Quentin was listening.

One guard pointed a pistol at him, the other a torch. More unintelligible orders were shouted. Bruce instinctively took his hood down and raised his hands. They grabbed him and pushed him to the concrete pavement. His bag was removed and the first guard started emptying it. More shouting. A bottle of water and a bread roll dropped next to him. Bruce looked as the torch was shone inside before he was dragged back to his feet. The rucksack was thrown back at him.

The second guard grabbed his ear, pointing to the earpiece that was inside, yelling at him in Mandarin. Bruce stopped transmitting.

Quentin's voice sounded in his ear, as if from within his very soul.

'Play the part of a deaf person. It's your hearing aid. *Zhùtīngqì*. Ju-king-shee.'

'Ju-king-shee,' Bruce repeated.

'I'm deaf. *Wǒ lóngle*. Wo, long-le,' Quentin coached.

'Wo long-le!'

The pair stepped back and released him, shrugging to each other.

Thirty metres further ahead a couple were also being questioned. Bruce watched as they were led away. A girl and a guy, maybe early twenties, dressed for clubbing. Perhaps it was the chic black clothes that had framed them.

A call came over the guards' radios. They took hold of Bruce, marching him towards the road where a minibus screeched to a halt in front them. *Shiiit!*

'Artemis, you still hearing me?' came Marc.

Click, click.

'Kite is with me, safe. We're in the van and we have eyes on you. We need to get you back before you enter the system, otherwise the game's up, big time. Stay tuned.'

Click, click.

Bruce pictured Martine next to Marc, her LALO wing bundled in the back of the van.

The guards shoved him into the minibus. He quickly scanned inside the vehicle. Up front were two goons, then the couple in black. The two guards climbed aboard to join them in the back. He stayed his reflex to leap straight back through the closing door when he caught sight of one of the guards with his pistol trained on him.

The muddle of guards and prisoners faced each other from the padded plastic seats that ran down either side. The minibus set off along Xizang Road. Bruce assumed they were headed for police headquarters.

Xizang Road was a dual carriageway, peppered with traffic lights along its straights. At the second stop, Marc's voice came through his earpiece.

'Artemis, we will come alongside at the next lights and fire some shots. We need them to speed away with their heads down.'

Click, click.

'Have you got your backpack?'

Click, click.

'You need to be wearing it. Harness fastened. When I tell you, get to the back doors, open them and stand with your back facing out. Going parachuting, understand?'

Click, click.

Holy moly. How was this gonna work? In the shadows between passing street lights Bruce slid his rucksack on, tightened the shoulder straps and silently fastened the chest and leg straps. The minibus slowed down for the red lights.

Bruce glanced towards the back windows, watching for a move. A set of headlights rounded the following vehicle and drew up alongside. Bruce watched the van. Its window opened. As the lights changed, he spotted an arm appearing. Black sleeve. Martine. She pointed the Glock, pausing for a split second. He ducked in his seat just before she fired five quick rounds, aiming high, shattering side windows but avoiding bodies, engine, tyres and fuel tank.

Panic erupted inside the van. The driver hit the accelerator in an effort to get away. Everyone else was on the floor in the back, keeping as flat as possible.

'Doors, now!'

Bruce sprang up, stepped over a guard and one of the couple, then yanked the handles. The doors flew open. He turned, hung on tightly to the roof frame and positioned himself as instructed, feet on the edge, back facing out. A guard looked up, open-mouthed. He went to point his pistol but Bruce kicked out, knocking it away as the vehicle picked up speed.

Marc remotely activated the ripcord. Bruce felt the kick from the deployment mechanism breaching the pack and ejecting the canopy. The slipstream took the wing, wrenching it open with the snap of a spinnaker catching an ocean breeze. He was lifted out and clear, the cool night air rushing upon him in a void of tranquillity, the minibus slipping away below. He climbed to forty feet before the canopy stalled. He swung to the vertical and then it tilted forward, letting him back to earth.

As he landed in the road, a car blasted its horn and swerved to avoid hitting him. Marc and Martine skidded up beside him while he frantically weaved the chute around his arms to gather it in. Another car swung to miss him. Another blast from a horn droning by, the vehicle's wake so strong it nearly ripped the silk bundle from his grasp.

Their side door rattled open. Martine hopped out and dragged Bruce into the van. Marc floored it, taking the first available turn to disappear.

'You okay?' Martine asked, as she held Bruce while the van lurched from turn to turn.

'Yes, I'm fine,' he said, trying to catch his breath, trying to slow the adrenaline, to think straight. 'Can't believe what you all just pulled off. And well played with the translation, Rostam. You still with us?' he added, with a finger to his earpiece.

'Pleasure to be of service, my boy!' cried Quentin.

'Marc, I guess you figured I wouldn't wear that LALO wing if I knew you could deploy it remotely.'

'*Exactement*. But then again, perhaps you would.'

'It helped that they were municipal guards – security stooges, not regular cops,' said Martine. 'Otherwise, it might have been a different story. They didn't check your papers or photograph you?' Bruce shook his head. 'They probably intended to do all that at the station.'

Marc drove to a pre-determined location, a deserted steel mill near the port. Martine and Bruce climbed out and took on food and water, Bruce picking some grit from his dry bread roll. Police sirens echoed in the district behind them. His sweat was starting to dry and the adrenaline rush had become exhaustion. His legs had turned to lead.

'Stand back,' said Marc. 'Don't breathe this stuff in.'

They walked away, upwind, watching with intrigue as Marc sprayed chemicals over the van. Ten minutes later he went around again, this time spraying water from a ten-litre pressurised container, scrubbing the bodywork with a long-handled brush to remove the remnants of dark blue paint. Beneath it a coat of white emerged. He changed the licence plates and did a close final check by torchlight. Finally, he opened the side door and motioned for them to come aboard.

'Beijing, anyone?'

29

Far away from the hijinks in Shanghai, James Tavener was feeling upbeat.

From Sardinia he had headed for Paris, to a top-floor apartment just off Boulevard Haussmann. The spacious two-bed was in prime real-estate territory, purchased with the proceeds from the sale of the Rothwell lists. With no finance owing and no tenants in residence, he had mothballed it as a European bolthole, but one with style and culture all around. Inside was adorned with high alabaster ceilings, parquet floors and original fittings. Outside, aromas from nearby restaurants rose above the hubbub of crawling traffic, punctuated by the occasional car horn, distant shrill from a traffic officer's whistle, or a busker's violin.

Tavener removed the dust sheets and kept out of sight for a couple of days, watching for surveillance activity. He spent his time researching his target. The strongest lead was Lucien Martell's reputed connection to the French Olympic fencing squad, but that soon turned out to be a dead end. Whether it was poor record-keeping, the passage of time and changes of staff, or overblown claims about

Martell's links to the top of the sport, no-one had heard of him at Noisy-le-Grand.

Tavener's belief that Martell was a common French name brought a welcome surprise. There were only an estimated one to two hundred people registered as Martell in the country. He had only met Lucien in passing, but recalled that he sounded French. Of course that didn't mean he lived in France. What else could he do but follow the path until it ran out?

With some digging into occupations, addresses and net worth, Tavener was able to whittle the numbers down to a few likely suspects. Starting with the cognac house founded in 1715 by Jean Martell, Tavener at once felt his objectivity slipping away, indulging the prospect of how such an establishment could fit the Architects' Club brief so perfectly. It had heritage, with more than whiff of drama. Jean Martell was born in Jersey, an acknowledged smuggling spot in those days. The house would be well connected, have land and property, and a business of sufficient scale to provide both funds and cover for off-the-books activities. Tavener even considered taking a tour of the distillery, just to get close.

But the clock was ticking, running down on his chances of taking revenge while the trail was warm and running up on him being identified by Chinese intelligence. He had to make gains, but in the right direction, and that was not the House of Martell.

BEAUMONT

* * *

It was late Sunday evening, fourteen hours after their dramatic escape in Shanghai, when Bruce, Marc and Martine rejoined Lucien and Quentin in the basement of the Jianguo hotel. Having rotated drivers, they were sufficiently rested to conduct an immediate debrief with Beaumont, where Lady Margaret, Greg Pitman and Ying were ready on the VTC.

'Our time in China is finite,' said her ladyship. 'Bruce very nearly got caught. The stakes are rising. We are very much in familiar *unfamiliar* territory. They know a security breach has occurred; they might not know that data was actually taken. This could go in any number of directions, potentially beneficial or harmful to the operation.'

The eight conferred over the possible outcomes of the Shanghai operation.

'It would be usual to change compromised information, or associated plans,' said Quentin. 'Think Hitler and the Ardennes offensive. The secret plans fell into allied hands and he was forced to change – to a bad option in that instance.'

'Which paid off, thanks to allied incompetence,' Bruce put in.

'Correct, but let's not overdo the comparison. They won't change the list. That isn't the issue. It hinges on whether Tao finds out. If he does, what might he do? Bring his plans forward? Would that be possible?'

'Do you think Tao will definitely find out about the breach?' asked Lucien. 'It seems to me that a culture of fear permeates the government – the country, no less. The Director of Works would be hung out to dry ... or literally hung.' He smoothed his chin between fingers and thumb, contemplating, looking around the others for a reaction.

'But could he control what the system monitors in Beijing would have detected?' said Bruce. 'Surely they would be part of Tao's internal spy machinery. And would Tao have a suitably trustworthy replacement available to take over what must be an enormous and most secret portfolio?' Nobody answered. The permutations were multiplying with every question.

'Our mission is definitely creaking,' added Greg Pitman from the Beaumont end. He was met with silence. 'I'm not saying that anything more could have been done,' he continued. 'It's just a reality we must face. But is there any point in pursuing our plan to record Lin's voice so that *Dēnglóng* can be triggered? Tao will be ready to quash it, and probably round up anyone implicated in it.'

'Maybe, but I believe that we should continue with the plan,' said Quentin. 'Tao will be guessing at who took, or *tried* to take, information. But remember that Shanghai is a melting pot for investment and property development. The Directorate of Urban Planning could be targeted for a host of reasons. And if Tao is paranoid and thinks the perpetrators are foreign intelligence, such as CIA or MI6, then what might he think they would do with his list?

Probably use it as leverage: the threat of exposure in return for de-escalation. A tactic to buy time while the West figures out what to do with him. Point is, nothing is certain, except if we do nothing failure is guaranteed.'

The Beijing team returned to their cover roles at the embassies and kept a low profile for the next few days. By the weekend, with no unwelcome visits from the authorities seeking to revalidate work permits and entry visas, Marc began the groundwork for the next task under Plan A – recording Marshal Lin's voice.

Voice recognition had been developing steadily in the mainstream since the early 1970s, but Marc had access to another corporate prize: pioneering software that could *replicate* voice in real time. Sure, code existed to record, segment and reconstitute voice messages, but it lacked the dynamism to respond in the moment, to hold a live conversation. The prototype of Verbiage was the holy grail for a UK-based boutique software firm, whose founder was a Club associate. Still under development, the package was set to propel the firm into the big time and the big money, so it was the most confidential of industrial projects. However, an exception would be made for the Architects' Club. The founder would rather the world remained stable and healthy so he actually had a market in which to sell.

The increasing risk to the Beijing team's activities meant that operational security had to increase. Mid-week dinners where all gathered had to stop. Only the two sub-groups met in public, never the whole team, with Quentin and Marc acting as the conduit between them. The Jianguo basement became the single place where they could all come together.

*   *   *

Ritan Park covered a modest ten hectares on the northwest edge of the Jianguomenwai Embassy Compound. Crisscrossed by neat paths, it hosted picturesque ponds, low-key historical and religious sites and a handful of Western restaurants, all under a canopy of weeping willow, cypress and biloba.

Quentin knew that the restaurants would be watched now, so he had initiated a routine of evening strolls around the park, passing the throngs milling around the entrance to the Temple of the Sun. This provided an opportunity for him to meet with Marc to talk in person when other channels would not do.

He found Marc sat alone on a bench, with a view through the trees down to the café by the largest pond. No room for others to sit, no paths nearby, no CCTV coverage. Perfect.

'How are preparations?' he asked as he sat and offered Marc a mint humbug.

Marc shook his head. '*Non, merci.*' He turned to look at Quentin. 'I think I have a way in. Kite found a contact list on the files recovered from Shanghai, which I ran through a translation program: key names that, I guess, the Director needs to have access to.'

'Go on.'

'It includes Marshal Lin – his outer office and direct line.'

'Top drawer!'

'The telecoms exchange within the Defence Headquarters site is secure. But for calls outside Beijing it looks like they get routed through the main China Telecom system.'

'Which is in Beijing? And less secure?'

'*Exactement*. It will not be easy, but there will probably be fewer guns around. My concern is that the signal quality is good enough for the software to work.'

Marc skipped through the location, site features, and how exactly he would break into the network to eavesdrop on the marshal.

'Perhaps I will have one of those humbugs after all,' he said. Quentin offered the open bag again. Marc passed him a hand-drawn copy of the site plan by dropping the folded slip of paper into the sweetie bag when he took his treat.

They paused to consider what had been discussed. A young couple appeared a few metres in front, passing through the trees arm in arm. The girl was about to look round at them when Quentin cleared his throat and fired a filthy spit onto the grass. She recoiled, turning back to her partner, and they moved on apace.

'Proof that commonplace doesn't mean accepted,' Quentin said with a smile.

Marc resumed, 'One advantage is that China Telecom is new, founded a year ago. Things will still be fluid. I did a visual yesterday. They appear to have some temporary exchange units in the yard. Building works are ongoing in a massive side building. I think that's where the switch gear is going long term.'

'Easier to infiltrate.'

'*Oui*. But I need to go again, to monitor security routines.'

'Let me know when you've got everything you need. Then we can shape the task, brief the boys and girls.' Quentin slapped Marc on the knee. 'Good work, monsieur. *Au revoir.*'

30

The next morning, Friday, 12 July 1996, began another stifling day in central Beijing. Quentin bought a copy of *Apple Daily* from a street vendor on the short walk to work along the Guanghua road. He couldn't believe his eyes as he scanned the headline: MARSHAL LIN XIANGQUIN ARRESTED AS TENSIONS ESCALATE WITH TAIWAN AND THE WEST.

His frustration was compounded by bewilderment when he reached the entrance to the New Zealand Embassy to find a queue spilling out into the car park. He turned to another contractor to enquire what was up.

'Apparently we're all having our photo taken. Again,' said the man.

'I don't get it.'

'Sounds like the Chinese are setting up face recognition at all their border controls, so they want current photos of all visa holders.'

'But they can't be in the embassy doing this?'

'Oh no, of course not. That's our people ... always obliging.'

Quentin computed what it all meant. It was getting ugly. If a face recognition system was rolled out to all ports of entry and exit, then false passports would be a big risk.

He looked about him as the queue shuffled forwards. The timing of Lin's deposition, and the nature of it, was alarming. Scanning through the leading article, no definitive reasons were given for Lin's removal. 'Acting contrary to the national interest … pending trial.' The fabrication went on.

Lin's anointed successor was newly promoted Marshal Zhou Kai. The report didn't flinch in its characterisation of the man known as The Bull. He had been brutal in dealing with dissent and had a track record of widespread internment, torture and summary executions, especially of ethnic minorities. The worst part was that, as a soldier, internal security was not even his remit. It appeared that others gave him free rein to do the dirty work he relished, all in the name of the Party and the people. Tao had brought an ultra-nationalist alongside, which fitted with the strategic ugliness of the Phoenix programme.

Word soon got round the others about Marshal Lin and the face recognition programme that would be underway in every embassy within a week. Plan A would have to be ditched: they wouldn't be able to fake an operation order from a guy who was behind bars.

The extra care they took in communicating was evidently wise, but it caused excruciating delays in proceedings. The flow back and forth of information about

Lin, the need to abort Plan A and devise a new one, begged for more interactions to overcome blockers and pitfalls and to give subtlety and sophistication a chance. But, as embassy workers, a flurry of meetings after such sensational news would be suicide. Now they were being watched, for sure.

The means of meeting, therefore, had to be through something routine, prosaic – even repugnant; something to bore, divert or repel prying eyes.

The Australian Embassy had recently acquired a vacant neighbouring building, which was strongly rumoured to have been used by the MSS masquerading as the area's services management offices. Its former residents had left the place in squalor. The Aussies welcomed any help they could get from friendly embassies to help clear rooms and fill skips.

Bruce suggested this would be a good meeting place, and so, at suitably random times, he, Martine and Marc would cross paths. As they toiled away in the basement of the three-storey concrete lump, they could discuss their plans in hushed voices, all preceded by Marc's judicious sweep for surveillance devices left by Chinese intelligence, of course.

It was on the following Monday morning, three days after hearing the news about Marshal Lin, when they first met at the vacant building. Having worked up a sweat and looking suitably dusty, the three paused for a drink and a snack in a windowless storeroom full of cheap office furniture that stank of mould and rat piss.

Marc coughed in the fetid atmosphere, but then began to speak. 'First thoughts are to stick with exposing the leader's intent but change the approach to containing him. No *Dēnglóng* now. We must build a solid portfolio of evidence of his madness – what he really has in mind – and expose it at the right time and place to the right audience. A suitably large audience, to achieve ... how shall I put it? ... *une masse critique*.'

'You mean, instead of seizing control via the operation order, he is basically arrested by his own people when enough of them are prepared to act against him?' said Martine.

Marc nodded, then coughed some more. 'This place is truly disgusting, Bruce, but I suppose I shouldn't complain.'

'Sorry about that,' said Bruce with an apologetic smile. He paused for a moment before continuing, 'The new guy, Marshal Zhou, he sounds like a proper militant from what Rostam read in the paper. Could we use the WASP to record a meeting between him and the President – the two guys running the show? And they aren't going to be talking about their holidays, are they? We should get some red hot evidence. Is it possible?'

'*Oui*, if we know when they will meet,' said Marc, pursing his lips as he contemplated Bruce's suggestion.

'If we know the marshal and President are both in town maybe we can get the device on station and wait. Can it do that?'

'*Oui.*'

After further discussion, Marc was eager to share Bruce's idea with Quentin. He smirked as he set off for their developing routine of walking in the park together. Their cover was a clever one. Normal pattern of behaviour. Neat. And the suspicion of a gay relationship would skew how the authorities saw them, or so they hoped. Neater still.

When Quentin arrived at Lucien's apartment, he relayed the suggestion and confirmed his opinion. 'I like it,' he said, sat across the plastic-topped table. 'Bruce has come up with a potential winner here.'

'Proof of the President acting behind the backs of the CCP could be the clincher,' Lucien mused, rubbing his chin. 'Imagine it alongside copies of the bunkers' list, the master programme directive and the virus appendix.' He stood, stretched his arms high above his head and let out a yawn, then wandered to the window and parted the blinds, suspicious of who might be around. 'And I have something to add,' he went on, turning back to Quentin. 'We get Marshal Lin to give a recorded message about the truth and peril facing not just the Chinese people but the whole world!' Quentin sat up. Lucien didn't wait for a reply. 'We then send the recording to the editor of *Apple Daily*. And in case Tao's spies try to muzzle the story, it would also go to all members of the CCP Central Committee.'

'Well! That would amount to a media Mexican stand-off, the newspaper and the Party both knowing that this was the biggest deal in modern Chinese history. Both knowing that the other had possession of the recording. It's bound to become public – but how, and the consequences of how, would be up to the Party.'

Back in his room, Bruce stripped for a shower. As the water warmed, pattering upon the crazed porcelain tray, he pondered their situation. Plan B was as optimistic as they could have dared, given the lack of other options. But success was far from certain. If it worked, surely Tao would be deposed and a de-escalation of tensions would follow as the CCP rowed back from his insane vision for the world.

He blew out a long breath. Another headrush of excitement entwined with terror awaited. He stepped under the flow, pulled the curtain across and set his face upwards, inviting the water to slap away his doubts.

At Beaumont a hasty VTC with Lucien and Marc had brought her ladyship up to date with the surprise developments and the suggested new plan. It meant much to do for the trio in France, and everything hinged on Ying. Lady Margaret pushed back from the monitor and briefly widened her eyes, trying to process the seismic shift that had just occurred. She turned to Ying and Greg.

'Where might Marshal Lin be incarcerated? What do you think has happened here?'

For a moment Ying stared down at his hands, which were folded in his lap, and then began to speak.

'The difference between Tao and Lin is that the soldier understands the barbarity of war and the politician does not. Tao just *wishes* he was a hero,' he said slowly. He paused to consider his words before continuing. 'My instinct is that Tao has gone too far and Lin has challenged him. But Tao is a master of manipulation. He will make Lin a scapegoat for anything he chooses, and Lin will have no way of defending himself – unless he comes to trial, which might never happen.'

'That's your instinct, and I value your instinct highly, Ying,' said Lady Margaret. 'Could there be any other possibilities, however? ones that would prevent us getting his cooperation, I mean.'

'I don't see how. Lin is a reasonable man. His lifelong friend has cast him aside in shame and humiliation. The only way back from that – maybe the only way he carries on living – is with Tao gone. Lin will not stand by to see the world destroyed for one man's madness.'

She took in his words, weighing them, looking for opportunity, searching for hope. 'And what of Marshal Zhou? His character? What if he also objects to the President's vision? if one can even call it that.'

'That is the very bad news. Zhou is a thug, and worse, he has no family, so he will not care who perishes as long as it's not him. He was an orphan who beat a path to power by inflicting all manner of cruelties in the name of the Party. It was obvious that he was just taking out the anger of his childhood abuse on others. But he stood out and got results, which is how he advanced so far. President Tao's plans give Marshal Zhou even more opportunity for advancement and vengeance.'

'My God,' said her ladyship, putting a hand across her open mouth. 'Then we have to look to Marshal Lin to give us something compelling, irrefutable.' She gazed ahead, lost in thought. 'Where might he be held?'

*   *   *

Shanghai's Tilanqiao prison had had many names since its foundation in 1903. Originally the Ward Road Gaol, the American-inspired design held up to eight thousand inmates at its height. By the mid-nineties, nearer to three thousand occupied the ageing edifice. While the inmate population had dwindled, its reputation as the harshest prison in China had not. The choice of location to incarcerate Marshal Lin was obvious and political. President Tao wanted everyone to know, and everyone to see, that he held no fear.

Gathered around a mahjong board in Marc's studio apartment, Marc, Martine and Bruce chatted over the plan.

'We're going back to Shanghai, then, of all the prisons in China,' said Bruce. 'Not ideal after last week's furore.'

'At least we have some familiarity with the locale. It's barely two kilometres from the Urban Planning Directorate,' Martine replied. 'And Ying reckons that Lin will be kept in the high security wing – solitary confinement, by any name.'

'Which reduces the maths dramatically. He estimates about a hundred cells in high security now?'

'*Ja, stimmt,*' Martine nodded.

'I'll go ahead of you two next week,' said Marc. 'Set up a base somewhere and watch the staff in the wing come and go. Should be ready for our first move soon after you arrive for the weekend. Meanwhile, you can relax, while I go to listen to the President and Marshal Zhou.'

*   *   *

At 6 a.m. on Monday, 22 July, Marc pulled up under cover of the same derelict warehouse that was the drop-off for the previous venture into Marshal Lin's Defence Headquarters. It was within range – just – and the area was as deserted as before. He opened the case, set the device upright and looked around in case anyone was watching. The WASP launched, disappeared on its way and manoeuvred into the new head of the People's Liberation Army's private office before his staff had arrived. Windows were still cracked open at night to let in cooling air, ready to start the next day, which made Marc's job much easier.

He positioned the microbot on top of the blinds, from where it would capture a view of the whole room and the faces of anyone sitting there. Then all he could do was wait and pray that all conversations were not held at the President's residence. That was definitely out of range.

The hours drifted by and Monday drew to a close, with Marc watching through the video feed whenever the WASP's motion sensor detected activity in the room – a power-saving measure. Monday was his day off from his embassy role, but from Tuesday he had to take holiday. By Wednesday he had resigned himself to swapping with Bruce, whose shift pattern allowed it.

On Thursday morning Bruce took up position in the van. It had been driven a kilometre or so from the area used by Marc, to avoid setting a pattern but to keep the target in range. He was feeling tense. The nightmare knock at the window to see the faces of Chinese police or internal security surrounding the van was an image he struggled to put out of mind. He poured himself a cup of tea from a Thermos as the laptop and WASP booted up and synced.

A minute later he launched the device. Watching the video feed, he hardly dared to breathe. The flight to the building allowed him to sense the controls, which was fine in the open, but Bruce could feel the tension overcoming him as the picture showed the target getting closer. His hands felt like they had turned to concrete, with intended delicate inputs registering as spikes in motor speed and erratic changes of direction. The picture jumped and sometimes the headquarters disappeared from the screen altogether. *Regulate your breathing, Bruce ... it's just turbulence.*

Three minutes later the WASP was closing fast on its giant host. Now came the challenge of navigating the partly opened window. Bruce felt himself getting hot but couldn't spare a hand to loosen his collar. Beads of sweat formed on his forehead as he guided the device through the gap and set it down on the top of the window blinds, as instructed. He put the controls down, reached over and lowered the van window, then gulped mouthfuls of water from his bottle, hands shaking.

The day dragged by, with Bruce seeing nothing all morning. Presumably Marshal Zhou had business elsewhere, probably the presidential palace. Bruce sighed in frustration. What if the motion sensor or video had failed? He had no way of telling. He could but trust the machine and keep an eye on the battery level.

At 2.15 p.m. the video feed blinked into life on Bruce's screen. He donned a headset and observed. He could see the marshal dashing around, gathering papers and finessing the position of armchairs that were already perfectly set. A tray with glasses and a jug of water was brought in. This was promising. Then, at 2.30 p.m., President Tao was ushered into the office by a member of staff. Bruce hit record.

The men sat in the armchairs, giving a clear view of Marshal Zhou's face and a side view of the President. Bruce turned the volume up, his heart pounding, anxious that the two men could be heard.

His concerns were soon allayed. As the video feed settled he could hear the President's voice loud and clear. But as he listened, Bruce realised the bigger challenge: they were speaking in Mandarin. How would he know what and when to record? He let the recording run. It was all he could do. As the men spoke he noticed his intuition and acuity sharpening, watching and listening for body language and voice inflexions that suggested emotion, importance.

The conversation progressed. Bruce kept watching to ensure it was being saved to the laptop's external drive. He would also need twenty percent battery remaining to extract the bot.

Twenty minutes later and the external drive was sixty-two percent full; battery at thirty-eight percent. Bruce felt flushed, his eyes running dry from not blinking. How far could he push it? They needed this footage and it was all down to his judgement on what was being said. Would any of this yield a result?

'Come on, come on ...' he muttered.

Seventy-nine percent disk; twenty-six percent battery.

The pair were still going strong.

Bruce took in a lungful of air, held and released it to encourage calm. He took the decision that he would shut down at twenty-two percent battery and wait till the room was clear to extract the bot. Just agreeing to himself where to cut brought a curious comfort.

Sunlight was flooding into the office. Marshal Zhou stood up and went towards the window, out of view. Bruce heard the sound of blinds being lowered. *Shit*.

Ninety-one percent disk; twenty-three percent battery. Bruce was about to shut it down, but then the men rose from their seats, shook hands, and the President departed with Zhou in tow. Bruce decided to stay live, continuing to watch the office, just in case by happenstance they returned and divulged something more. Two minutes later, Zhou returned, grabbed his cap and headed out, closing the door behind him.

'Thank fuck,' Bruce said, exhaling. He hit stop.

He gingerly launched the bot, brought it down and round towards the open window and spied the two-inch gap remaining under the blinds through which he had to fly. He edged towards the gap, trying to relate the camera position to the bot's tiny rotor blades above it. He closed in. The lower edge of the window frame withdrew from view at the top of the screen, then Bruce heard a zinging noise, followed by a clatter.

The picture juddered and fragmented before returning to normal. Bruce's mouth turned to sand. He peered at the screen, trying to figure out what had happened. When he tilted his head it became clear. The WASP was lying on its side in the darkness under Marshal Zhou's desk.

SAM EARNER

Battery: nineteen percent.

31

Bruce couldn't believe it. The mission hung by a thread. He paged Marc: INCIDENT.

Marc appeared thirty minutes later, the spluttering two stroke of his moped rasping into earshot along the gravel side road to Bruce's location in a derelict grain store. He concealed the moped between some large bushes, walked the last few yards to the van where Bruce was waiting inside, and climbed in.

Bruce explained the situation. Marc listened without judgement or expression. Bruce was relieved that his teammate's mood was calm, professional. No sneer or recriminations for the physics guru. Too much was at stake, and it was evidently not the Club's way.

'Is this recoverable?' he asked. 'Otherwise, we have to go in. *I* have to go in, I guess.'

Marc raised a hand. 'One thing at a time, *mon ami*. This system wouldn't be much use if we lost the bot every time it crashed.'

He adjusted the laptop screen and began accessing menus. Bruce watched him work through different settings, back and forth, assessing the bot's status, orientation and circuitry before making adjustments and selections. He held back from asking questions.

'Okay, let's hope this works,' Marc said at last. 'The blades have collapsible hinges that work with the direction of rotation to prevent excess damage if they hit something, but the motor can run in two directions to redeploy the blades. Because it's lying on its side, I hope the restart sequence will roll it upright. It worked during testing.'

During testing? Never for real? Bruce held his breath. Marc restarted the video feed, then opened the recover menu and clicked start.

They heard a snick as the lead rotor blade spun and hit the felt-tiled floor. The picture rotated and the bot appeared to right itself, with a slight wobble.

'That's step one,' said Marc.

The machine's hum sounded through the laptop speaker, then Marc gently lifted it off.

Bruce spotted the battery level. 'Sixteen percent left. How ..?'

'*Shhh!*'

Marc turned the WASP and brought it out from under the desk. As it rose they caught a view of the marshal's outer office. The staff were going about their business, oblivious to the secret visitor next door. He turned it to the window and was faced with the exact same challenge that undid Bruce. The pair were glued to the monitor as Marc moved it under the blind. The lower edge of the window frame was level with the centre of the screen. Bruce bit his lip, in turmoil as Marc looked to be flying the bot into the frame.

At the last second, Marc fed in some collective, pitched the nose down, and manoeuvred the tiny craft over the sill and under the window frame, like driving over a humpback bridge.

He turned to Bruce. 'Well? Get going! I'll bring it as close as possible, but you need to recover it. Catch it, if you can.'

Bruce scrambled from the van and sprinted past the industrial ruins into a field of long grass, weeds and brambles. He couldn't hear the WASP over the traffic noise from the Fuxing road, but after half a minute he spotted the black speck coming rapidly towards him. He dashed to intercept its course, nearly tripping on debris in the uneven ground. At the last moment, the rotors became audible, then they cut out. Bruce shifted into position and caught the WASP with cupped hands, drawing it into his chest. He fell to his knees among the undergrowth, clasping the precious creation as if the fate of the world depended on it.

That evening the footage was passed to Quentin for an assessment. He returned to Lucien's apartment so his translation could be interpreted by two minds, a more objective approach.

Lucien watched Quentin's face as much as the laptop screen, trying to stay his curiosity. After five minutes he couldn't hold back any longer.

'Is it gold or chicken feed?' he said.

Quentin raised a hand for him to be quiet. He needed all his concentration. When the recording finished, he picked up a notepad from his lap where he had jotted down elapsed timings for specific points in the video. He returned to the recording, stopping about three quarters through it.

'This part ...' he ran a few seconds of footage, then stopped and translated the words for Lucien.

'*Are you familiar with the relevant components of Phoenix, Marshal Zhou?*'

'*Yes, Your Excellency. And I have the latest reports for you on the completion of our protective facilities, nuclear offensive programme, and stance* ... or maybe it's position he means ... *in the South China Sea ...*'

He forwarded to the next time stamp. 'I think this is the gold you were hoping for, Lucien,' he said, resuming the recording.

On the screen Tao turned to his top soldier with a beaming smile. Quentin added some theatre by impersonating the men in his translation, starting with an exaggerated squeaky voice for President Tao's haughty oration.

'*No, Marshal, there will be no more than the one hundred Phoenix bunkers that are now ready for use. There is no time. Such must be our sacrifice.*'

Then he switched to a gruff, gravelly monotone for Tao's chief bulldog, as he called him, growling: '*And our second wave attack, Your Excellency? A total response to their measured first strike? using our short half-life warheads?'*

Back to Tao's squeaky voice again. *'Precisely so, Marshal.'*

He stopped the playback. 'I think that should do it, don't you, *mon ami*?'

Lucien jumped up and clapped his hands in rapture. *'Excellent!* Surely that is enough.'

While Marc had saved the day, and Bruce had bagged the evidence, the team had missed their window for executing the next part of the operation, which had been planned for that weekend: to extricate Marshal Lin. They couldn't all book holiday at the same time during the week, there would be too much room for suspicion. But weekends largely went unnoticed. So they bided their time till the following Wednesday, when Marc would go to Shanghai to prepare for the mission.

Lucien and Quentin spoke with Lady Margaret and the Beaumont team every other day. Apart from Ying's vital contributions to ongoing business and planning, the significant discussion focused on the rising political and military tensions centred on the Taiwan Strait. Evidently Marshal Zhou had initiated the first moves to enact President Tao's blockade.

It had begun with a few smaller Chinese naval vessels entering the area and challenging shipping via radio. Questions were posed that were neither overtly hostile, nor sensitive or difficult to answer. Passage was permitted when the target vessel played ball. They were conditioning the outside world, who put up with the farce while searching for routes to de-escalation.

But the outside world was not just watching, it was preparing too. The USS *Carl Vinson* battlegroup was diverted from the Persian Gulf to station off Hong Kong, three hundred nautical miles from the Taiwan Strait. When the Chinese started patrolling the Strait, the US President sent two cruisers to dock at Taiwan's naval bases at Tsoying and Makung. In a break from tradition, he chose strength over pacification, seeking to call President Tao's bluff and raise the political stakes for him at home: attack Taiwan and you attack America. Little did he know that Tao *wanted* provocation and escalation.

*   *   *

The basics of the Shanghai trip would be like the previous mission. Same grotty grade of accommodation, different place.

Marc would observe the high security wing of Tilanqiao prison from a vantage point among the mass of high rise development in the city centre. The plan was that he would identify a suitable access target, a staff member, who one of the team would intercept outside the prison so that a microcam could be concealed in their uniform or equipment. That would provide views inside the facility, crucially including a list of prisoner cells and means of internal access.

Having set up and spent Wednesday and Thursday observing the prison, it soon became clear that the plan would not work.

It was late on Friday that Bruce, accompanied by Martine, Quentin and Lucien, joined Marc in the living area of the studio apartment to hear what he had discovered. He surveyed the room, taking in the fifties-style powder blue kitchen units, the filthy four-ring electric cooker and the raffia blinds covering the windows. Martine ran a finger along the arm of a threadbare sofa, as if checking whether it was safe to sit on or a biohazard. He made eye contact with her and tilted his head. *What did you expect, Martine?*

There was just enough room for three to sit on the mustard-coloured sofa. A cheap veneered coffee table covered with a layer of dust stood in front of it, beyond which Quentin pulled up a pair of metal-framed laminated wooden chairs from the kitchen table. Lucien had made tea. He set the mugs on the table. 'Help yourselves to milk and sugar,' he said with chuckle. There was neither.

Marc brought his hands together with an enthusiastic clap.

'Okay, let's start. The high security wing is a modern build. It's a steel and concrete structure, with a courtyard where prisoners can exercise ten at a time for thirty minutes a day,' he said, hovering the tip of a pencil over a sketch of the layout. 'The exercise yard has a high cut-resistant fence around it with the usual measures: barbed wire, lights, etcetera. The main prison walls are even higher – about six metres – and enclose the yard within the overall prison site. There are two guard towers overlooking the back of the prison. Each has a manually operated searchlight.'

Quentin slurped a mouthful of tea. 'You said the camera access wouldn't work?'

'Ah, *oui*. I mean, *non*. The walls are too thick, and I cannot get close enough for the feed to be received. No good.'

'Bugger.'

'However, there is a potential vulnerability.' Marc pointed to a side door on the section joining the wing to the main prison. 'The guards come out of this fire door to smoke. Presumably they can't smoke inside because there are fire detectors. They just stand a few metres from the door, keeping it slightly open.'

'So we go in using the suits? Drop on the guard and raid the place?' said Bruce.

'Yes, it's what I think,' said Marc.

Martine shook her head. 'They aren't going to open up just because you go in guns blazing or have a guard as hostage. There will be compartments. These are Chinese. They will let you kill whoever you want. They won't open up.'

The conversation went on, turning over every eventuality, estimating all possibilities. By late in the evening they had agreed on a plan. Nobody much liked it, but they were compelled to stay ahead of President Tao and Marshal Zhou's deliberate escalation, which affirmed that Phoenix was coming.

The next morning Bruce woke coughing from the dust and mould spores that hung in the air of the decrepit studio. Breakfast was an awful concoction of rice and dried fish, which was the best Quentin could get from the nearest street market. They drowned the mash-up with tea and coffee, then readied for a tour of the area and a visit to Marc's observation post high up in an apartment block above the prison.

The team was careful. The authorities had everyone on record with up-to-date photos, presumably by now loaded onto a shiny new database. Martine covered her head, and the five strung themselves out along the recce route so that none was spotted with another. They used five different access points into the sprawling apartment complex, only coming together again in the OP on the tenth floor.

Marc had rigged up a pair of pale grey curtains at the door from the apartment's sitting room to its small balcony. Recessed between deep side walls, the balcony was contained by metal railings through which a nylon sheet had been woven, three feet high, grubby, white and wind-torn, an attempt to provide a modicum of privacy from the murderers, rapists and doubtless political prisoners who might pry from their concrete purgatory below. The position allowed the five to huddle unobserved, crouched low, with a grandstand view over the prison and high security wing.

Far below, the exercise yards were filled with inmates shuffling round the perimeter of the main complex. They wore drab grey prison uniforms with black Chinese characters inked on their backs.

'Is that their names on their fatigues?' asked Bruce.

'Numbers. Just numbers,' Quentin replied.

To the right, in the smaller internal yard that Marc had described, was a group from the high security wing, striding around, making the most of every second's worth of fresh air and space.

'Wait a moment,' said Bruce as he focused a pair of binos. 'Is that Lin? ... at the back?'

'Think so,' said Martine. She lowered her scope and looked at the photo Marc held up. 'That's our guy.'

'Pity he's so far away. The thought had occurred to me of whether we could dart him,' said Bruce.

'What?'

'You know, like a blowpipe. Infect him. He gets ill – not too ill – and is taken to the infirmary where it'll be lower security. And we get to him there. I know that wouldn't normally work. It's too far and the projectile would be found, but you folks have a habit of surprising me on the equipment front. All fronts for that matter.'

'You folks? You are one of us, you know, Bruce,' Martine said.

'Hmm, I guess I feel I've got further to go yet. And a lot more physics to learn.' He grinned at Marc.

'The main thing is he appears to be fit and we will need that when we exfiltrate,' said Quentin.

Lucien eyed them all, one at a time. 'Seen enough? Let's head back and get the kit ready. We go in tomorrow night.'

32

It was 01:00 on Sunday, 4 August 1996. Bruce drew in a deep breath, held it, then released it as he set off with the others. The five crept out of their accommodation and climbed into the van. As Marc departed for the drop-off point, in the back Bruce struggled into his AG suit, fighting to get into the all-in-one construction, rolling around as the van turned, accelerated and braked. Martine and Quentin were having similar fun beside him.

'One is getting too old for some of the more juvenile parts of the job, methinks,' Quentin muttered, as he slumped against Bruce. 'Apologies, dear boy. Doing my best here.'

Lucien sat up front. Tonight he would direct the mission and act as tactical reserve alongside Marc who would run the tech and support functions. Quentin would lead the infiltration team.

At last Bruce had got himself zipped into the suit. He was already sweating and he wasn't even out of the van yet. He squinted to see out through the front. Rain was streaming down the windscreen, with the wipers hardly making a difference.

'Can you believe this?' he said. 'We're going to have to watch for slips – literally.'

'Slipping over isn't the problem. We need a guard to come outside for a cigarette, remember, which won't happen if it's pouring with rain. Otherwise this show's not even going to start,' Quentin replied.

Ten minutes later Marc swung into an underground car park. Quentin, Bruce and Martine jumped out and the vehicle wound its way back up the ramp and away. The infil trio pulled their helmets and gloves on, zipped their cuffs and checked that each other's compressed air backpacks were secure.

Quentin checked around for any observers. 'Weapons … Ready!'

They cocked their silenced H&K MP5 sub-machine guns and then their backup Glock pistols. Safeties were applied.

'Switching to image-intensified view,' he said, completing the preparatory orders.

'Team Three. I will stay on, er … organic thermal, if it's all the same to you,' Bruce said.

'Suit yourself, old boy. Least you'll spot a cigarette!'

In a flash of near panic Bruce realised what a distraction he would be if he failed to bring his mind's thermal vision to life. Another deep breath and release. He conjured the heat picture and then made sure the explosive charges he had been given were secure in their pouches.

They filed through the car park and emerged onto the back street from where they would launch. Rain pattered on

Bruce's helmet, but it was falling less heavily now. He checked the time on his head-up display: 01:17. Two minutes later Lucien came on the net and did a radio comms check. They were ready.

'Go!' he ordered.

They lifted off. The unreal sensation of being a weightless puppet returned to Bruce. He felt the special alloy lift points pulling him silently upwards, past the glow of street lights from the alley and into the cover of darkness. The enhanced earphones allowed sufficient noise from the slipstream passing over his helmet for situational awareness, like someone blowing softly into his ears. Bruce had to trust that their noise cancellation of peak volumes and higher frequencies would work if any shots were fired.

He returned his thoughts to the job, the target. They rose over the fifteen or so storeys of the buildings between them and the prison, constantly scanning for anyone who might spot them. The cloud base reflected the hue of light pollution, so wherever possible they moved in the shadow of high rise.

Bruce looked down to his right, spying the tenth-floor apartment with its tatty cover on the balcony railings – Marc and Lucien's observation post. The two men had concealed themselves well under some dark material that appeared to be just another piece of rubbish thrown outside and forgotten.

The three hovered to assess the situation. There was no movement in the yard for the high security wing, which was under floodlights. Rain continued to fall steadily, a sparkle of diamonds twinkling around the beams. The guard towers were manned, their searchlights standing idle. No prison guard outside the fire exit enjoying a cigarette, however.

Quentin's voice crackled in Bruce's ear. 'Proceed.' They moved towards the target, staying high. 'Safeties off.' Bruce slid a finger onto his MP5, which was slung across his chest, then pushed the catch fully forward.

The descent to the prison was fast and near vertical. All three set down on the high security wing, a ripple of boots ringing on the galvanised metal roof as they made contact. This time Bruce landed gracefully. He froze, looking for a reaction from the watch towers, but the rain and distance meant nobody would have heard a thing. He moved to the edge of the roof and located the electrical junction box for the floodlights covering the exercise yard. He attached a small charge and switched on its receiver.

'Zero, charge one set. Repeat, charge one set.'

He doubled back to rejoin Quentin and Martine, now poised in the shadows above the fire exit door. The rain eased further and after another five minutes it stopped. They waited. Bruce used the brief lull to focus his thoughts on creating an inner calm. His few experiences of firefights showed how brain function can quickly switch to its survival modes, creating freeze, flight, fixation or panic. He listened to his breath, felt the slowing of his heart rate, and watched the streaks of water pooling then running from the metal roof under his boots.

Lucien transmitted, shattering Bruce's meditation. 'Be ready. Someone will be gasping for a smoke by now.'

Another two minutes crawled by. Then the door mechanism squeaked and the door swung open. Below them the dark shape of a prison officer's cap contrasted with the lighter shade of his uniform as he pushed the door to behind him, stepped away a few paces and lit up. A long plume of smoke billowed into the air.

'*Un moment*. There might be more,' warned Lucien.

Half a minute later Quentin whispered the command. 'Now.'

They floated down behind the guard in silence. Bruce brought his MP5 into the aim and covered the doorway, with a partial view inside through a gap. Martine covered Quentin. The guard continued to draw and puff, in splendid ignorance of what stood at his back. Martine had her pistol trained on him. Quentin stepped forward and landed a blow to the back of the man's head, sending him to the ground with a clatter, unconscious. The cigarette tumbled from his fingers and sizzled out in a puddle.

They turned and joined Bruce.

'Ready. Go!' said Quentin.

Bruce pulled the door back and entered first, the others with weapons pointed in close combat postures beside him. A short corridor opened to a small reception area. No-one was there. He spotted light from a room ahead on the right and the sound of people talking.

'I think access control is on this corner,' he whispered. He crept ahead a couple more steps and saw the facia of the control booth. 'There's a window. Glass looks armoured.'

'We go in through there,' said Quentin. 'The door will be tougher. Blow the window.'

'Preparing charge two...'

They had no time to peek through, to see who or what was behind it. A false move would mean the cavalry getting called.

Bruce approached on all fours and set himself underneath the enclosure. He peered up at the thick plate glass above him, looked back to the others and gave a thumbs up. Quentin and Martine nodded back. They dared not even whisper in their helmets.

Bruce got the charge exactly as he wanted it in his grip, with a hand on each of the limpet levers. Staying below eyeline level, he attached the charge low on the window. Inside, someone spoke in Mandarin, then there was a pause, followed by the scrape of a chair across the floor. A face appeared at the window and looked in horror, straight down into Bruce's black visor.

The guard yelled, but Bruce had already dropped flat to the floor, detonator switch in hand. He fired the charge.

The space shook. Plate glass flew into the access control booth and smoke occluded everything. Bruce was amazed how his earphones cancelled much of the blast noise. He looked up to see Martine gliding over him into the booth, like a slow-motion hurdler, a jet of air from her pack thrusting her forwards as she fired two short bursts of silenced machine gun fire into the space.

Quentin stepped past and was ready at the door to the cells, machine gun trained ahead. A buzzer sounded and the magnetic lock disengaged. He heaved the door back and entered the corridor.

Bruce got up and looked into the booth. A guard was inside flat on his back, sprawled across a desk, eyes staring to the ceiling, motionless. His butchered body was peppered with bullet holes, and here and there his flesh was charred and shredded from the blast and shards of plate glass.

'Which cell, Team Two?' Quentin yelled to Martine.

She crunched upon the debris, turning to the far wall where there was a plan of the wing on a whiteboard. In each cell were Chinese characters. '*Scheisse!* Mandarin!' She opened the internal door to the booth for Quentin. He dashed in beside her and studied the plan.

Bruce glanced in to see what they were doing but as quickly turned back to cover the reception area and corridor connecting to the main prison block.

'Cell Twelve. Along on the left,' said Quentin, heading out. 'Keys or button to open it?'

Under the debris and shards of glass was a large control panel with pairs of red and green buttons. He paused for a reply.

BEAUMONT

'Go!' said Martine. She hovered a hand over the release button for Cell Twelve.

Bruce withdrew from the reception area and teamed with Quentin in the corridor. They stalked ahead with guns readied. Cell doors stretched down each side, a symmetry of steel and concrete, maybe thirty in this section. The only light was a mean glare coming from a line of white units strung along the ceiling centreline.

A guard rushed into view at the far end, firing his handgun wildly. They crouched to either side and returned bursts of automatic fire. The guard's chest and legs were punctuated by splatters of blood, the splintering of bones audible among the silenced shots as he collapsed. Bruce held his aim, ready for the next attacker, but none came.

The prisoners started thumping their cell doors and yelling, drowning out the buzzer and lock release at Cell Twelve.

'Open!' came Martine's voice in his ear.

Bruce ran ahead, adrenaline surging through his body. He grabbed the door handle, pulling it open to reveal Marshal Lin stood at the back of the cell, arms raised in defence, only visible by the light from the corridor. He wore the same style of grey fatigues as the prisoners in the exercise yard two days ago. He face was drawn, lined, like a heavy smoker, or someone with a terrible hangover. Images of torture flitted through Bruce's mind, but there were no obvious injuries. Perhaps solitary was enough.

Quentin entered the cell, lifted his visor and spoke in Mandarin.

Lin eyes narrowed. 'I did not ask to be rescued!' he answered in English. Perfectly good English, Bruce noted.

'Tell me, Marshal. How *would* you ask?' replied Quentin. 'Let's go!' he said, glancing at Bruce and tilting his head towards Lin. He pulled his visor down.

As they grabbed him, he tried to resist. 'What are you doing?' Quentin cried. 'Do you want to save your people? I'm talking about *Phoenix*.'

Lin's eyes widened as he stared into the satin black helmet. He relaxed his grip and gave a curt bow of the head in acknowledgement.

Martine's voice came over the radio: 'We got company!'

Bruce could hear the muted thump from her silencer as she returned fire. Then came the explosion of a grenade.

'We must use the other fire escape,' she cried.

Quentin led them out of the cell. Bruce looked to where the dead guard was lying ahead. The way out.

'Go, Team One. We'll cover you,' he said to Quentin.

'No, I'll cover you both. You're carrying him, okay?'

'Roger.'

'Team Two, get out of there. Time to fly,' Quentin transmitted.

Bruce watched Martine emerge from the access booth while giving the final shots of suppressive fire. She pulled the pin on another grenade and rolled it through the main door into the lobby before closing it behind her. Another boom resonated beyond it.

'Let's move!' she shouted.

Bruce and Martine led Marshal Lin towards the exit. Bruce radioed Lucien and Marc. 'Zero, we are about to exit building. Fire charge one.'

Martine unclipped a spare harness from her gear and signalled to Lin to step into it. At first he looked confused, but she grabbed his ankle and fed his foot through the first opening, then he got it.

Behind them exchanges of fire resumed, with Quentin holding the reinforcements at bay with judiciously aimed double taps to preserve his ammunition. They heard charge one explode.

Bruce shoved the bar to open the fire door and they broke out into the darkness of the yard. He and Martine stood on either side of Lin, clipping two straps each between his harness and theirs, ready to lift.

Searchlights swung onto them for a few seconds before being extinguished by Marc with a silenced sniper's rifle. More shots whistled into the watchtowers, killing two guards who were waving their rifles around, desperately trying to locate the shooter.

Heavy fire started coming down the corridor and Bruce turned to see Quentin slump to his knees in the doorway, unable to reload or reach for his backup weapon. He shuddered as rounds struck him.

'Go ...' he groaned into his microphone before keeling over.

'Fuck!' cried Bruce.

'Let's go, Artemis!' Martine shouted.

Bruce realised. No time. Accept it.

'Ready!' He clenched his jaw. *We're leaving him?*

They eased the controls of their anti-gravity suits and felt the strain of Lin's weight bear through the karabiners. Lin grabbed at the straps, his face cast with horror as they rose.

Martine turned to him and spoke the only words of Mandarin that had ever stayed with her. '*Xiāngxìn wǒ.*' Trust me.

Once they were rising and stable with the load of their passenger, Bruce looked back down to Quentin as he lay on the ground. His head was a mess of conflicting emotions. He couldn't bring his thermal vision to life, so he used the helmet's image intensification system to confirm the unthinkable. His teammate, and so much more than that he had come to realise, was prone, motionless. Bruce stifled the scream of anguish, of self-loathing, a volcanic rage at having failed to bring Quentin with them.

He continued to watch, straining to see as they slowly turned away from the scene. Prison officers spilled into the yard, three or four surrounding Quentin, the others, maybe six or more, pointing guns and casting torches around in search of their enemy. Marc released a few more carefully aimed shots, sending them back for cover, while the trio continued their ascent and transition to the evacuation rendezvous at the underground car park from where they had started.

*   *   *

By early Sunday evening, after driving for another fourteen hours along the highway from Shanghai, the remaining Club team and their guest reached the environs of Beijing. They made for a designated safe location near the Yongding river, twenty miles west of central Beijing.

After Lucien's sombre call to Lady Margaret, in which he relayed the contrasting outcomes of the mission, the long journey gave time for discussion with Lin. Bruce reflected that, like many senior soldiers around the world, a prerequisite for holding the highest military office was the ability to speak a foreign language. Often English was preferred, and Lin spoke it well. Without Quentin, it was critical to this element of the operation.

Lucien explained what had happened, who they were, and why Lin was now a free man, of sorts. Lin said nothing and just looked back at Lucien with suspicious eyes.

'You sure he speaks English?' Lucien asked Bruce.

'Definitely.'

Bruce observed how Lucien handled such a unique and vital situation. They needed Lin onside, and getting a video statement from him would be invaluable. But Bruce suspected that Lin was sceptical about the explanation they gave for not being CIA, or any other state intelligence service. He couldn't blame him. Of course Lin would suspect it was a sophisticated ruse to get secrets, confessions, or whatever might play into the hands of the West. But Bruce also knew what President Tao had become and where he was heading, and that was the bind that Lin must have been contemplating.

There was simultaneously a risk and opportunity for the Club. Lin appeared unmoved by the vague, euphemistic description of 'a long-established, independent community dedicated to world peace' that Lucien had given. The jump suits, machine guns and other-worldly capabilities overshadowed such innocence. Say too much, and they could expose the Club for no gain. But say enough, and Lin might become an associate, notwithstanding his long-term fate.

Offerings of water, snack bars and cigarettes were eventually accepted by their guest. So too was a change of clothes. Bruce wondered whether there was a moment when the man made up his mind about them. Was it when Lin leaned forward to stare at the floor, letting out a groan – of concession? of defeat? or was it acceptance that he had to trust them? A casual onlooker might say it was just fatigue. Bruce intuited otherwise.

All Lucien could do was hold his nerve and persist with patient, skilled persuasion. Everyone agreed that the doomsday clock was running down. There was no other play for either side.

BEAUMONT

At last they reached the hills of Guangsigou, where Lin would be hiding out for the next few days in a hut a couple of kilometres from the road. Marc stayed with the van, while Bruce and Martine deployed as area defence, he scouting ahead and she acting as rear guard. Between them Lucien walked with Lin.

As they approached the hideout, Bruce looked back and registered the change of expression wash across Lin's face in the final metres. Was it shock, surprise or disappointment? Likely all three. The Ritz this was not. A single living space within a wooden shack, its one window an opening covered with gauze. The site was buried among the jumble of huge bushes and forbidding scrub that covered the hillside. Shade was afforded by the canopy of pines that reached up from the rocky terrain.

Bruce and Martine closed in around the hut, keeping watch while Lucien deposited the basics of food and shelter. Despite the desolation of the place, the exchange of one prison for a temporary other, Lin confirmed a change of heart.

'I will give you your statement,' he said to Lucien.

Lucien smiled back. 'It will be *your* statement, Marshal. For your people and the people of the whole world.'

33

In Paris, James Tavener's efforts were starting to show promise.

His first assumption was key: Lucien Martell would have needed somewhere to stay during the years he had, apparently, *not* spent coaching the French Olympic team. Very good. A man of his means would probably have a residence in the city, which saved James all the bother of ringing round hotels with a bogus story, hoping for a lead.

Tavener contemplated which came first for Martell, the fencing or the Architects' Club. It was an academic distinction. With no other solid line of investigation, he visited the French national archives in Fontainebleau in search of past telephone directories for Paris. He had to wade through twelve years of directories before finding *Martell, L. M., 23 Rue Parmentier, 93460 Gournay-sur-Marne.* It was barely two miles from the headquarters of the French Fencing Federation.

Gournay-sur-Marne was a leafy, low-rise suburb that seemed left in the past. Avenues were thick with linden trees that ran along gravel sidewalks and obscured the view into most homes. The urban layout was based on a system of roadways radiating from circles in a progression of Haussmann-inspired geometric blocks. It was a quiet, soothing retreat from the noise and bustle of the city centre only ten kilometres to the west. Sundays were quieter still.

Tavener pulled up a hundred metres from the address, which lay at the end of the street on the far side of a large roundabout. He had a direct view of the gates to the driveway, but the house was largely hidden behind greenery. He thumbed a mint from a pack, slipped it into his mouth and waited.

The expectation was that the property had long been sold. Perhaps a conversation with the new occupants might get him Lucien's main address. Failing that, another round of research, deception and – worse case – a rifle through city property records in the dead of night might be required. The options fermented in his mind.

An elderly lady shuffled into view in his rear-view mirror. She was squat, wrapped in a head scarf and woollen coat, despite it being August, and stooped over her shopping trolley. The trolley shook and twitched as it crunched over the rough gravel path and she bobbed along with its rhythm. Tavener stretched back against the headrest, partly out of discomfort, partly out of the tedium of watching her crawl by.

But he was intrigued.

She reached the gates of number 23, passed them by and entered the house next door. He set off after her.

Her home was a modest affair with few windows, perhaps a two-bed. It needed renovation and was almost lost in the overgrown shrubs. Tavener pushed through to the side door and knocked gently on its flaking surface. A voice called back from inside. She was on her way. Feet scuffed across a stone floor, then the door rattled open.

'*Oui, monsieur?*'

The accent and croakiness in her voice had Tavener paying careful attention. He summoned his best, but somewhat stale, French.

'*Je suis un ami de Monsieur Martell. Vous souvenez-vous de lui?*' Her expression set with concentration. She remembered him, alright. '*Du numéro vingt-trois?*' Tavener added.

'Ah, Monsieur Martell. *Oui! Mais ça fait si longtemps.*'

Yes, it probably had been a long time. But did she know where he lived now?

'*Savez-vous où il habite maintenant?*'

'*Sa famille vivait dans l'Est.*'

In the east… of France? '*Où dans l'Est, madame?*'

'*Près du Salève. J'oublie le lieu, monsieur.*'

'*Ce n'est pas un problème. Merci beaucoup, madame.*' He slipped a ten franc note into her tiny wrinkled palm and beamed a smile. '*Au revoir, madame.*'

Near Salève. He could work with that.

*   *   *

BEAUMONT

The Beijing team had returned to the basement of the Jianguo hotel. They were exhausted.

Bruce and Martine slumped into a pair of hotel dining chairs, with kit bags and equipment set down around them. Marc opened the laptop and connected cables while Lucien shuffled his chair to the table in the centre of the room and hurriedly dialled into the secure VTC. Lady Margaret answered, soon joined by Ying and Greg.

The momentous events of the last twenty-four hours had turned the conference into a historical landmark, even by the Architects' Club's standards. They had busted China's top military man out of a high security prison. The video statement by Marshal Lin had already been sent to Beaumont via encrypted email over a private network, as per protocol. But they had also lost one of their most senior exponents. With AG suit.

Lady Margaret went straight to business.

'Good evening, Lucien, everyone. Am I to assume that your discussions with Marshal Lin were productive? I have just this minute received your transmission.'

'*Bien sûr*. Most productive, my lady, if a little rough around the edges.'

'How so?'

'It's only that he looked less than presentable, like an escaped con, which was unavoidable. We did our best to help him clean up. And the setting – the backdrop inside the shack was far from ideal. Some might attempt to counter by saying that he was being held captive and was speaking under duress. But the actual message, his performance, was excellent, under the circumstances.'

Lucien paused while she considered his comments.

'Very well. It sounds like we have as much as could have been hoped for.'

'Yes, and we even managed to include him referring to a package of information to be presented to the relevant persons, but that was necessarily vague. We must keep our options open until we know exactly what we have as a total body of evidence, and therefore who would be best placed to receive it.'

'Of course, as we had envisaged.'

Her attention turned to Quentin. What exactly had happened? Was he dead?

Each came forward in turn to give their account. Each had a different perspective in the blur of action during the escape.

'He fell down? Fell over, or collapsed, Bruce?' Lady Margaret was searching for a glimmer of hope among the details.

'Fell to his knees. He had taken a barrage of hits. Then he toppled over.'

'Was he breathing?'

'He managed a final order – for us to get out with Lin. He sounded weak.'

'I guess it has left him,' she said, almost under her breath.

BEAUMONT

The Beijing group glanced at each other. They weren't supposed to know his situation, but Quentin made no secret of his extraordinary past. The experiments, his body's ballistic resistance, the aftermath.

Bruce broke the silence. 'What about his suit? The Chinese have it now – and him to question about it.'

'Marc? Is there a chance that it could be damaged and not work?' Lady Margaret said.

'Hmm, only a small chance. But in any case the electrics run on a network which gives redundancy in case you get hit. When I saw he wasn't going to get out I remotely activated the kill switch. That can be turned back on, but only if you know the code for the pack.'

'And would he know the code?'

'*Oui*. Everyone knows that, or should,' Marc said, glancing at Bruce.

'But if they work out the technology … It's as big as discovering nuclear power!' She brought both hands to her mouth, aghast.

'It will take them ages to figure it out. Why anyone would be running around wearing compressed air packs will confuse them. They won't be expecting anti-gravity materials. They won't be able to identify the materials, and if they do, where would they get more? That would be tricky.'

'Were you observed taking off?' she asked.

'*Non*. The only external observers were the guards in the towers. I shot them before Martine and Bruce launched. By the time the other guards emerged they were out of sight. There is a chance that people from some of the other apartments might have seen us, but who will believe them? That district is rife with alcohol abuse ... and other substances.'

'Let's pray that Quentin is alive, and then that he can resist interrogation, God forbid.' Lady Margaret sank back, away from the camera. Her distress was palpable.

Nobody spoke for a moment. It was clear to Bruce they hadn't a clue about whether Quentin had survived. And how he would fare in interrogation was anyone's guess. It would depend upon what was done to him.

'We should have left someone in Shanghai to observe if he is moved from the prison,' said her ladyship.

'That's the downside of having an enduring cover,' said Martine. 'We have to work. And we're running low on holiday time.'

'True, but we must remain firm, now more than ever. I know you all understand that. We are entering the end game. Ying expects that President Tao will keep Lin's escape under wraps, gambling that he will remain in hiding. If word gets out, he will blame America, of course, and try to use it to his advantage. Privately he might suspect that military contacts loyal to Marshal Lin were behind it. We must realise that in the short term we have made things worse. Tao will probably accelerate his plans.'

BEAUMONT

They watched as Lady Margaret stood and walked away from the camera, shoulders dropping, a brief shake of the head before returning.

'Do you need another team member to complete the operation?'

Eyes turned to Lucien. '*Oui*, my lady. Without Rostam we are critically limited in what we can do.'

There were many activities to cover, whether managing Lin at the safe hut, preparing content for the big exposé, or delivering that content without getting caught.

The team at Beaumont conferred. Muffled exchanges were heard and Lady Margaret waved her arms in apparent frustration. She turned again to the camera.

'Greg Pitman will come over, posing as a tourist. Three month visa,' she said. Greg appeared beside her on screen and gave a brief wave.

Lucien grinned. 'Moonstone, welcome!'

'What about getting Quentin out?' Bruce interjected.

'Normally that is exactly what we would do. But we are short on time and resources. We don't know where he will be. And wherever that is, he will be too heavily guarded. We must stick to the mission, Bruce,' Lady Margaret said. 'Believe me, if we could, we would.'

'If Greg is here, what about protection at Beaumont?' asked Lucien.

'There's someone I can call upon.'

34

Quentin Saxelby's return to consciousness was punctuated by pain and bright lights. He could taste the chemicals in his system even though his mouth was dry. Blurred vision and watery eyes, a searing headache and stinging across his torso made him take his time in coming round.

The surgical lamp hanging over his bed was blinding, but Quentin noticed the slight movement on the left out of the corner of his eye. Then the rustle of a newspaper being folded. He kept his eyes closed to buy time, lying still in coarse pyjamas with blood soaking the stitched wounds in shoulder, ribs and stomach.

The voice began in English.

'How do you feel, Mr …?' Then the first pause.

Quentin played groggy. He *was* groggy. The eyes stayed firmly shut. He coughed and winced in discomfort.

'Hmm, we saved your life. You were hit four times. Lucky to be alive, Mr …?'

The MSS officer – it had to be an MSS officer – knew to make a careful start, to save as many cards as possible for later, should they be required.

'May I ask your name? You can tell me your name. It would help.'

Another cough, eyes staying sealed.

'Who wanted you to do this? They abandoned you without any consideration.'

The chair scraped on the floor as the man rose. Water was being poured into a glass.

'Here, you need to drink.'

Quentin did need to drink. He partly opened his eyes and sipped, as his captor worked on building the relationship, like shaping a lump of clay upon a potter's wheel.

'What is *that* about? I am intrigued. Were you planning to leave Shanghai's most secure prison on a motorcycle?' The officer chuckled.

Quentin presumed that the AG suit was in the room. It would make sense. Having it there aided questioning; details could be pointed out, responses could be stimulated by the constant reminder that they had it, they had him. He knew when to let out some line, though.

'Yes,' he wheezed.

'Yes what? Who sent you?'

'Yes ... motorcycle. I was set up. Lied to.'

'I see. And what is the backpack for. Compressed air. Why?'

'To breathe ... for fire or smoke. CS gas ...' Quentin tailed off, exhausted already. They couldn't go to work on him yet. Not strong enough. That's what he hoped, at least.

The minutes stretched into an hour. Quentin was making it last well, or as well as he could have expected. But he feared that his thinking reflected his injuries: it was shot.

The MSS officer's impatience grew. The mood changed when Quentin made a bold but unwise move.

'These leathers, why do they have metal in the cuffs … and shoulders, and …' Quentin heard the suit being handled '… knees?'

'For fighting.'

'What? How does that work?'

'I hit you with them.'

'That's ridiculous.'

'Not my idea, old boy. Why don't you ask the double-crossing fool who designed it?'

'And who is that?'

Quentin shortened his breaths, shallower, quicker, feigning stress, building the moment.

'Zhou.'

'Which Zhou? Marshal Zhou Kai?' Quentin nodded. The officer erupted in laughter. 'Why would he help Lin? Now, I *can* tell you what Zhou would do with you if he was here. Why do you lie? I have been hospitable towards you. Now you insult me. I know you work for the West. CIA? But you are quintessentially English. Did I say that correctly? Probably a contractor. A deniable asset, not on anybody's books.'

And so it began.

They were joined by two other men who dragged Quentin out of the bed and along a dark corridor. There was nobody else around. He hadn't a clue about location, the time or even what day it was.

BEAUMONT

The interrogation room had been prepared with chairs, restraints and two tables at the side. One had drinks and snacks, even a packet of cigarettes. The other had a range of items meant to intimidate, plus a medical bag.

Beatings came first.

Quentin struggled to maintain focus but realised they only allowed short breaks so he could recover, ready for more. They didn't take him to another cell, then to wake him, to sleep deprive him. They had no time for that part. They were in a hurry. Presidential orders?

The stress and exertion of the beatings made him pass out frequently. Water would be thrown into his face. Sometimes they let him drink, to give him just enough strength. Sometimes they poured the water onto the floor as he gasped for fluids, just for variety, like music.

Through the fog, Quentin knew his real dilemma. The longer he held out, the more time would pass and the less potentially valuable he would be. At some point they would give up and execute him.

They stripped him to the waist.

The irons came next. A couple of fingernails, small stabs, a few cuts. But that didn't last long. Out came the cables and electrics.

'I hope you don't mind, but it will work better here,' said the MSS officer. He attached the crocodile clips to the bleeding ends of Quentin's fingers. The blood would aid conductivity.

The current was intolerable. Quentin screamed but the sound was choked off as every muscle in his body went rigid. Bones cracked with the tension. Sweat poured off him. He fell over in his chair. They undid the leather buckles at his wrists and ankles to get him back up more easily. He was so drained that they didn't bother to fasten them again.

When he passed out, Quentin came round to the sensation of a needle being withdrawn from his arm. He suddenly felt awake again. Adrenaline.

A knock came at the door and proceedings paused. The officer spoke briefly with the visitor, then returned and stood in front of Quentin. He held up a photo.

'So, you work at the New Zealand Embassy? Why don't you try again and tell me who sent you.'

Quentin stared back at his tormentor with venom in his eyes.

He was electrocuted again, screaming again, this time with one long roar until the current was cut. Quentin let his head fall forward, eyes shut.

The assistant with the needle approached and tried to inject him.

'It won't go in ... what has happened to his skin?'

'His face!' cried the officer. 'There must have been a reaction.' He lifted Quentin's head to see if he was alive.

Quentin's eyes opened, burning with rage. He snatched the syringe from the assistant's hand and stabbed it into the officer's neck, sending him reeling back in terror. He leapt to his feet and grabbed one of the assistants by the throat, crushing his windpipe and squeezing the life from him. The other assistant had turned white with fear. He fumbled wildly for his gun but was too slow. As the first man slumped to the floor, Quentin scooped up a six-inch blade from the table and thrust it up and under his adversary's jaw, deep into his skull. He held it there for a moment, keeping his victim slightly aloft, while he peered into his eyes and watched him depart. The man's arms went limp and Quentin let him drop.

The MSS officer shuffled in the corner. Quentin turned and a shot rang out from the officer's pistol. They both fixed on Quentin's chest and watched as he dislodged the bullet from his rhinoceros hide with a bloodied finger. It fell to earth, striking the stone with a leaden tick. The officer's eyes followed it, staring at the squashed stub of metal, in paralysis, in terror. In resignation. Quentin lunged forth and slashed the man's throat.

He reached down and studied the officer's wristwatch. Amateurs. The Casio read 23:14. He took the pistol and readied it for anyone who might appear, slipped into the corridor and returned to the treatment room. The AG suit was still there. It was *all* still there, strewn over a couple of fraying canvas chairs: boots, gloves, helmet. But no guns.

Quentin grabbed the pack and slid back the cover on the control panel. What was the code? His head swam. He took a moment to think, reaching over to glug water from the jug beside the bed. Of course, it was *that* number. The only number that ever mattered to him. His love's number. He keyed in the six digits and a green indicator lit. Battery good, electrics workable.

A couple of minutes later, after the usual struggle to get into the suit, Quentin crept out of the room in search of an escape route. He switched on the image intensification view in his helmet and selected auditory enhancement to better hear what might be ahead.

The first door was underlined by a slither of yellow light. Night shift? No sounds came from within, so Quentin eased the handle and entered. Empty. There were four CCTV screens showing views of the perimeter. Parts of the outside seemed familiar. He cast around for clues, then spotted it on a pad of headed notepaper: *Tilanqiao*. He was at the same prison.

To his left was another, heavier, door through which he heard footsteps growing louder. The owner appeared in the monitor. Quentin moved to the side, out of view. The door opened and a guard walked in. Quentin struck him in the throat with the side of his hand, sending him down, clutching for breath. He thumped him on the back of the head and knocked him out.

The screens showed that outside was clear. Each of the four monitors corresponded to one of four zones marked on a switchboard to the right. It included controls for lights, gates and other electrically operated systems. He tried the row marked as external lights for Zone 2. The corresponding picture went dark.

Quentin strode out, brought the suit controls into place and lifted off.

Getting out of Shanghai, whether by day or night, would be difficult. Go too far by air and he would be spotted – if the thrusters could manage to go far. The operational range was two kilometres at a hundred metres above mean sea level.

Quentin racked his brains to recall the geography of Shanghai. He needed a safe route to arrive at a public phone in a quiet area, ideally with a motorcycle parked nearby to quell interest in his leather suit. Fat chance. Then he could call Beijing for a pickup. That was incentive enough to get moving.

35

Gathered in the contrived opulence of a private lobby on the first floor of the Great Hall of the People, President Tao Wei invited his comrades to sit. The six men settled into plain leather armchairs arranged in a semi-circle on a plush red carpet and under a vast chandelier, behind them a bird's-eye view mural of the Forbidden City framed by marble columns.

Tao had called the Politburo Standing Committee together to hear his plans for the evolving situation with America and the West. He knew all too well that a united inner circle would be the basis of stability and reassurance within government and throughout the country during these challenging times.

His audience included Marshal Zhou Kai, in the appointment of First Vice Chairman of the CCP Central Military Commission, and Jiang Sheng, Chairman of the Standing Committee of the National People's Congress. The latter led a body of 155 members who constituted the highest organ of state power and the legislature of China.

As always, His Excellency spoke first.

'Comrades, as you know, our pursuit of Chinese harmony continues, as it has done since Chairman Mao reunited a country that had been bled dry by Western invaders. It is unsurprising that with progress comes resistance and denial by those who cannot accept our rightful standing as a mighty and ancient nation.'

Zhou smiled warmly, savouring his leader's words. Mr Jiang wore a neutral expression, a reflection of the respect he was obliged to give and the concern he felt moved to acknowledge about the President's ambitions.

'You have witnessed the arrogance and hegemony that America continues to display, most recently by sending two of her largest battleships to moor in Taiwan,' Tao continued. 'This desperate demonstration serves only to strengthen our resolve to reassert our rightful kinship with Taiwan and enjoy unfettered agency with her. That is why we began setting conditions for re-engagement by managing international transits through our waters.'

He paused and examined his subordinates' reactions. All bar one wore expressions of support, offering solemn nods of acknowledgement. Jiang Sheng looked to the floor. Tao would not allow that.

'Chairman Jiang, do you wish to share your thoughts?'

Jiang made eye contact, then lowered his head in deference. 'No, Your Excellency. I was merely concentrating on your words – waiting for what you were going to say next.'

A shadow passed over Tao's face. 'Hmm. Well, I have conferred with Marshal Zhou on the most appropriate way to … to *guide* the Americans away from affairs that do not concern them.' Another pause, another examination of reactions from the group. 'We will invite them to remove their battleships from our shores. Does anyone wish to discuss this approach?' His laser stare swept across them.

Zhou sat up and glared across at Jiang, daring him to challenge the President, but Jiang spoke up anyway.

'Your Excellency, I suppose the simple question to begin is what if they refuse? I mean, do we have contingencies for negotiation? Perhaps suspending the checks on shipping in the Strait as a show of goodwill?'

Tao erupted into laughter.

'Chairman Jiang, this is why we have taken so long to emerge from the shadows. We will not take our place by *trying* to become strong. We must show that we are already strong. Then the world will understand. I am in no mood to negotiate with America. They will leave or they will face the consequences!'

The men exchanged furtive looks. None dared to speak. Jiang continued, however.

'I understand, Your Excellency. Strength is indeed a virtue. Then, may I ask, should we advise the Elders of your great endeavour?'

'The Elders? No. How will we grow with the chains of antiquity hanging around our necks? They are an anachronism, the legacy of a bygone era,' said Tao.

'They still have influence in the Party, Your Excellency. Their wisdom is respected.'

'And your counsel is noted, Chairman Jiang.'

The speech resumed, with ever greater fervour and less rationality. It was a pointless exercise. The committee was there not to be consulted but to be told. They sensed the mood and read the threat: support the President or be branded a traitor.

One hour later, Tao had finished with them and they knew the Party line. The road ahead was going to get bumpy, but how exactly China would navigate it remained to be seen. That was the preserve of His Excellency and his henchman, in whom all were to place their trust and loyalty.

*   *   *

Marc had just drifted off to sleep when his mobile rang. He reached out an arm, fished around on the bedside locker and picked up. The number was unrecognised. He rolled onto an elbow, half sitting, half lying and prepared for whatever was coming next.

'*Allo?*'

'Talisman? It's Rostam.'

Marc bolted upright. He moved the phone to his other ear to listen better. Quentin's voice was hoarse but he was alive! The abridged protocol suggested that his teammate was short on time. No surprise. But what was this call? A ruse forced by his captors?

'*Allo, mon ami!* It has been a while. Have you enjoyed any good dinners lately? I know you like your food,' Marc said with a forced laugh. It was a coded challenge. 'No dinners' would mean 'I am under duress'.

'Many, thanks. Look, I'm out, in the clear. Need a lift, if it's not too much trouble?'

'*D'accord! Bien sûr.*'

'You should bring some supplies too.'

Marc knew this was a reference to medical supplies. *Merde!* He would have to call in sick and hope no-one came round to check on him. They fixed a RV at the location where Marc had washed the van down to change its colour during the previous mission – the deserted steel mill near the port.

It was a conscious decision to make haste not speed. The thought of another giant round trip starting in the dead of night was crushing; turning up missing something vital was unthinkable. After splashing water on his face, Marc methodically packed the food, water, bandages, painkillers, clothes, antiseptics and rehydrating fluids that Quentin would need. After ten minutes he was on his scooter, duffle bag across his back, making for the Jianguo to get the van and head back to Shanghai. He would alert the others of the seismic news en route.

*   *   *

Greg Pitman arrived in Beijing on a red eye, his BA flight touching down at 06:45 on Tuesday, 6 August. He pulled his black North Face holdall off the baggage carousel, slung it over a shoulder, then threaded through customs to the taxi rank outside. He was staying at the Great Wall Sheraton hotel on Donghuan Beilu in the embassy district, posing as a mature tourist of means.

Bruce had arranged to meet him at noon in a popular eatery crowded with lunchtime diners. He arrived ten minutes early and sat at a small table in the back room, separated from the rest of the restaurant by a beaded curtain, mercifully distant from the continual flow of waiters going to and fro the kitchen, with its ceaselessly banging door and peeling black paint held on by a film of grease. As Bruce's watch flipped to 12:00 the curtain parted and Greg entered. A nod was sufficient.

'I hear moonstone is highly regarded in these parts,' Bruce opened. 'Is that true?'

'I heard it was used in a mosaic of Artemis, no less,' Greg said with a grin. 'At your service.'

'And yours, sir.'

Bruce hardly knew where to begin.

'So, the breaking news is that, right now, Talisman is bringing Rostam back from Shanghai,' he said. 'As you know, he was shot and captured, but survived and has since escaped. That might invite questions about whether you are still required on the team here, but that's above my pay grade and I guess will depend on Quentin's condition.'

A waiter approached, flicking open a notepad to take their order. Greg gestured for Bruce to choose. Two roast duck pancakes with plum sauce and two mineral waters were sufficient for pen to be stowed and menus removed. The waiter headed back to the servery.

'As the only fluent Mandarin speaker, Quentin is vital,' Bruce continued. 'Perhaps you could cover deployed activities in his place, especially now he'll be a wanted man. What do you think?'

Greg tapped an index finger on his nose, pondering.

'Lady M is probably not going to want me heading back having just got here. We are into the endgame now, all things equal, and that usually means a peak of effort, which means more troops required. And, as you say, with Quentin on an arrest list – and more likely under a kill order – he's gotta stay out of sight. Plus, if he's injured then somebody else needs to take his place on active tasks.'

The waiter brought their meals, proving that from chaos can come magnificence. Bruce loaded the first duck pancake and tucked in. 'Wow! Food's better than the décor then. This is delicious.'

Over the next half-hour they continued discussing the operation. Marshal Lin was still holed up in the mountains, while Martine was engaged with Lady Margaret and Ying in crafting the information package cited in Lin's video statement. Lucien was preparing the mission to release the package, which involved all manner of contingency planning and preparations. Greg would definitely be able to assist him with that.

'Who is with Lin now?' he asked, as he puzzled over all the moving parts.

'Nobody. Plan is to visit him every two days. Man short, remember,' Bruce replied.

'I get it, but he's at risk. And in the likely showdown in the Great Hall – if enough people buy this – they'll want to hear from Lin in person. Tao will hope there's little chance of him appearing and that he's fled to save himself. We have the advantage in that regard, and therefore he is a prized asset.'

'You are right, of course. We need to arrange something better for him while the last pieces are put in place,' Bruce said thoughtfully. 'I'm due to see him tomorrow. Do you want to join me?'

'Absolutely. The man could be the lynchpin for this whole operation. By the way, do you guys get access to the news? Tao has put his bulldog on the stage – Zhou issued an ultimatum for the Yanks to get their cruisers out of Taiwan.'

'We figured things would accelerate, although there's no way of telling what the plan might have been regardless. What's the Americans' response?'

Greg stroked his chin. 'Well, cautious. Clever, in fact. They let the Taiwanese do the talking. Their minister of foreign affairs said the vessels were part of a liaison visit, resupplying before rejoining the *Carl Vinson* battlegroup on exercises.'

'Neat. Keeps Tao as the aggressor. Ball's back in his court then.'

Bruce dabbed his lips with a napkin. 'Better get the bill.'

Next day the rendezvous was the tourist site at Shijingshan Gujianqun, west from Beijing's centre, by the Yongding river. The site was famous for its stone monuments depicting ancient demigods and its expansive gardens and ponds.

Bruce arrived first. He strolled through the gardens for a while, taking a few happy snaps before settling on a wooden bench in a picnic area under the trees and enjoying some spring rolls from a hot food stall.

Greg emerged fifty metres from Bruce and stopped to drink from a fountain. When they made eye contact Greg meandered away and was soon out of sight. Bruce set off via a different route, back to his Bultaco scrambler. As soon as Greg appeared, they climbed on, Bruce kickstarted the two-stroke and they sped off along the five kilometre trip to the hut. Scarves were pulled up over their faces and conical rice hats held in place to obscure their Western looks as they rattled along the gravel track into the hills.

The track became stony and then steep, too steep for Bruce's riding skills with a pillion. He slowed and cut the engine.

'This will have to do,' he said.

'How far to go?'

'A mile, give or take.'

Bruce pushed the bike away, deep into nearby bushes. He returned to Greg. 'This way.' They walked off the track and into the cover of trees. Bruce tried to pick out the path through the undergrowth that he had taken when they first brought Lin here.

With about two hundred metres to go, he raised a hand. They crouched down. He produced a scope and scanned the approach to the hut. Woodland adorned with flat-crowned Greeting pines was broken by small clearings, with rocky outcrops among the rambling scrub. A breeze stirred the vegetation and the chirps of tree sparrows echoed around them.

'Okay?' Greg whispered. 'Bruce?'

'The surroundings appear to be clear, but where's Lin?'

He drew back from the eyepiece and handed the scope to Greg.

'Perhaps he's having a nap, or just staying out of sight. Only one way to find out.'

'Hmm, something's not right.'

'Then we move out and round to detect anyone lying in wait.'

They did as Greg suggested, circling to check potential vantage or ambush points, but found nothing.

When they crept into the hut, Bruce's concerns were confirmed.

'Shit! Where the hell is he?' he said.

The cramped space was empty and the few items left to sustain Lin had been taken.

Greg searched for clues among the discarded food wrappers and water containers in vain. 'What happens now?'

'That's anyone's guess. He might have been captured. Maybe he fled, to get out of China and watch whatever unfolds from a safe distance.'

'Fuck it!' Greg said angrily. He flung an empty plastic bottle into the dirt. 'Without Lin, this whole thing can be denied as a fabrication. They'll claim his video statement was forced.'

36

Marc and Quentin arrived back at Marc's studio apartment in Beijing's embassy district in the early hours of Thursday morning. They would have been earlier but Marc had to rest for a couple of hours on the way back. He was shattered.

It was against protocol for Quentin to stay with him, but his accommodation was under police investigation. With no immediate alternative, Marc set Quentin to recover from his ordeal properly. He had provided sachets of electrolyte rich fluids in lieu of a drip during the drive back. Quentin's epidermis had still been too tough to take a needle.

By 10 a.m. both had got some sleep and were ready for breakfast. Marc busied himself setting places and serving cereal, eggs and toast in the sitting area. He turned on the TV across the room.

'What the hell?' he exclaimed.

The China Central TV news channel was relaying images of the USS *Arkansas* and USS *Shiloh* on fire and partly sunk.

'What is he saying?' he asked Quentin, who was lying on the sofa, eyes riveted to the screen. Marc turned the volume up.

'Er … response to US aggression … Chinese sovereign territory ... So they've come out and said it then.'

'What else? Keep going.'

'Oh it's more of … you know, the obvious. But how did they do it? Those ships have all sorts of capabilities, including anti-submarine warfare.'

'How many deaths?' Marc asked.

Quentin paused to hear more commentary from a passionately nationalist newsreader.

'Hmm, nothing being said on that. Very wise. But look at it, there will be hundreds at least, just from the blasts.'

The USS *Arkansas* had listed heavily at its moorings and was billowing smoke. Munitions were detonating in one of the ship's magazines, flames spewing round bulkheads as if formed of pure liquid. Scores of men flailed in the water, some wreathed in burning fuel.

'*Mon Dieu!* This is war.'

They continued to watch the propaganda, finally remembering to tuck into the food. Marc apologised for the eggs going cold, but Quentin dismissed the apology. 'Hardly your doing, old boy!'

'Anyway, you look better,' said Marc. 'Your pupils are normal now, no pinpoints. Skin has eased too.'

'Well, that's something. Interesting though. Last time I was in this state it took years to leave me. Although can't say as I like sunlight much right now. Not as bad as before, mind you.'

BEAUMONT

'It was telling that you disabled the guard in the control room.'

'Meaning?'

'You didn't kill him.'

'Ah, didn't need to. Didn't *wish* to. Thinking rationally through the mist – is that what you're getting at?'

'*Oui.*'

'You mean can I be trusted on the operation now? I understand ... I think the answer is yes.'

That evening the whole group gathered in the basement of the Jianguo hotel for a VTC with Beaumont. It was against good practice, but they accepted the risk since it would be the last full gathering before the final phase of the operation.

The VTC connected and Lady Margaret appeared, looking drawn, dark circles under her eyes. Behind her to one side sat Ying. She took a moment to compose herself, lightly smoothing a hand over her hair.

'Firstly, Quentin, thanks be to God for your safe return! I look forward to hearing the full details of your escape when you are all safely home.'

'I think it's a case of thanks be to Quentin, my lady. And I might leave some details to the imagination,' Quentin replied with a snort of laughter. 'But thank you. I am pleased to be back and feeling recovered.'

She peered back from the Beaumont ops room, as if trying to reassure herself that he really was recovered.

'That is truly good news. Of course we will have to play you differently, now that you are a most wanted man. You are vital to the mission – not least as our only Mandarin speaker. To my mind that fits a covert role alongside Marc providing operational support. If you concur.'

'Understood, my lady. And I have done as much before. I have no problem with staying out of sight.'

'Next, the bad news: Marshal Lin,' she continued. A murmur of frustration came from the group. 'Quite … As you know, we intended to use the video statement to bolster the information pack – words from the horse's mouth to give credibility to the message and its contents. But we also wanted Lin available in person in case live witnesses were called to substantiate the claims. That is now impossible. We will have to proceed with the information pack and video and hope for the best.'

'What else can we do? If Tao has attacked American warships, the fuse is lit on this whole crisis,' said Quentin.

'That is true, yet we should reflect that our mission has met the intended schedule. Next Thursday is the biannual session of the National People's Congress. If we can succeed at releasing the package at 16:00 on Wednesday, it will allow time to reach and be read by recipients, but come too late for a counter campaign to be run by Tao.'

She coughed and took a sip of water. 'Excuse me.' The glass was carefully set down. 'Ying has suggested that he be available by VTC in case events run in our favour and the assembly seeks to corroborate claims against the President by calling witnesses while in session.'

'But how will he patch in to the Great Hall?' Bruce asked.

'Ying has the contact details. He knows how it works.'

Ying raised an A4 size printout. Bruce guessed it was a staff list or services directory recovered from their raid on the Directorate of Urban Planning in Shanghai.

'We have email addresses for the Standing Committee of the National People's Congress. Ying can advise on where to find terminals to access accounts, so that the information can be distributed from inside the intranet, bypassing firewalls and external server data limits. You should have received the information now.'

Martine gave a thumbs up to the camera. 'We have it. Thank you.'

'Lucien, you will be mission lead on comms during the CCP session.' Lucien raised a hand in acknowledgement.

'Bruce, Martine and Greg will therefore be on point, firstly to access the network and distribute the information package, then to deploy on the ground near the Great Hall to provide a comms link and be ready to act if Lin or any other significant players appear, or if anyone tries to scupper proceedings.' She paused for her directions to be absorbed. 'Our best hope is that it all comes out in session. We need a genie that cannot be put back in its bottle. Questions?'

Three hands went up.

'Greg.'

'My lady, have you any news about what the Americans will do next, following the attacks on their ships?'

'The basics are fairly consistent. Both CNN and the BBC World Service report that the *Carl Vinson* battlegroup is heading towards the Taiwan Strait. What I noticed from some brief aerial footage was how dispersed were the ships. Very far apart.'

'Is that for the reason I think?' Bruce interjected. 'To mitigate a tactical nuclear strike?'

'It would fit the scenario,' said Greg. 'The Chinese fleet as currently deployed would be greatly overmatched by the Americans. If Tao wants to try for a knock-out blow, then he would probably use a mini-nuke. However, tactical nukes will destroy remarkably few vessels in blue waters if they are well separated, although separation brings other complications, such as manoeuvre, comms and logistics. The biggie is that it fits the Phoenix playbook: if Tao attacks, then the US could well retaliate with a nuclear strike, but it would be limited.'

'And give Tao the green light for a total launch,' said Bruce.

'Exactly. And it gets worse. For a carrier group like that, they are effectively already there. The five hundred kilometres from their holding position is to the middle of the Strait. They could reach it in half a day.'

'Meaning?'

'Meaning they had better take their time or we will be out of time. This could all be over in less than twenty-four hours!'

Her ladyship leaned into the camera, motioning her hand downwards. Calm.

'I sense that we will be afforded the time we need. We must be resolute and follow the path that is set before us.'

The VTC ended.

Lady Margaret sat back in her chair for a moment's silent contemplation. They couldn't force the matter. Distributing the material immediately would risk it being quashed before the six-monthly session of the CCP. There would be no chance of calling a special session a few days early either. Never mind how on earth one might invoke the authority to do so, the logistics of getting thousands of delegates in place sooner prohibited it. Finally, there was the small matter of accessing the intranet to send the package.

She could feel the stakes rising for her team as if it infected her very skin. Bruce had nearly been lost to the Shanghai police but kept his head, followed the plan, and enabled his own rescue. Quentin was nearly lost to God in a firefight, but the indestructible man somehow found a way back. They had won Marshal Lin's compliance but not his confidence. Would they see this through before President Tao pushed the button? And who would be standing at the end to see it done?

Of them all – and she felt conflicted about loving them all because deep down it was a mother's love – it was Bruce that cut her inside. He was his mother's son, doing what he was born to do. Still, she felt a stab of dread at the thought of him coming to grief. She wouldn't be able to forgive herself if that happened.

Ying whispered at her back. 'Would you care for some tea?' It brought her back to her senses.

'Thank you, Ying. Some Chinese white tea would be most welcome, if you will join me?'

He stood, gave a small bow and left the room, his footsteps shuffling away upstairs.

It was Lady Margaret's special insight that had steadied the team. Her overwhelming instinct was to go with the plan that was unfolding. She intuited that the Americans were moving, but they would also take every opportunity to slow the escalation. She sensed that they too were betting on the situation coming to a head in the Great Hall of the People. All of China saw what had happened in Taiwan, what their leader was capable of. The hope was that he would be challenged. But he had to be deposed too. Surviving a challenge would make Tao even stronger, even more intimidating to his subordinates.

She stood, tidied the papers on her desk and thought about her team returning to their preparations, readying for the first recce of an access point from which to send the golden email.

Through the weekend and into the start of the following week, the Americans did what the Architects' Club and the world had hoped for. They stalled some more.

The USS *Carl Vinson* battlegroup split into two parts. The carrier led half the force to the east, midway between Okinawa and Taiwan. The consensus was that this was to stay out of range of anti-ship missiles. But it also bought time and complicated the picture – seemingly to keep Tao guessing.

The other half of the carrier group stopped three hundred kilometres from the Strait, in a close holding position. And there it was, a stand-off between two global powers with chests puffed and stares locked. The world's press had reported the crisis somewhat phlegmatically until the cruisers went down. Now it was all Cuba 1962. And it was. But Cuba ended in negotiation and Tao was all about annihilation.

There was another round of security inspections at the embassies. It reached the German Embassy on Wednesday. Email day. In the temporary checkpoint set up in a large gazebo across the street from the embassy building, Martine sat on a hard plastic chair to face her inquisitor over the wooden trestle table. There must have been ten such stations. A strong wind had taken hold, flapping the white canvas sides of the gazebo, its metal frame squeaking as dozens of sandbags struggled to hold it down. Traffic raced by, adding noise and fumes.

Visas were checked and more photos taken. They were being openly checked against a database on MSS officers' laptops. Martine called her itinerary to mind, ready to account for the past week in detail. She thanked God that the Club's collective attention to tradecraft, in its every mundane, obsessive detail, was an endemic part of the culture. She showed off her blonde hair and striking looks. The liberal use of scarves, hats and sunglasses meant no such identity would have been spotted whenever she was out in public on a task.

She glanced at her watch. It was a quarter to two.

'Have somewhere to go?' The officer said.

'*Ja*. In fact, I have.'

'And where is that?'

'Work.'

After ten minutes of hapless questions sneered from behind her open passport, she was allowed to go. The desperation to catch Quentin could almost be tasted in the air, mingling with the smoke-infused breath and perspiration emanating from the official.

But she did have somewhere to go, and by three o'clock she was on her way out of the embassy, heading to rendezvous with Bruce and Greg.

37

The Standing Committee of the National People's Congress comprised 155 people. It was one of many distribution groups hosted on the email server of the Beijing Administrative Area's intranet. As Ying had explained, the intranet was rapidly becoming the most popular means for party and government officials to communicate within a secure local digital environment. The feature of value to the Club was that the intranet also hosted all manner of humdrum functions, such as facilities management, transport and security. Greg and Marc had reconnoitred security points in remote or infrequently used locations that Ying estimated would have the same terminals and intranet access as were used by officials in government offices.

By the time Martine arrived at the Jianguo hotel to meet the others, the game was already over. Greg unlocked the metal basement door and she slipped quietly in. Marc and Bruce were huddled over the laptop.

'What's up, guys? Are we good?' she asked. 'Just us for now, is it?'

Greg shook his head, then nodded. 'We are not good, and yes it's just us for now. Lucien and Quentin are making their preparations at Lucien's place.'

'So why not good?'

Greg motioned a hand to invite Marc to explain.

'We placed hidden cameras at four locations to keep watch over the potential targets,' he said, pointing to the camera views which were clustered in a two-by-two grid on the screen. 'See here and here – these sites are PLA Guard warehouses, basically stockpiles for the army. They are rarely visited, just for the occasional equipment check, turnaround, etcetera.'

'So, what's with all the traffic?' Martine said.

'It looks like they're using it for parking coaches and staff cars for NPC members. We should be pleased there'll be a good turnout tomorrow, I guess, which is very unusual. Normally only the five-yearly Party Congress gets a full house. It helps our mission if the Party membership wants answers for what's happening with the US and Taiwan. But it means today's plan is a no-go.'

'What about this one?' she said, pointing to the image of a lone security officer sat in his hut behind closed chain-link gates. 'Is that a computer monitor?'

'Can you zoom in?' Greg asked.

They leaned in as Marc tapped the keys.

'There – looks like he's logged on,' said Greg, squinting to confirm that the screen was lit. 'If it's a habit among security at that location it could make our task easier.'

BEAUMONT

'I get it,' Marc said. 'We just don't need another fleet of buses showing up there too, or anything else unexpected.'

'We'd better keep Beaumont informed. The package will have to go out during the early hours of tomorrow morning,' Greg continued.

'That will cut it very fine,' said Martine. 'Many might not even get to their emails before the conference.'

'Not so sure,' said Bruce. 'It's a fear culture, remember. I would expect folk to check their emails in case of last minute changes. We just need enough people to open it to start the snowball.'

At 03:00 everyone was in position. Lucien was observing proceedings from the Jianguo hotel basement. Marc and Quentin had dropped Martine and Bruce near the fence line of the target site. Next was Greg, out of the van as if on a parachute jump, disappearing into the foliage before Quentin had even closed the door after him. Marc then drove on to a covert position about half a mile away.

The site was a disused airfield, its hangars believed to be used as storage facilities. It lay near to the northeastern expressway, about ten kilometres from central Beijing. The revised plan had Greg covering as lookout and sniper if things got ugly. But his first task was to construct a diversion, so any unexpected visitors would be sent away to enter via the other entrance, a three-kilometre detour to the far side of the airfield. He set up the diversion signs and mini barrier at the junction with the main road, which was out of sight from the security hut. Then he moved into cover among the undergrowth, with an elevated view of the hut which was about one hundred metres away. It was a cramped cubicle with visibility of the road into the site, just big enough for two people and with sliding windows on three sides.

What had everyone on tenterhooks was that the security hut was manned but the gates were closed, inside which was also a vehicle barrier. Since it seemed nothing was expected to arrive, why man it? Marc had logged the duty shift timings. The guard changed every four hours, leaving them three hours clear, in theory.

Lost in the black expanse of open ground bordering the airfield, Bruce and Martine scanned the fence line. The night was still, the clouds above them hardly moving.

'Team One and Two. Ready,' Bruce whispered into his mic.

'Team Three. In position. Diversion set,' came Greg.

Bruce and Martine paused for a few minutes, watching for observers, before scaling the fence and heading in. No nifty AG suits tonight. They wore balaclavas and head cams and were on radio comms so that Quentin could do his magic and make sense of the Chinese characters on the email system.

Bruce radioed again. 'Team Three, how are we looking for an approach?'

'It's a go, assuming the guard stays put. Currently hunched over a newspaper,' Greg responded.

'Roger. Out.'

The pair made a dash for the hut, staying in the blind spot of its back wall. Crouching low against the weathered prefab side, Martine retrieved the first piece of equipment from her backpack. She uncoiled the plastic tube from around a compressed gas bottle and fed it into an air vent near the floor. She looked to Bruce and gave a curt nod, her eyes reflecting the glow of light escaping from the hut. Then she opened the valve.

They flinched as the gas hissed before becoming a quiet flow when the tap was opened wider. Bruce timed the flow of halothane into the hut. After thirty seconds he clicked his radio Pressel switch three times, asking Greg for a situation update.

'Keep going, Team Two. A few more seconds, if the supply will last,' said Greg. 'He's starting to lean forward onto his desk. Stand by.' Another ten seconds went by. Martine looked at Bruce and shook her head as the gas flow weakened. 'Oops. He's out. Flat on his desk. Clear to move.'

Martine let out a sigh, wiped the condensation that had formed around the bottle and stuffed it back into her bag. They sped round to the door and entered, staying low, with the door open so that they did not succumb to the gas.

'Keep that screen unlocked while I get the gear out,' said Bruce.

Martine shifted the mouse and peered at the Chinese version of Hotmail, while Bruce produced an external hard drive, battery pack and decryptor. He plugged into a port on the rear of the base unit.

'Ready.'

Martine adjusted her headcam. 'Zero, this is Team One. You on?'

'Roger. And I have a good view of the screen,' said Quentin from the van.

He guided Martine through the mouse moves and clicks needed to open a new mail and select the distribution list for the correct standing committee. She started to attach the package of four pdfs and two videos comprising the Phoenix Programme Directive; Appendix D: *The People's Medicine*; the Phoenix bunkers' occupancy list; a transcript and video of President Tao's conversation with Marshal Zhou, and Marshal Lin's video-recorded statement. It would be slow.

They hit a glitch. When Martine went to upload the attachments a password request popped up.

'*Scheisse!*'

'It's okay,' said Quentin. 'Team Two, you need to connect the decryptor.'

'One mo. Got a better idea,' said Bruce. He rifled through the paperwork on the desk top, then carefully lifted the guard's arm to free a notebook, which he flicked through. It did not contain what he was hoping for. He got down on all fours, then lay flat on his back on the floor to inspect the underside of the desk.

'*Was tust du?*' cried Martine.

'Yes, what's going on, Team Two?' Quentin said.

Bruce reached up, peeled the Post-It away and held it in front of his camera. 'What does this look like, Zero?' he asked Quentin.

'Good work. Could be the password. Try it.'

Martine keyed in the characters, which was still a complex procedure, even with Quentin spelling out every move from root shapes.

'*Ja, fantastisch!*'

They were in.

The next and final heart-stopping moment arrived.

SEND.

The progress bar crawled along at the bottom of the screen. Bruce looked to Martine, remembering their op stealing the Phoenix bunkers' list in Shanghai and how long that transfer took. And that was just a text document. They held their breath.

Bruce kept watching, fearing that a watched computer never delivers. When it reached ten percent he said, 'Does this mean the file sizes are okay? It's just about transfer rate now?'

Marc's voice sounded in his ear. 'Yes, it looks like that.'

'Just gotta sit it out then. Going to be a while,' said Bruce.

'I estimate another eight minutes.'

Bruce and Martine instantly turned to the guard. His breathing was slow and deep. Martine quietly slid a hand inside her pack and brought out a box similar to a spectacles case. Upon opening, it contained a syringe and small bottle of chemicals. She pushed the syringe through the lid and drew a measure of solution.

'Just in case,' she whispered to Bruce.

Another couple of minutes went by. The guard suddenly moved his hand. His breathing paused, then he grunted and let out a long snore. Martine was poised to inject him in the thigh, but he resumed deep, regular breathing.

'What's the status, Team Two?' came Marc's voice.

Bruce realised he'd been so focused on the guard he had forgotten to monitor the email delivery progress. He looked up. The bar read a hundred percent. A few seconds later the email had gone. Quentin watched the pop-up confirming transmission.

'That's it! Message sent. Well done, team. Now get the hell out.'

'Clean exfil, Two,' said Martine to Bruce, her eyes fixed on him for a second.

Bruce opened the door wider to allow more air in and they checked everything was in place: the Post-It, papers and notebook, mouse, newspaper. Then their own items were gathered and stowed.

Bruce and Martine slipped out of the hut leaving the security officer to his slumbers, closing the door and retracing their steps to the fence. On the other side awaited the same open field, beyond which Marc's van appeared. They crossed, climbed aboard and sat back, relieved. Ecstatic.

'Job done!' said Bruce. 'Flippin' awesome.' He puffed out a great breath of relief.

Martine slapped him on the thigh. 'That was acceptable!' she said with wry grin.

Marc pulled away slowly, taking his time, keeping it all calm and controlled. 'Just got to collect Greg,' he said, 'and all will have gone off without a hitch.'

They had done it! Package away without detection. One hundred and fifty-five of the most senior officials in the Chinese government had access to a new truth. Their lives would now be shaped by a new reality.

Bruce grasped Martine's hand, gave it a light squeeze, a celebratory shake. She pulled her balaclava off and returned a beaming smile.

Suddenly Greg's voice came across their earpieces.

'Team Three. Heading RV Wolf. Got company.'

Bruce sat up and moved forward to peer out of the windscreen. Up ahead an army jeep was stopped at the diversion sign, its headlights shining at the bogus barricade, illuminating spots of drizzle that had started to fall. A soldier climbed out and strutted back and forth, breaking the beam of the headlights, walkie-talkie in hand.

Marc passed by, heading for a fallback pickup point three hundred metres further on. As they reached it, Greg stepped out from behind some trees. Bruce opened the side door and he clambered in.

'Bollocks! Last thing we needed,' he said.

Quentin rubbed his hands together, upbeat. 'Look at it this way. They'll probably radio the hut or head down to the gate to find out what's going on. It will look like he fell asleep. He will be an idiot for not spotting someone putting up signs on his patch.'

Greg tutted. 'And that's the point. He might look like a twat, but what if they suspect something serious – and they are a suspicious lot over here. Worst of all, what if the guard checks his emails and sees something big has been sent. What then? Could he recall the email?'

'Don't think so. We've certainly ruined that boy's life, no doubt about it, when they see which email account it came from. My guess is it's too late for anyone to stop it now. Someone will already have seen it in their inbox. This culture? I would bet on it.'

'Guess the only real downside then, is that Marc has to ditch another van,' Bruce said. Laughter broke out. Even Greg conceded to hope, letting the tension of the night begin to ebb away.

38

When James Tavener made the journey east and realised the Salève was a mountain ridge, not a town, he was not disappointed. Something felt right, harmonious even. He decided to use the apparent setback as an opportunity to get a bird's eye view of the surrounding area. Disguised under a floppy grey hairpiece, flat cap, dark-rimmed round glasses and a few days' stubble, he pulled up in the little blue Renault near the Col de Pitons, the highest point. At over 1300 metres it was a popular spot with panoramic views. The gravel car park was busy, with families milling around taking photos and enjoying packed lunches.

Tavener reached for his binos and map and made for a vantage point away from the gaggle, looking northwest. There, barely one kilometre below him, was the village of Beaumont. Beyond it lay similar small hamlets, such as Présilly, Feigères and Neydens. In the opposite direction was Le Sappey.

He focused the binoculars and systematically scanned the buildings at each location. The undulating terrain obscured some areas from view, but having studied the various architectures around the centre of each settlement, usually marked by a church, Tavener identified three prominent residences of interest: two in Le Sappey and one in Beaumont. The iconic chateaux stood head and shoulders above other properties in their respective areas.

Asking around who lived where was not an option – it was literally too close to home – so he would move in and observe each house, waiting to see a familiar face. With his plan set, James Tavener left to buy supplies and find a room to rent for his operating base.

The logic of killing two birds with one stone meant that he reached the chateau at Beaumont last. He trekked the five kilometres from Saint-Blaise on foot, backpack over a shoulder, to hide in a copse overlooking Lucien Martell's family home. There he sat, nursing his Thermos of tea, chomping on a baguette filled with Comté and quince jelly, and rubbing a sore ankle that had become inflamed by the walk.

Eventually he got what he had been waiting for. But it wasn't her ladyship who emerged from the house. The man who appeared from a side door for a stroll around the grounds was of Far Eastern appearance. Tavener felt a rush of panic. The Chinese, *here*?

He checked about him, ditched his tea and hurriedly stuffed his belongings into the rucksack. If it was a trap then the worst thing to do would be to bolt. As he looked around he saw and heard no more than the meadow grass rolling with the breeze and the rustle of leaves. Minutes passed before he considered another explanation for the presence of a Chinese man. A single individual. The Hong

Kong file. The sting at the Breidenbacher. When the virus was released, it failed. How could anyone have got on to him? Stopped that? Could this be the escaped official from the Hulunbuir lab, under *her* protection?

He lifted the binos again and examined the man's demeanour. Which was he, MSS or fugitive? His expression, the carefree pleasure of taking in the air without so much as a glance around his environment, suggested to Tavener that he was no spy. He was green. This was the official. This was the place. Beaumont.

* * *

It was Thursday 15 August. The day of the National People's Congress had arrived. In Beijing the Club team members woke early, turning on television sets in their apartments to monitor coverage of the build-up at the Great Hall of the People. Crowds were already gathering around Tiananmen, a mix of native Chinese and tourists from around the world. It was seven o'clock.

As Bruce chomped a bowl of muesli, he spotted Martine's blonde head among a long queue of press waiting to have their ID checked before entering the building. The clock was really ticking now as one by one the team would play their final cards to complete the operation. It was only a matter of time before Martine's unforgettable looks would have someone asking why an administrator at the German Embassy had turned up as press at the Party conference. This was not the place to be risking disguises.

By eight o'clock he was ready to go. He took one last look round the apartment then picked up his baseball cap and checked that the camera was secure where Marc had fitted it in the logo. He plugged a wireless earpiece as far into his ear canal as he dared to push it. The mini radio transceiver was incorporated into a Walkman containing a tape of Pink Floyd's *Wish You Were Here*. Fingers crossed the authorities wouldn't get the joke.

The only items available to them for this op were hidden cameras and wireless comms. There was no place for weapons, or anything that could be picked up in a spot search by any of the thousands of police and security service personnel now swarming the centre of the capital. He stepped outside, closed the door behind him and set off for Tiananmen Square.

Lucien, Quentin and Marc were operating from the van. The security operation around the conference meant they were forced to stay well back, this time on the edge of Ritan Park in the embassy district, which was ignored by the Chinese authorities during such an important national event.

The mood in the van was sombre. They had all seen enough missions to know how easily things can implode. Months, even years of painstaking work could turn to dust in a heartbeat. A single missed step, failed message, unpredicted move, and when the pivotal moment arrived the situation could crumble.

'We're all packed up then?' said Quentin.

'*Oui*. No going back now. Everything that we are not using today is boxed and ready for my contact at the Jianguo to ship, when I say,' Marc replied.

'Your contact, whoever he is, is worth his weight in gold. How does he avoid customs?'

'Same way you did. Same way everyone does, follow the contraband route. Pay other trustworthy people and it goes down as clothes for the poor of Vietnam or motorcycle parts for dealerships in Seoul. That's where it's going anyway. Into more safe hands, then back to Europe.'

The radio crackled with a first contact from Tiananmen.

'Zero, Team One. I'm in. Radio check, over,' Martine whispered from whatever private spot she could have found. They guessed in the ladies' room.

Lucien responded. 'Okay, over.'

'One. Out.'

He checked the time on his Breitling. 09:30.

Bruce and Greg followed suit with radio checks from their positions on opposite sides of the square. Kick-off was 10:00.

Bruce stood in the back line of a crowd about six deep on the opposite side of Tiananmen from the Great Hall of the People. He wanted to blend in, be absorbed by the blob, which meant living with the din of cat chatter as a hundred different languages squabbled to be heard over each other. The aroma of takeaway coffee and sweet breakfast pastries from street vendors mingled with body odour and cheap aftershave. A gust of wind swept through the square, lifting and billowing towering red banners that draped from the walls of the Great Hall. Bruce felt the hairs on the back of his neck stand up, a sense of premonition swirling in the breeze.

He took a sip of water and looked on as a guard of honour formed up in the middle of the square. At 09:55 the pomp climaxed as the Central Military Band of the PLA struck up and the presidential motorcade swung into view. Bruce sharpened his focus, his pulse quickening.

The weather was glorious, and President Tao appeared to savour the attention, waving like royalty from the open roof of his personal limousine. Onlookers cheered, cameras flashed, and the line of police, arms linked, swayed with the weight of the crowd.

The President descended from the car like a conquering Roman emperor from a golden chariot. He swept up the steps to the grand entrance, turned and paused for a final acknowledgement of the crowd and world media before entering the Great Hall of the People.

Inside, Martine was taken aback by the scale of the place, despite having prior knowledge from their research and planning. The auditorium was full. That meant over three thousand CCP members were seated on each of the lower floor levels and the balcony, plus two and a half thousand in the gallery. On the dais were the 155 members of the Standing Committee of the National People's Congress. The press corps was set up at the rear of the lower floor, left of the central aisle.

Everyone rose to their feet as the President entered the hall followed by the senior officials of the Politburo Standing Committee. That was Martine's cue to thread her way to the aisle along which Tao had entered and station herself on the edge of a section of reporters. This, she hoped, would be the route taken by any other special entrants who needed an easy way through the crowd. She fitted a standard earphone into her other ear for a live translation of proceedings, courtesy of CNN.

The President reached the stage and signalled to the membership. All took their seats and the session was underway. The first hour was taken up with a succession of formalities. Such large organs of state as the Chinese Communist Party and National People's Congress inevitably involved an ebb and flow of changing appointments, she supposed.

At last Tao walked to the podium to make his address, his large frame towering over the party members behind him. He paused and scanned the audience before speaking.

'Comrades, life in China has never been better,' he began.

Martine listened as he catalogued the advances achieved under his rule: how many people had been lifted from poverty, how trade had improved and accordingly the improvement in China's role in the world and in Asia in particular. Then he turned to matters of national strength and sovereignty, to America and Taiwan. Martine lifted a hand to rub her nose. 'Here we go,' she muttered into the wrist mic, imagining Lucien, Quentin and Marc also tuned into international news coverage.

'Now the world knows that we will act to respect our territorial integrity!' came the words booming over the auditorium.

Keep going, thought Martine. Then what? Say it …

But what they wanted never came. The President skilfully generalised the topic, raising specifics into abstractions. With a full ten thousand people present, of whom those sat behind Tao had been sent the golden email and were waiting to hear whether World War III was coming, President Tao postulated that the near future was in America's hands. He and China would never be the aggressor, only the honourable defender of its rights.

'… remember, we built the Great Wall to keep our enemies out. Not to contain them, nor to invade!'

The delegates rose to their feet and gave a standing ovation that lasted a full five minutes.

Quentin radioed Martine. 'Team One, what's the reaction among the NPC Standing Committee members? What is Jiang Sheng doing?'

'Team One. Nothing,' she said with a sigh.

On the dais, Martine picked out the slim, well-groomed figure of the Chairman of the Standing Committee of the National People's Congress. He would have received the email. But did he open it? Did anyone ask him about it? *Surely*. It was explosive. Perhaps he had raised it with the President before the conference, only to be put down? Was the fear culture so powerful that the people's representatives would rather risk oblivion and trust to vain hope than challenge it?

On a vast screen behind the stage an overhead projection of Chinese characters and English appeared: LUNCH.

The audience began to disperse. Martine stood on tip toe, trying to watch the stage as reporters and delegates jostled to head out. She watched for a few more moments, looking around and over heads as people filed past her. Jiang Sheng reappeared, making his way through the cluster of officials around the President.

'Hold on,' Martine resumed into her wrist mic. 'Jiang appears to be having a word in the President's ear.'

The contact lasted only a few seconds, ending with the President's brusque gesticulations sending Jiang on his way.

Martine ducked down and pretended to search in her bag as a mass of reporters continued to tramp by. She retrieved a tissue and held it over her nose while she spoke.

'*Scheisse*. Doesn't look good. I am guessing Jiang just asked the Pres if he's going to talk about what happens next with Taiwan and the Americans. It was a bit far for me to sense, but the aura around his head seemed to be on fire – whatever he said was really important to him. It *must* be about the conflict. But Tao shut him down.' She glanced up to make sure nobody was observing her.

'Roger,' said Quentin. 'Not looking good. Not one bit.'

She blew her nose then kept the tissue in front of her face. 'Can we do something when they reassemble?' she asked, a note of desperation creeping into her voice. 'Such as using the recording of Tao's voice to trigger *Dēnglóng*?'

'The army won't buy that,' Lucien replied. 'They'll wonder why he would do such a thing when he's on stage leading the assembly. No. We need someone to spill the beans.'

'Or get Ying on the VTC, on the big screen? He can say something. Can we do that?'

'No, Marc can't control their VTC. They must dial out, speaking of which, have you got the envelope?'

'*Ja*, but for what now?' Martine let her hands fall in frustration.

Lucien's tone was rising too. 'They have to help themselves and kick this off. Jiang, or someone, must act, say something, call witnesses. Won't be another chance. They're acting like a bunch of frightened sheep!'

She brought the wrist mic back up to speak. 'They're gonna be dead sheep soon. Us too.'

39

'Check in, Two and Three,' Lucien ordered.

Bruce responded first. 'Team Two. Nothing. Out.'

Then Greg. 'Team Three. A vehicle has stopped on the corner of East Side and Qianmen. Pulled up onto the pavement. Over.'

'Zero. Why significant? Over.'

'Three. It's a black S-Class Mercedes. Darkened windows. Not subtle. Call it instinct. Will monitor. Over.'

'Zero. Roger. Out.'

Greg saw the delegates who were outside smoking extinguish their cigarettes in the prescribed bins and file back inside.

Martine returned to her place as the auditorium refilled for the afternoon session. The screen above the stage had changed from LUNCH to show the remainder of the conference timetable: reports from the regions and awards. She smirked. Doubtless the reports would confirm the success of the President's directions on political reform, economic growth and social developments. Then the conference would, presumably, leave on a high note, after a wealth of awards and titles were conferred on anointed sons of the regime. No daughters, just sons, she bet.

After ten minutes, the President walked onto the dais and bid the assembly to take their seats.

Then she could see it. The first seat at the front of the NPC Standing Committee block was empty.

Martine brought her hand up, lightly pinching the bridge of her nose between thumb and forefinger. 'Team One. Something's up. Eyes on targets, guys,' she whispered.

She surveyed the stage, then casually scanned around the auditorium checking for anything out of the ordinary. Something was coming. She could feel it.

The President initiated the formalities with consummate stage management and eye contact to all quarters of the audience, high and low. It was the start of another commanding performance. When his sweep of visual engagement finally ranged widely enough to his left he noticed the empty seat. Jiang Sheng's empty seat.

He stopped mid-sentence, staring at the chair. From his mouth came nothing but a void of silence, peppered with mutterings of hesitation, contrasting with the eloquence of just moments before. Martine held her breath. The spell had been broken. The President looked about the stage, then turned to the auditorium floor, squinting against the stage lights towards the doors at the back. Was he hoping to find Jiang dutifully returning to his seat? or to escape?

The quiet was absolute, the atmosphere thick with conspiracy. Slowly, the audience allowed itself to stir. A cough echoed from high in the gallery, the rustle of paper came from the balcony. A murmur started to roll through the space.

Outside, Bruce pushed back against the man next to him as the crowd swayed. His voice broke over the net.

'Team Two. Large number of military vehicles entering the square. They're shifting! Estimate fifty troop carriers. Maybe more. Still coming into view.'

'Roger that. On your toes, people,' came Lucien.

'If this is what I think it is, I'll try to get inside,' said Bruce. 'Back up, Team One.'

'No stupid risks, Two.'

Bruce squeezed his way to the front, stopping at the linked arms of police officers glaring back at the crowd. Fifty metres ahead the troop trucks squealed to a halt and their tailgates began slamming open, with platoons of armed soldiers jumping down. An officer with a loud hailer led the way towards the Great Hall and began shouting in Mandarin.

'Are you seeing this through my cam?' Bruce radioed.

'Bugger me!' said Quentin. 'It's *Dēnglóng*! They've called it. The military are taking control of parliament.'

Such an event was unprecedented in China's post-revolution history. The uncertainty and confusion could be seen in the faces of the police, trying to hold back the crowd while turning to see what was happening behind them as the military arrived. After a few seconds the crowd surged and their line broke. The mob began to spill past them under its own momentum.

Bruce pressed forward to stay at the front of the advancing mass. As the troops climbed the steps towards another line of police ranged in front of the entrance, the police commander yelled an order. The officers raised their weapons to stop the advancing soldiers.

Bruce screamed and pushed forward, as if fleeing into the building. Those around him instinctively reacted and within seconds hundreds were yelling in panic and rushing for cover, past the soldiers and up the steps. The police line disintegrated and Bruce broke into the lobby, concealed among the hysterical mass.

As the crowd flowed through the entrance hall and into the auditorium, police grabbed them, lashing out with batons and wrestling them to the ground. Bruce dodged his way through, burying himself within the knot of bodies. In the commotion he fell to the floor. He covered his head, holding his cap in place, then crawled into a row, past the legs of delegates trying to move back from the intruding crowd. When he had distanced himself from the throng, he stood up to find suited Party members looking him up and down. One grabbed him and tried to push him back into the aisle. Into the hands of the police, Bruce assumed. But it was too late for that.

Behind them, soldiers burst into the hall. Their commander led the way, raising his loudhailer and speaking in Mandarin.

Quentin sounded in Bruce's earpiece. 'He's announcing martial law under the *Dēnglóng* protocol, same as he did outside.'

Bruce removed his baseball cap and shuffled towards the aisle, pretending to comply with the Party member who had seized him. The man let go. Bruce moved back along the row and stopped on the edge of the aisle.

The officer in charge lowered his loud hailer. Nobody spoke. When his men had taken positions around the hall he went to the foot of the stage and waited.

President Tao's face was twisted in conflict between revulsion and terror. He cast about him, looking for salvation. At his left, out of the stage wings, Jiang Sheng appeared.

'What is this!' the President spat at him. 'Explain this … this travesty!'

Bruce watched, transfixed, as Jiang Sheng continued to approach the President, upright, arms at his sides, expression neutral, unintimidated. *Unintimidated. Because you got the place locked down. Because you're gonna blow the lid on this thing.*

Martine looked over the shoulders of reporters to see their live-feed monitors. The nearest she recognised immediately: RTL. To her right, ABC News. At left, RAI of Italy. The small screens showed that everything was going out to the world live. Police officers started grabbing at cameras and reaching to pull plugs and dismantle equipment. They were met with a flurry of rifle butts and shoulder barges. The shocked news teams recoiled at the ugly confrontation. But as quickly as it began, it ended. The police backed off, wiping bloody noses and holding cracked ribs.

Having backed away from the ruckus, Martine returned to her vantage point and stood on tip toe, looking for Bruce. Where was he exactly?

Nobody was paying attention to Bruce now. With the disturbance between police and soldiers behind him over, he watched again what was unfolding on stage.

Jiang Sheng took to the lectern. All motion ceased in the hall; all eyes turned to him.

The only sound was the air conditioning swirling softly in the ceiling and the hum of the PA system, with the word REPORTS beneath Mandarin characters projected fifteen metres high on the screen.

Jiang turned to the screen, then back to the audience.

'There is only one report that matters today.'

Ignoring the President, Jiang Sheng bowed to the six other members of the Standing Committee, which included Marshal Zhou, and then to the eight Elders, known as the Eight Great Eminent Officials, who sat on the other side of the dais. He returned to face the audience.

'I have ordered *Dēnglóng*. I did this because this morning the Standing Committee of the National People's Congress each received information of grave concern. I wish to verify this information here, today, because it represents an imminent threat to our country and to the whole world. I am referring to President Tao's Phoenix Programme.' Gasps sounded around the auditorium.

'This is all lies,' Tao shouted. 'A conspiracy to deflect us at the vital moment!'

Jiang met the President's bluster with a stone face. 'His Excellency is requested to respect the protocol which *he* endorsed. His Excellency will be given full opportunity to respond when the case has been stated.'

Tao thrust his fists towards the floor and strutted in a circle, furious.

Jiang Sheng requested that the email attachments be projected on the big screen. He gave the audience a summary of the Phoenix Programme, as conceived by the President. Then, with every passing image of Tao's most secret pages, he developed the picture, explaining how all subordinate projects were working in isolation towards a cataclysmic outcome.

The delegates became progressively roiled. A few called out from the floor. As the information multiplied the mood darkened. When an overview of the Phoenix protective facilities was shown, with no evidence of plans for further building, the shouting became pervasive.

Tao couldn't take any more. He stepped back to the lectern and pushed Jiang aside.

'This is conjecture. The information is distorted. Where are the witnesses!'

'Wow,' said Quentin over the net. 'Cat's out of the bag, I would say.'

Greg transmitted, 'Team Three. We have movement from the black Merc. A detail has surrounded the car … It's Lin. Confirm, Marshal Lin being escorted towards the Hall. Over.'

'Could be the clincher.'

'You got a full tank of fuel to get us out of here afterwards, Zero?'

'First things first. We're not there yet.'

*   *   *

Tavener had spent a full twenty-four hours watching Beaumont, reluctantly dashing back to his accommodation for more food and warm clothing. He was confident he had the measure of the place.

Nobody seemed to be on the defensive, and just three people had come into view: the Chinese official, her very-much-alive ladyship, and a second female with long unkempt dark hair and scruffy clothes. Probably house staff. And no Lucien Martell, or any other man for that matter. The hens were in the coop and the fox was ready for breakfast. It was seven in the morning. He felt providence at work. This was the moment.

Tavener packed up his few items, checked his pistol and started along the selected covert route to the house. He sneaked a look through windows, spying some sort of sitting room – it was small, maybe a snug – then the kitchen, before reaching the side door. He grasped the handle and turned it.

The door was unlocked. Tavener wrenched it open, thrust the pistol ahead and stormed into the kitchen.

He swept the gun back and forth over the scene, but nobody was there. A stack of crockery sat beside the sink. He picked up a half-finished cup of coffee from the kitchen table; it was almost cold, but not quite. The house was deathly quiet. Where were they?

Creeping through the kitchen and into a corridor, Tavener paused and listened after every few steps. He eyed doorways, ready for any to spring open and shooting to start. He came upon a large room to his right, with sofas, a grand old dark wood table, and an imposing limestone chimney breast sporting a pair of crossed sabres. It was also devoid of life.

Further along the corridor was a staircase to the first floor. A murmur was audible in the distance. He craned his neck to listen over the banister, to who might be above, only to realise the sounds were coming from behind a wooden door under the staircase. With a gloved hand, he eased three fingers between door and jamb and pulled. The hinge squeaked and he instinctively yanked it wider to get it over with. Inside were steps leading down to the basement, from which voices could be heard. He recognised Lady Margaret. The other voice was male and sounded as if it was the Chinese official.

Tavener crept down the stone steps and into the gloom of the cellar till the secret beyond was revealed. Lady Margaret and the official were in the dingy light under a low ceiling, sat in front of a computer and a bank of monitors, with phone lines, files, paperwork and other paraphernalia dotted around. On the monitors were images from the BBC World Service news and a blank VTC screen. As he inched forwards another screen came into view displaying quadrants of colour images from CCTV outside the house.

'Good morning, my lady,' Tavener announced himself.

Lady Margaret and the official jumped in fright, then froze, before turning to face him.

'What? Did I surprise you? I thought your clairvoyant powers would have seen me coming a mile off.' He grinned at the stunned expressions. 'Nevertheless, what a joy to find you here, all tucked away and keeping busy. Is that what you've have been doing all this time, while pretending to the whole world to be dead?' Then he spoke to the official. 'And, if I'm not mistaken, it has been even longer since we last met. Am I right, Chen Ying?'

40

Tavener looked at Lady Margaret.

'Where's the housekeeper?'

'Um, fetching tea,' she said, struggling to get the words out.

'Impossible. Just came through the kitchen. No-one there,' he shot back.

'I ... I don't know. That's where she was going. Perhaps she needed the bathroom.'

The cellar door squeaked again, followed by the click of women's shoes upon the steps.

Tavener raised the pistol to his lips. *Silence.* He withdrew into the shadows as the footsteps grew louder, the tinkling of bone china crockery accompanying the housekeeper's approach. She entered the ops room with a laden silver tray.

'*Allô ... Du thé, madame,*' she said.

Tavener emerged, pointing the gun. 'Put it down over there.'

The woman jumped, upsetting the contents of the tray. A tea cup rolled over the edge and smashed on the flagstones.

'*Madame!*' she cried.

'It's alright, Marie-Claude.' Lady Margaret got up and helped the trembling figure set the tray down on the desk.

The woman put her hands to her face and shook, trying to stem the tears.

'Oh, for God's sake, woman. Just sit over there. *Assieds-toi là!*' Tavener waved the pistol towards an empty chair in a recess, away from Lady Margaret and Ying. She scurried past, the back of a hand covering her mouth in distress.

'That's better,' he said.

He addressed Lady Margaret. 'You know I'm not one for formalities, or wasting time, so I'll come to the point. You have cost me rather dearly in time and money. Oh, and freedom, for that matter.'

'Freedom? I think that is your doing. If one chooses to lead a double life with the criminal underworld—'

'Shut it! Just shut your haughty proclamations. I wouldn't be marked by Chinese intelligence if you had stayed out of the way. But I suppose you were saving the world from ... from what? The Chinese knowing what MI6 have on their virus programme? I made most of it up anyway, you fool.'

'And we just extended that strategy. But you got your money all the same.'

He sniggered. He had got his money.

*   *   *

Around 2.30 p.m. local time, some seven hours ahead of Beaumont, Mr Jiang announced that he was calling his first witness. The crowd by the centre doors parted and Marshal

Lin entered wearing khaki dress uniform and escorted by four soldiers.

He tried to take it all in. Camera lights and lenses swung onto him, a sea of faces loomed, a mass of bodies stirred in anticipation. Lin straightened himself and strode ahead.

He didn't see it at first, lost in the clutter. A tall blonde woman emerged into the aisle and held out an envelope. Lin's focus went to her – her hair, her face, then followed her outstretched arm to the white paper addressed with the words written in Mandarin – *Trust Me*. He paused, grasped the paper and gazed into the eyes of its bearer, the one who stole him into the night sky. He folded the envelope, slid it into a trouser pocket and walked on.

Applause rippled around the membership as he came into full view and ascended the steps to the stage. Marshal Zhou turned red at the sight of his predecessor, his jaw twitching with anger.

'Comrade Lin, welcome,' said Jiang Sheng into the microphone. 'Please come and join us.' He waited while Lin mounted the stairs to the stage and slowly walked across to the podium. 'Marshal Lin Xiangquin, would you please explain to our members what you have explained to me.'

Lin began his account, haltingly at first. He had never addressed the assembly in such numbers. An irresistible urge to glance around at Marshal Zhou returned the only thing it could have. A snarl, as if Zhou wanted to leap from his chair and strangle him. Yet Lin held eye contact, like a civilised being contemplating the primal savagery of a beast in a cage. When he realised the audience was hanging on his every word, he turned to the front again and found his voice. They want the truth, he thought. Now it is time.

'It is my shame to have acquiesced for so long, suppressing my misgivings about President Tao's grand vision. My recent incarceration is but one piece of evidence among the catalogue that proves his vision was intended to achieve one thing, to serve one man: President Tao's place in history as the Chinese ruler of the world. And China, and the world, would pay the ultimate price for this.'

He told them about the PRD virus – a deliberate manifestation – the first attempt to subdue the West without conflict. Next, Taiwan – the sea blockades and military escalation. Then came a summary of his visit to the Beishan Mountain bunker and the short half-life nuclear warheads intended to enable a survivable war – but one where only point one percent of Chinese citizens were part of the plan. When he said that individual family units had been allocated, and included provision for illegal family sizes, it was clear who would get invited into the ark and who would be left to perish.

The auditorium descended into chaos. Papers were strewn around, obscuring the view across the floor like confetti. Ten thousand voices erupted.

'Think we may have started a revolution,' came Lucien's voice over the radio.

'That's the price when people appease a dictator for too long,' said Greg.

When Marshal Lin concluded his account he stepped back from the podium and stood aside. Jiang Sheng returned to the microphone and raised a hand asking for calm. Slowly, as the final outbursts from the balcony faded, he invited the President to respond.

Like replacing a scalding saucepan to a flaming stove, the assembly boiled over when President Tao got up. He approached the podium but had to wait for the tumult to subside before he could speak.

'This is a conspiracy that has misrepresented and exposed our closest secrets at the worst possible time for China.' The sound of hissing grew across the crowd, drowning out some of his words. The President leaned closer to the microphone and pressed on. 'Everyone who had a hand in this treason will receive the harshest justice.'

With the claims out in the open, his main line of defence was to request independent verification: witnesses. Other witnesses. He asserted that as a fugitive Marshal Lin – now merely Lin Xiangquin – was unfit to be heard. In fact, he continued, under the *Dēnglóng* protocol, today could only serve to confirm a basis for a formal investigation and subsequent trial, should a worthy case be identified.

'So I ask, have you any other independent, honourable witnesses to support your claims, Comrade Jiang?'

Jiang Sheng and Marshal Lin made eye contact. Lin nodded and went to the front of the stage, descended the steps and spoke to the officer in charge.

'Has the Director of Works arrived yet?'

'I will check, sir.'

The officer hurried off towards the exit, radioing as he went.

'Is that all you have? And he's not even here,' the President blustered. He looked over to Jiang Sheng: 'I demand better than this!'

'You better have something, Lin, or I'll put a noose around your neck this time!' Marshal Zhou barked from his seat.

Marshal Lin raised a hand, requesting a moment's patience, then he took the envelope from his pocket and opened it. Inside was a single sheet of paper. He scanned the message:

> *Comrade Chen Ying, formerly Programme Lead at the Research Facility, Hulunbuir, is waiting on VTC. Direct dial +334 55 76 34 24.*

His face set for moment, trying to recall the name. The images of devastation as the labs burned during the Chinese New Year celebrations made the connection. Chen Ying was the one who got away.

He conferred with Jiang Sheng, who immediately lifted a handset on the podium to speak to the audio-visual suite set behind angled windows like an air traffic control tower, high at the back of the auditorium. He instructed them to fire up the VTC and get it on screen.

The VTC screen lit up with an incoming connection request. An overseas number.

Tavener lowered his gun and studied the monitors. The BBC World Service was showing coverage from inside the Chinese assembly. He flapped the gun at the screen.

'Turn that up.'

Lady Margaret raised the volume, her eyes on the VTC, its connection request waiting to be answered.

'… unprecedented scenes of a showdown within the Communist Party conference this afternoon … amid an apparent military coup … connected with recent escalation of tension between China and the West …'

A moment passed as Tavener joined the dots. She read his expression, watched the cogs shunting round.

'I spy an opportunity,' he said. 'I suspect that Ying is about to play a pivotal role. Am I right? Only your organisation could put itself in this position.'

He stepped forward and poured himself a cup of tea. 'My lady? Milk first, no sugar? Did I remember correctly? Let's have tea first. Then perhaps we can come to an arrangement.' Tavener was revelling in her turmoil, savouring the torment. Twisting the knife would come later. 'So ... did I remember correctly?'

'You did. Pour one if you will, although I have rather lost my thirst. Please understand, Mr Tavener, that you are about to put your own life in peril along with everyone else's if you interfere now. There really is no time.' She let out a little cough, her lungs brittle with stress.

'Ah yes, I must remember that I am also on this planet that you are about to save. Bound to the fate, and prostrate before the greatness of the ancient order of the Architects' Club.'

The call kept blinking, waiting to be answered.

'You see, I could do very well if this call is what I think it is,' he continued. 'Get the MSS off my back. Make a very tidy penny, I expect.' He took a sip of tea, then raised the cup. 'Bottoms up!'

Lady Margaret reached for the VTC controls. 'I have to answer this.'

Tavener towered over her and pressed the gun to her temple. 'Sit down! I say what happens.'

Lady Margaret froze, then did as ordered, slowly turning her head sideways, shrinking under the muzzle. Marie-Claude was watching from the shadows, eyes staring back from above the hand that remained clasped across her face, as if she was stifling a scream.

Tavener took another mouthful of tea, reached inside his jacket and produced a small black notebook. He flicked to the back and found a number. 'Don't mind if I use your phone?' He lifted the receiver and punched in a string of numbers.

Lady Margaret studied the incoming VTC number, as if emblazoning it on her eyes. All she could do was wait. The wisps of steam rising from her untouched cup of tea offered a curious calm, a meditation, as she memorised the number.

The call stopped. *Connection terminated.*

She huffed and turned to Tavener, wondering what he was doing and whether she might have a chance to call back. He was peering at his notebook, punching numbers into the keypad, then hanging up and starting again.

'Sod it,' he mumbled.

He screwed his eyes tight, trying to focus. He started to sway. A hand went to his forehead as he leaned over the desk.

'Bitches!'

He swung the gun round at Lady Margaret. She blocked it as a deafening crack sounded, the ricochet sending Ying and Marie-Claude diving for cover from the stray bullet. Lady Margaret landed a side-palm strike to his throat, prising the pistol from his grasp as he clutched his windpipe and dropped to his knees, energy leaving him with every passing second. He thudded onto his back, staring up at his assailant, powerless.

Lady Margaret reached for a pack of antiseptic wipes and two pairs of medical gloves from a shelf. She gave a pair to Marie-Claude, wiped the pistol clean and handed it to her.

'Can you deal with this?'

'*Bien sûr*,' replied Marie-Claude, taking the gun.

Marie-Claude stuffed the gun into her belt, kicked off her shoes, stood at Tavener's head and took hold of his collar, then dragged him away into the wine cellar.

Lady Margaret reset herself at the desk and invited Ying to take his place in front of the video camera. She dialled the number.

41

Ying appeared on the screen, towering over the stage. President Tao at once recognised him and rushed under the image, flailing his arms as if to block Ying from view, shouting wild protestations at another unfit witness, another enemy of the Party.

From his perch on the armrest of an aisle seat, Bruce looked about him. The crowd had lost patience with the President. His objections were becoming a time-consuming distraction, a ruse to derail a process that had never before been attempted. Bruce turned his attention to the stage where two soldiers were ushering the President to Jiang Sheng's seat. Tao's resistance stopped short of allowing himself to be manhandled, the ultimate insult to his fast-diminishing authority.

The atmosphere was nearing fever pitch. Most of the ten thousand delegates were back on their feet and it was difficult to hear what was being said on stage. Ying tried to speak but his opening lines were drowned out by swelling applause as word got around that he was the official that had escaped from Hulunbuir. He waited for the clapping to subside, then started afresh, Bruce listening to his words translated by Quentin over the radio net.

'I am Comrade Chen Ying, leader of the research programme at the Hulunbuir bioweapons facility. Together with Comrade Wu Qiang, the chief virologist, I was directed by President Tao to synthesise vectored bioagents,' he began.

More applause followed when they learned how he had risked his life to prevent the PRD virus from killing millions, how his fallen comrade had altered records of its design and then arranged the destruction of the lab as a desperate measure to thwart the President's malign intentions.

As he concluded, attention shifted to the auditorium floor. In Bruce's ear Quentin's voice crackled with more news: 'From the TV feed it looks as though we have the Director of Works and the Chief Nuclear Engineer arriving in the hall.'

Bruce stood and turned back to see the President's reaction. Tao's mouth dropped open, his shoulders slumped, and he looked across to Zhou, seemingly in search of a miracle.

The Great Hall resonated with waves of cheering and stamping of feet. The two new witnesses stopped halfway along the aisle, just a couple of feet away from where Bruce was standing, and waved to the audience on either side. Bruce joined in the applause.

The pandemonium was quelled when an elderly gentleman rose and walked to the front of the stage, holding his hand aloft. The delegate next to Bruce nudged him, pointing and wearing a broad smile.

'Kang Jie. He is one of the Elders,' the man said.

Bruce recalled conversations they had had about the Elders, the senior figures who used to provide a guiding light for the leadership before President Tao took power. Kang Jie was the only former Supreme Leader among the eight, a respected dignitary who had tried to navigate the difficult years of a communist country evolving in a globalised world.

He kept his hand in the air, appealing for quiet, then went to the podium.

Quentin's voice continued the translation in Bruce's earpiece.

'My fellow citizens, there is no precedent for what we are witnessing today. We have only our principles and the protocol of *Dēnglóng* itself to guide us through such a time.' Kang Jie's tone was dry and sombre, but somehow tinged with warmth and empathy.

It was as if everyone had stopped breathing, such was the peace that befell the assembly.

'*Dēnglóng* was conceived to protect us from calamity, in whatever form that may arise,' he continued. 'Military force in this circumstance has one purpose: to enable rationality to endure. We have seen sufficient evidence that there is a case to answer and that our President's current intentions for Taiwan and the West are unsound.'

Tao leapt to his feet and pushed past the soldiers guarding him. He grabbed the microphone from Kang Jie. 'This insanity has exposed our secrets and forever harmed our interests!' he shouted. 'I order that this conference ceases and the traitors be arrested, for the protection of the government.' The soldiers seized him and pulled him back, with one resetting the microphone for Kang Jie to continue.

'No, Tao Wei, *you* have forever harmed our interests, and *Dēnglóng* does not exist for the protection of the government, it exists for the protection of the constitution, which you have long forgotten.' Kang Jie held his focus on Tao, allowing his words to register. 'Communism is no different from any honourable ideology in its intent: it ultimately seeks that all may live in freedom, equality and peace. But you have bound the country's interests to your own, and perverted your authority to serve only your legacy.'

Cheering resumed in the hall. Bruce looked about him again, deafened by the ruckus which had turned into an outpouring of joy, of relief. Party members nearby were breathless with celebration, hoarse with chanting. *Out! Out! Out!*

Kang Jie raised his hand a final time. Again his request was respected and silence fell.

'A formal enquiry and subsequent trials will be commissioned. These will be announced to the membership in due course. That is when testimonies will be formally admissible and due process can resolve this constitutional and political crisis.'

Marshal Zhou had had enough. He stood and moved forward, glancing to Tao, then to Kang Jie, finally glaring at Lin. 'If none of this is admissible today, then let me act in China's real interests,' he declared before drawing his automatic from its holster and firing at Lin, who crumpled to the floor holding his stomach, his hands running red with blood.

Bruce watched in disbelief as Zhou then aimed at the central aisle. He looked across at the Director of Works and Chief Nuclear Engineer who were stood frozen with terror. Just as the shot rang out, he launched himself at the director. The soldiers followed suit, throwing themselves on the chief engineer as another round was fired. It missed, splintering the wooden back of a seat. A rattle of pistol shots echoed as fire was briefly exchanged. Screams filled the auditorium as everyone dived for cover.

Rolling onto his back and off the man he had shielded, Bruce slumped to the carpet clutching his left shoulder which had been punctured by a bullet. Blood oozed from the wound, soaking his jacket, running down his arm and covering his hand. His gaze went back to the stage and he looked directly into the empty, staring eyes of Marshal Zhou's corpse. The officer in charge stood at the foot of the steps like a statue, his pistol still trained on the dead man.

It was carnage. When the firing stopped, heads popped up from behind seats and everyone made a dash for the exits. People climbed over seating and each other, the aisles became gridlocked and doorways were blocked as they panicked and crushed themselves to a standstill. The soldiers protecting the director and chief engineer – both unharmed – had got up and formed a ring around them, and Bruce too, keeping them from being crushed in the stampede.

Bruce was getting cold, beads of sweat forming on his brow. His mind began to wander, but he recognised it and focused on staying awake. Through the forest of bodies he spotted Martine's blonde head as she made her way towards him, thrusting her way against the tide.

She knelt down beside him. He was breathing and conscious. Good. She looked around for something to staunch the wound. Among the debris was a discarded cotton scarf. She pushed it between his shirt and jacket to absorb blood but not contaminate the entry wound.

'Team One. Artemis is hit, but walking wounded, I hope. There's a mass panic to escape from here. Will try to extract via another route. Over,' she said into her wrist mic.

'Team Three. Let me know where you exit and I will come to assist,' Greg replied.

'Zero. We will bring the transport to suitable RV when exit point is known. Out,' came Lucien.

Martine put an arm around Bruce. 'Can you stand?'

He grunted and trembled as he got his legs under him. 'Christ, I feel like Bambi on the ice.'

'Stay strong. Gonna get us out of here.'

Bruce held on as best he could, feeling his strength trickling away, aware of Martine scanning around for potential ways out. Through the gathering fog in his consciousness he noticed President Tao in the custody of four soldiers, two of whom flanked him, locking his arms. They were leading him away towards the wings on the left, past another group of soldiers who were giving first aid to Marshal Lin. She guided Bruce towards the stage. They struggled up the steps and made to follow members of the NPC Standing Committee who were slipping away via the stage wings to the right.

'Keep going, Bruce. I might have a way out.'

Bruce's head bobbed around to look behind them. 'W-watch out!'

Two men in suits caught hold of Martine, one on each shoulder, pulling her back and causing Bruce to fall.

'Halt! You're coming with us,' said the first man. He had a revolver trained on her.

She spun round to face them. Bruce kicked out, hitting the man in the ankle. The man stumbled and lost aim. Martine speared him with a side thrust kick into his sternum, sending him flailing back down the steps.

She parried the second man's attempts to draw his weapon with a back fist strike to his face, breaking his nose. He dropped the pistol, raising his arms in defence. A front kick between the legs followed. Then a reverse punch to the mouth sent him down, squealing in agony, hands going to his bloody mash of teeth and lips. She stepped in, snatched his gun and stuffed it into the back of her jeans.

The scrap shocked Bruce back to life. A burst of adrenaline kicked in and he was up and moving. Martine got an arm under him again.

'Think I'm okay,' he said, breaking into an awkward run, holding his damaged shoulder.

They headed to the back right corner of the stage. Most of the delegates had left, and when they reached the emergency exit only a trickle of confused faces remained to watch them as they sped by.

'Team One. We are out. Northwest corner, heading for the rear service road,' Martine transmitted.

'Go to RV Stag,' said Lucien, code for the nearby Sichuan restaurant hideaway.

As fast as it had returned, the adrenaline waned again. Bruce was turning pale, clammy.

'How far?' he gasped.

'Just a couple of hundred metres. If they can get through the roads then timings should be good,' Martine replied.

'Struggling now.'

'Don't talk. Just concentrate on your balance.'

They crossed the service road. The area was deserted, as though the focus of the world was on Tiananmen. They heard footsteps sprinting up from behind. Martine strained to see who was after them this time, ready to draw the gun.

'It's okay! It's me.' Greg's words were a solace. He joined them and supported Bruce from the other side.

'Thank God. He's getting heavy and losing blood.'

The trio struggled on till they entered a small street along which they would find the Sichuan restaurant. Bruce lifted his head.

'How much further?'

Greg suddenly steered everyone a sharp right turn into an alleyway.

'Here we go. This leads to the back of the restaurant. Should be secure for a while till they arrive.'

A minute later, the restaurant's back gate opened. Brief eye contact was the mutual acknowledgement between the team and their female ally. The woman led them to a secluded seating area behind the kitchen. Out front the clientele was swelling as folk started to disperse from Tiananmen in search of refreshments.

Greg used the few Chinese words he knew and the international language of hand gestures to request clean cloths to replace Bruce's bandage.

On the counter next to them a TV was looping recorded footage from inside the assembly. As he watched from a distance the magnitude of events hit home to Bruce. Greg glanced up periodically while fixing his wound. Of course he would have no idea what things looked like in the hall, Bruce realised.

'Wow, really?' said Greg as he watched the President strutting around in a tantrum. 'No way …' China Central TV news was showing unedited coverage of the shooting.

'They didn't waste any time using their newfound reporting freedoms then,' he remarked.

Martine helped Bruce take a sip of water. 'Easy, not too much at once.'

Their radios came alive.

'Zero. ETA two minutes. Apologies for delay. Over.'

'Three. Roger. Out.'

Greg and Martine helped Bruce shuffle along the side entrance out to the street. An ambulance drew up. Quentin jumped out of the back and held the rear door open.

'Ready?'

They clambered in. Lucien looked over his shoulder from the front passenger seat to check they were safely aboard. As Marc pulled away, Martine asked what had happened to the van.

'Ah, no go with that thing in the centre today,' Quentin replied.

'And?' Martine looked around. Their kit appeared to have been transferred.

'And, er, we needed something that would be allowed to move through the centre.'

'You stole this? And now it's red hot, with a big target number painted on the roof. We aren't gonna get far. Bruce needs attention too.'

'It's okay,' Greg said. 'Good move in one respect – we have medical supplies and equipment, and I'm a trained field medic.' He hooked Bruce up to a drip and started replacing his dressings. 'Mind if I have a prod around that shoulder of yours, Bruce? See if the bullet's anywhere accessible?' He donned a face mask and surgical gloves. Bruce groaned.

42

Connection terminated. Lady Margaret was lost in contemplation in front of the blank VTC screen. Beside her Ying sat quietly watching the international news, which continued with sensational reports of the meltdown in China's parliament. 'Paralysis', 'Humiliation' and 'Climbdown' were among the emotive words being splashed along tickertapes. The western hemisphere was waking up to a new order in the East.

'Do you think that's it?' she asked Ying. 'Is it enough? And what about Lin? What if he dies?'

Ying brought his hands together as if in prayer. 'What is it you say in the West: the game is up? There is no going back from this. Tao will be put under house arrest. Kang Jie will probably stay as caretaker leader, if only for the sake of stability.'

'But he has no formal authority.'

'He has *power*, and power lies where it is given. People forget that. They think power is taken. Power is never taken.'

'What matters is that Tao can no longer prosecute his goals and send us all to hell in a mushroom cloud,' she concluded.

BEAUMONT

From deep within the wine cellar came a call for assistance. Lady Margaret stood.

'Perhaps it would be wise for you to retire upstairs, Ying. Please make yourself comfortable. You know where we keep the tea.' He got up, bowed and went on his way. 'And it's probably best if you close the door up there,' she added.

She took a small case from a cabinet beside the desk, went through the cellar, past the steps and into a large space where she found Tavener and Marie-Claude. Barrels and wine racks lined the perimeter. In the centre, under the yellow glow of three conical metal pendants, Tavener lay paralysed. He had been positioned upon a thick sheet of metal about the size of a coffin lid, under which was a tough piece of plastic that covered most of the floor. Marie-Claude stood over him, pistol aimed.

'And how is our uninvited guest? Any trouble?' Marie-Claude shook her head. '*Bon*,' said her ladyship.

She opened the case, filled a syringe, stooped over and injected him in the arm.

'You'll note that I didn't take the clinical precaution of rolling your sleeve up. Apologies in advance for any infection that might result.'

Tavener's eyes were all he could move. His fury was evident in their watery bloodshot contortions, rolling around in cups streaked with dilated vessels.

'I know you can hear me. I just needed to make sure the rather minimal dose you drank with the tea hadn't worn off. We know what would happen then, don't we, James?'

He was dribbling from a corner of his mouth, straining to speak, but all that came out was an incoherent moan.

'One might, in a situation like this, be consumed by the need to understand motive: *why*, Mr Tavener, *why*. But that question has been resoundingly answered. Indeed, it occurs to me that you have fallen foul of the primary motivators you would once have used to recruit spies: money, ideology, coercion and ego – although perhaps not ideology in your case.'

He attempted to move his limbs. Fluid ran from his nostrils. Another groan of anguish, or was it anger?

'Now, mercifully, I do not need anything from you. Not money, nor information, not even a confession. But I will indulge myself in a couple of ... let's call them formalities. I can be one for formalities, as you know.'

She returned the syringe to its box and placed it atop a sherry barrel.

'You shot Philip Roberts and Jenny Noble-Franks. And one of your hired thugs murdered Colonel Malcolm Hunter. They could have just tied him up, but hey-ho, what goes around ...'

His eyes narrowed in confusion.

'Did you also kill young Rory McIntyre on Crib Goch? Did he get too close to your prize?'

The snot blew in and out from his nostrils as his breathing became panicked, rage giving way to terror.

'Well, I have a surprise for you, Mr Tavener.'

Lady Margaret stepped aside and Marie-Claude walked round to take her place at his feet, looking straight into his eyes. She lowered the pistol, reached up with her other hand and slowly drew away the wig of long dark hair.

'You'll need to use your imagination where the make-up is concerned, Mr Tavener.'

He turned pale as he stared into the face of Jenny Noble-Franks. She knelt and lifted his trouser leg to expose the old injury. 'How's the ankle?' Then she stood and lifted her blouse to reveal the crude deformities in the skin across her stomach where a bullet had entered and hasty stitches had been applied. 'One-all, I suppose.'

He yelped like a goat that sees the blade.

Lady Margaret resumed: 'If you're wondering *how* – how did it come to this? How did we know? I would offer a point of principle. *Ceteris paribus*, one fighting for survival will be more motivated, careful and even bold, than one murdering for money, power, or glory, whatever that is. Our organisation has always fought for the survival of humanity, and living that way tends to keep you on your game. You, however, blinded by greed and arrogance, made too many mistakes.'

Tavener's body relaxed. Had he conceded to defeat? Was he listening to her sermon out of curiosity, perhaps because these might be the last words he would ever hear?

Lady Margaret recalled that night in 1987 at the multi-storey car park in Bristol, the disaster when Tavener's true colours were revealed, but for far too high a price.

'Philip Roberts did all the right things when he suspected something was up – Jenny suddenly rushing off, but nobody knew for what.' She studied Tavener's eyes, perceiving a change in mood. As if he wanted to hear the other side of the story. His ego couldn't let it go.

'Dearest Philip called on Greg Pitman to back him up,' she continued. 'Greg, as you probably found out, had previously spent months watching over Jenny to protect her from kidnap, interrogation or execution – courtesy of your paymaster, I have since assumed. So, this night Greg gained entry to a house across the street from the multi-storey to where you had lured Jenny. From its roof terrace he had a view of the events that unfolded there. You wondered who saw you that night, I'll bet.'

Tavener grumbled and attempted to move.

'Greg described to me how you and Jenny came to blows, then dear Philip rushed in to save her, but you were the better shot. Quicker. You killed Philip with a bullet to the head and intended the same for Jenny if she didn't spill the beans about the Club. How am I doing?'

Lady Margaret glanced at Jenny, sensitive to her feelings about reliving painful memories. But Jenny's eyes were bright. This was a catharsis. Her ladyship continued.

'Jenny's saving grace was spearing you through the ankle with a blade. That was just enough for you to fire at point-blank range, more as a reflex, I imagine, because you were not too discerning about where you aimed. Her massive blood loss and your serious injury must have led you to believe that was good enough, so off you hobble to your car, leaving the scene. But no attempt to remove the bodies. I suppose that was because you were so badly hurt.'

Watery snot was running in streams down each of Tavener's cheeks. As he breathed, the occasional bubble would form, inflate and pop at a nostril. His pallor had worsened, on his brow lay a patina of sweat. He wants to know, she thought, but he doesn't like what he's hearing.

The account unfolded further. As Tavener drives down to exit the car park, he passes Greg, now driving up to rescue the others. Greg is faced with the task of removing Philip's body and getting Jenny to a surgeon. Dear Jenny then spends the next eight years in hiding: missing, presumed dead, with no family contact whatsoever. That was the price of life with James Tavener at large.

'So, to the present. I should admit to being quietly impressed that you got here. I wondered whether all the havoc wreaked in the organised crime world, courtesy of the disinformation you sold in the Rothwell lists, would have caught up with you. You did your homework to find Lucien's former residence in Paris. However, he kept his neighbours close, and dear Madame Durand didn't like the look of you, James. Even had she not called, yes, I *was* expecting you. My vision is quite good these days, with all the practice I've had. And finally, today, you evaded all the dummy CCTV cameras but didn't spot the swanky new hidden ones. Money well spent.'

He appeared to purse his lips, then he let out a cry.

'What's that you say? Let me guess. You're curious about the part when you interrupted the vital VTC call? If I knew you were coming why put that crucial moment at risk? The whole charade of being caught off-guard etcetera? That was partly bad timing: I couldn't tell exactly when you would appear. But it was Jenny's ardent wish to look you in the eye, and I wanted you to have the opportunity to think on your actions. We couldn't subdue you physically – bit thin on manpower here, as you can see – so it had to be chemical. It was risky, but I knew you, your hubris. And you didn't disappoint.'

Tavener threw an arm out to the side.

'The dose is wearing off,' said Jenny.

He was writhing upon the cold metal sheet.

Lady Margaret looked to her. 'I'm done.'

Jenny stepped over him and glared down. 'I'm not spending another eight years hiding from you, Mr Tavener.'

He squealed in horror as she raised the gun.

Crack!

43

The team's escape from Beijing was running into trouble. Marc sped along, wringing all available power from the wheezing diesel motor. The ambulance swung from side to side as he made last minute turns to avoid a growing net of road blocks.

In the back Bruce was lying face down on a stretcher with Greg holding a bottle of antiseptic fluid and cloth, prodding his injury, trying to locate the bullet. Marc flung the vehicle around another street corner causing the fluid to splash over the gaping wound. Bruce screamed in agony.

'Marc, can you drive just a little more steadily, please?' said Greg.

'Not if you want to get out of this place alive, *mon ami*.' Marc glanced into the mirror. 'I'll try.' In the passenger seat Lucien said nothing and kept checking around for pursuers.

Hanging onto the lowered side rail of the stretcher opposite Bruce, Martine gulped water from a plastic bottle and wiped her mouth. 'He's losing blood. Can't you give him something?'

'I need to remove the bullet and stem the flow. Then maybe I could administer morphine, but we really need him compos mentis for when we go on foot,' Greg replied. He looked into the front at Lucien who had a mobile phone to his ear. 'I presume we will be going on foot at some point?' he said, raising his voice.

'Yeah, what's the bloody plan, Lucien?' Martine cried.

Lucien listened for most of the minute-long call, before exchanging a few muffled words and hanging up. He took the phone from his ear.

'Okay, the plan is that we are leaving by private air charter, but somewhat *unchartered*, if you follow me.'

'*Nein*, not really. Details, please.'

'Our ... shall I say ... sponsor, owner of the Jianguo, has rather kindly agreed to loan us his Learjet. We're heading to Osaka. Then it's up to us to get home.'

'Well, that is very generous. Taking a risk, isn't he?'

'He's relaxed about it. He thinks the current turmoil is adequate for this to go unnoticed – if we don't get caught at the aircraft. He is very pleased with us, apparently. He's already looking forward to an uptick in business.'

Martine paused for a moment before responding. 'Ah, okay. That is very good, apart from the part where the airport will be the first place they secure if they suspect spies trying to flee the country.'

'True,' said Quentin. 'However, the authorities would have to immediately connect the ambulance disappearance with foreign agents, whose presumed next move would be to flee via an international airport, which is a rather obvious move in itself.'

'They are dumb. Such subtleties would be lost on them. With the meltdown in the Great Hall and this vehicle on the loose they will shut everything down until they have something or someone. We have to assume the airport is off limits,' Martine retorted.

Lucien looked round from the front seat. 'Perhaps they will not expect anyone to enter via the opposite side of the airfield to the main terminal, from where private aircraft fleets operate. That's where we are going.'

They soon left the city centre, Marc skilfully weaving through the route he had hastily planned. Encounters with police vehicles dwindled till they appeared to be in the clear. With eyes on the mirrors, he allowed himself a moment's relaxation, settling into his seat while they threaded towards the airport's eastern gate from the direction of the Chaobai river.

Greg interrupted the calm. 'Got it!' With a satisfying *ting* he dropped the deformed bullet into a metal surgical bowl.

Bruce cried out and was on the verge of hyperventilating. He was running with perspiration. Martine reached over and dabbed his back, neck and brow with a cloth.

'Well done, Bruce,' said Greg. 'Going to seal this now. Not too big a wound, actually.' He poured more antiseptic. Another howl. Then he set about stitching.

The final mile along the main perimeter road brought silence inside the vehicle. Everyone held their breath and watched for hostiles.

A small queue had formed at the roundabout by the airfield entrance. Marc inched forwards. He was three vehicles from the turn when a police van swung into sight two hundred metres behind them.

'Hang on everyone!'

Lucien studied his side mirror. 'But surely we'll make it—'

'*Non.* Too slow. He will spot us and we will be trapped.'

Marc hit the blues and twos, broke from the queue and forced his way through and into the site. The police van didn't react at first, but when Marc killed the lights and sirens their suspicion was roused. On went their lights.

'*Merde!*'

He floored it, racing down the entrance road and into the network of hangars and office buildings. The police van was little faster than the ambulance.

Lucien scanned ahead. 'We need to take a right up here, then first left to get out by the taxiway on the other side of these hangars. Then it's a right again and go to the end of the row.'

Marc made the turns and accelerated for a final sprint towards the huge open doors. As they rolled in, the doors began to close behind them.

He pulled up beside the only aeroplane, an executive jet, where a man in a dark grey suit was waiting. They clambered out. Martine and Quentin helped Bruce while Greg gathered various items of medical kit. Bruce was pale, his head hanging down. He didn't speak.

'Our mutual friend extends his thanks and invites you to use his plane,' said the man.

'Please pass on our sincerest thanks for his great generosity,' Lucien replied.

The siren from the police van could be heard as it roamed around in search of them. Lucien turned and gestured to the ambulance.

'Can you take care of this?'

The man smiled and bowed, then looked past him. Across the hangar were three other men, ready beside the open doors of a large shipping container.

'Sorry about the mess in there,' said Greg, as he unloaded items from the ambulance onto the spotless sealed concrete floor. Inside was strewn with bloodied rags and it had been emptied of any potentially useful medical supplies.

They helped Bruce up the few steps into the Learjet, then Greg ferried the purloined medical kit aboard. Marc ascended the steps, followed by Lucien. They turned to wave goodbye to their saviours. The large doors to the airfield began to open. The cabin door thudded shut and the aircraft lurched as the tow truck started pulling.

Once outside the engines spun into life. They taxied and waited for their departure slot. A three-minute interlude for a hastily submitted flight plan was a miracle by the airport's standards, borne of a culture where the well-connected had influence. But for those onboard every second felt like torture.

With the green light from air traffic control, the plane rolled ahead, turned onto the piano keys and lined up for take-off. The team relaxed into the plush leather seats and looked out across the apron where a stream of police vehicles was rushing into view, a constellation of lights sparkling under the afternoon sun. The aircraft's engines roared to full power and it accelerated away.

The euphoria of being airborne, watching Beijing fade from view as the Learjet climbed and circled to the southeast, was short-lived. Bruce was deteriorating.

Greg had wasted no time preparing for the worst-case scenario. He monitored Bruce's blood pressure, pulse, breathing and pallor, knowing that he had lost more blood than if he'd been treated by a regular medical team without the car chase.

Martine was growing concerned. She looked intensely at Greg but said nothing. He was busily tying lines and a drip into place above the reclined leather seat on which Bruce lay.

Greg bit his lip, pensive. 'He needs blood.'

Quentin turned to Greg and Martine. 'And?'

'One of us will need to give him a pint, otherwise … I can't be certain.'

The little colour in Bruce's face had run to grey, shadows hung under his eyes and blue tinges had developed around his lips. He was semi-conscious at best.

Lucien said, 'What do you need?'

'He's A positive,' said Martine. Marc raised an eyebrow. 'We talked. He mentioned it once.'

'I'm B,' said Greg. 'Christ, this is like drawing straws.'

He turned to Marc.

'AB.'

'Lucien?'

'Group B. Sorry.'

'Nein!' cried Martine. '*Scheisse*. I'm AB ...'

Greg shook his head. 'Fuck. Fingers crossed ... Quentin?'

'O negative, old boy. Well, someone's got to save the day.'

There was a collective sucking of teeth. The others didn't speak for a moment.

'What?' asked Quentin.

Martine said what they were thinking. 'What about the pilot?'

'Eh? Otherwise engaged, my girl. And anyway, why? What's wrong with my blood? All we've got, by the sound of it.'

Martine looked to Marc and Greg. 'We've got just under three hours to Osaka. Can this thing fly on autopilot while we take his blood?'

'I don't know. Very risky. He will be light-headed for a while. And if anything crops up with air traffic …' said Greg, rapping his fingertips on the arm of the seat. 'Just ask him what group he is.'

Martine went to the cockpit and knelt by the pilot. When she returned it was with a definitive shake of the head.

'He won't say, but he informed me that he is already illegal, flying solo. He doesn't also want to be prosecuted for not being at the controls.'

'Guys, what's the problem here?' Quentin persisted.

'Quentin, no offence, but … well, you as much as told everyone yourself … about the experiments, years ago. What happened to you,' said Greg.

'But I recovered, old chap.'

Quentin realised that Marc was avoiding eye contact.

'Ah, the penny has dropped. You're referring to my rather dramatic jail break I assume.'

'*Je suis désolé*. I had to tell them,' said Marc.

Quentin waved it away. 'No problem. Yes, you did. It's fine.'

'Still gotta decide, and quickly, guys.' Martine pointed to Bruce. His eyes were closing.

'No choice,' said Greg. 'He won't make it without a transfusion.'

Five minutes later he had rigged Quentin up and begun to extract his blood.

'Even this is not ideal,' said Greg as watched the red trickle threading its way into the collecting bag. 'A pint probably isn't enough, but these are field conditions. It should certainly make a difference though.' He ran the back of a hand over his forehead, wiping away the perspiration. 'Of course, all the usual screening and treatments to make sure the blood is clinically safe can't happen here. To be fair, I have never attempted anything like this before, under these conditions. It's crude, to put it mildly.'

While extracting blood was relatively quick, the infusion took nearly the rest of the flight. But it worked. Bruce came to, his vital signs recovering until he opened his eyes and realised properly where he was. A dull ache throbbed deep in his shoulder where the bullet had been extracted. His left arm had been put in a sling. His lips looked dry. He was weak.

Opposite, Martine, Marc and Quentin watched him intently, while Lucien spoke with the pilot. Greg leaned in and offered him some water. 'Need to keep hydrating now. I had you on a drip, but you're looking much better and we'll be landing soon. How do you feel?'

'I feel alive, which is the important thing. Well done, Greg.' Bruce took the bottle and swallowed a few mouthfuls. 'Thanks, all of you, for getting me out. Guess I owe you my life.' He stared ahead for a moment, lost in thought, head still swimming. They had done it. They had really done it. Hadn't they?

'And well done to you, Bruce, for saving who will undoubtedly be a key witness in making sure *former*

President Tao never sees the inside of a government building again,' said Quentin. 'Apart from a prison, that is.' They all laughed, Bruce wincing and putting a hand up to his shoulder.

On arrival, Bruce was transferred to a private medical facility in Osaka and given a full examination, more blood and antibiotics. He would remain under observation for twenty-four hours while the team made arrangements for returning to Beaumont.

44

Bruce, Quentin, Martine, Marc, Lucien and Greg had travelled separately, via different routes from Osaka and Tokyo, to wend their way back towards the soaring black tower of Château Beaumont.

It was a mid-August afternoon. The lawns around Beaumont were parched but the meadow under the Salève ran with long blades of grasses and wild flowers that ebbed and flowed with the summer breeze. A hazy sun hung behind wisps of cirrus. Sparrows and house martins screeched and chased each other through the tall pines bordering the estate.

Lucien was the last to arrive. After taking his luggage upstairs and freshening up, he joined the others who were gathered in the living room. Martine, Greg and Marc sat on a sofa opposite Bruce, Quentin and Ying. They pretended to sip cool glasses of real lemonade but watched furtively as Lucien hurried back and forth with ice buckets and bottles of Dom Perignon. Lady Margaret likewise was flitting about, laying platters of finger buffet delicacies upon the broad coffee table.

'Are you sure we can't lend a hand, my lady,' asked Bruce.

'Well, you sure as hell can't!' Quentin roared, flapping an elbow into the air like a bird with an injured wing. Bruce's arm was still confined to a sling.

The others laughed.

'I am quite all right, thank you, Bruce,' Lady Margaret replied. 'I do really wish to serve you all, even though it is but a gesture in light of what you have achieved.'

'The mind boggles at what we must achieve to qualify for a black-tie dinner, my lady,' Quentin said, creasing with laughter.

'Save the universe?' added Martine.

Her ladyship smiled and gave them a dismissive shake of the head.

'We will, of course, enjoy a proper celebration soon. This is just for today, now that the last of us has returned.' She looked at Lucien with a warm smile.

Lucien raised his glass to her in acknowledgement. It was indeed good to be back at Beaumont. Home.

He turned to Ying. 'Is there any news on how things are working out in Beijing?'

Ying set down his lemonade. 'I contacted some trusted colleagues. It appears that calm has been restored and that President Tao's plans have been stopped. I mean formally. Forever.' His chest rose and fell as the emotion swelled within him. 'My people, all the people of the world, have been saved.'

BEAUMONT

For a moment it was as if the room had slipped into a trance. Eventually Ying brought his hand up across his mouth and cleared his throat.

'Jiang Sheng has taken the role of caretaker from the former leader, the Elder, Kang Jie. A full party congress will be called in the autumn to review the memberships of the Politburo and the National People's Congress Standing Committees. The culmination of that process, most significantly, will be to appoint a new leader to succeed Tao. Oh, and Marshal Lin Xiangquin is reported to be stable in hospital and is expected to make a full recovery.'

'I am pleased for Marshal Lin. He is a good man. The rest makes sense, I guess, but what about the investigation, and trials?' Lucien asked.

'They will go ahead as planned. No dates for trials yet. The investigating team starts immediately. Apparently they have already been appointed, but I do not know the names.'

The others listened, reminded that everyone's efforts hung by the thread of time, by what the Chinese did with what had happened. Bruce wondered whether culture would dictate habit, and the old ways would continue, starting the whole ideological cycle again. Another leader, another vision; new doctrine, the next dictator in the making.

'And what about you, Ying?' asked Martine. 'Will you go back? *Can* you go back?'

'I was contacted on the VTC number. I am requested to report as a witness, and I sense this is my path. I will go.'

'You should be up for a hearty promotion and a medal, I'd say,' said Quentin.

'It looks like the authorities are sharing a lot more information with the media now,' said Lucien.

'They are, and not just what the leader wants the world to know,' said Ying. 'There was a strong sentiment among many of my friends that a brighter future lies in openness and trust with the rest of the world. Then we can have better relations and better trade.'

'Would that not ultimately mean democracy?' said Lucien.

'Perhaps, but one step at a time. Many feel this should be the nature of things, but that constitutes a wholesale change of national identity. Have you ever changed your identity, Lucien? Your real one, I mean,' Ying said with a chuckle. 'It will take time.'

'Of course,' said Lucien. 'And what's the situation with Taiwan now?'

'Taiwan? Ha!' Ying opened his arms, hands outstretched. 'After all the funerals for the hundreds of American servicemen and women, and after the time it will take to remove those missile cruisers from the harbours, it will then take a century for the shame to pass. Taiwan will be left in peace.'

Lady Margaret returned and set down the final trays of food: this time a medley of coronation chicken finger sandwiches, smoked salmon and cream cheese blinis, and prawn Marie Rose vol-au-vents. With a final adjustment to the buffet, she stood up.

'I think we should begin.'

'Hear, hear!' said Quentin.

Lucien popped a magnum of the 1969 and filled crystal flutes, which her ladyship served, beaming with joy.

'Quick, get it down so we survive the speech!' Quentin snorted.

Lady Margaret grinned back and waited for the laughter to subside. She raised her glass. 'No speeches, just a toast – to you all. To a mission accomplished. To the Architects' Club. Long may we serve.'

'To the Club!'

The conversation resumed, as the champagne flowed and they savoured the food. They had finally reached a point of letting go, chatting over the light and dark moments of the operation. It was the beginnings of laying to rest the ghosts of what was, and what might have been.

Bruce was healing. He couldn't believe that it was always that same shoulder, the one that had suffered at the point of Rostam's dagger, the one that was smashed upon Rothwell's squash court floor, courtesy of Jez Picher. Most of all, as the casual glances came his way, Bruce knew the others were wondering one thing in particular: was he the same now that he had Quentin's blood in his system? He felt okay. Fortunately there were no signs of scleroderma. 'Avoid overdoses of adrenaline, dear chap,' had been

Quentin's warmest advice. 'But then again, perhaps not, depending on the circumstances.'

Bruce's contemplation was broken by Martine, who caught his eye, mystifying him, just as she did when they first met.

'Everything okay, Bruce?'

'Er, yeah. Guess so, certainly will be once this is back to normal,' he said, shrugging his bandaged arm and trying to shrug off the doubts.

'What's next for you? Where you gonna go?'

Bruce's expression flickered with confusion. 'My next mission will be with you ... with *us*, I mean. Isn't that how it works?'

The others had paused their conversations and were listening.

'You can't go on missions all the time,' Lucien cut in. 'I don't wish to disappoint, but your life expectancy wouldn't be very good if you did that. And, thank God, we don't have *problèmes dramatiques* like this all the time.'

Marc finished eating a vol-au-vent. 'We take time off after missions, Bruce,' he said. 'Maybe months, if you can find things to do, places to go. You will be well rewarded, if you understand me.' He looked over at Lady Margaret who was sitting on the arm of a sofa. 'You can visit me, if you like, in the south of France. Ride horses.' He focused on Bruce's injury. 'But maybe not straightaway.' Another outbreak of giggles ensued.

BEAUMONT

Lady Margaret rose and excused herself. She went out into the corridor and took a moment to think. Last chance. Was everything in place? She thought about the triumph of Jenny returning to a normal life, to her family. But that came with a price: answering all the questions about how, when and why. She and Jenny, aided by Lucien and Marc, had long since crafted cover stories, one for her family and for the authorities in respect of a missing person, the other for public consumption.

The public explanation would run along the lines of a Shirley Valentine episode. Pressures of work and home caused a form of breakdown. She snapped and disappeared to rural Spain to escape it all. But, with time, the fairy tale crumbled and finally she felt ready to return.

The private story was also a fabrication, intended to satisfy the police file and fulfil the trust of Charles and her family. In classic tradecraft style, the lie ran as close to the truth as possible but was factually insulted from it. The narrative would be that Jenny had secretly agreed to support an MI5 investigation into money laundering by an organised crime syndicate. She was compromised and her life was threatened. She entered MI5's version of witness protection, which was more covert than the norm. Recent events meant that the risk to Jenny had passed and she could return home. The story would be fielded and corroborated by Dawn Shepperton at Thames House.

Nothing more could be done now. Lady Margaret took a deep breath, then headed down to the operations room.

Two minutes later she peered around the living room door. The mood among the others was gripped by a moment of anticipation.

'Bruce, may I borrow you for a moment?' she asked. 'Please carry on, everyone. Chin-chin!'

But no-one uttered another word. All eyes followed Bruce as he walked to join her. When he exited the room, Quentin whispered into his glass, 'Does this mean a return to Rothwell? I do miss that place.'

Lady Margaret led Bruce next door to the study and sat him in a soft leather armchair.

'Bruce, there's something I need to explain, something very important that I have been unable to share with you until now,' she said. 'I sincerely hope that you will understand and accept the way things have turned out.' She let out a heavy sigh.

Bruce's face crossed with bemusement and concern for her ladyship, who obviously had something big to offload.

'I wouldn't worry, my lady. After what we have been through nothing could surprise me, short of my own mother walking through that door.'

She looked to the ceiling, choking back the tears. Her voice was about to crack.

'There's someone I would like you to meet.'

About the author

Sam Earner is a former British Army officer, now providing consultancy services in the defence sector. He trained in Neuro-Linguistic Programming and has studied Ken Wilber's works on Integral Theory since 2002. He read Aeronautical Engineering at Bristol University and has a Master of Defence Administration degree from Cranfield University. Sam is married to Debbie and they live in Somerset as loyal subjects of a female ginger cat.

Printed in Great Britain
by Amazon